Lanterns

PREVIOUS NOVELS BY PATRICIA VERYAN

The Mandarin of Mayfair
Never Doubt I Love
A Shadow's Bliss
Ask Me No Questions
Had We Never Loved
Time's Fool
Logic of the Heart
The Dedicated Villain
Cherished Enemy
Love Alters Not
Give All to Love
The Tyrant
Journey to Enchantment
Practice to Deceive
Sanguinet's Crown
The Wagered Widow
The Noblest Frailty
Married Past Redemption
Feather Castles
Some Brief Folly
Nanette
Mistress of Willowvale
Love's Duet
The Lord and the Gypsy

Lanterns

PATRICIA VERYAN

St. Martin's Press
New York

96B8299

Library of Congress Cataloging-in-Publication Data

Veryan, Patricia.
    Lanterns / by Patricia Veryan.—1st ed.
        p.   cm.
    ISBN 0-312-14640-x
    I. Title.
    PS3572.E766L36   1996
    813'.54—dc20   96-20052
                                                             CIP

First Edition: October 1996

10   9   8   7   6   5   4   3   2   1

CHAPTER I

<SUSSEX, ENGLAND>

SUSSEX, ENGLAND

Autumn, 1818

o, I hasn't forgot what I promised." Arthur Warrington peered through the gathering dusk and said in a half-whisper, "But it's not quite dark yet. 'Sides, the castle doesn't frighten you, Friar, mighty warrior that you are."

They were very close to forbidden territory now. Lanterns loomed up, a gloomy immensity, black against the darkening sky, stretching from here to the very edge of the cliffs. Arthur scrambled over a low and crumbling wall, then paused briefly before squaring his slight shoulders and flinging his cloak back so as to come at his sword. His companion sprang onto the wall and he hissed, "They've got her in the Haunted Castle, sure's sure. An' we must come to the rescue, y'know." The sword managed to catch itself in his cloak, but he succeeded in wrenching it forth at last, and waved it in the approved fashion while proclaiming "Forward!" in an unapproved whisper.

Misunderstanding, Friar Tuck leapt to engage the whirling weapon. He was told sternly to stop "playing about," whereupon he sat down and sulked.

"Come on," said Arthur urgently. "You mustn't d'sert me

now, Friar. I'm the bravest outlaw what ever was, but I can't fight all the wicked Sheriff's men at arms all 'lone!" A thought striking him, he muttered, "I wonder why they call 'em men at arms. Everyone's got arms." He glanced at Friar Tuck who was now preening his whiskers and added apologetically, "Well, almost everyone. Anyway, we'd best get on, or Etta will fuss an' Aunty Dova's sure to blame—"

The sentence died away and would never be completed. Arthur Warrington, aged almost five, was struck to terrified silence, and Friar Tuck, of the ginger-and-white persuasion, shot back over the wall without a thought for poor Maid Marion.

Somewhere amid the ruins of the Haunted Castle a door had opened and closed again. Briefly, figures had been silhouetted against a glow of light: two men, who now carried a shapeless burden across the low bridge towards a coach and four that had waited in the shadows.

A deep voice said curtly, "You know what you are to do, Mac?"

"Aye, sir."

"You'll be careful? We want no witnesses."

The second man, who talked like Hamish who'd been their gardener in London, said, "I well ken that, forbye!"

There was a faint sound. A moan perhaps.

Arthur's trembling knees seemed to melt under him so that he slid down and crouched beside the wall. But despite his thundering heart he peeped over the top.

"Whatever happens, she must never be found. You understand me?"

"Aye, sir."

The furtive pair had reached the coach, a spectral shape with no lamps lit. Arthur could see only their outlines as a third man held the door open, and they lifted their burden inside.

The Scottish voice grumbled, "This grim, glum, bogle-ridden ruin isnae a safe place for ye tae bide, sir, and ye knows it. I've nae wee joy in the Big Smoke, but I'd sooner see ye there! If Ti Chiu comes sniffin' aboot—"

"London's too noisy," interrupted the first voice impatiently. "And Ti Chiu would create less notice there, whereas here he'd stand out like a sore thumb, as would his master. Be off with you!"

Arthur ducked lower.

The carriage door slammed, the horses snorted and pawed eager hooves at the cobblestones, and there was the sound of a window being let down.

"But, how can ye manage tae—"

"Have done! Daniel—go!"

The crack of a whip. Heavy wheels crunched and rattled, leathers creaked, and the hoofbeats became a steady and fading pounding.

Straining his ears, Arthur heard not the faintest sound of footsteps, but when he dared to peep over the wall again the man who'd stayed was nowhere to be seen.

It was a long time before he summoned the courage to creep from his hiding place, and not until he was well up the slope did he dare follow the example of the craven Friar Tuck, and make a mad dash for home

<hr/>

The dower house, a square and spacious dwelling, was situated at the northwest corner of the Lanterns estate. Although more than a mile inland, it had been built on rising ground and in good weather offered an unobstructed view of the English Channel and the French coastline. It was a far cry from the luxurious elegance of Sir Lionel Warrington's London mansion, but his elder daughter, Miss Marietta Warrington, blessed with the happy facility of making the best of things, had come to think that they might have done a great deal worse than to have settled here.

"No matter what you say, there is absolutely no reason for them to call here so often," she remarked now, as she crossed the large kitchen to set the teapot on the tray with gentle care.

The old silver tea service, besides being a thing of beauty, was a relic of their former life and as such was to be handled reverently. "What could Sir Gavin Coville possibly find to interest him here?" she went on, keeping her voice low. "Our home is humble—"

"Now," put in Fanny, looking glum as she extracted warm scones from a baking pan.

"—And he is not the type of man to have formed a *tendre* for dear Aunty Dova."

At this Fanny uttered a shriek of mirth, clapped a hand over her mouth, then said between giggles, "She is in there now, you know, and Sir Gavin is being very polite, but I can scarce wait for the day when he sees her go into her dance. Already, he judges her ripe for Bedlam!"

Marietta, who was deeply attached to her high-spirited younger sister, tried to look stern but was undone by the sparkle in the big hazel eyes and failed to repress an answering smile. "He can have very little in common with my father, and he certainly must be aware that Papa suffered a great loss on the Exchange."

"On the tables at White's and Watier's, more like," said Fanny with a sniff. Noting Marietta's slight frown she knew she had been disloyal to their beloved but disastrous parent and added hurriedly, "Next you will say that our landlord has a *tendre* for me!"

Marietta hurried into the dining room, and returning with the tea strainer, said rather tartly that she had no intention of saying such a thing since Sir Gavin was merely acting for Lord Temple and Cloud, who was really their landlord, even if he never showed his face at Lanterns.

"And hopefully never will," said Fanny. "He couldn't live in that awful old place and would likely want the dower house back, and then where would we be?"

"Besides," said Marietta, continuing with her train of thought, "Sir Gavin is too old even for your ancient spinster sister. Why, he's likely the same age as my father! And even if

Mr. Blake Coville should have an interest in you, Fan—"

"Oh, do stop," said Fanny. "The reason why Sir Gavin and his son come to see us is perfectly obvious to any idiot"—she thrust the sterling silver cake plate in front of her sister's nose—"unless she be blind as several bats."

Marietta glanced critically at the face reflected in the highly polished surface. It was, she thought, a quite nice but unremarkable face. The nose was slim, the cheekbones were high but a trifle too broad. The mouth? Well, that was not too bad, and with a pleasant curve to the rosy lower lip. But it was a resolute mouth, and the chin below it could boast not the vestige of a dimple and was too firm. The eyes, with their thick black lashes were, she had to admit, very satisfactory, and a faint glow of approval stirred in their green depths as she considered her hair. The soft near-black curls were truly her crowning glory and shone like silk, nicely setting off her very light and clear complexion. "Hmm," she said.

"Hmm, indeed," exclaimed Fanny, lowering the impromptu mirror and filling it with small cakes and biscuits. "You never will admit how lovely you are. Mr. Blake Coville's eyes light up when you come into view. And small wonder."

Marietta added cups and saucers to the tray. "*Much* wonder," she argued. "Save for Jocelyn Vaughan, and Alain Devenish, who has vanished into the country somewhere—"

"Like us," inserted Fanny with a sigh.

"Like us. Where was I? Oh, yes—Except for Vaughan and Devenish, Blake Coville must be London's most eligible bachelor."

"And most handsome. Who is Jocelyn Vaughan?"

"Heir to Lord Moulton, and cousin to Lucian St. Clair. Do you not recall when he came home from the war so badly wounded, and when he recovered all the ladies were in a flutter for fear he would wed Alicia Wyckham?"

Fanny shrugged, re-filled the kettle, and put it on the hob. "For myself, I have no interest in highly born gentlemen," she declared loftily. "They are all stupid. I shall marry a poor professor, or an artist, or some plain and humble man with a brain in his head. But I care for your sake, dearest. Despite your looks, you—er—"

"I am four and twenty, and too old to attract an eligible suitor." Marietta took up the tray. "But you are only nineteen," she added, "and in spite of what you say I expect at any day to hear you admit you have become interested in some dashing young Corinthian." She laughed at Fanny's look of disgust. "Never fear, I don't mean to press you. But I would very much like to help poor Papa, you know. Someone must save him from the odious widow!"

Fanny crossed to open the door and murmured with a shudder, "Heavens, yes! How selfish I am. One of us must marry well and tow us out of the River Tick, as Eric would say. Please find a smile for Blake Coville, dearest! You cannot pretend you are indifferent to the gentleman."

Marietta turned away to hide the sudden rush of colour to her cheeks. "You have been reading too many of Mrs. Meeke's romances! Bring the cakes and the scones, Fan. And do try to remember that we are poor as church mice and I have no dowry to recommend me to any gentleman."

Walking along the passage into the drawing room she refused to judge it as any less than a most comfortable and welcoming chamber. Because of the chill of the late afternoon air, she had told Bridger to set a fire, and now the tangy aroma of woodsmoke hung on the air. Sir Gavin probably judged the furnishings shabby, but they were also immaculate, the woodwork glowing, and the rugs and several *objets d'art* clearly having come from a gentleman's home.

A casual onlooker might have been surprised to note that when she and Fanny carried in the tea trays only three of the several gentlemen present rose to their feet. A closer look would have revealed the fact that five of the other 'guests' were breathlessly still. Indeed, they had never drawn a breath at all, for they were life-sized dolls, carefully costumed and having surprisingly realistic features.

The Covilles were far from inanimate however. Both hand-some men, when entering a room side by side they'd been known to bring all conversation to a halt. At forty-eight, Sir Gavin's figure was trim, his dark brown hair was as thick and curled as crisply as that of his son, and the touch of grey at his temples emphasized rather than detracted from his good looks. His dark eyes were large, and some doting ladies had described them as 'velvety,' but they were also shrewd and intelligent. Blake Coville had inherited his father's height and build and his mother's deep blue eyes, and a smile lit them as he hurried to take the tray from Marietta and carry it to a low table.

His gaze flickered over her admiringly. He was aware that, apart from their groom, the Warringtons could not afford to keep full-time servants, and that they maintained only one old and antiquated coach and three hacks. Even so, the various family members still contrived to keep up appearances and dressed well. This afternoon Miss Marietta looked charming in a gown of primrose silk, beautifully embroidered above the hem. Following Fashion's edict, the skirt was in the new slightly shorter length which allowed a glimpse of shapely ankles (and Miss Warrington's ankles were very shapely indeed), while the neckline was cut higher to the throat than had formerly been judged stylish. If either that creation, or Miss Fanny's pale green muslin gown was self-made, as his father believed, Blake could only suppose that somebody in the household must be an exceptional seamstress.

He wondered that they could find the time for dressmaking, for they seemed always to be working. If one chanced to pay an early morning call, Miss Marietta might be found dusting or mending or helping the village woman who came in twice a week. Miss Fanny was likely to be rolling out dough or preparing vegetables in the kitchen; and Sir Lionel would be puttering about in his basement workroom busied with one of his "inventions." As for the widowed aunt who lived with them, it still made Blake uneasy to find that lady, who must be at least fifty, digging industriously in the vegetable gardens and holding merry conversations with the products of her labours. Peculiar, was Mrs. Emma Cordova, no doubt about that.

"You should not have gone to so much trouble, Miss Marietta," he now said in his pleasant voice. "Uninvited guests need not be catered to, you know."

Sir Lionel Warrington was always delighted to receive callers, and he beamed expansively. When he had married, he'd been judged a fine figure of a man, but the years had taken their toll, and after his adored Elsa had died giving birth to Arthur, his broad shoulders had bowed a little, and the abundant black hair had thinned even as the waistline had thickened. At forty-nine, uneasily aware that his character was not strong and that his gaming had brought disaster down upon them, he had become absent-minded in some respects—such as meeting the tuition costs for Arnold, who was at Harrow; and for Eric, reading for his degree at Cambridge. But he was also aware that despite his failings he was loved, and, loving in return, counted himself in many ways a fortunate man.

"It is our pleasure to have friends around us, ain't it, m'dears?" he said heartily.

His two daughters agreed with polite promptitude.

Sir Gavin Coville smiled his thanks, and told the sisters that they came like bright sunshine into the room. His ponderous gallantries always amused Marietta. She sat at the table and began to pour the tea, noting that Aunty Dova's light brown hair was even more fly-away than usual, but that she looked quite well in a mulberry velvet gown and was responding politely to their guests.

Praying that there would be no embarrassments, Marietta said, "I hope you will always feel assured of a welcome here when you are in the vicinity."

"You are too kind." Sir Gavin accepted the cup Fanny carried to him. "But I fear this is an odd hour to pay a call. I trust we do not intrude upon your time. We had to be in the neighbourhood on a, er—matter of business." His voice died away, and he stifled a sigh, but as if recollecting himself, went on hurriedly, "And since we were close by, we could not refrain from coming to see how you go on here."

"We go on well, I thank you," said Sir Lionel. "Not perhaps as well as in days gone by. But . . . quite well."

Mrs. Emma Cordova, her round face full of mischief, confided to the "lady" beside her, "They really came to look at Lanterns, you know." Turning to Sir Gavin she added without a pause, "Did I introduce you to Mrs. Butterfield, sir? You likely have met her son. Captain Butterfield is the most delightful young man." She leaned forward and putting up a concealing hand, whispered behind it, "The most frightful gossip, you know, but a gallant soldier."

Sir Gavin said with kindly gravity that he was acquainted with the lady, but not with her son.

Blake found these inanimate 'guests' hilarious and had to struggle to keep his countenance. He did know George Butterfield, and said that Mrs. Cordova was quite correct about that young gentleman's tendency to gossip.

"Well, you know," said Sir Lionel excusingly, "I always think that for all their faults, gossipy folk at least show an interest in others."

Sir Gavin stared fixedly at his son who was showing an interest in another scone, and Blake at once drew back his hand. Sir Gavin smiled. His smile became fixed when Mrs. Cordova demanded bluntly, "And why this sudden interest in Lanterns, sir?"

"Emma!" murmured Sir Lionel, embarrassed.

"It is, after all, my step-son's estate, dear ma'am," Sir Gavin pointed out.

"It is now," agreed Mrs. Cordova. "Not that his poor papa ever dreamt the title would come down to his son. Of course he did not, since he died when he was twelve years old. I don't mean that Mr. Paisley died when he was twelve years old, else he'd never have had a son, would he? I mean he died when the *boy* was twelve."

Sir Gavin corrected patiently, "Eleven, actually, ma'am.

Perhaps you are confusing the fact that he was twelve when I married his poor mama."

"I am never confused," responded Mrs. Cordova with questionable accuracy. "If I were, I might not have noticed that you were not used to visit Lanterns as often as you've done these past few months. What's to do, sir? Is Lord Temple and Cloud come to look over his home at last?"

A grim expression darkened Blake Coville's handsome features. Fanny gave her sister a long-suffering glance, and Sir Lionel moaned faintly.

If Sir Gavin was annoyed, however, he maintained his aplomb, murmuring with a smile, "Now whoever told you that, ma'am?"

Mrs. Cordova seized one of many trailing wisps of hair and thrust it under her cap. She then took up her teacup and waved it towards an extremely ample 'lady' who occupied a fireside chair. "Mrs. Hughes-Dering," she said. "And if there is anything worth knowing, from the shires to Brighton to Bath, Monica knows it, I promise you."

"Well, that is true," agreed Sir Lionel, who numbered the real and extremely formidable dowager among his friends.

Blake, still looking grim, said, "Then perhaps the lady can tell us of the whereabouts of my step-mother, which is more than—"

Sir Gavin's voice cut across the bitter words like the crack of a whip. "You forget yourself, sir!"

There was an instant of stunned silence.

Blake flushed scarlet, and mumbled an apology.

Marietta and Fanny looked at each other in amazement. Their hire of the dower house had been arranged with Sir Gavin's steward a year previously. They had not met either of the Covilles for several months after they'd moved in, but a recent visit had been followed with rather surprising frequency by others. They had never known Sir Gavin to be anything but poised and gracious. In fact Fanny had said he was "Sedate, serene, and bloodless, and quite without any human emotions."

He was not sedate now, and to see that distinguished countenance distorted with passion was shocking.

Engrossed in his troubles, Sir Gavin put a hand across his brow and bowed his head.

Mrs. Cordova rose, pushed back her untidy hair and spread her skirts. In a thin but not tuneless voice she began to sing, and as she sang she danced slowly around the centre of the room.

"Oh, no!" moaned Fanny, *sotto voce*. "Aunty Dova's off!"

Blake Colville's jaw dropped and he stared, clearly dumbfounded.

" ' 'Tis better,' " trilled Mrs. Cordova, " 'to have loved and lost . . . than never . . . to have loved at all . . .' "

Sir Gavin's head jerked up, and he stared at her, his eyes intent.

Sinking to a deep curtsy before him, she murmured, "Is that not so, sir?"

He said tensely, "Then—you know, ma'am?"

Blake snapped, "How could she know? Nobody knows!"

"Ah," said Mrs. Cordova, drifting back to her chair. "But nobody knows what I know. I know . . . things . . ." She pounced at another of her inanimate friends and demanded saucily, "Is that not right, Sir Frederick?"

Blake pulled his chair closer to Marietta and murmured, "Sir Frederick? Is that supposed to be Freddy Foster? Be dashed if it don't bear a strong resemblance to the silly clod— Er, what I mean is, are they friends?"

"They were, before we left Town. Mr. Coville, pray do not judge—I mean—Aunt Cordova was my mother's sister, and she is the dearest creature, but—it is just that—well, since she lost her husband, you know . . ."

"Married some Spanish fella, didn't she?"

He had spoken with no more than mild curiosity, but she was at once defensive. "It was a very happy marriage, but he went back to fight against Bonaparte and was killed at the Battle of Salamanca. Aunty has never quite recovered from the shock."

Coville slanted a glance to where his father was now talking earnestly to Sir Lionel. "Is that when the poor lady started making these—er, effigies?"

Marietta shook her head. "It only began after we moved down here. Aunty Dova is very warm-hearted, and she misses her friends terribly. So she decided to pretend she can still chat with them, just as if—"

A cry of anguish interrupted her, and she was dismayed to see Sir Gavin bow forward in an attitude of despair.

As swiftly as she started up, Blake was before her, bending over his father and patting his shoulder comfortingly. "Now, sir, you must not upset yourself so. I thought we had agreed not to speak of the matter."

Sir Gavin groped for a handkerchief, and dabbing at his eyes gulped, "I—I know. But—the lady seemed to . . . That is, she said she knew . . . something, but Sir Lionel says . . ." He shook his head, unable to finish the sentence.

Sir Lionel hurried to the sideboard and poured a glass of brandy for the distraught man.

Shocked by such a display of emotion, Fanny crept to take her sister's hand and said nervously, "Dearest, perhaps we should allow the gentlemen to be private."

"No, no. Pray do not let me frighten you away." Sir Gavin sipped his brandy and set the glass down. "I do most humbly apologize for . . . for that disgraceful outburst. But—" His voice shredded. "You had as well know the whole. It is my—my dear wife, you see. She has been—stolen!"

After the initial outburst of dismay and sympathy, Sir Lionel exclaimed, "I can scarce credit that so dreadful a thing should take place! How did it happen?"

Blake said sombrely, "We know very little. Three weeks ago at some time during the night Lady Pamela vanished from our London house."

Incredulous, Marietta said, "But surely someone must have seen or heard *something!* Did no one notice a—a carriage pull up, or a door close, or something of the sort?"

Sir Gavin shook his head. "Alas. Nothing."

"In the heart of *London?*" exclaimed Sir Lionel. "I'd have said such a crime could not go unnoticed!"

"True," said Blake harshly. "Unless the criminal chances to be an expert in such matters."

Marietta searched his grim face. "Has there been a demand for ransom, then? Do you say you suspect someone?"

"We've not been approached for a ransom. But we know—"

His father raised a silencing hand. "It is one thing to suspect, Miss Warrington. But as to proving it . . ." He shrugged. "We cannot be sure."

"Cannot be sure?" cried Blake impatiently. "What other explanation is there? Who else could get into the house, know where to find her, and spirit her away? Who else had a motive?"

"Who, indeed?" Sir Gavin said with a sigh. "We have kept the matter very much in the family till now, but I will confide in you, my friends, and hope your aunt may be able to help us." He took a deep breath, as though nerving himself. "It is, you see, that my dear wife's mama had settled a considerable sum upon her grandson—my step-son, that is to say. But it was left in trust. Young Paisley was not—er, pleased when I married his mother. I tried, but"—he shrugged helplessly—"I failed, alas. The boy took me in dislike and wished to live elsewhere. He demanded his inheritance. My wife loves him devotedly, but she was forbidden to hand over the monies until he reached the age of five and twenty. He stalked out of the house in a rage fifteen years ago, when he was but eighteen years of age."

Mrs. Cordova sang softly, "But he's come home again . . . home again."

They all stared at her.

Sir Lionel pursed his lips and murmured, "Jupiter, but Paisley stayed away more than a day or two, didn't he! Fifteen years? Why, he must be—let's see . . ."

"Three and thirty," supplied Blake. "But he's lived hard, and looks older."

"Which has nothing to say to the matter," said his father in another sudden burst of irritation. "The point is that his attitude was—was quite unacceptable. He insulted me, which was not important save that it upset my dear wife. Lady Pamela has been ill for some years and her nerves are not— Well, at all events, she became hysterical and said she would not sign over his inheritance until he apologized. Paisley is a man of—of a most violent nature. He demanded his rights, and so bullied my wife that I was forced to have him ejected from the house."

"Pretty behaviour!" exclaimed Fanny, her romantic heart moved by the dramatic tale. "What manner of man could treat his mama in such a fashion?"

"My step-brother," muttered Blake, frowning, "is capable of any villainy!"

Sir Gavin said wearily, "Now, Blake. We do not know that."

"We know that Lady Pamela disappeared the very next day! And that she's not been seen since!" Blake sprang up and paced to the fireplace agitatedly. "He has taken her, I tell you! And means to force her to sign over the monies."

Marietta said haltingly, "But—surely, he is by now of an age to claim his inheritance?"

"Exactly so," said Sir Gavin. "But the thing is, you see, that there was a condition to the bequest. His grandmama, knowing how wild and undisciplined was his character, stipulated that in the event he should behave in such a way as to bring disgrace down upon the family name, then my wife was to use the money to establish a home for orphaned children."

His eyes very wide, Sir Lionel asked, "And *has* Paisley disgraced the family name? Oh, your pardon! I should not pry into your affairs!"

"You do not pry, sir. Have I not asked for your aid?" Sir Gavin said. "Paisley is, alas, of a revolutionary turn of mind. Heaven only knows the type of men with whom he has associated these fifteen years. He has been involved in some very dark doings: the kidnapping of a young lady a few years back, a prominent and wealthy French nobleman who was hounded to his death, an ugly scandal in Brittany—to name but a few disgraceful incidents."

"Well! If that don't beat the Dutch!" muttered Sir Lionel, flabbergasted.

Her eyes very round, Fanny breathed, "He must be a monster *veritable*!"

Marietta asked, "Then you believe Mr. Paisley, or I should say Lord Temple and Cloud, has kidnapped the lady so as to force her to make over his inheritance."

Sir Gavin nodded miserably. "It would seem so, Miss Warrington."

"Why, it's wicked!" declared Sir Lionel. "It's more than wicked! Be dashed if it ain't downright evil! You must find your wife, sir!"

"We have tried, heaven knows," said Blake. "We've had men searching. We've scoured Lanterns from roof-tiles to cellars, but—"

"Lanterns!" Alarmed, Marietta cried, "Oh, no! Do you think he has his mama here, then?"

"We'll not be safe in our beds with such a man in the neighbourhood," exclaimed Fanny, turning pale.

"Pray do not be worried, ma'am," said Blake reassuringly. "He is not there. Nor is my poor step-mama. After her disappearance, as my father said, we fairly turned the wretched old ruin inside out."

Sir Lionel asked, "What do the authorities have to say? I fancy you've Bow Street and the local constables searching for the rogue?"

Blake looked sternly at his father. "As they should."

"No!" Sir Gavin's response was vehement. "I'll *not* have my wife's name bandied about the newspapers! I'll not have a *whisper* of scandal touch our family! I have hired men privately. We shall find Lady Coville, I promise you!"

"Perhaps," muttered Blake. "Assuming my brutish stepbrother ain't frightened the poor creature into her grave!"

Fanny gave a squeal of horror.

Sir Gavin said remorsefully, "Alas, we are alarming the ladies. I should have known better than to confide such a terrible story. But—" He rose and turned to Mrs. Cordova, who was carefully rearranging 'Mrs. Hughes-Dering's' gown. "Ma'am—you seem to have some knowledge of our trouble. If there is anything you can tell us—*anything*—we shall be eternally in your debt."

Sir Lionel said supportively, "Now, Emma. If you really do know anything that will help Sir Gavin, you must tell him, my dear."

Mrs. Cordova giggled, and murmured archly, "Such a handsome man, Monica, do you not agree? Shall I help him? What is it you wish me to tell you, sir? Is it about my radishes? Ah, lots of folk would like to know how I grow such magnificent radishes. My late husband was very fond of a radish now and then." Her face grew sad. "I heard you say you had lost your wife. You have my sympathy. To lose the one you care for is dreadful. Just dreadful."

He gazed into her kind but vacant eyes, then glanced at Sir Lionel, who gave a gesture of helplessness. Nodding resignedly, Sir Gavin said, "I fear we have overstayed our welcome, sir. We shall leave you in peace."

Mrs. Cordova hurried out to alert the Covilles' coachman.

Sir Gavin looked very sad as he said his farewells. In the large and chilly entrance hall, he asked, "Warrington, do you think your sister really has any knowledge of my wife?"

"She might." Sir Lionel hesitated. "There's no way of telling. Most of the time poor Emma is quite rational. She has the warmest heart. A very good woman. Such a pity."

Following, with Marietta beside him, Blake Coville said, "Well, now you know our dark secrets, Miss Warrington. Shall you deny me next time I call?"

"As if I would! You have my sympathy, rather. I shall pray for the safe return of your step-mama."

They turned into the entrance hall. The two older men had

passed outside, and Blake took Marietta's hand and drew her to a halt. "You are too good. Dare I impose on you to keep an eye on the manor house and let us know if you see any sign of my step-brother?"

"It would be our pleasure, sir. I only wish we could do more. Or that I knew something that would help."

"I do!" A small, muddy, and untidy figure darted at them from behind the thick draperies that closed off the draughty hall in cold weather. "I know *all* about it!" declared Arthur, jumping up and down in his excitement. "I tried to tell Bridger, but he wouldn't listen and said I was not to 'sturb you. Friar Tuck an' me—we saw the villins drag the lady out from the Haunted Castle of the Sheriff of Notting—"

"Arthur, you rascal!" said Marietta, realizing belatedly that she had neglected her small brother. "I thought you were in your room! Have you but now come home?"

"I bin home ages 'n ages. I hided in the curtains and heard everything what you said, an'—"

"Oh!" she gasped. "How dared you! Up to bed, young man! At once!"

Mrs. Cordova hurried to join them and took the boy by the hand. "He is not to blame, Marietta. We are. Come, scamp! Oh, how dirty you are! You must have had a lovely time. No, never mind spinning any of your tall tales, it's wash and bed for you, my lad."

"But I *did* see," he wailed. "An' I'm hungry! I hasn't et for weeks, I 'spect!"

Watching as he was led, protesting, away, Blake said in amusement, "An active imagination, has he?"

"Very active." Marietta held out her hand. "Good evening, Mr. Coville. Truly, I am sorry for your trouble."

Holding that small and not very well manicured hand in both his own, he said, "I thank you. And—I am permitted to call again? You will like to hear if—I mean *when* we find my step-mama, no?"

"Oh, yes indeed!"

Still holding her hand, he said, "And if your aunt *should* remember something, anything at all, may I beg that you send word? We stay with the Dales at Downsdale Park."

Downsdale Park was probably the most palatial of the nearby residences, and Lord and Lady Dale, extremely haughty, were said to entertain nobody below the rank of baronet. 'How lowly our home must seem to him,' thought Marietta. But she said, "Of course. We will notify you at once."

She tried to disengage her hand, but he held it captive a moment longer, half-smiling into her eyes in a way that made the breath hurry in her throat.

"You are so kind," he said softly, and bowing his curly head pressed a kiss on her fingers. "Truly, our steward did us an inestimable service when he was able to interest Sir Lionel in this property. *Adieu*, lovely Miss Warrington. I shall count the hours to our next meeting."

Painfully aware that she was blushing, Marietta bade him goodnight and closed the door.

Her father had to knock quite loudly before she recovered her wits sufficiently to let him in.

CHAPTER II

T he breeze set the clothes flapping on the line, and Marietta had to struggle to settle the prop firmly. She had toiled with the wash for most of the morning, and the thought of it falling and having to be done again made her cringe. She was late hanging it out to dry because Mrs. Gillespie, who should have come today, had not appeared. Probably, she had suffered another of her 'rheumaticky spasms.' Spasms, Marietta thought resentfully, that originated in a gin bottle. Mrs. Gillespie was, in fact, a less than satisfactory helper, but she was willing to come on Tuesdays and Thursdays, for a comparatively meagre sum, and when she was not suffering from her 'spasms' worked hard and seldom broke things.

The clothes smelled clean, and if the breeze held they should dry nicely by sunset. Marietta stretched wearily, and straightened her aching back. She had awoken in the night and for at least an hour had been quite unable to go back to sleep, thinking of poor Lady Pamela Coville and her wicked son, but with her thoughts wandering often to the dashing Mr. Blake Coville.

It seemed that each time they met she was more attracted to the gentleman whom common sense decreed she should dismiss from her mind. He was the beau ideal of London. Rich, handsome, perfectly formed, the heir to a baronetcy, and as kind and mannerly as he was well born. In other words, the target of the eagle eyes of countless match-making mamas. When she was near him, it seemed that his every thought was of and for her; indeed he was so obviously admiring that Papa was becoming hopeful of his spinster daughter finally making a match that would restore their fortunes forever. Poor, foolish Papa. Blake Coville was a gentleman in the fullest sense of the word, and was likely courteous and attentive to every lady he met. As for Miss Marietta Warrington, she might be passably pretty, but she had no fortune to recommend her. Fortune, indeed! Far from a fortune, she had a large family to be supported and not even a small dowry to lure a husband!

Reluctant to go back inside she stole a few minutes to wander about and enjoy her surroundings. The dower house faced southwest and had the advantage of the Channel view. The rear was lovely also, its lawns and gardens blending into broad meadowland threaded by a sparkling stream, and framed by the emerald swell of the Downs. Beyond the cutting gardens Aunty Dova had worked miracles in what she termed her 'food field,' and vegetables were thriving, the rows neat and weedless. In the flower-beds the brilliance of roses was contrasted by the bright simplicity of daisies, marigolds lifted glowing faces to the sun, and pansies peeped shyly from the borders. The afternoon was warm and several birds splashed and cavorted about in the birdbath, while Friar Tuck crouched under a stone bench, fancying himself invisible, and preparing for another of his frequent and unfailingly futile charges.

A flock of starlings flew past and soared upward. How blue was the sky. Such a glorious day. If they were still in Town, she thought wistfully, she would likely be driving down to Richmond Park with Tim Van Lindsay, or Freddy Foster, or— But the past was—past. This was today, and there was much for which to be thankful. They were all together in a nice house in a very beautiful part of God's very beautiful world. Most of the money from the sale of her own and Mama's jewels, the London house, and their horses and carriages, had gone to Papa's creditors, but she'd been able to salvage a little that was earning a tiny bit of interest in the bank. The hire of this house had been unexpectedly affordable. Her beloved brother Eric had sacrificed the Long Vacation to stay in Cambridge and tutor three young students, thus helping with his tuition costs. The rather surprising amount of income earned by "Madame Olympias" and her crystal ball—which she referred to as her Mystical Window Through Time—went towards Arnold's fees at Harrow. By practicing very strict economies the wolf had been kept from the door, but for how long, Marietta dared not think.

Not one to wallow in gloom, she straightened her shoulders. Worrying would not give them back the carefree life they had known in Town. And, after all, how many poor souls crowded into rotting, filthy slums would think the Lanterns estate and the dower house an earthly paradise?

The sun was beginning its westward slide down the blue bowl of the sky, and she had promised to spend some time with Arthur after his nap. She avoided the side door and hurried around to the front. Aunty Dova was sure to ask her to finish "Lady Leith," and she could not just now, for she must go and seek out the witch's hat.

She turned the corner of the house, and halted, staring speechlessly at the eager-eyed young gallant who was tethering two saddle horses at the foot of the terrace steps.

Blake Coville, clad in a beautifully tailored riding coat and buckskins, snatched off his hat and hurried to meet her, smiling hopefully. "I know you've far more important things to do than go for a ride with me, Miss Warrington. But it's such a lovely afternoon and—won't you please take pity on a lonely man and let me persuade you?"

Marietta's tell-tale heart began to pound unevenly. Horribly conscious of her faded pink cotton work dress and crumpled apron, and equally aware that she must look hot and untidy, she stammered, "Oh! You are—very kind, but—but I'm afraid—"

"You are too busy. How well I know it! Each time I come you are working. It will do you good to escape for a half-hour.

If you care not for my own disappointment, consider the poor mare. She's longing for a run."

Marietta's eyes flashed to the 'poor mare.' What a splendid creature, her chestnut coat sleek and shining in the sun. And, oh, how she would love to go for a ride. She stifled a sigh and said firmly, "In this house we all have to work, Mr. Coville. Our circumstances do not allow for 'escapes.' "

"Oh . . . of course," he said, looking crestfallen. "I was thoughtless. But—I'd hoped you might spare me just a little of your time. I'll bid you good day, ma'am."

He smiled ruefully and turned away. And he was young and very good to look at, and he had been so kind as to bring that beautiful little mare. And the poor man must be so anxious about his step-mama; it surely would be heartless to refuse if she could perhaps turn his mind from that worry for a little while. Having thus cunningly circumvented conscience, "Wait!" she cried.

Luckily, her riding habit was still stylish and fit well, although she noted that it was a trifle more tight across the bust. "You are becoming positively buxom, my dear," she told her reflection as she dusted a hare's foot across her nose. "A bucolic, rosy-cheeked and bosomy country wench!" Without appearing to be devastated by this assessment, she snatched up her neat hat and her riding crop, and hurried down the stairs.

Outside, Coville stood by the horses, chatting with Fanny, who wore a simple and outmoded peach-coloured round gown, and had tied a pink scarf over her thick black tresses. Marietta smiled to herself. Little Fanny undoubtedly had given not a thought to her appearance, or, if she had, supposed herself to be a proper dowd. She would have no least notion that an old gown could not make her look anything less than the very essence of glowing, vital youth and beauty.

Coville turned eagerly as Marietta approached. Fanny turned also and gave her sister a whimsically knowing glance, while saying lightly that she thought it most kind of Mr. Coville to bring such a dainty mare. "You cannot know, sir," she went on, "how my sister loves a spirited horse. In Town scarce a morning passed but that she was up and riding in the park with one beau or another long before the household was awake."

Coville grinned and bent to cup his hands and toss Marietta into the saddle. "I'll keep that in mind," he said, walking around to mount his own tall chestnut.

Leaning to her sister, Marietta murmured, "You saucy little rogue!"

"I told you," teased Fanny, her eyes sparkling.

Marietta reined the mare around and the pretty creature frisked and curvetted, tossing her head eagerly. Briefly, Coville looked anxious, but before he could speak, a shrill cry rang out.

"Etta!"

Marietta's gaze flashed to the upstairs window from which Arthur leaned, his conical wizard's hat perched on his dark curls. "Oh, my!" she exclaimed contritely.

"You *promised*!" wailed the boy.

"Dearest, I did! I am so sorry. But I'll just go for a short ride and then come straight back."

"You said I'd be Merlin an' you'd be the wicked witch when I waked up and we'd go broomsticking an' find goblins in the wild wood! You *promised*, Etta!"

"Never mind," said Fanny quickly. "I'll be a witch for you, Arthur."

A shriek rang out from somewhere in the house. "Fanny! The muffins!"

Fanny gave a gasp, and flew.

"You get ready, Arthur," called Marietta. "I'll be home quick as quick!"

The boy drew back from the window, looking rebellious.

"Oh, dear," she said. "I did promise the little fellow. Perhaps—"

Coville said firmly, "No, ma'am. Arthur has you all day and every day. We won't be long away, and it will not hurt him to wait a little while. You need a rest from your labours, Miss Marietta. And I need your kind and gentle company."

He smiled at her blindingly, then led the way along the drive-path. Hesitating, Marietta glanced back. Her aunt came to the door and waved to her. Aunty Dova was so good with the child; she'd soon restore his spirits, and, as Mr. Coville had said, they wouldn't be out long. Marietta urged the mare to a canter and joined Coville, her sense of guilt fading as they rode side-by-side through the golden afternoon.

He headed north into the Weald, maintaining a steady pace. They skirted picturesque Cloud Village, passed thatched cottages and occasional farms where labourers would pause to wave to them. And as they went they chatted idly of Princess Charlotte's sad death, of the scramble of the royal dukes to marry and produce a new heir, of London and people they both knew. Time slid past, unnoticed. They were following a lane shaded by great beeches when a big black stallion galloped to the fence of his field, and cantered along beside them.

"He wants to join us," said Coville.

"Yes," agreed Marietta. "But not at this speed."

He grinned. "I'd thought this was the rate at which you ladies like to ride in Town."

"It is the rate at which we are *obliged* to ride, rather. But we are not in Town, are we?"

Coville had a glimpse of her laughing face, then she was away.

"Hi!" he cried gaily, and was after her at the gallop.

Neck and neck they rode; along a river-bank, thundering over a rustic wooden bridge, up a rise, and down again, to follow a lush shallow valley, the wind sending the ribbons of Marietta's hat flying out behind her and rippling the skirts of her riding habit. They passed a field of cows, brown and white, chewing placidly, great mild eyes turning to them as they raced by. Marietta crouched lower, exhilarated by their speed and by the smooth gait of the little mare, until at length they approached a field bathed in sunlight where two haystacks rose in golden dignity.

Coville shouted for a halt.

"Oh!" gasped Marietta buoyantly. "How grand that was! Thank you so much!"

He smiled at her, admiring the becoming flush on her cheeks, and the sparkle in the clear green eyes. "It is I who should thank you, ma'am. Shall we rest the hacks for a space?" He led the way through the open five-barred gate and towards the haystacks and, dismounting, lifted Marietta from the saddle. She sat on a hay bale while he loosened saddle girths and straps and secured the reins to a fence post.

Returning to throw himself down beside her, he said, "You're a fine rider, ma'am. But I hope you never venture such speed in Hyde Park."

"I would be in deep disgrace, no? Oh, how lovely it is. Look at those great woods over there. Where are we, sir? Are we liable to have someone's keepers after us with pitchforks?"

He chuckled. "Never fear, I'll defend you. That is the Ashdown Forest. And I believe this is one of several farms owned by a friend of your father—a Mr. Innes Williard—so I doubt we're in great danger of being taken for trespass."

Marietta's smile faded.

Quick to notice, he said, "Am I mistaken? Do they not cry friends? Oh, egad, one can never trust the word of a gossip!"

"I did not say they are not friends. Though I cannot think why people should gossip about such a matter."

"When a gentleman has a sister who is a handsome and wealthy widow, people will always find cause for gossip, ma'am."

"Thank you, sir," said Marietta demurely. "I'll own my aunt is handsome, but I'd not thought her name was being bandied about."

Coville gave a shout of laughter, saw the faint pucker of her brows, and choked back his hilarity. "Oh, forgive me, I pray. I feel sure your aunt has—er, her share of admirers. But I must confess I referred to Mrs. Isolde Maitland. I was told she has publicly expressed her admiration for a certain . . . neighbour."

Marietta's lips tightened. 'Or for any man who will bring her the title she covets,' she thought, and said coolly, "My father, in fact."

Leaning on one elbow and looking up at her, his eyes still dancing with laughter, he said teasingly, "Aha! And you do not care for the lady."

"I said no such thing!"

"You got all starched up and said it silently. Do you not wish to see Sir Lionel re-marry?"

"No! I mean— Oh, it is not that at all!"

"Then it is that the widow is lovely, but a fortune hunter. Or—a shrew, perhaps?"

"If the lady were a fortune hunter, Mr. Coville, I think she would not choose my father to admire." Irritated, Marietta took up her riding crop. "Could we start back now? I must—"

"Whoops," he said teasingly. "I am desolate! I have made you cross with my nonsense. I shall win back into your good graces by offering my services."

She stared at him.

"No, I mean it, Miss Marietta. You will need help. A lady who is lovely and determined and clever can be very dangerous, you know."

"I don't," she said tartly. "But I suspect you have had experience along those lines, sir."

Unabashed, he nodded. "Oh, yes, indeed. Sufficient that I can be a powerful ally." He leaned closer and said in a sinister half-whisper, "I shall give you some hints that will enable you to quite defeat the widow's machinations. Unless, of course," he added irrepressibly, "your sire has a raging passion for the lady."

The picture of her shy and gentle father nourishing a raging passion, wrung a spurt of laughter from Marietta.

Coville gave an exclamation of relief. "I think I am forgiven!"

"And I think you are very naughty!" She tried to look stern. "And have made me speak of something I should not."

"You are much too kind and sweetly natured to be anything

but delicious. And I am yearning to change the subject to one that really interests me. Tell me about the most lovely and fascinating lady I have ever met. Your likes, dislikes, friends, foes, where you grew up, whether you enjoy country life or miss Town, if there are other Warringtons in the neighbourhood, what you think of Lanterns, who—"

"Mercy!" she cried, amused and touched, but throwing up her hands. "How can I answer so many questions?"

"Then answer one for today, and I shall ask you another when I call to take you riding tomorrow morning, and another the next day, and so on."

He was lying on his side, head propped on one elbow, long legs stretched out, all lithe grace. With that warm smile lurking in his blue eyes, he seemed very sincere, but was she really the most fascinating and lovely lady he had ever met? She doubted it, but it was nice to hear and it was some time since any gentleman had told her such things. She had ceased to be fascinating and lovely, it appeared, when Papa ceased to be a wealthy man. The handsome Mr. Coville was an accomplished flirt, but he made her feel pretty and desirable again, and she would have been less of a woman not to enjoy his attentions. She said lightly, "You surprise me, sir! I had not supposed that you and your papa were in the district for a long stay."

He sighed. "Sadly, that is true. But I will be riding this way as often as I can, regardless of our present—problems. Still, perhaps we should condense my list a little. Let us have the first and the last. What are your likes—your especial likes—and what do you think of Lanterns?"

"Hmm," she said, wrinkling her brow. "My first especial 'like,' of course, is my family. I think you've not met my two brothers, Eric and Arnold, for Eric stays at Cambridge, and Arnold has just left us to spend the rest of the summer with friends. As for your second question, I do not know Lanterns. I've seen it, of course, but it looks so big and gloomy, and as if it might tumble down the cliffs at any moment."

"Part of the moat has already done so. Have you never gone there?"

"Goodness, no! The ghost stories might just be true, and I would purely dislike to meet one."

"Should you? I'd love it! But say truth now. You must have some curiosity. I'd thought everyone in the county had poked about down there. Haven't you seen any treasure hunters?"

"No! Is there supposed to be buried treasure, then? How exciting! Do tell me. I'd not heard that tale."

"You've not missed anything worthwhile, for it is so much fustian. If there were a whisper of truth to the legend the treasure would have been found ages ago. That's how old it is. Some ancestor of my step-mama is supposed to have brought it back from the Crusades."

"What, exactly? A chest full of gems? I'd think that would be difficult to stow away. Especially for so long a time."

"I agree. No, it's supposed to be a picture. Something that belonged to—"

"Ah!" she exclaimed, clapping her hands in triumph. "Excuse me, but I do remember! It is called *The Sigh of Saladin*, no?"

"Jolly good. Not a large piece of art, so they say. But all worked in gold and gems. Worth the proverbial king's ransom."

"No wonder everyone tried to find it. Why was it called *The Sigh of Saladin?*"

"Lord knows. If my rascally step-brother ever shows his nose hereabouts, you can ask him. He likely knows all about it, since it was his ancestor who won the thing."

Marietta said, "Perhaps we should start for home, Mr. Coville. I'm afraid my little brother will be thinking I have quite forgotten about him."

He sighed. "Why ever is it, I wonder, that beautiful young ladies are always overly endowed with pestiferous little brothers . . . !"

"It sounds as though you have suffered from that restraint very often, sir," she said merrily. "But I promise you I would not

for one instant be without my own little brother, although—"
She paused, tilting her head as, faint with distance, a church bell
sent out its mellow announcement. *"Three?"* Startled, her eyes
opened wide. "No, surely it cannot be?"

He pulled out his pocket watch, and nodded. "It is. You have
made the moments fly past. But the sun won't go down for
hours yet. We still have time to ride as far as the forest and—"

"No! I must go back at once. I'd not dreamed we had been
out so long. And only look, the sky is beginning to be hazy. If
fog rolls in from the sea—oh, dear! I will be properly in Arthur's
black books, poor mite!"

Coville helped her to her feet and said kindly, "You should
not fuss over him too much, Miss Marietta. You love him, of
course, but he is a boy after all. And if he's like most small boys
he has quite forgotten your plans and is by now deeply involved
in some scheme of his own."

To an extent, Mr. Coville was correct. At that same moment
Arthur had abandoned his Merlin role, but he had not at all forgotten the original program.

"It's 'cause she's a girl, I 'spect," he said mournfully. "Eric says
they're all 'like. You 'member him saying that? It was when his
Everlasting Love gave him back his lock of hair, an' it was tied
up with a piece of string, 'stead of in the locket he gave her."
He took off the wizard's hat and looked at it forlornly. "Etta
promised she'd come back quick. 'N that was hours an' hours
ago." Shedding the long robe with the half moon and the stars
sewn on it, he said, "We gave her lots of chances, Friar. We
waited an' waited, din't we?"

Friar Tuck paused with one back leg flung over his shoulder, and peered up at the child's wistful face, but he made no
comment and resumed the business of tidying his nether regions.

"Fanny said she'd play," went on Arthur, "but she goed down
to help Papa 'stead. An' Aunty Dova forgot and went to her caravan." He sighed heavily. "You can't blame them, I 'spect.
They're all so old, an' I'm just a little boy, an' I'm not 'portant.

Even when I tell them *reelly* 'portant things, they won't listen. If I was 'portant, they'd listen. An they'd have time to play. But I'm not. So I'm goin' to run away an' find another boy."

He opened his cupboard and dragged out his Running Away Sack. Merlin's robe was the first thing to go in. Then came Robin Hood's doublet and cloak, his picture book of stories, his pirate flag with the skull-and-crossbones, and his black eye-patch. The suit of chain mail that Aunty Dova had fashioned out of some long chains they'd found in an abandoned cowshed followed. He took his nightshirt and the pair of bedsocks Fanny had knitted for him for Christmas, and in case it rained he added his Sunday hat. The sword, bow and arrows, and wooden pistol stuck up a bit at the top, but they wouldn't fit any other way. Next, to the larder to commandeer a wedge of cheese and the end of a loaf. A tray of jam tarts demanded instant attention and he lingered over these forbidden fruits, half hoping Fanny would come in and catch him, but he heard her laughing down in the basement with Papa, and he went back upstairs, feeling scorned and unwanted.

He was gathering up his sack when he remembered the helmet. Eric had made it for him out of an old saucepan, and Aunty Dova had found some very tall plumey feathers in a trunk in the attic and stuck them on top. It was a fine helmet, but when it was added to the rest the Running Away Sack seemed much heavier than it had been when he'd set off for London last year to find Harry Rogers, the gardener's boy. It was because of the chain mail, prob'ly, he thought, which was new since last year. Still, he was bigger now, and should be able to get there, 'stead of having Etta and Papa come and fetch him home. With a considerable effort, he succeeded in throwing the sack over his shoulder.

After he picked himself up, he had to admit that the Running Away Sack with the chain mail inside was just too heavy. If he couldn't carry it as far as the door, he prob'ly wouldn't be able to get it down the stairs. He pondered the matter, but it was Friar Tuck who found the obvious solution by suggesting with a roll-over and a stretch that he wear the chain mail, and thus lighten the sack.

"That's a sp'endid idea," he said, beaming. " 'Sides, I'll have to have some lightness left, so's to carry my spear!"

The suit of chain mail was not easy to put on, but after some convulsive wriggles and a lot of puffing and blowing, he was ready at last. He decided to wear the mighty helm also, and when he scanned himself in the cheval-glass in Etta's bed-chamber he looked so strong and tall that his spirits picked up considerably.

Friar Tuck raced in and leapt onto the bed, being a Mad Beast.

"That's a good Mad Beast, Friar," acknowledged Arthur. "But you can't be that today, 'cause if I'm goin' to be Sir Lancer Lot, you'll have to be Sir G'waine." An idea dawned, awesome in its nobility. "What we're goin' to do, Sir G'waine," he declared, "is leave a legend 'hind us. We'll do a Deed of Shivery— like the knights of old did. *Then* they'll 'member us! An' they'll be sorry!"

Inspired, he found the coil of rope he had used to tie Etta to the tree when she was captured by The Dragon. He made quite a number of winds around the sack, and luckily he was getting better at knots. It wasn't easy to lift the sack through the window without dropping it, but at last he overcame that hurdle. Having lowered the sack most of the way to the ground, he made his way downstairs and clanked across the hall. Everyone, it appeared, was stone deaf.

He wasn't able to straighten out the once-tall fern where the sack had landed, but he apologized to it politely, and with Friar Tuck bounding after him, he set out on his quest, staggering a little, and tripping over his lance occasionally, but forging onward.

The third time he had to rest he was quite tired, and dozed off for a little while. He was surprised when he awoke and found that the sun had fallen into the fog. He ate his bread and cheese and watched Lanterns begin to blur as the fog rolled in. "Oh, Sir G'waine," he breathed, enraptured. "We're goin' to do the best Deed of Shivery what ever was! They'll be *glad* to play with us after this! Even Papa!"

CHAPTER III

y love!" Mrs. Cordova had come in at the back door just as the front door opened to admit her niece, and they met in the hall. "Had you a nice time? Has Mr. Coville left? You should have invited him to stay and dine with us, or at least have a few words with your father."

"He's chatting with Papa now. But I think he is anxious to get back to Downsdale Park."

"Bother, bother, bother!" Mrs. Cordova shook out the voluminous black satin robe she carried and inspected it anxiously. "I knew some of the spangles were coming loose! The poor boy must worry so for his step-mama. Were you able to lighten his spirits?"

"There was little need. I think he conceals his feelings very well, for we scarcely spoke of the lady. Where is—"

"Which does but prove how clever you are, Etta. You will make someone a good wife. Ain't that so, Warrington?" she added as her brother-in-law came in the front door.

"Oh, very true." Sir Lionel beamed at Marietta and slipped an arm about her. "Clever puss! You have quite captivated young Coville. He could not say enough good of you. Which is understandable, of course. But you must try to keep him in the vicinity, child. He is greatly admired in Town, you know, and if he were to go back, there's no telling—he might forget you. And we cannot have that, now can we?"

Marietta pointed out gently, "You know, Papa, I have left my salad days behind and I have no fortune to bring to a marriage. Perhaps you should not refine too much on—"

"Pooh! Nonsense! You are the prettiest young lady in all Sussex, and would grace the home of any gentleman. Besides, Sir Gavin is rich as Croesus—or was it Midas? Well, no matter. Much the young fellow needs dowries. He is properly smitten, I'm sure of it. With luck, m'dear, you'll be Mrs. Blake Coville before the year is out!"

Envisioning a rosy future which included a fine London house and the restoration of his servants, horses, and carriages, Sir Lionel patted his daughter on the back, beamed at his sister-in-law, and went down to his workshop humming blithely.

Watching her niece, Mrs. Cordova asked, "You do like Mr. Coville, don't you, dear?"

"Yes, very much. Who could not?"

"Enough to marry him?"

For a moment Marietta did not answer. Then she said, "Do you know, Aunty, I really don't believe I shall ever have to consider that possibility. Now do pray tell me, where is Arthur?"

"Goodness, I don't know. With Fanny, I suppose. I shall have to find some thread or I'll lose these spangles. I had quite forgot that Mrs. Stroud had made an appointment with Madame Olympias this afternoon." She giggled. "Luckily I got to the caravan before she did. Do you think they suspect it is me, Etta?"

"No, I don't, for you keep it very dark and mysterious in your caravan. Besides, between your robe and turban, and the funny accent you use, to say nothing of all the paint you put on your face, I would not know you!"

"Even so, I'm glad we put it about that the great Grecian mystic likes to escape from London occasionally, and that we make a little extra money by permitting her to keep a caravan on a corner of our property. It is—not completely unbelievable, do you think?"

"I hope very much they go on believing that, Aunty," Marietta said with a smile. "In view of the advice you give to people we would be liable to have some very angry visitors if ever the truth came out!"

"But—Etta!" protested Mrs. Cordova, stung, "I really *am* a mystic! I only tell my clients what is revealed in the Mystical Window Through Time. Or what it is best for them to believe. I do not hurt or deceive anyone."

"No, dearest, of course you don't. You just bend the truth a trifle. And you give them a good dramatic performance for their money, which they very much enjoy. Now I really must go and find Arthur. I had thought he'd be waiting for me."

"He must be with Fanny. Do you know where the child has got to, Mrs. Hughes-Dering?"

Not waiting for Mrs. Hughes-Dering's 'reply,' Marietta went down to the basement. Sir Lionel's workshop was incredibly cluttered and a magical place for a small boy, and despite endless warnings not to touch, there were temptations everywhere that proved irresistible to a curious mind and a pair of astonishingly quick little hands. Arthur's last visit to the workshop had ended in disaster. The memory of her father's singed hair and eyebrows and his enraged howls that the child would burn the house down caused Marietta to hasten, but her apprehensions proved groundless. Fanny was there, fascinated by her sire's new invention, an as yet unperfected device to remove fleas or head lice. She told her sister gaily that Friar Tuck had taken a very dim view of the invention when they'd attempted to test it on him. As for Arthur, she supposed he was in his room.

Marietta's premonition that something was amiss communicated itself to her aunt, and together they went upstairs. Once again, Arthur was not to be found. The state of his room confirmed Marietta's fears. "Only look at this mess!" she exclaimed. "His Running Away Sack is gone, Aunty Dova! Poor little boy, I really let him down! And only look how the fog is rolling in. I must go after him before it starts to get dark!"

"Oh dear, oh dear!" moaned Mrs. Cordova, accompanying Marietta to her bedchamber. "I shall have to tell your father, and he will fly into a fit as he always does!"

"Then don't tell him just yet. With luck I may be able to find Arthur and fetch him home before Papa misses him."

"You're never going outside wearing *that?* For pity's sake, child! You will look a proper figure of fun."

Marietta agreed but put on the black cloak and the witch's hat and told her aunt that Arthur might forgive her if they played at goblin-catching en route home. "Besides, who will see me? We are the only people living on the estate at the moment, and Sir Gavin and Mr. Coville are halfway to Downsdale Park by this time."

"I will be so anxious! How shall you know which way to go?"

"Oh, I fancy he's off to Town again and he usually drops things as he gets tired, which should give me a trail to follow. Would you be a darling and take in the wash?"

Mrs. Cordova agreed to perform this task. She shook most of the dust off the things she dropped and hid them at the bottom of the pile, and after she had carried in the laundry basket she went in search of a needle and thread so as to repair the robe of the Great Grecian Mystic. She sat on the drawing room sofa beside her friend, 'Captain Miles Cameron,' and said comfortably, "Now do tell me, dear boy, are you not glad the war is over at last . . . ?"

❦

The tall man who slipped out of Lanterns' massive front door remained in the arched recess for a minute or two, watchful and silent, as one with the deepening shadows of the mist-shrouded afternoon. When at last he emerged, his movements were smooth and catlike. He wore riding boots, but there was no sound of jingling spurs, no rattle of a pebble as he seemed almost to drift down the time-worn steps. He turned aside from the bridge that had once been the drawbridge, and followed a weedy sunken garden that encircled the house. In olden times this had been the moat, but through the centuries the sea had eaten away the cliffs and now the south end of the moat was gone and the sunken garden was cut off by a low wall at the very brink of the cliff.

The tall man rested long, thin hands on the wall and looked down at the rocks far below and the waves that swept in to swirl over them, only to sink down and retreat again. The sea was quiet today. The house was quiet, too. The doctors had said he needed quiet. Doctors! But this time, at least, they'd managed to remove the musket ball from his back; perhaps because he'd told them he'd not endure another series of their excruciating efforts. He watched a seagull swoop over the beach and wondered why it was not perched on a buoy or a post somewhere with its fellows. A loner, he thought wryly, as he had been for most of his life. By its very nature his occupation dictated that he have few friends. As to enemies, Mac was right, he had more than enough of those!

The gull swooped low, and alighted some distance along the wall. It moved its feet up and down, half turning to view the human from the corner of a beady eye.

Amused, the man sketched a salute. "Good afternoon, sir. Or is it madam? Jolly good of you to drop in. Allow me to introduce myself: My name is Diccon. But perhaps you came to call upon Mr. Fox?"

The bird uttered a squawk and regarded him warily.

"No cause for alarm. You are perfectly welcome to share the wall. What? Going already? I'll find you some bread if you'd care to stay for tea."

Of whatever gender, the gull refused the invitation and with an impressive spread of its wings departed, to be quickly swallowed up by the thickening Channel fog.

Diccon's thoughts turned inward once more. It was a strange road he followed through life. A road that had earned him more than his share of hard knocks, and that seemed of late ever more solitary. But nobody had forced it on him. He'd followed where his interests led, and, whatever else, the years had certainly not been dull. And yet, what had he to show for it all? At an age when most of the men he knew were comfortably wed and had set up their nurseries, here he stood on a chilly autumn after-noon, keeping company with an unsociable gull (not even a bird of paradise!) and with his back reminding him that he'd do bet-ter to go inside and light a fire. He heard a distant and familiar summons and smiled faintly. There was always Mr. Fox, of course, to scold him for moping about feeling sorry for himself. He pushed away from the wall and stood straight. He'd go and see what—

He sensed rather than heard someone behind him. Had he been at the top of his form he'd have been aware of an intruder a few seconds earlier. The lapse cost him dearly. Before he could turn, something smashed into his back bringing pain so savage and blinding, that it forced an anguished cry from him. But be-cause he lived with danger his reaction was instant and efficient. He crouched and spun about, caught a glimpse of a blurred but decidedly bizarre figure, waving plumes, and a lance poised for another attack. Furious, he wrested the lance aside with a force that sent his attacker spinning into the wall to slump there, un-moving.

It had been a surprisingly easy victory, but, taking no chances, Diccon held the lance poised and ready while he moved closer to his assailant. His vision was clearing. He was bewildered to discover that the 'lance' was a headless broom-stick. With a horrified gasp he viewed the still form of a small boy, a battered saucepan topped with long plumes sagging on his head. A large ginger-and-white cat sprang up onto the wall, froze as it encountered him, then went tearing off.

"Aah! You monster! You hideous brute! What have you done?"

Turning unsteadily to meet this new attack, Diccon reeled. A witch, complete with high-pointed hat and long black cloak was rushing at him. "Madre de Dios!" he gasped, fearing that his brain had become disordered.

The witch flew to kneel beside the boy. "Arthur!" she sobbed, "Oh, my dearest! What did he do to you?" She lifted the pseudo-helmet from the child's head, revealing a very small white face and closed eyes. Smoothing back the tumbled dark curls, she turned like a tigress on the man who dropped to one knee beside her. "Do not *dare* to touch him!" There was a note of hysteria in her voice and tears poured down her cheeks as she clawed at his hands. "You've *killed* him! You murderous, *monstrous* man!"

Diccon hid his terror that she might be right, and said coolly, "Try not to be so ridiculous. And don't pull at him, you'll make him feel worse."

She fought him madly, and he took both her flying hands and held the wrists in an iron grip. "Stop, or I shall be obliged to slap you!"

Between the fog, the deepening dusk, and her tears, Marietta couldn't see him very clearly, but she had an impression of a gaunt face, unruly light brown hair, and piercing, very pale eyes. She choked back sobs, and fought for control.

The deep, cold voice said, "That's better. I think he's just stunned, but we must get him home. Is he yours? Who are you? Do you live nearby?"

"He is . . . my brother." She watched as he felt for a pulse and explored that pathetic little figure with steady, practised hands. "How could you . . . strike him like—like that?" she demanded.

"I don't think anything's broken. If you saw it, then you must know that he came at me from behind."

"But—he is only a *child!*"

"Yes. Well, he was uphill from me and didn't look like one with that damned great thing on his head. I thought— Never mind about that." He took off his coat rather awkwardly and spread it over the boy. "I'll go and get a horse poled up. How far away is your home?"

"Less than two miles."

He said inexplicably, "Then Mr. Fox will do," and walked away, his head a little bowed and his steps rather erratic. Over his shoulder he called, "Don't go mauling him about. He'll do better to lie quietly."

"He'd do better had you not struck him!" she retaliated.

There was no response. He disappeared into a great frowning door of the manor, and Marietta hovered over her brother, holding his small hand, and praying.

The 'hideous brute' returned quite soon but instead of a team he led a small, shaggy donkey harnessed to a cart. Marietta's suspicion that he was a penniless wanderer using Lanterns as a temporary haven was reinforced.

He left the leathers trailing, and came to bend over the child. She said with loathing. "I'll lift him, thank you very much!"

Her outstretched hands were again thrust aside. "Madam," he said icily, "I appear to have won an ignoble victory. I do not propose to watch you drop my victim and then blame me for any further damage."

"I am perfectly capable of lifting him, and I do not want you to touch him with your—"

"Murderous hands? You will discover how murderous they are if you do not stop being ridiculous. Move!"

He had not raised his voice, but the steel in the tone convinced her that he was quite capable of attacking her, and she drew back.

He bent and slipped an arm under the boy's shoulders.

Arthur moaned, and his eyelids flickered and opened. Confused, he muttered, "I slew the . . . villin, Etta. But I hurt. Is I . . . dying?"

"No, no, dearest," she said over the lump in her throat.

"You won the battle but lost the war, old fellow," said Diccon in a tone that surprised Marietta. "We're going to take you home with the wounded."

"On a . . . gun carriage?" asked Arthur faintly.

"Just so. Now I'm going to lift you, and if it hurts you can yell. Soldiers do yell, sometimes."

The suspicion of a grin tugged at the boy's mouth. "You did," he said. "You yelled—very loud."

"Hmm," said Diccon, and lifted him into the cart.

Arthur whimpered.

The donkey emitted an ear-splitting bray.

Marietta gave a gasp, and Arthur clung to Diccon's coat, his eyes wide with fright.

Diccon said, "It's just Mr. Fox. He's a donkey, but he worries."

"Oooh," whispered Arthur. "You got a donkey!"

"I have. When you're feeling better you shall ride him, if you like."

"If you ever come near us again, my papa will take his pistols to you," said Marietta through her teeth. "He likely will, anyway!"

His bored glance flickered from the peak of her hat to the hem of her cloak. "One wonders," he drawled, "if you ever say anything sensible, Madam Witch. You might better tell me with whom you stay."

She had quite forgotten her costume and her face flamed. She said angrily, "We do not stay with anyone. As I told you, our house is not quite two miles northeast. It is called—"

Incredulous, he interrupted, "The *dower* house? The devil you say!"

"Instead of swearing, perhaps you could set your donkey in motion."

He offered a hand. "If you will hurry up and get in, I'll do so."

Marietta refused his assistance but found it difficult to climb into the cart wearing the voluminous cloak. Chagrined by the awareness that the monster had viewed a good deal of her limbs, she was breathless by the time she knelt beside Arthur. "We're going home now, dearest," she murmured. "Be brave. You'll soon feel better."

"He does feel better," said Diccon, climbing to the seat and chirruping to Mr. Fox. "He made a jolly fine charge. Though I'd be interested to know why."

Arthur whispered, "He's got a donkey!"

⚜

Pausing on the landing, Sir Lionel was considerably taken aback to see that the insensate villain who had attacked his child had seated himself in the front hall. Usually mild-tempered, Sir Lionel stiffened, his plump cheeks flushing with wrath. "I wonder at your gall, sir!" he snorted, proceeding down the stairs. "I say, I am amazed and confounded! One might suppose that having so brutally dealt with my little son, you—"

Diccon came to his feet and interrupted, "How does the boy go on? Is he badly damaged?"

"He will recover." Irked because he had for some reason felt compelled to respond to the authoritative tone, and also because he was obliged to look up at this crude individual, Sir Lionel added, "No thanks to you, sir! You are fortunate I do not call you out, but—"

"Did he tell you what happened?"

Sir Lionel puffed out his cheeks and said, somewhat deflated, "He did. Otherwise, I promise you, I would—"

"Yes. Well, of course you would. Any father worth his salt would. I'll not distress you by staying. I just wanted to be sure he was—"

"Good day, sir!"

Diccon frowned, but nodded and turned to the door.

"A moment, if you please!"

A large lady was running down the stairs.

Diccon checked, eyeing her rapid advance uneasily. At such a headlong pace her flowing draperies constituted a distinct hazard.

"Look out!" shouted Sir Lionel.

Diccon sprang forward and was in time to catch her although her size and speed sent him staggering.

"Thank you!" she gasped, regaining her balance. "Not that I should feel beholden to you, of course, since you were so cruel to my darling Arthur. But— Ah. He has hurt you, I see! Is that why you struck him?"

He looked at her curiously, wondering if she had mothered the lovely witch he'd driven home. Certainly, she indulged herself at table and affected an odd style of dress, but he suspected that this lady once had been a beauty. He was startled then to realize that her big dark eyes were fixed upon his own unblinkingly. Disconcerted by a sudden feeling that she could see into his mind, he replied, "I—thought he was someone else. May I ask if he makes a habit of attacking strangers?"

"He has a vivid imagination and spends much time in his make-believe worlds. Which is not such a bad thing, the real world being what it is. . . . But he has never attacked anyone before."

"Did he say why I caused him to change his behaviour?"

"No. Do strangers make a habit of attacking you from behind, Mr. . . . ?"

Diccon stood very still, meeting her penetrating gaze narrowly. "My name is Mallory Diccon—"

Irritated, Sir Lionel interrupted, "I do not care what your name is, and I see no call for this discussion." He marched to fling open the front door. "If you take my advice, sir, you will leave this area without delay. Lord Temple and Cloud, who owns this estate, is returning to the neighborhood momentarily, and will no doubt set his dogs on any vagrants who loiter about."

Diccon bowed and left them.

⚜

So I crep' up a'hind him," said Arthur, pale but bright-eyed as he lay on the sofa in the withdrawing-room next morning. "An' then I charged into battle on my trusty steed."

"You must have been going quite fast to hit him so hard." Marietta dusted the mantelpiece clock carefully. "You might have knocked him over the edge, you know. Didn't you think of that?"

"I jus' thought he was a bad man. An' I wanted to rescue the lady. The one you was talking about."

It occurred to Marietta that although his retaliation had been far more violent than was justified, Mr. Diccon had some small basis for complaint.

Arthur saw her faint frown, and explained, "I wouldn't have been going so fast, but when my trusty steed started to run, well, my armour was awful heavy, an' going downhill like that, I couldn't stop. If he *had* falled—"

"Fallen, dear."

"—fallen over the edge, would he have been killed stone dead?"

"Yes, I'm afraid he would." Marietta laid down her duster and went to sit on the sofa beside her brother. "And that would have been a very terrible thing, Arthur. Something you would never be able to forget for as long as you lived. Because when a life is taken, it brings pain and grief to many other lives. You wouldn't want to cause anything like that, would you?"

"But s'posin' he was a bad man?" he said earnestly. "A *very* bad man. S'posin' he'd hurt someone else? Even someone you loved? Wouldn't it be right to make him dead then?"

"But he's not a bad man, my dear one. He's just a wanderer who's borrowing Lord Temple and Cloud's house because he doesn't have one of his own. Still, I know what you mean. That's why we have the Watch, and the constables, and Bow Street to punish people who do very bad things. We don't punish them ourselves."

"Oh. But there's not a Watch or a Bow Street here, is there Etta?"

"There's Constable Davis in the village." With a sudden vision of future embarrassments, she added, "But if we had absolute proof that somebody had done something evil, we'd still talk it over with our family before we bothered Mr. Davis. And above all, dearest, we don't *ever* deliberately hurt anyone. You might have hurt Mr. Diccon quite badly, hitting him in the back like that. Will you promise to be more careful in the future?"

He hung his head, and nodded.

Marietta stroked his curls fondly. He was such a sensitive, lonely little boy, too often left to himself in his 'make-believe world,' as Aunty Dova had said. He had already paid a high price for his actions and she had no wish to make him feel crushed with guilt. "Were you pretending that Mr. Diccon was the Sheriff of Nottingham?" she asked kindly.

Arthur sighed. "I 'spect ladies don't know much 'bout things. Robin Hood doesn't wear chain mail. It was Sir Lancer Lot who was jousting with the Black Knight."

"I see. Then you didn't really think Mr. Diccon was a bad man, did you?"

He considered this in silence. Then he raised his angelic blue eyes to meet hers. "He's got a donkey," he said simply.

Fanny came in. "I'm baking you a gingerbread man, wounded hero," she said, offering a skewer and a shallow pan to her brother. "Would you like to make his face?"

Only too willing to oblige, Arthur took the skewer and with great concentration began to give the gingerbread man a very toothy grin and two big eyes.

Fanny smiled at her sister. "I see he's well on the road to recovery. Is Mr. Coville coming to pay a call today? I'd thought he meant to take you riding this morning."

Marietta had thought the same thing, but said they had formed no definite plans.

"D'you know what I think?" said Fanny. "Your devoted swain is a Bond Street Beau and believes no civilized person rises before noon."

Mrs. Cordova trotted across the entrance hall waving a bulky parcel. She had left the front door wide, and brought a breath of warm air and a flood of sunlight with her. "Only look what I found on the terrace!" she panted.

"Aha!" exclaimed Fanny. "I mistake the matter, and the devoted swain has called already!"

"But I do not have a devoted swain," said Mrs. Cordova, puzzled. "Do I?" She peered hopefully at her amused nieces, then laughed. "Oh, I see! Wicked girls that you are!" Inspecting the parcel she added, "And this is not for you, Marietta. It's addressed to 'Master Arthur Warrington.' "

Arthur gave a whoop and reached out. Rending the brown paper, he was suddenly very still, gazing and gazing. Mute, he held up a small leather sword belt and scabbard. The two-edged sword was wooden but beautifully carven, the hilt set with a great imitation ruby.

"Oooh!" he breathed, springing up. "Quick! Quick! Help me put it on, Etta!"

She laughed. "What, over your nightshirt?"

"Jus' to see if it fits," he said eagerly.

Searching the paper, Fanny teased, "There's no card, but I suspect Mr. Coville believes that the quickest way to a maiden's heart is through her little brother. And you are blushing, Etta."

Mrs. Cordova had also picked up a piece of the wrapping. Turning it in her hands she murmured, "I think you are in the wrong of it, Fan."

Marietta looked at her sharply.

"It's from the Black Knight," cried Arthur, wrenching forth the sword. "An' it fits jus' right! Oh, isn't it sp'endid!"

Marietta frowned.

Mrs. Cordova pointed out, "Under the circumstances, it is kind in him."

"He might better have sent a book, or a toy," said Fanny primly, "rather than a weapon of war!"

"Wheee!" squealed Arthur, leaping about and flourishing the sword with vigour. "I mus' go and get dressed!"

Mrs. Cordova took the boy to the stairs, glanced out of the front door, then hurried back to the withdrawing room. "You will want to change also, Etta. Mr. Coville is riding through the lodge gates! My, what a handsome creature he is!"

Running to peep at the "handsome creature," Fanny closed the front door and called, "Only one horse, Etta. You won't need your habit."

Marietta fled to her room. She put on a pomona green and white muslin morning dress, tidied her hair, brushed a hare's foot over her shiny nose, and hoped Papa would not attach too much importance to this visit.

In the entrance hall, Blake Coville waited. His well-cut riding coat was blue, his linen like snow, and immaculate moleskins clung to his muscular legs. He was a sight to make any female heart flutter and Marietta's heart was no exception as he took her hand and said admiringly, "How charming you look, Miss Warrington. Your father has given me leave to take you for a short stroll. May I beg that you will agree?"

All smiles, Sir Lionel stood nearby, nodding encouragement, and when Marietta said she would go and fetch her bonnet and a parasol, he told her triumphantly that he had already sent for those articles. Mrs. Gillespie came puffing from the back stairs, her square face flushed as she offered the dainty bonnet. Embarrassed by such a display of eagerness, Marietta tied the ribbons hurriedly and avoided Mr. Coville's eyes.

Outside, the air was already quite warm. They followed the drive-path around to the back of the house, then walked through the gardens and into the meadows.

Coville took Marietta's parasol and put it up for her. "You are not provoked with me for suggesting that we walk?" he asked. "I had intended to bring a mount for you, but—alas! there is no time!"

Disappointed, she asked, "You are returning to London, sir?"

He nodded and said with a sigh, "Our steward sent a footman with an urgent message. A foreign potentate has arrived at Carlton House in connection with a matter vital to Britain's interests, and since my father has travelled widely and chances to be acquainted with the sheikh. . . ." He shrugged ruefully.

"Your papa is asked to handle the business, is that it? You must be very proud to be the son of so important a gentleman."

"Yes. Well, I am, of course. But to leave Sussex at this particular time is"—he sighed again—"is very far from my own wish, Miss Marietta." He offered his arm. "May I be permitted to address you so?"

Well aware that eyes were watching from the windows of the house, she slipped her hand onto his arm and said, "In private perhaps, Mr. Coville."

He patted her hand. "Then, in private, I must be Blake. Yes, I know that is being very forward, but you must know how very lovely you are, and how much I admire you. I am so glad we are friends. I only wish—" A worried look came into his eyes. "There's no use wrapping it in clean linen—I wish my step-brother was not coming back at this particular time. You will take care, ma'am?"

"Good gracious," she said, smiling at him. "I am in peaceful Sussex, Mr. Coville. Not aboard some East Indiaman being pursued by Portuguese pirates!"

"I know. But—may I beg that you will do something to set my mind at rest?"

Temple and Cloud must really be a bad man. Pleased that Mr. Coville should be so concerned for her safety, she asked, "Such as?"

"If by any chance you hear that Paisley, my step-brother, has come to Lanterns, will you get word to me? Your father has my direction. I'll come at once, I promise you."

Astonished, she protested, "No, really! You are very kind, but his lordship cannot pose a threat to me, or to my family, surely?"

That frighteningly grim look was in his eyes once more. He said quietly, "He is the most dangerous man I have ever known. I would hold no lady safe within ten miles of him! And you stay here, ma'am, on his land. I know you must think I exaggerate. I do not. Quite apart from Paisley, there are treasure hunters to be guarded against. If you see anyone lurking about Lanterns—"

Marietta started.

He drew her to a halt and peered into her face. "What is it? Never say you've already seen trespassers down there?"

Mr. Diccon hadn't really meant to hurt Arthur, and had been so gentle with the child afterwards. And Arthur was overjoyed with the sword. Somehow she could not bring herself to betray their trespasser. "After all you have told us," she said, "I would be terrified to go near the old place." Coville looked unconvinced, and she added, "Besides, surely your step-brother would not choose to live in such an old ruin?"

"There is no telling what mischief he may be brewing. I

could not bear that anything untoward should happen to you, or to your family." He pressed her hand and said earnestly, "While I'm away I shall hold your lovely face always in my mind's eye. And I'll count the hours till I can return and find you safe."

It was a good thing, thought Marietta, knowing her cheeks were hot, that she had more common sense than to refine upon such behaviour. If she allowed herself to interpret his remarks as she knew Papa or Fanny would do, it would be very easy to believe that Mr. Blake Coville's heart was being ensnared by a penniless girl with a large family to be provided for.

CHAPTER *IV*

I am quite aware that I'm not going fast enough for you," said Diccon wielding the curry comb with steady strokes. "But I've already taken care of Orpheus, and what you fail to realize is that I'm not supposed to be doing this at all. Someone should be waiting on *me*, rather!"

Mr. Fox brayed softly, turned and lowered his head to lean it against his owner's chest. Diccon staggered, and swore. Mr. Fox looked at him anxiously. Pulling the donkey's ear, Diccon soothed, "It's all right. Don't fly into a pelter. I'm not quite steady on my pins yet, is all."

Reassured, Mr. Fox permitted his head to be turned aside again and his grooming recommenced.

It was a brilliant morning. The sky was a deep blue against which white clouds billowed majestically. The warm air was heavy with the scents of blossoms and the clean salt tang of the sea. Birds hopped and twittered, bees buzzed, and Diccon grumbled.

"Only listen to all that peace and quiet! The place is like a blasted tomb! Yes, I know that's how it is supposed to be. It wasn't yesterday afternoon, though." He chuckled, and the curry comb slowed. "We didn't know about that little brat and his family in the dower house, did we, Fox? As well we found out. We'll have to be more careful, especially when Yves comes back. Can you imagine that rogue's reaction were he to rest his eyes on the delectable witch?"

Here, the curry comb stopped altogether, and Diccon leaned on the donkey's back, an amused twinkle in his eyes. "Did ever you see such a little beauty? But what a termagant! Likely that's why she's unwed. No man wants a shrew for a wife. She may perhaps be betrothed, in which case heaven help the poor fellow! We're happy in our bachelor life, aren't we, Fox? Though it would be grand to have a little scamp like young Arthur about the house. If one had a proper house. And to have a gentle lady to confide in, and love, and who would care about us." He considered that wistfully, then uttered a snort of derision, "Who'd want us, eh? A battered bachelor short on those two vital necessities, looks and lettuce. And—your pardon, but facts are facts—a donkey."

Mr. Fox tossed his head and brayed, and Diccon laughed. "Insulted you, did I? Very well, I'll stick to my task and then I mean to go and poke around the old wing. You never can tell, there might really be a *Sigh of Saladin* lurking about. If we were to find that, my friend . . . ah, then things would be different!"

He finished his grooming, turned the little donkey out to graze, and walked back to the manor. It would take a small army and a large investment to restore Lanterns, but with typical Scots industry MacDougall had attacked the littered kitchen in the 'new' wing so that the enormous room fairly shone with cleanliness. Diccon filled the coffee pot at the pump and set it on the stove to heat while he 'poked around.' One of the first improvements, he thought, must be to have running water laid on.

The broad passage was gloomy and deathly still, and the chill from the flags struck through the soles of his boots. The rooms he passed were shuttered and dark. At the end of the corridor a massive sweep of stairs led to the railed balcony of the first floor and beyond spread the immensity of the single-storey hall that connected the old and new wings. He walked softly across it, his ears straining against the solid wall of silence. At the far end an iron-bound door opened onto three wide stone steps worn by age and leading down to the most ancient part of Lanterns. It was even more gloomy here for there were no windows on this level, the only light filtering down from the stair-well to the upper storey, and from one room where a block had tumbled from the west wall. The stone floor was uneven, and the smell of damp and decay hung thickly on the air.

The farther he progressed the more noticeable was the deterioration, and he halted in the vast chamber that had been the original great hall, saddened because the poor old house had come to such a state. Yet it still retained traces of former glory. A rusting suit of armour sagged on a small dais and the walls were hung with several broadswords, a crossbow, a mace, and a mighty war axe, their grim dignity marred by cobwebs. Three chests, a very long table, and benches set on either side of the outer door had survived, thick with dust. At the southernmost end of the room a narrow flight of stairs led to the upper floor and en route provided access to the minstrel gallery, which was supported by sturdy beams.

Here, in the twelfth century, the mighty Simon, Lord Cloud, had held court, surrounding himself with knights and squires and men at arms, and lovely ladies who wore flowing robes and wimples and busied themselves at their tapestries. It was this same nobleman who was said to have come home from the Third Crusade with the *Sigh of Saladin* as a wedding gift for his bride. If legend spoke truth the jewelled picture had been hidden when Lanterns was besieged by invading French during the war that ended in 1217. Part of the house was burned during the desperate fighting and Lord Simon and the squire who had hidden the picture were slain. If such a treasure had actually existed, it was never seen again, but the tale had been handed down through the centuries and in the event that it was based on fact, surely the picture would logically have been hidden here, rather than—

The sound was no more than a whisper, but he heard it, and sensed also that he was no longer alone. With not a second's hesitation he raced soundlessly back to the main entrance and peered outside. A ginger-and-white cat was slinking in through the hole in the wall. The knight who attempted to follow was making a good deal of noise due to chain mail and a dropped helmet. The latter having been replaced, he tried again and succeeded in getting one leg through the space.

Amused, Diccon growled, "Advance and be recognized!"

There came a startled yelp. The cat shot out through the wall and fled. The knight backed away then crouched behind a stone urn, his plumes waving above it betrayingly.

Diccon choked back a laugh and called, "Only Sir Lancelot may pass this way! If you are he, show your sword."

A tremulous voice said, "I'm he," and a small wooden sword waved beside the plumes.

Diccon stepped from the entrance arch. "Welcome, Sir Knight. Are you on a quest?"

"Y-yes." His eyes very wide, Arthur came into view but pressed back against the urn. "I'm a shiverous knight," he explained. "So I've came to 'pologize for jousting with you without telling you we was jousting."

Diccon managed to keep his countenance while offering a profound bow.

"An' to see your donkey," said Arthur, venturing a step closer.

Watching the hopeful little face, Diccon knew it was unlikely that Sir Lancelot had obtained permission to come here. Still, it would do no harm to let the boy meet Mr. Fox, at least. "This way," he said with an inviting gesture.

Arthur came to join him, peered in through the door, then stepped back a pace. "It's awf'ly dark."

"We can follow the moat around to the kitchen door on the other end, if you wish."

"Ooh," breathed Arthur. "Is this a moat? It's all dried up."

"To a pirate, perhaps. But to a knight of the round table it's full to the brim. Every good castle should have a moat, don't you think?"

Impressed, Arthur nodded and walked a little closer to the tall man. "We got one, y'know. It's behind the barn." Brightening, he enlarged upon that stretch of the imagination. "A dragon lives in it. Has you got a dragon, Mr. Diccon?"

"You should call me Sir—er, Gawaine. My dragon has gone flying off somewhere, I'm afraid. Probably in search of lunch. Speaking of which, I do have a kitchen. And I believe there is a seed cake lurking about. Perchance you would share my board, Sir Lancelot?"

"A'right," said Arthur, happily. "But I'd rather have some cake, if you please."

❧

Shameful, I calls it!" Mrs. Gillespie set the iron on its heel and handed the folded tablecloth to Marietta. "This'n needs a darn, Miss. The squire should call in the army and chase the varmints out." She folded her arms across her bosom, tucked in her chin, and arranged her sagging features into the expression that said she knew Important Things. "*If* they be humings, that is to say!"

"Not—human?" Seated at the kitchen table working her way through a pile of mending, Marietta smiled. "Come now, you never believe the ghost stories about Lanterns?"

"Aye. There's them as laughs." Mrs. Gillespie nodded grimly and took up her iron again. "But my mister's seen lights in them there ruins o' dark nights."

Marietta had occasionally observed Mr. Gillespie making his way home from the Seven Seas tavern after his "lunch" and could well believe that there was no limit to what he might see later in the evening.

Some of her scepticism must have shown in her face because Mrs. Gillespie lowered her voice and added bodingly, "And there's bin moans and howlings heard, and shadows what creeps and slithers about! And there's a stranger there now! A mighty *strange* stranger! Very tall, he is, and bony and with eyes like chips of ice what glow in the dark, so my mister says. *And* Cobbler Higgett, likewise! Moves about like a shade—not a sound he makes!" She shivered. "Makes you think poor Mrs. South's in the right of it after all!"

Marietta snipped her thread and folded the repaired pillow slip. It was typical of country folk and their superstitious natures, she thought. They had so much of kindness and generosity, yet their outlook on life was very often rather shockingly narrow.

"You ask that foreign fortune-teller lady what leaves her caravan here," said Mrs. Gillespie, annoyed because Miss Warrington hadn't risen to the bait. "*She* knows, surely. Second sight, that one's got!"

Marietta smiled inwardly. "What could Madame Olympias know?"

"Why about poor young Sam South. Hasn't I said it? They thought as he'd run away to sea, but Mrs. South says she saw him in a dream, and he was being kept in a cage down in the cellars at Lanterns, and the room was full of demons and witches, all tormenting the poor lad. After his immortal soul, they was! No doubting!"

Incredulous, Marietta said, "But—it was just a dream!"

"Mayhap it were, Miss, and mayhap it were a warning! Not a week later they found Samuel's scarf there, what his ma had just knitted for him! And how did it get there? That's what *I'd* like to know!"

Marietta frowned, and, uneasy despite herself, said, "Then Constable Davis should take some men and search the horrid old place!"

"Aye, and so he did, Miss. Two months ago while you was in London. That's when they found the scarf. They kept on looking for the boy, and when they went back . . . the scarf was gone!" Her voice lowered dramatically. "Vanished clean away in just them few minutes!"

"Oh. Well, even so, I don't see what that has to do with the man who is living there now."

Mrs. Gillespie put her iron on the hob and glanced cautiously to the door. "He's come back!" she hissed. "Old Nick, is who he is! Come back to get some more souls!"

The thought of Mr. Diccon being taken for Old Nick drew a laugh from Marietta. She said merrily, "What rubbish! I have met the gentleman, and I promise you he is no more of a demon than is my papa!"

Bristling, Mrs. Gillespie changed irons. "P'raps you're right, Miss. But if it was *my* little boy, I'd not let him go wandering off down there all by hisself! No, indeed!"

Marietta stood and with a chill edge to her tone said, "If you refer to Mr. Arthur, he is in the back garden, using his crayons."

'Hoity-toity!' thought Mrs. Gillespie, but said nothing.

Marietta went out into the fresh radiance of the morning. Arthur's sketch-book lay on the blanket she'd put out in the sun. The breeze riffled the pages and stirred the swing under the mulberry tree, but of the boy there was no sign. It was silly to pay heed to Mrs. Gillespie's gloom-mongering, but she went inside and climbed to his room. Five minutes later, troubled, and wishing Aunty Dova and Fanny had not gone into the village, she set out.

He wouldn't have gone there again—he *wouldn't!* Not after what had happened yesterday. But she remembered the light in his eyes when they'd rested on the sword that morning, and remembering also his awed voice murmuring, "He's got a donkey!" she walked a little faster through the lodge gates.

When she came near to Lanterns she paused, her eyes searching the weedy grounds and the great sprawl of the house. There was no sign of her brother, or indeed of any life. Mrs. Gillespie's superstitions were nonsense, of course, but the silence was rather unnerving, and she found herself unwilling to go down there. Instead, she called, her clear voice echoing briefly, then dissipating, as if blown away by the breeze so that the quiet seemed more intense than before. Surely, if Arthur was here, he would have heard her? But the house was so old; the walls were likely very thick and might blot out sound. She started down the slope with slow reluctance.

Last evening she had been so fearful for her brother that she'd paid little attention to the house. Now, she scanned it curiously. It was a long structure. The wing closest to the edge of the cliffs had been constructed with stone blocks, and pre-dated the newer addition by, she would guess, several centuries. The first Lanterns had been a rectangular, westward facing, two-storey hall with a high-pitched roof, probably a later improvement, dramatised at the far southern end by a great gable. The only windows, which were tall and narrow, were high up, at the first-floor level. The newer addition was very large and far less stark, its brick and timber quite charming, in fact. It rose to the same two storeys as the original pile and culminated in another great gable. A single-storey central wing connecting the buildings was evidently the principal entrance. It was dignified by a great round-headed front door, recessed under a stone archway and approached by a low bridge, that might at one time have been a drawbridge. There were more and wider windows, several of which were broken and had been boarded up.

She was intrigued to see that the manor had originally been protected by a moat, of which traces still remained in the form of overgrown sunken gardens threaded with stepping-stones. About a hundred yards east of the manor were the sagging remains of a gigantic barn and several outbuildings.

Indignation gripped Marietta. The original wing, of course, was past hope, and looked ready to tumble down the cliff at any moment, as the southern end of the moat appeared to have done. But the newer part of the house, although also very old, had once been beautiful, and could be again were it not so shamefully neglected.

The gable of the north wing towered over her. Hesitating, she had the sudden conviction that she was watched. She looked about uneasily. A clump of tall hollyhocks by the ruined barn swayed suspiciously. Chilled, she could almost hear Mrs. Gillespie's ominous words: "He's Old Nick. . . . Come back to get more souls!" Impatient with her skittery nerves, she thought,

'Do stop being so silly, Marietta Warrington! The hollyhocks moved because the breeze blew them, of course!'

She left the drive-path which led to the low bridge across the moat and the central front door and walked back instead to the stepping-stones. Negotiating them with care, she made her way around the end of the house to what she judged to be the tradesmen's entrance. There was no response to her knock, and lifting the latch she pushed the door open. Surprisingly, it did not creak, and she stepped into what must have been the scullery. It was unoccupied, as were the buttery and pantry, and the gigantic kitchen, which was astonishingly neat. She gazed uneasily at the fire which burned in the stove. Again, she called, and again there was no response. She should leave at once, but she was curious now, and she went on, peeping about at a succession of dark and empty rooms, constantly surprised by the excellence of craftsmanship that had gone into the construction. She had wandered across a very large entrance hall when at last she had an indication that she was not alone. She checked, listening intently. The closed door before her must lead to the older wing, and from beyond that door faint sounds became identifiable as running footsteps drawing ever nearer. There was an unmistakable stumble, accompanied by a frenzied panting and then a blood-curdling shriek.

Marietta's heart jumped into her throat. She turned to escape, but paused. Suppose the runner was her brother? She bit her lip, looked around desperately for something with which to defend herself, and snatched up the only article within reach, a wooden and comfortingly solid music stand. She had only time then to shrink against the wall to one side of the door before it burst open. Another piercing shriek rang out. Arthur raced past, head thrown back, legs pumping frantically. Heavier footsteps were following.

A male voice roared, "You can't escape, you varmint! Stop, or—"

Somewhere beyond that voice a door must be open because

light was casting a shadow on the dusty floor—the shadow of a terrifying figure with one upraised arm brandishing a great two-edged sword.

To shock and terror was added rage. Marietta flailed the music stand with all her strength at the murderous creature who plunged through the door after her brother. Her fingers tingled at the impact. Caught squarely across the chest, the pursuer reeled backward, tripped on the steps, fell heavily and sprawled face-down, unmoving.

Another shriek rang out. "*Etta!* What has you gone and done?"

Her breath fluttering, Marietta cried, "It's—it's all right, dearest. You're safe now, but . . . No! Stay back! Keep away from him!"

The boy eluded her outstretched hand and raced past to drop to his knees beside the fallen man and pull at one unresponsive arm. "Sir G'waine! Get up! Do *please* get up now! Oh, do!"

A dreadful suspicion began to dawn. Shaking, Marietta wavered down the steps. "Arthur—what are you doing here? Did that man—"

"He's not a 'that man'!" The boy's eyes were tearfully accusing. "I found him for a new friend. We was playing. He was Sir G'waine, but now he's being the Black Knight and he makes it much better than Fanny does. He didn't do nothing bad, Etta! And now, you've gone and *killed* him dead!"

The room swung around Marietta. She was suddenly icy cold, but she forced the faintness away, and bent over her victim. He had discarded his coat and waistcoat, and the white shirt had ripped in his fall. She saw a crimson stain on the fine linen and was sickened by the fear that he had fallen on that great sword. She said in a far-away voice, "Arthur, you must—you must help me, dear."

"Yes, but why did you do it?"

"I thought— But never mind that now. Can you find your way to the kitchen? I think I saw a water jug. Bring it to me as quickly as you can."

Sobbing, the boy ran off.

Marietta knelt beside the injured man and took up one thin hand, searching for a pulse. She could have wept with relief when she detected the beat, rapid but firm. She put down his hand gently and tried to turn him, but although there seemed to be not an ounce of fat on his lean body, he was far from frail and she lacked the strength to discover where else he was hurt. She widened the tear in his shirt and, investigating, gave a gasp. He had evidently suffered a recent injury and the fall had broken open the wound a little, but it was not the torn flesh that so appalled her, but the long scar that angled from his left shoulder; the mark on his right side that looked like the imprint of a horseshoe; the evidence of a healed bullet wound above it.

"What 'ave it 'appen to my Diccon? *Tiens!* Is 'e shot again?"

The voice at her ear almost made her jump out of her shoes. With a muffled yelp of fright she jerked around and found a small dark man standing beside her. "Oh! How you startled me!" she gasped.

Looking into what he later described as "the face of a heavenly angel," his dark eyes grew round with admiration. He tore off a knitted stocking cap, said, "Good day, mademoiselle," and repeated his question.

He was unmistakably French, and to judge by his great hip boots and the thick scarf knotted jauntily around his throat, was probably a fisherman. "Are you his friend?" asked Marietta prayerfully, and when he pursed his lips but gave a rather droll nod, she said, "Thank heaven you have come! Would you please help me? If we can lift him a little, and get his shirt off, I'll tear it for a bandage."

"Aaiee! That is where the doctors they 'ave at last take the musket ball out from 'is back!" he said as they managed to remove the shirt. Startled, Marietta jerked her head up and stared at him. "Me, I am Yves," he said as if that explained everything. Tearing the shirt into strips, he added, "Did my Diccon, 'e fall and cause these damages? We all try and tell 'im it is too soon to come down 'ere! But you know 'ow 'e set 'is mind, just like Monsieur Fox!"

"Musket ball?" echoed Marietta. "Was he in the war, then?"

"But yes. At the great battle." He grinned. "But then, my Diccon, 'is life it is one long battle, *hein?* You will know this, being—" He broke off, pausing in his efforts to eye her uneasily. "You *are* my Diccon's *chère*—"

Her face flaming, Marietta interpolated, "I most certainly am *not!*"

At this point Arthur came back, clutching the water jug. He was very pale, his eyes enormous, his face tear-streaked. He glanced at the Frenchman disinterestedly. "Hasn't Sir G'waine waked up yet? Is he killed? Your face is all red, Etta."

Marietta had no doubt that it was. She concentrated on bathing the wound gently, and said she was sure Mr. Diccon would be all right, especially now that his friend had come to help him.

"But this Yves, 'e cannot remain, mademoiselle." The little Frenchman propped Diccon's sagging head against his shoulder and looked troubled. *"Par grâce!* You 'ave see the cut 'ere above 'is temple? And—ay! there is the most big lump! One 'opes the 'ead it is not broke."

Marietta's hands shook. "One hopes very much," she said unsteadily. "But at all events, he cannot be left alone here. I'll have to send for my father's carriage and take him to our house."

"But, no, mademoiselle. In this, Yves 'e can 'elp. The big one, Yves will not try. But Monsieur Fox 'ave not mind the cart, and 'e will take my Diccon to your 'ome. Yves will feed the rest while 'e can."

Distracted with worry because Mr. Diccon had shown no sign of reviving, Marietta scarcely heard him and he went off to return very shortly with the donkey harnessed to the cart. Between them, they managed to lift the unconscious man inside, this procedure causing Mr. Fox to hang his head and set up a doleful braying.

Yves imparted with a confidential air, "It is that 'e worries."

He took a note from his pocket, read it over, then offered it to the donkey, who devoured it and seemed comforted.

Arthur scrambled into the back of the cart to sit by 'Sir Gawaine,' and Yves handed Marietta up to the seat. "Mademoiselle, she will not to disturb 'erself," he said kindly. "This Diccon, 'e should be dead many times. 'E not die now. I think."

She forced a smile and thanked him. Guiding Mr. Fox up the slope, she glanced back. Yves was leading a magnificent grey horse from the old barn. Forgetting her worries for a moment she murmured, "Oh, what a beautiful animal!"

Arthur said, "That's Sir G'waine's charger."

She said incredulously, "Are you sure, dear? It looks to be a very valuable animal."

"He says it's a bad-tempered rogue," said the boy. "It's called Awful."

She couldn't imagine anyone naming a fine horse in such a way, but she said nothing. Perhaps because dear Mama had died so soon after he was born, little Arthur had been slow to start talking. Even now, he tended to mispronounce or mis-use words that most five-year-olds would have mastered. He would catch up, of course, for he was a very bright child in many ways. Probably, he was mistaken about the horse, or perhaps his imagination was ruling him again and it belonged to somebody else. Certainly, it was not an animal to be owned by a poor vagrant.

❧

Diccon had not recovered consciousness by the time Marietta drove into the stableyard at the dower house. Lem Bridger, their sturdy groom and general factotum, was preparing to scythe the lawns. It was a task he loathed and he was only too willing to abandon it. Easing Diccon's limp figure over his shoulder, the sturdy ex-Navy tar carried him into the ground-floor room that had, in a more affluent household, belonged to the housekeeper.

Marietta sent Arthur to fetch one of his brother Eric's nightshirts and take it to Bridger. She was in the kitchen, assembling hot water and medical supplies when the groom came in to advise that he had put Mr. Diccon into the nightshirt and that he was comfortably in bed. When she enquired anxiously if the sick man had awoken, he shook his head, and asked if he should ride into Eastbourne and fetch Mr. Wantage. Marietta did not much care for the apothecary, who was very haughty and, or so she thought, of an unsympathetic nature. When possible she preferred to consult Dr. Avebury in Brighton, but the busy doctor would be unwilling to ride all this way, and to take Mr. Diccon such a distance would surely worsen his condition.

She walked to the back door with Bridger and asked if her father was out. Sir Lionel, he imparted with a twinkle, had gone for a drive with Mrs. Maitland.

It was typical of the perversity of fate, thought Marietta, that the handsome widow should have called while her father was alone and unprotected. Shy in the presence of most females, and having no least desire to marry again, Sir Lionel was well aware that Mrs. Maitland had determined to become the new Lady Warrington. He usually made a frantic dive for a hiding place when she arrived unexpectedly, but he was far too well bred to be rude to her, and without sufficient warning to escape, or the supporting presence of his family, must have been helpless before the wiles of the pushing woman. Marietta could only pray he would manage to get through the drive without being manipulated into a proposal.

Starting down the scullery steps to the stableyard the groom said he'd saddle up Spicy, their twelve-year-old chestnut mare, who could reach quite a good speed when handled firmly. He paused then, staring at Mr. Fox and the cart.

Marietta said, "I'll unharness the donkey after I do what I can for Mr. Diccon. Why do you look so puzzled?"

"Well, it's not what you'd expect of a gentleman, is it? Doesn't Mr. Diccon have a horse?"

"Why would you think he is a gentleman?"

"His clothes, Miss. Fine linen, too. It don't fit with that cart!"

She pointed out rather impatiently that many gentlemen who had suffered financial reverses still clung to their pride, and that of more importance than Mr. Diccon's background was the need to bring help to him as soon as may be. At once apologetic, Bridger ran off to the stables.

Returning to her victim, Marietta found that his pulse was steady, but there was no sign of a return of awareness. She decided not to disturb her bandage and stood by the bed, regarding him worriedly. He was not a handsome man, and yet there was something proud and compelling about that lean face. The forehead was high, the eyebrows heavy, the hair thickly curling and an unremarkable brown. His complexion was clear, the skin rather sunken under the cheekbones, and alarmingly pale at the moment. Deep lines were etched beside the thin, high-bridged nose and between the brows. The jaw was well-defined, the chin strong and unyielding. It was the face of a man who has known his share of trouble, but in sleep he looked younger than she had at first thought, and there was a weary droop to the thin lips that made him seem less formidable and ruthless.

"So here you are!" exclaimed Sir Lionel, coming down the corridor in a great state of agitation. "If you *knew* what I've been through with Mrs. Maitland! How you could all have abandoned—" Drawing level with the open door at this point, his aggrieved tirade ceased. Shocked, he cried, "What the deuce—? Why is that horrid fellow in my house again? Are your wits gone a'begging?"

Marietta gave a hasty account of what had happened, and her father's wrath cooled slightly. "Hum," he said, frowning down at the unconscious man. "Well, you've no cause to blame yourself, child. Anyone would have thought the same. It's the boy's fault. He had no right to go traipsing down there after what happened yesterday! I sometimes wonder if the only skill your Aunt Dova has taught him is how to wander away. But never mind that. As soon as this fellow wakes, he must be sent packing. By rights, he should be driven from the neighbourhood. We want no vagrants hanging about."

"But, Papa, the poor man has been twice hurt by us. If you *knew* how hard I hit him!"

Sir Lionel grinned. "With your reticule?"

"With a music stand. But it looked to be mahogany," she added thoughtfully. "And as I recall, it was most beautifully carven."

"Whether 'twas mahogany or bacon has nothing to say to the matter. The fellow's a penniless rogue, I've no doubt, and—"

"And was at Waterloo, sir. The poor soul is fairly covered with scars!"

Impressed, Sir Lionel's brows lifted. "Is that so? By Jove, if he was one of Wellington's fine lads—" In belated comprehension, he demanded, "How do *you* come to know of his wounds? Be dashed if he's not wearing one of my nightshirts! Etta! You did not—"

"No, no, Papa. It is Eric's nightshirt, and Bridger undressed Mr. Diccon and put him to bed."

"How did Bridger know he was at Waterloo? The fellow bragged of it, I don't doubt. Not that I'd blame him."

"He said nothing of it. His friend told me. I was hoping he would consent to stay and care for him, but Monsieur Yves had to—"

Her father interrupted sharply, "A Frenchman?"

"Yes, sir. But he seems a good sort of man. And he has a most magnificent grey horse. Arthur thought it belonged to Mr. Diccon, and he says it is called Awful, but I rather doubt—"

"Orpheus," corrected Diccon faintly.

"Thank heaven!" cried Marietta, hurrying to bend over him. "How are you, now, sir?"

Diccon's head seemed to have been arranged into two pieces, and his back was almost as spiteful, but he managed to answer, "Not as dead . . . as you might wish. You are a very . . . violent family, I think."

"Not so," said Sir Lionel. "My daughter thought you were some monster attacking the boy, is all. An honest mistake."

"All . . . in the eye of the . . . beholder."

Marietta's cool fingers rested on Diccon's brow. "I am truly, truly sorry," she said. "I doubt Arthur will ever forgive me."

"I hear you've taken some wounds," said Sir Lionel. "Your friend, Yves, said—"

At this, Diccon started up, gave a gasp, and sank back again. "*Yves* is here?"

Sir Lionel nodded. "Said you was at Waterloo. True, sir?"

"Yes. But—"

"By Jove! You've all my admiration! Your rank?"

Diccon said impatiently, "What? Oh—major. Had Yves any . . . message for me?"

Marietta said, "You are hurting yourself. Try not to talk. Your friend said something about feeding the rest, whatever that may—"

"*What?*" Diccon dragged himself to one elbow. "He can't leave them there!" he panted fretfully. "I must get up . . . and—"

"Now, now," said Sir Lionel, putting an arm about his shoulders and lying him back down. "Don't upset yourself so, poor fellow."

Aware of her sire's intense patriotism, Marietta was still astonished by such a transformation. One might almost think him to have just discovered that Major Diccon was a dear friend.

"Bridger shall carry any word to your Frenchman that you desire," went on Sir Lionel. "Ah, yes. I have you now, you rascal! I've not seen your face in the dark of the moon, of course, but I did set eyes on that splendid grey of yours a time or two. Now, tell me—when shall I receive my consignment? My cellar is dashed near empty!"

With a sense of overwhelming relief and repentance, Marietta thought, 'Old Nick, indeed! Why, he is nothing more sinister than a free-trader!'

CHAPTER V

In the nick of time Marietta restrained the billowing sheet and slid a clothes-peg over the sagging centre. It would be nice, she thought, to have had Mrs. Gillespie for three days this week. With an invalid in the house and extra wash to be done she was badly needed. Even more badly needed, however, was her own attention to the ever increasing pile of bills in the kitchen drawer. Her desperate juggling of one debt against another was nerve-wracking, but she'd managed somehow. Until now. Yesterday evening Papa had given her a bad fright.

He'd been playing chess with Major Diccon, and when laughingly accused by his opponent of taking risks with his queen, had replied that there were times when risk was justified. "A fellow assesses the odds," he'd said heartily, "and if they're promising he takes the plunge as a good sportsman should. Nothing ventured, nothing gained, eh? Why, just last month I—" He'd cut short that remark, slanted a guilty glance at Marietta, and laid one finger beside his nose, grinning at Diccon in a "mum's the word" fashion. Her blood had run cold, for it had sounded horribly like another of his disastrous wagers, or the gaming that had swept away home and fortune and reduced them to a less than shabby-genteel existence so far from Town and the luxurious life they'd known.

Not that she really minded living in the country. If truth be told, although she'd not realized it at the time, she'd begun to be bored by the sameness of the *ton* parties, the gossip, and the endless pursuit of pleasure. Here, instead of bricks and hot pavements and crowded streets with grime and soot everywhere, there were lush fields and trees and green velvet hills, and pure clean air. And there was no time for boredom. They all were busy, and tired at the end of the day, and they took pride in their achievements, as she thought they deserved to do. Still, there was small chance that her pretty little sister would find an eligible husband in this quiet corner of Sussex, and if Papa had plunged them even deeper into debt, heaven only knew how she was to keep them from Debtor's Prison.

She found that she was still holding the sheet, and, sighing, released it and went to peep over the hedge that concealed the side yard from the gardens.

Major Diccon was sleeping on the chaise Bridger had set under the apple tree. Three days had passed since the apothecary had ruled that he'd suffered a concussion and must not be moved for a week at least. He had scoffed at that verdict and insisted that he would not intrude into their lives in such a way. His attempt to leave, however, had ended in collapse and he'd been packed back to bed again, willy-nilly. She felt responsible for his injuries and had said firmly that he must let them try to make amends. Fanny had complained that they had enough to do without having to care for an invalid. Neither Papa nor Aunty Dova had objected, however. As for herself, having had some experience in nursing the males in her family, she had been pleasantly surprised to find that Diccon was neither fretful nor demanding. He was, in fact, the soul of patience, even when she suspected that he was tired. Arthur was seldom far from his side and would coax the invalid to talk about the people and ways of the foreign lands he had visited. The Major spoke in a slow drawl and used words sparingly, but his accounts were spiced with a droll humour that would set the little boy giggling, and were so interesting that they all would listen. Often his tales ended with Sir Lionel entering into an intense debate with him on some aspect of the story, and Arthur complaining to Marietta that Papa had "stolen Sir G'waine"!

Aunty Dova also chattered at their invalid, drawing him into exchanges of Society gossip with her 'friends' that frequently became hilarious. Diccon neither patronised the lady nor displayed the least sign of condescension during these odd chats, but actually seemed to find her fascinating. Only yesterday during one of their 'three-way' discussions in which he was answering for 'Sir Freddy Foster,' Mrs. Cordova had gone into whoops of laughter and had said merrily, "Oh, but Major Diccon has Freddy to the *life*, Etta! Absolutely to the life!" Fanny had responded, "Perhaps they are good friends. Is that so, sir?" Diccon had given her his lazy smile and murmured, "It would add enormously to my consequence if that were the case, do not you think?"

Marietta turned with a start as she heard her name called. Fanny was coming to join her. She felt ridiculously flustered to have been caught watching the invalid, but Fanny said lightly that she'd come to help with the wash and to escape Arthur's chatter. "All he does is talk about the Major. I declare the child is positively bewitched!"

Marietta smiled. "He does seem to have taken a great liking to the man. And you have not, I think."

"I'm sorry he was hurt, but," Fanny shrugged, "I'll own I'll be glad when he has gone away. He is too—too devious."

Holding one end of another sheet, Marietta asked, "In what way?"

"In every way!" Together, they hung the sheet, and Fanny said, "Have you not noticed that whenever something comes up concerning his background, he evades? Never a straight answer. That business about Freddy Foster, for instance. I asked if he knew Sir Frederick, and instead of a simple yes or no, he managed to avoid answering altogether. I tell you, he has something to hide!"

Suspecting that what he hid was a close acquaintanceship with kegs and bales of illicit goods, Marietta refrained from comment. Irked, Fanny took a towel from the basket and snapped, "Oh, you may smile, but were I in your shoes I would make haste to depress his pretensions, for it is certain that Papa will have none of him as a suitor!"

Marietta was taken aback. "As a—*what*? Fan, you cannot be serious! The man has never so much as looked at me in that way!"

"Not while you face him, perhaps. But when you do not see, he can scarce tear his eyes from you, and I've sometimes spied an expression in those cold eyes of his that is more like fire than ice! I'll not deny that he can be charming. But, consider dearest, he is little better than a vagrant, with not a penny to his name! It will not serve, and you know it!"

Marietta laughed. "No, really! How can you be so foolish? Do not have us betrothed only because I'm sorry for our treatment of him."

"What about his horrid treatment of a little child?"

"You know that was unintentional. Only think of how he must have felt when Arthur slammed that broom into his back. And I might very well have killed the poor soul because of my silly suspicions! But he scarcely even taxed me with it!"

Fanny gave a scornful little snort. "Perhaps he is enjoying his convalescence too much to risk jeopardising it."

"That is unkind."

"If it is, I am sorry. But I do not like to see you so—so intrigued by a very ordinary man who is so much older than you are."

It was true. Marietta did find the Major intriguing. She said slowly, "I'll admit I think him very far from being ordinary. Do you never feel that his is a very strong and commanding nature? Yet he is willing to play childrens' games with Arthur. I would like to know more about him. Besides, I doubt he is more than a year or two older than Blake Coville."

"Mr. Blake Coville has as good as offered for you. Mr. Innes Williard is absolutely besotted and you'll not fend off an offer from him for much longer. Either of them is a hundred times to be preferred over a man who is a considerable enigma! And if the Major, or whatever he is, is so strong and commanding, why has he only a little donkey between himself and destitution?"

Marietta answered defensively that Major Diccon also possessed a magnificent grey stallion, to which provocation Fanny tossed a pretty shoulder and went off in a huff.

Shaking out a bolster cover, Marietta wondered why she had become so annoyed by her sister's remarks, and whether, if she really had to choose between Major Diccon and Innis Williard, she would—

"So here you are, my pretty!"

One of the gentleman in her thoughts was close behind her, his bluff voice causing her to swing around hurriedly. "Mr. Williard!" She shook his hand politely. "My apologies. Was there no one in the house to greet you?"

"Pshaw, I do not stand on ceremony, Miss Marietta." His ruddy face was wreathed in a grin and his bold dark eyes devoured her hungrily. "Don't worry about my seeing you in your apron. I think we're on such terms that I need not be shy about finding my way to your side if my knock at the door goes unanswered."

Marietta tried unsuccessfully to free her hand and wished that he would not stand so close. As usual, he was clad in the latest fashion, but his garments seemed never quite to fit properly, and for all the fobs and seals and the great ruby ring on his square hand, he had none of the quiet elegance that the Major managed to achieve in a plain coat and riding breeches. She dreaded that Fanny might be right and Williard meant to offer. He must be closer to Aunty Dova's age than her own, and although many ladies admired his rugged good looks, she could not like his loud voice and aggressive manner.

She said, "You should have been properly received, sir. But I think my papa could not wish me to be private with you here. If you will be so good as to release my hand, we can—"

Instead, he held her tighter, his eyes glittering as he thrust his face close to hers. Words tumbled from his lips and he all but panted, "Much your papa will care if I have you all to my-self for a minute. He likely thought to dodge me, but he need not have worried. I don't mean to press him for payment. What is money, after all? And if we can keep it in the family, my dear, why—"

Marietta wrenched free and made for the back door. Surely Papa had not been so unwise as to borrow from this man? "You must discuss financial matters with Sir Lionel," she began.

Moving very fast for such a husky individual, Williard was before her, blocking her retreat. "Come now, sweeting," he said, affecting a persuasive manner. "There's no need to be coy. You're no green girl, and I've been about the world! You know my feelings for you, and I'd thought you would like a double wedding. Sir Lionel and my pretty sister, and you and—"

Enraged, she interrupted, "You forget yourself, sir! If you have spoken to my father in this matter, he has not mentioned it to me! Nor have I given you any cause to suppose I would welcome a declaration from you, much less one offered in such terms and in so improper a way! Be good enough to let me pass!"

He did not like to be crossed, and at this his dark brows drew together. Marietta's cheeks were flushed, her eyes sparkling with wrath, her head held very high. She looked even more de-sirable, but that she would react in this way to his very gener-ous proposal was as annoying as it was unexpected. Isolde had agreed with him that the chit would be overjoyed by such a grand chance, but whatever Miss Warrington felt at this mo-ment, he could not think it was joy. Resentful, he pointed out, "I do not ask about a dowry. Did you remark that? I know your father is properly in the basket. If you are ashamed that you bring nothing to the union, do not give it a—"

"Pray have done, sir! Had you approached my father in the correct fashion—"

"Do not take that tone with me, my girl!" His hand shot out and grasped her wrist. "I do you the honour of offering you my name, and you dare to turn up your nose? You should have left those high and mighty airs with the dim-witted London beaux who are easily fooled! You do not fool me! Your father lost five thousand guineas to me, and has begged for time. I'm a patient man, and for your sake would be willing to wipe out that debt, but do not try my patience too far, or—"

"What a pity about your ears."

With a startled oath, Williard whipped around to face the owner of that sardonic drawl.

Marietta, who had been stunned by the amount of Sir Lionel's indebtedness, pulled her hand free with a gasp of relief that at once became apprehension. Major Diccon stood watching them. He looked haughty and contemptuous, but he was also pale and had been ill. If Mr. Williard lost his temper, as was his habit, the Major would be no match for him.

"Who the devil are you, and what are you doing here?" roared Williard, his face assuming a crimson hue.

Diccon said icily, "I am a guest in the home of Sir Lionel Warrington. I cannot think that you have a similar claim." His lip curled, his eyes raked Williard from head to toe, and he added, "I believe you must not have heard Miss Warrington desire you to move aside." His voice sank to a purr. "Do so!"

With a snort of rage Williard stamped forward and swung his heavy riding crop high. Diccon's eyes narrowed, and he crouched slightly.

Alarmed, Marietta stammered, "Thank you, M-Major Diccon. I feel sure Mr. Williard is—is leaving now."

What Williard read in Diccon's face she could not tell, but his impassioned glare faded, he lowered his hand and growled, "Major, is it? Well, you're a damned impertinent jackanapes, whoever you are! But I'll not discipline you in front of the lady." He turned about and stamped towards the gate in the hedge, blustering, "Your father won't thank you for this day's work, I promise you, Miss Marietta!" Diccon took a step toward him, and Williard hurried for the safety of the gate. Passing through, he shouted, "Set one foot on my land, fellow, and my men will know how to deal with you, major or no!" The gate slammed behind him.

There came a burst of soft applause from the house. Mrs. Cordova stood in the open scullery door beaming at them. "Oh, well done, Major!" she trilled. " 'Faith, but you properly frightened the creature! Do you not agree, Etta?"

Marietta said, "To say truth, for a minute, sir, I really thought he meant to attack you."

Diccon smiled his lazy smile. "Then I must be thankful I was able to bluff him. He's a big fellow. I only hope I did not step in where angels would fear to tread."

In Marietta's ears was the echo, 'Five . . . thousand . . . guineas. . . .' She said with an effort, "Oh. I mean—no! You were most kind, and I thank you."

He bowed, watching her worried face gravely.

Mrs. Cordova said, "And I thank you, too, sir. I never liked that man! Which reminds me—you have a caller with a horse, Major. He would not come in, and is waiting on the terrace. It is the man who waits, you understand? I suppose the horse also waits, but—" She gave a sudden shriek of laughter. "My, how confusing this becomes! His name, he says, is Monsieur Yves, and something is causing him the greatest distress."

"He said that?" asked Diccon sharply.

"Oh, no." Mrs. Cordova held out her skirts and essayed a risky pirouette on the step. "I could tell. I often can, you know." She murmured in a far-away voice, "I see many more things about people than they suspect. You must let me tell your fortune, Major."

"It would be my pleasure, ma'am." Mrs. Cordova beamed at him and hurried down the steps, and he said hastily, "But for the present, I beg you will allow me to rob your vegetable garden." Receiving her permission, he bowed slightly and left them, walking briskly to the neat rows of vegetables and then around to the front of the house.

"He stole a carrot," said Marietta. "Did you see the horse? I only caught a glimpse, but it's a beautiful animal."

"And costly." Mrs. Cordova nodded. "It would be interesting to know how he came by the creature." Another pirouette and she murmured, "I fancy most men tread softly around our major. I wonder why he does not want me to tell his fortune."

⚜

Yves' shaggy little pony and Orpheus were tethered at the lodge gate, and as the two men left the terrace and started down the drive-path, Yves halted. " 'Allo? 'Allo?" he said, annoyed. "I do not care to make the shout. It is truth that beside you Yves is always as if walking in the ditch, but if you could your mind remove from the *très belle* mademoiselle, you might 'ear those things I say."

Diccon flushed slightly. "A proper fool I should be to allow my hopes to drift in that direction. I apologize if my mind wandered. Now tell me—have you finished the deliveries?"

Yves directed a much-tried look at the sunny skies. " 'Ave I not said it? Your beast I bring to you now, for we sail tonight."

"Tonight! There'll be a moon, you fool!"

"And the more large fool I, if we stay."

The grey stallion nudged his master's shoulder and whinnied a greeting, and Diccon caressed the silken neck affectionately before giving in to rank flattery and offering the carrot in his pocket.

Watching this fond reunion Yves said solemnly, "They come, *mon ami*. Two with the long memory who love not this Yves, but who love much less my Diccon."

"They're not alone." Diccon shrugged. "Likely at least half a hundred men would rejoice to hear of my departure from this world. Yet I live."

"Ah, but suppose I tell you that a week since these two they sail from a small French fishing village at dead of night? Sup-

· 77 ·

pose I say that one 'e is very tall and very white—like the dough? And the other"—he threw his arms wide—"much of a Chinese walking mountain?"

Diccon stiffened and stepped away from the velvety muzzle that was tickling his neck. *"Monteil?"*

"Mais oui!" Yves nodded vigorously. "This same Monsieur Imre Monteil who vow your death. The monstrous Ti Chiu, also! If you 'ave wisdom, you go very fast away. Like me."

"Nonsense. Wherever he may be going, Monteil would not dare to set foot in England again. And even if he did, he'd never think to look for me here."

"Do you forget that this evil one was so thick as inkle-weavers with the mighty Claude Sanguinet? Like as not 'e still 'ave many spies, and if 'e desires a man to find—that man is found! Listen, *mon ami!* To stay in this place—" Yves offered the dramatic and all-encompassing shrug that covers every imaginable situation and can be achieved only by a Frenchman. *"Ce n'est pas la peine!"*

"Not worth *your* while, perhaps," argued Diccon. "But you worry too much. Besides, I can't leave until I have word from Italy."

"Ah, well. On your own 'ead be it. What more can Yves do? And your fine Orpheus?"

"I'll ride him down to Lanterns." Diccon stifled a sigh. "It's time I went back there, at all events."

"Mais non! You must not be alone! 'Ow shall you manage the beasts? And if—"

"Jove, what a gloom-merchant! MacDougall should return at any day, and I'm well rested. I thank you for taking care of my animals. When may I expect the next shipment?"

"To this place? You may not. The Swiss, 'e know I work with you, and because of our—er, conspirings, 'e 'ave lose much of the money which 'e love! Me, I do not like to be dead, *merci!*" Wringing his friend's hand, Yves said mournfully, *"Au revoir,* my Diccon. I will tell you again that it is the great pity you are too sure of your own self. You are good. But not an army, *mon ami*. Send me words when the Monteil go back to 'is—what is it you say?—'is lair! Or, better, when 'e meet 'is doom!"

Diccon was irked, but he knew better than to try to change the mind of this droll but stubborn individual. He promised to "send words" as asked, and watched the Frenchman stride rapidly down the hill. He was a fiery little gamecock; a typical Latin, ready to imbue every situation with drama, but a devilish good man in a scrap, just the—

There came a soft footfall behind him. Involuntarily, he whipped around.

Carrying a large tin bowl, Marietta exclaimed, "My, but you are so sudden!"

The sunbeams filtering through the branches of the laburnum tree awoke a bright sheen on her dusky hair and deepened the green of her eyes. Alarm touched the delicate features that he found almost too exquisite to be real. He had frightened her. 'Fool!' he thought, and straightened at once, smiling a greeting.

"I promise you I mean no harm," she said. "I came to see your horse. He is splendid!"

"Yes. Ah—he is."

In the course of his chequered career he had mixed with all classes and conditions of people and often his life had depended upon his ability to say the right thing at the right moment. His quick wits had never deserted him. Until now. The nearness of this slim girl seemed to reduce his brain to glue, and his desperate attempt to find something charming and ingratiating to say failed miserably. He recovered to an extent and intercepted her outstretched hand as she moved towards Orpheus. "You must let me introduce you, ma'am. He sometimes forgets his manners with strangers."

Still holding that small hand in his own, breathing in the faint sweet scent she wore, and wretchedly aware that his own hand trembled betrayingly, he reached out to the horse. Orpheus tossed his head and rolled fierce eyes at the newcomer.

"Behave, you rascal," said Diccon. "Miss Warrington is a friend." After a suspicious sniff, the big grey quieted and permitted that his nose be stroked.

Marietta had not missed the look of awe that had dawned in Diccon's eyes, and was quite aware of the tremor to the long fingers that held her hand as though it were fashioned of sheerest crystal. In company with every female since the dawn of time, she knew when she was admired. In this instance it was a nice feeling, especially since he made no attempt to stand too close, as he might so easily have done. He released her hand very carefully, as though fearful of breaking it. With an inward smile she thought that this tall, shy man was a far cry from the deadly individual who had faced down Innes Williard, or the brusque stranger who had only a few days ago remarked that he wondered if she ever said "anything sensible." She said lightly, "You are very handsome, Orpheus. But I wonder what you would do if your master had said I was an enemy."

Diccon smiled. "That is something you will never discover, ma'am, for I never would tell him such a rank falsehood."

"I think I am fortunate! Is your friend going away, Major? Do you wish us to stable Orpheus for you?"

"No, no! I'd not impose— I mean, it is time— it's past time I went—er, home." He untied the reins, then reached for the bowl Marietta carried. "Let me take that. It's too heavy for you." He peered at the contents and wrinkled his nose. "Gad! What is this stuff?"

"Mash for the chickens. And you cannot carry it and manage Orpheus as well. Will he allow me to lead him, do you think?"

"Yes. So long as I am close by."

She took the reins and started along the side drive-path that led to the barn and stableyard. "Oh, how beautifully he moves! Would you let me ride him? I love a spirited animal. Now why must you look so aghast? I have a very good seat, I promise you."

"Then I shall begin to train him to accept a side-saddle, Miss Warrington."

"Another polite evasion, Major?"

He looked startled and she said laughingly, "Oh, yes. I am aware of your devious ways, but I will not tease you. As to your going back to Lanterns, that is quite out of the question until you are better—unless you've someone to help you."

"You're very kind, but I am much better, I thank you. And my man will be rejoining me within a day or two."

His man? She hid her surprise and decreed serenely that until then the Major must remain at the dower house, and that there was plenty of room for Orpheus in the barn. "It will make very little extra work for Bridger, for we only keep three horses, nowadays." She heard the note of regret in her own voice and added hurriedly, "Now tell me why you call him Orpheus, if you please."

"Like his namesake, he is a music lover."

Marietta patted the glossy shoulder of the big horse. "He sings, no doubt?"

"Not really. Cannot follow a tune for the life of him. But—in a sense he does follow a tune."

"You are going to have to explain that, Major."

Greatly daring, he said, "If you will come to Lanterns and visit me, I'll show you. One picture is worth a thousand words, so they say."

"The picture of you putting Mr. Williard to flight was worth many thousand words." Her smile faded into a troubled look. "I am sure you . . . heard."

"I'd not intended to eavesdrop, ma'am. But his voice carries, and I thought you might—er—"

"Be grateful for some interference? I was, indeed. Your rescue was very well timed. Had my brother Eric been there, he would have done exactly the same."

"He is abroad, Miss Warrington?"

"No. At Cambridge. We'd hoped he would come home for the summer, but he took on two students cramming for Responsions, and was unable to break away. Arthur adores him, and was terribly cast down. But Eric tries to—to help with expenses, you see."

"He must be a fine fellow."

"Yes, he is, and full of high spirits; always ready for any escapade, the more reckless the better. I am very sure his friends had some jolly scheme for the Long Vacation that he would far rather have shared than spending the summer days tutoring."

They had reached the barnyard, and a small army of chickens came rushing to meet them with much squawking and a flurry of dust and feathers.

"If you will be so good as to tether Orpheus," said Marietta, "I'll divide up the mash and you will see how impolite are the table manners of our flock."

Five minutes later, Diccon retreated from the yard and leaned against the fence brushing straw and feathers from his breeches. "They're savages," he said breathlessly.

"And carnivorous," she agreed.

He inspected the back of his hand. "I thought that great red brute would go for my throat!"

She could not restrain a chuckle. "That was Gentleman Jackson." And recalling how Diccon had dodged about, trying to put down the smaller bowls while the flock surged about him, she said, "I'm sorry he pecked you, but I think he grew impatient."

"Impatient! He was downright murderous! I'm very sure Jackson would never behave in such a way!"

She closed the gate and asked, "Do you know the great man? Eric yearns to meet him."

"Most young bucks do. He's a grand fellow. And considering I did exactly as you bade me, I fail to see why your rooster became so hostile."

She thought triumphantly that she'd found one more piece of the puzzle that was this enigmatic gentleman. He might be a humble free-trader, but he knew the much-sought-after boxing champion. She explained, "He became hostile because he was— er, baffled by your terminology." Diccon raised an eyebrow enquiringly, and she said, "As I told you, sir, one does not summon fowls by calling 'Chicken, chicken.' "

He grinned and untied Orpheus. "No, but when I called, "Here, coop, coop, coop," following orders, they came at me like Ney's cavalry. Now, will you tell me what I'm to do with my friend, here?"

Before she could respond Mr. Fox came plodding towards them, with Arthur mounted on his back. The boy, red-faced and out of breath, wheezed, "I must . . . talk with . . . Sir G'waine! P-private!"

"Ar-thur . . . !" said Marietta, recognizing the signs.

"Oh, *do* go 'way, Etta! It's . . . it's men talks!"

"Now that's a sure way to make the ladies curious," advised Diccon gravely. "Besides, it's not quite polite. What we have to do, Sir Lancelot, is to beg your sister's pardon, and ask if we may be excused." With a hopeful glance at Marietta, he added, "Just for a little while."

CHAPTER VI

D isgraceful, sir!" trumpeted Lord Ignatius Dale, his dark eyes protruding alarmingly and his whiskers vibrating. "I say it again—dis-grace-ful!"

As cool as the short, round peer was inflamed, Diccon faced him on the terrace of the vast stone pile that was Downsdale Park, and drawled, "There is not the need, my lord. I heard you the first time. I brought Master Warrington here to apologize for trespassing, and—"

"Not - the - *need?*" bellowed his lordship. "Not—I say *not* the *need*, sir? What, I wonder, Mr. Whoever-You-Are, would you fancy constituted a *need?* That undisciplined young savage lurking behind you, sir, brought that confounded mangy little ass trampling all over my grounds, sir! It consumed my peonies! My *peonies!* M'wife dotes on 'em, d'you hear me?"

"Along with most of the county, I do, sir. But—"

"Eh? Why, Devil take you, sir, how *dare* you, sir?" Purpling, his lordship howled, "I said m'wife *dotes* on 'em! And the poor soul is laid down on her bed with the vapours, from the shock of seeing that damned *ass* leering at her through the window of the breakfast parlour while she was eating her eggs, sir! All along the terrace the mangy damned brute trampled his dirt! And not content with eating m'confounded *peonies*, and putting m'lady into the vapours, what must the damnable—"

Diccon lifted one hand to halt the flow. "Guard your tongue, sir! There is a child here."

"By George, don't I know it!" Dale shook clenched fists at the impervious sky. "The brat's dumb brute ate m'papers, you stupid bl—" he checked with a fuming glance from Diccon's hauteur to Arthur's terrified face.

"Do you say Mr. Fox was inside your house, my lord?"

"Who the deuce is Mr. Fox?"

"My donkey is named for Charles James Fox. He looks like him, you see. Especially," added Diccon musingly, "when he wears his hat."

Staring at the donkey Lord Dale saw the resemblance to the great statesman, and almost smiled. "What I see," he snapped, recovering, "is that you are ripe for Bedlam, sir. You and that brat with you! A gentleman should feel safe in leaving important letters lying on the table of his own terrace. A *gentleman* does not have to put up with common trespassers, and donkeys, and runny-nosed brats daring to insult him on his own lands!"

"I will admit that Mr. Fox is partial to a paper snack now and then, and I am sorry for it if he ate your letters. But I fail to see that he insulted you, nor do I see that Master Warrington stands in need of a handkerchief. As for my social standing, should you perhaps be happier were you to be insulted by someone with a title in front of his name—whether or not he personally had *earned* the right to be addressed as 'my lord'?"

Dale scowled. "Why, you're a dashed revolutionary! I'll have you clapped up, be damned if I don't."

"Which won't get your letters back, will it?"

"No, and they were government documents, I'll have you know, and I hadn't even read 'em! By Jupiter, if I thought 'twould serve, let me tell you I'd have that confounded ass cut up and—"

Arthur gave a horrified yelp. "It wasn't his fault, sir! I only came here 'cause I thought Alan A'Dale lived here, but Mr. Fox din't know your letters was 'portant, and I'm *very* sorry, Lord, but please don't cut up his tummy!"

Dale glared at the scared child and ground his teeth. The donkey brayed shatteringly, dogs barked a noisy accompaniment, and from inside the mansion a faint scream sounded.

Diccon said, "You made your apologies very nicely, Arthur. Now go back to Mr. Fox. This noisy man is upsetting him."

Arthur fled.

Diccon turned back to the angry peer. "Now, see here, Dale—"

"Stay back!" raged his lordship. "You men—throw him over the wall!"

❧

An' then," said Arthur, kneeling on a kitchen chair and watching his aunt tape a piece of sticking plaster across Diccon's knuckles, "a lady comed out, an' she was all stiff, like a statue, but Diccon bowed to her, jus' like Sir G'waine would, an' he talked, an' she didn't seem so stiff, an' in the end they went to look at the flowers in the garden an' me an' Mr. Fox crep' away an' waited."

Coming in from the dining room where she had set out covers for luncheon, Marietta exclaimed, "Good gracious! Never say you were able to placate the mighty Lady Dale, Major?"

"After knocking down two of her footmen?" Whisking a fragrant mutton pie from the oven, Fanny said, "You must have a silver tongue, sir."

Diccon was quite aware that this very pretty girl neither liked nor trusted him. He said with a wry smile, "And if I remarked that your pie smells delicious would you think I was merely trying to win your friendship?"

"Oh, no," said Fanny coldly, "I would be more likely to say that you just proved my point."

He sighed. "And that properly sends me to the ropes."

Mrs. Cordova shook her head and left them.

"No one here wishes to do that, sir," said Marietta. "Indeed we all owe you a debt of gratitude." She ignored Fanny's stormy frown, and went on, "You must be eager to leave this house, for we have involved you in one disaster after another!"

Diccon tried without much success not to stare at her. A ribbon of orange velvet was threaded through her dusky curls, and she had changed into a gown of pale orange muslin, with a low inset yoke of snowy eyelet ruffles. Yearning for the ability to sketch, he murmured, "To the contrary, ma'am. I cannot remember when I've enjoyed myself so much."

"You must enjoy violence," said Fanny tartly.

Persevering, Marietta said, "In which case we shall have to disappoint you, Major. For the rest of your stay here, you are to enjoy peace and quiet."

Diccon smiled at her dreamily, then sprang up as Mrs. Cordova came puffing in again, carrying "Captain Miles Cameron."

"No, really Dova," protested Sir Lionel, entering the dining room in time to see her settle her inanimate friend into the chair Diccon drew out. "Not at table! What will our guest think?"

"Oh, the Major knows him." Apparently unaware of the sharp glance Diccon slanted at her, she added, "I invited Miles to luncheon because he has some news for us, and I don't want to forget. Now, if you will say grace, Warrington, we can get on. I am fairly famished!"

She appeared to forget "Captain Cameron's" news while she satisfied the pangs of hunger and chattered about Lord and Lady Dale who were both, she said with cheerful candour, "blighting" people.

In a low voice Marietta begged her father for a few moments of his time after luncheon. Sir Lionel smiled at her but looked uneasy and without answering launched into a prolonged monologue about the failings of the Prince Regent. Discussing "poor old Prinny's" increased girth, he chortled, "They say he's been obliged to leave off his stays, and is now so large that he can no longer even ride around the Pavilion grounds!"

Fanny giggled, but Mrs. Cordova looked shocked, and scolded, "Really, Warrington! That is scarcely a subject to be discussed at table with young maidens present!"

"Pooh!" said Sir Lionel airily. "My girls are not missish, and we're all family here. Well," he grinned at Diccon, "almost all."

"Which reminds me," said Mrs. Cordova. "Miles met our dearest Eric the other day!"

"Did he so?" Watching her eagerly, Marietta asked, "Was Miles in Cambridge, then?"

Just as eagerly, Fanny enquired, "Is Eric well?"

No longer surprised by their acceptance of their aunt's often inexplicable remarks, Diccon assumed that they were being kind and humouring the lady.

"He is quite well," replied Mrs. Cordova. "But Miles was not at Cambridge, dear. He met Eric in Town."

"Come now, Dova," said Sir Lionel tolerantly. "You know very well my son is at University. Cameron must be mistaken."

"Oh, no," she said, reaching for a ripe peach.

Fanny said, "Eric may have gone into London for a change. The poor darling has had little enough vacation."

"Now don't go putting on a Friday face, Etta," said Sir Lionel. "A young fellow must kick over the traces now and then. I'll warrant we both did, eh, major? Are you a Cambridge man, by the bye?"

"No, sir," said Diccon. "My schooling ended at Eton."

"Went straight into the military, did you? Well, it's a good life for a lad. One of these days, I'll have the story of how it is that an old Etonian and a major is now a free-trader."

Diccon smiled. "I doubt there is much I could tell you that you've not already guessed, sir."

Fanny said, "And we should not press Major Diccon to tell us things that he prefers to keep secret, Papa."

Marietta slanted an embarrassed glance at Diccon, but his expression was unreadable.

Taken aback, Sir Lionel exclaimed, "Secrets? Jupiter! I had no intent to pry!"

"Of course you did not, sir. And Miss Fanny is quite correct, for there are, you know, secrets"—Diccon winked conspiratorially—"and *secrets*."

Relieved, Sir Lionel laughed. "You rogue! I'll wager you could tell some tales. Without the ladies present, of course."

"Do you hear that, Miles?" Mrs. Cordova dug an elbow at "Cameron." "They are so unkind as to try and keep it to themselves." She leant towards Diccon and said, "I have been naughty, Major, for I peeped at your palm whilst you were sleeping one day. I mean to ask Madame Olympias to consult her Mystical Window Through Time, and then I will know *all* your secrets, I warn you!"

He groaned. "In which case, ma'am, I shall be wholly in your power!"

"Foolish creature," she said complacently. "You already are!"

⁂

Went red as fire." Sir Lionel chuckled. "Did you see? That young fella's got a colourful past, I'll warrant, and don't want your aunt snooping into it!"

"Perhaps." After ten minutes alone with her father in his cluttered workroom, Marietta was still striving to turn the conversation in the right direction. "But I want to—"

"He's got an eye for you, child." Sir Lionel took up a wooden object about a foot long that bore some resemblance to a miniature pair of fireplace tongs. "Plain to see. You must keep him in his place, m'dear. Oh, I know you think we stand indebted to him. And I'll own he has poise and polished manners. I like him, and I do not doubt he comes from good stock. But he has no prospects now, Etta. I cannot allow a prize like you to throw herself away on an ingratiating rascal, who is at best a penniless half-pay officer!"

"How can you say such a thing, Papa? I scarcely know Major Diccon."

"Just as well." He tightened the handles of his device, and snapped the flat ends at her playfully. "Fanny don't trust him. What d'you think of my flea trap, m'dear? I'll wager it'll sell like wildfire!"

Clearly, he had no intention of letting her come to the point. Marietta gripped her hands together and said with firm resolve, "Papa, Mr. Innes Williard called here this morning, and—"

"Now did he, by George!" Sir Lionel's eyes sparkled. "Another of your admirers, and a respectable one who—"

"Respectable! He attempted to force his attentions on me and was so horrid that had it not been for Major Diccon—"

"What's that? I hope Diccon did not overstep the mark? If he means to offend my guests, he must take himself off, well or no!"

Her cheeks flushed with anger, Marietta protested, "You must not have heard, sir. Mr. Williard was the one who offended. The Major came to my aid, as I am sure you or Eric would have done!"

"Well, of course, if Williard really—" Cornered and fuming, Sir Lionel stamped to the far end of the room and rummaged in a bin filled with scraps of wood and metal. "His sister is a very pushing female, but that ain't his fault. I doubt the man intended any offence, and you're too quick by far, miss, to fly into a huff. You're a very pretty girl, but you mustn't give yourself airs. If young Coville don't come up to scratch, Innes Williard's a jolly good substitute. Lots of ladies have dropped the handkerchief for him, and would be overjoyed did he cast a glance in their direction!"

"Then I wish them joy of him, sir! I find him repellent, and—"

"Repellent!" Frowning, Sir Lionel returned to the workbench and slammed down a metal bar with unnecessary force. "Here's a high flight! The man's a friend and neighbour! He's well-favoured, well-built, very plump in the pockets, and—"

"And an uncouth boor who did not hesitate to warn me that I must be nice to him since we're in his debt to the tune of five thousand guineas!" At this, her father paled and looked stricken. Running to catch his arm she said, "Papa! Is it truth? I try so hard to pay the bills and set aside funds for school expenses, but—"

"But I do nothing! Is that it?" Scourged by guilt, he pulled away and blustered, "I've given up my clubs. I don't patronize my tailor—faith, but my clothes are in rags! I sacrificed my carriages and horses. And—and do I complain when you ladies buy cloth and pattern cards and—and deck yourselves out in the latest fashions and fal-lals? No!"

"But, dearest Papa, you said we must keep up appearances, and we sew and mend all our clothes so as to keep expenses down!"

"Oh, aye, set it all to my account! I say nothing when you bring this fellow into our home to eat up everything in the pantry and cause me to be saddled with a great bill from that miserable apothecary! Despite the fact that Diccon nigh killed my son with his nasty temper!"

"You know how badly he felt about that! Besides, Arthur was much to blame. And it was my fault that the Major was hurt afterwards. In honour we were obligated, sir! You could not wish that—"

"So now my honour is challenged, is it?" Sir Lionel sank onto a chair and put a hand over his eyes. "That I should live to see my own daughter turn against me!"

Stricken, she sank to her knees beside his chair. "Never, dearest Papa! Never! You know how much we all love you."

"I don't know . . . why you should," he said brokenly. "You're perfectly right, and I'm a villain! I sought only to make a little winning, Etta! Williard is shockingly poor at cards, and I so seldom have the chance to play anymore. The stakes were low . . . I don't know what happened." His voice shredded. He caught her hand and pressed it to his cheek and said on a sob, "I do not deserve . . . your loyalty! You'd be better off if I were . . . dead!"

He was a weak and foolish man, but he had been a devoted husband and in their more affluent days nothing had been too good for his children. The shock of his beloved wife's death so soon after Arthur was born had shattered him, and although he had recovered and now seemed reasonably contented, his strength and self-sufficiency seemed to have been buried with Mama. But he was kind, and gentle, and meant so well. And she loved him.

She stifled a sigh, and kissed and comforted him. And knew that their one hope was that Blake Coville should offer for her.

❧❦❧

A wind came up during the night increasing in strength until it whistled in the chimneys and sent curtains billowing on their rods. Long schooled to react to any unusual sound, Diccon was wide awake with the first creak of a protesting floorboard. A door slammed somewhere, and from Mrs. Cordova's bedchamber, directly above his own, came the sounds of a casement being cranked shut. All then was quiet, save for the wind, but he could not get back to sleep.

He could see again that dainty orange gown, the ribbon in the soft curls, the brief look of alarm in the big green eyes when Mrs. Cordova had implied that Eric Warrington was in Town instead of being at Cambridge. Sir Lionel had accused Marietta of "putting on a Friday face." It would seem that she had good reason for anxiety. All three ladies worked long and hard, and it was very obvious that they had been accustomed to a far more luxurious way of life. When Marietta wasn't dusting, sweeping, polishing, mending, helping her aunt sew the effigies, or caring for Arthur, she had to organize the household and deal with tradespeople and duns. Miss Marietta, who deserved the very best the world could offer, had enough to bear. If this brother of hers was as rackety as her sire—

He frowned into the darkness. Sir Lionel seemed a fond parent, but he was the type of man who, having willingly shifted his responsibilities onto his daughter's slender shoulders, might not be above pushing her into a loveless marriage so as to restore his finances. It didn't bear thinking of that so exquisite a creature should be sold to a crudity like Innes Williard.

· 93 ·

He tossed restlessly. His occupation and an innate shyness had prevented him from acquiring a reputation as a ladies' man, but he was not a stranger to the fair sex. As an embittered seventeen-year-old he had loved deeply and with tragic consequences. Years after Grace's death, a dashing and seductive émigré comtesse had laughed at and teased her "charming boy," but taught him so much of the tender passion. Poor Danielle had then declared she'd taught him too well and that she couldn't live without him. His quiet and then firm reminders that she was a married lady and they must be discreet had been brushed aside. She had instead pursued him so blatantly that he'd been unable to avoid a duel with her husband, which had unleashed a regular hornet's nest of scandal in Mayfair and ire in Whitehall. He smiled nostalgically. Quite a woman had been the comtesse. Yvette in Normandy had been a very different type; youthful, uncomplicated, undemanding, not two thoughts in her pretty head, but glowing with *joi de vivre*. In Spain, the fiery Dolores had loved him devotedly—until she'd been taken under the wing of a wealthy rag merchant.

He had been fond of them all; and had loved only Grace. True love had not come to him again until now, when he was unable to claim it, and all but powerless to help the lady who had so completely stolen his heart. He should leave here quickly, and yet, if this was the only chance he would ever have to be near her, how could he bear to go? Well, he must, that's all, because the longer he stayed to admire her courage and resourcefulness, her kindness, her beauty, the harder it would be to break away. Yes, he would be sensible. Tomorrow, he would leave. Or, perhaps the day after. Meanwhile, his throat was dry as dust. He got out of bed and pulled on the dressing gown that Yves had had the foresight to bring with his clothes.

Candle in hand he crept along the corridor although the wind was blustering so that there was small chance of those in the upstairs bedrooms hearing him. Light still gleamed from the door to the dining room. He paused, then moved on more soundlessly than ever. The door was ajar. Cautiously, he pushed it a little wider.

Marietta sat at the table sifting through what must only be a pile of bills and making notes on a sheet of paper. He drew back as she stood and crossed to the sideboard. She took out an ornate ginger jar, returned to her chair, and shook banknotes and coins from the jar. The counting of these was obviously disappointing, and she bowed her head into her hands, looking tired and despairing. His heart wrung, it was all he could do not to go to her at once and try to comfort her. But he was a stranger, newly come into their lives. How mortified she would be if she knew he'd watched her.

He backed away, therefore, and returned to his room, seething with anger that she should have to sit all alone in the middle of the night, struggling with all those bills and that pitiful little pile of cash. Probably trying to scrape together the funds to meet tuition costs for a brother who had carelessly left school to "go into London for a change, poor darling." "I'd 'poor darling' him," he muttered savagely.

He sat on the bed and waited. About half an hour later he heard the stairs creak, but he let another half-hour drag by before venturing into the corridor once more.

There was no light in the dining room now, and the door stood wide. He groped his way to the sideboard and took down the ginger jar. . . .

❧

The thing is," panted Capitan Rodolfo as he helped Diccon lift "Mrs. Hughes-Dering" into the donkey cart, "there's not much good holding up a stagecoach if there's no one in it."

Diccon agreed to the wisdom of this, but pointed out, "We already have Freddy Foster and—"

"Sir Fred'rick," corrected Capitan Rodolfo, straightening the mask which had shifted around, blinding him. "Not "Freddy." We don't *know* him!"

"Sorry. I forgot. How many more passengers will we need?"

The dashing Capitan hesitated. "I 'spect such a famous high-wayman wouldn't bother with a coach 'less it had at least three victims. Eh?"

"Probably not. In that case, I think we'd better fetch out Lady Dora Leith. She's a passenger to delight any highway-man."

The Capitan looked dubious. "I dunno if Etta's finished her yet. We could bring Miles Cam'ron."

"We could. But Capitan Rodolfo liked the ladies, don't for-get."

"He did?" Astonished, the daring highwayman asked, "Why?"

"Well, he was a Spaniard, you know. A Latin." This evok-ing nothing more than puzzled incomprehension, Diccon said with a lurking smile, "Latin gentlemen are particularly fond of the ladies. Capitan Rodolfo always kissed them, before stealing their diamonds."

"*Ugh!*" exclaimed Arthur, revolted. "How 'gusting! Then I won't be *him!* Who else? I dunno if Robin Hood held up stage-coaches."

"I think they'd not been invented then, old fellow. You might consider The Dancing Master. He was very successful for a time, and so far as I know they never hanged him."

Arthur was dubious. He would prefer, he said ghoulishly, to be a rank-rider who had met his end facing his captors with a scoffing laugh before swinging on the great gallows known as Tyburn Tree. Diccon provided some more likely candidates, but Devil Dice was dismissed as being "too new"; the Hounslow Horror's preference to shoot his victims through the eye lacked appeal; and although his famous mare, Black Bess, was an in-ducement, Dick Turpin's humble start in life as a butcher had a certain lack of dash. Diccon wasn't quite as sure as his fellow-conspirator that Mrs. Cordova "wouldn't mind a bit" if her "friends" were borrowed, and he pointed out that time was pass-ing and it might be as well to press on with the scheme. Bowing to such logic, Arthur took off his mask and required that it be re-tied. "I'll change to The Dancing Master," he announced. "An' you're the stagecoach driver."

This being decided, they went in search of the third passenger, and "Lady Dora Leith" was carried out to the donkey cart-cum-stagecoach.

It was a bright, if rather cloudy morning. The wind was still blowing, flapping The Dancing Master's cloak as he climbed onto the seat beside Diccon. Lem Bridger had driven Marietta and Fanny to Cloud Village to pay the chandler's bill and purchase candles, chicken feed, oats, and other such vital necessities. Mrs. Cordova had intended to stay at home, but when she had suddenly recalled an appointment and hurried off to Madame Olympias' caravan, Arthur had seized the moment to fill the doomed "stagecoach."

The highwayman laid out the route, Friar Tuck joined the expedition and was appointed Stagecoach Guard, and, Mr. Fox having been bribed with an old shopping list, the conspirators set forth.

They had been gone only a few minutes when Sir Lionel wandered up from his workroom in search of someone to try out the new flea trap. The house had that oddly flat feel that tells of the absence of human beings. Sir Lionel shouted a few times, but then had a vague recollection of Marietta telling him that she and Fanny were going shopping. He supposed they must have taken Dova with them. Major Diccon also appeared to be off somewhere, probably with Arthur. It was good of the fellow to be so patient with the child, who seemed to regard him as his own personal property. He padded rather disconsolately into the withdrawing room. Not a soul. Not . . . a . . . soul! He brightened. This was his chance, by Jupiter! On the thought he ran up the stairs at quite remarkable speed, and within ten minutes was hurrying down again, clad in riding coat and buckskins.

Only yesterday when he'd admired Orpheus, the Major had asked if he'd care to accompany him on a ride, offering to take one of their hacks for his own mount. Sir Lionel flattered himself that he had been used to cut quite a dash exercising his big black in Hyde Park. Of course, Moonlight had not been quite as sprightly as Orpheus. A fine animal, though, and plenty of spirit for a nineteen-year-old. Still, like any other man, Sir Lionel did not care to make a spectacle of himself and had been secretly relieved when Marietta had forbidden that Diccon should ride yet, thus enabling him to decline the offer. The Major *had* offered, though, and if he had meant to limit his invitation to a time when they would ride out together, he'd not *said* as much. Exactly.

The stallion rolled his eyes and stamped about a bit while he was being saddled up, but made only a small show of biting, or flattening his ears. Sir Lionel utilized the mounting block, then guided the big horse out of the yard. The stallion tossed his head and snorted, eager to run. Sir Lionel's pulses quickened as he felt the power of the animal. If he was obliged to cling to the pommel a few times when Orpheus danced in a circle, why, there was no one to see, and he was at least keeping his seat. He managed to hold to a walk, then to a trot. When Orpheus broke into an impatient canter, his heart began to pound, rather, but—oh! the silken gait, the proud crest! What a horse! Perhaps, when they were up the hill a little way and past these trees he would dare to touch the smooth sides with his spurs. There, they were clear now, and—

An oncoming rider and a scream caused him to pull back on the reins, and his heart thudded into his boots. He knew that voice and thought a panicked, 'Devil take it, she's cornered me again!'

In this instance, he wronged the widow. Mrs. Isolde Maitland was a handsome woman with a superb figure, luxuriant auburn hair, and well-cut features. If her hazel eyes were bold, they were also large and bright, but they looked better than they saw. In fact, the widow was short-sighted, and as her brother repeatedly warned, she should wear her spectacles instead of hiding them in a drawer. She had not glimpsed Sir Lionel through the trees and was really startled when he burst into sight. It took only an instant, however, for her quick wits to seize this golden opportunity, and she said with a breathless little laugh, "My goodness, dear sir, you are so sudden! *How* you frightened me, you daring thing! You may go now, Murphy. I shall be quite safe with Sir Lionel." A brisk wave of her hand dismissed her following groom who rode off, hiding a smirk. "At least, I *think* I will be safe," she added coyly.

Sir Lionel said in a hollow voice, "You're far from home, ma'am."

"Can you guess why I so often ride this way?" she purred, urging her brown mare closer.

Orpheus snorted and bucked, and Sir Lionel clung desperately to the pommel. "Best not . . . venture too close," he gasped, surviving the threat without a marked degree of skill. "He's—he's somewhat of a handful."

"Ah, but not for such an accomplished rider as yourself." She narrowed her eyes, peering at the grey. "What a large creature! And how well you look in the saddle, dear Sir Lionel. Though, I vow, were I your lady I would be terrified to see you up on such a brute. But then, I was ever protective of those I . . . love."

Sir Lionel quailed inwardly, and took refuge in silence.

Undaunted, she swept on, "I'd no *least* notion you enjoyed a morning canter. I wonder if you will be so generous as to allow me to share your rides?"

"Oh, he ain't—ain't mine, ma'am," gulped Sir Lionel, allowing Orpheus to trot. "Belongs to a fellow who stays with us. Temporarily, that is."

"Ah, yes. My dear brother told me of your—er, guest. Not a very charming one, I gather. Poor Innes was rather hurt to receive such Turkish treatment at your hands. Under the circumstances. . . . But I told him that you'd not have allowed it for an instant! Sir Lionel Warrington, I said, is the very soul of honour, and would never permit his bosom bow to be insulted. Especially since our two families seem likely to become even more . . . close."

As if to emphasize her words, she leaned nearer. "I should

not flatter you, sir, but—I am just a silly girl with little will-power. So I will confess that I have such an admiration for you! It fairly wrings my heart to see a lonely gentleman struggling to deal with a large family without a lady at his side. Truly, you are the type to throw other men into the shade and make a girl's heart beat faster! Yes, I own it, though it makes me blush! My dear brother says I must not betray my feelings or you will think me fast, but I told him—no such thing. Sir Lionel Warrington has been about the world, I said. He would understand a lady's heart. I have no fears on that head, I said. And furthermore . . ."

On she went. Flapping her eyelashes at him in that appallingly coy way. The least misstep and she would claim he'd popped the question. And she wouldn't be a gentle and loving wife as darling Elsa had been, for Isolde Maitland cared not a rap for anything but the title. He could speak plainly, of course, and advise her to set her sights on some other poor fellow. Only, burn it! he owed Innes that confounded five thousand! If only he could escape! If only he'd stayed at home! She'd never have caught him had he not ventured out.

CHAPTER VII

Jus' give me time to find a good place to lurk, please," said The Dancing Master. "An' then you come, an' I'll jump out waving my trusty horse pistol, an' being a Very Vill'nous Rank Rider, an' I'll freeze your blood when I roar, 'Stand an' d'liver!' " He removed the "Guard" from his lap and climbed down from the donkey cart, practising his Villainous Scowl, then asked anxiously, "Has you brought something to d'liver?"

Diccon had persuaded Bridger to make a few purchases in the village, and he admitted to having some "valuables" stashed away, this bringing a beam to interfere with the scowl. "But you'd best not roar terribly loud, Villainous Rank Rider," he cautioned. "Mr. Fox is sensitive and we mustn't upset him."

The Dancing Master nodded, and hurried off along the lane scowling busily.

Amused, Diccon watched that hop, skip, and jump progress. A fine little chap was Master Arthur Warrington. Briefly, he dreamed a dream of himself and Marietta comfortably settled into a charmingly refurbished Lanterns, and with little children playing around them.

He started when there came a distant shout. He was forgetting his duties. The Guard was sound asleep. He grinned and slapped the reins on Mr. Fox's back, and the "stagecoach" rattled up the slope.

Safely hidden at the bend of the lane, pistol in hand, and mask in place, The Dancing Master waited, tense with excitement. The hoofbeats were confusing as they seemed to be coming from higher up the lane, instead of from below. But now they were upon him.

With a high-pitched squeal, he leapt from his place of concealment and roared, *"Stand an' d'liver!"* whereupon several things happened very rapidly.

Two riders cantered around the corner from the north at the same instant that the "stagecoach" arrived from the south.

Already irritable because of the slow pace and the human who bounced so ineptly on his back, Orpheus let out a scream of fright, and reared, his hoofs flailing at the air.

Diccon sprang up, shouting, "Out of the way, boy!"

Arthur hurled himself aside.

Friar Tuck awoke like an uncoiled spring and shot under Mr. Fox's nose, yowling a protest.

Startled, the little donkey brayed shatteringly and tried to bolt, causing Diccon to be flung back on the seat.

Trying to control her scared mare, whose nerves were not helped by the wild gyrations of Orpheus, Mrs. Maitland shrilled, "Warrington, hold your brute still!" She squinted at the donkey cart. "Isn't that . . . Dora Leith?"

Diccon grabbed for the reins, but the widow's piercing tones further upset poor Mr. Fox, who essayed a buck. The cart rocked wildly, and "Lady Leith" was tossed out.

Arthur had been correct. Marietta hadn't quite finished the "lady." In fact, parts of "her" were only tacked in place. The fall was fatal.

Mrs. Maitland's was not a kindly nature, but she had not seen this latest addition to Mrs. Cordova's collection, and believed she witnessed a decapitation. Her shriek was ear-splitting and sent Orpheus into a shy that propelled Sir Lionel into a soaring flight cut short by the law of gravity. Fortunately, his plump form cushioned the widow when she slid from the saddle in a dead faint.

Marietta and Fanny had encountered Innes Williard in the village, and the gentleman had insisted that he and his head groom escort their coach on the return journey. They came upon the scene in time to see Sir Lionel sprawled in the dirt, clutching the widow in his arms.

"Papa!" cried Marietta, trying to open the coach door.

"*Whatever* are you doing?" gasped Fanny.

Not one to miss an opportunity, Mr. Williard thundered, "Unhand my sister, sir!"

"Eh?" said Sir Lionel, dazed.

Escaping the coach and running to bend over her sire, Marietta asked, "Are you all right, Papa? Whatever happened?"

"Sir Lionel very gallantly saved Mrs. Maitland when she fainted and fell from her horse," said Diccon, battling laughter.

"As usual you talk rubbish!" Mr. Williard dismounted and thrust the reins at his groom. "M'sister never fainted in her life. And if she did," he contradicted himself, dropping to one knee beside the widow, "there must have been some damned good cause."

Recovering, Mrs. Maitland moaned, "Oh, oh, oh," and threw her arms around his neck, wailing, "Poor woman . . . she has lost her head!"

"And so have you, by the look of things," snapped her insensitive brother. But for the first time, catching sight of the unfortunate figure in the ditch, he recoiled, aghast.

"No, no. Pray do not be distressed, ma'am," said Marietta, kneeling and taking one of Mrs. Maitland's hands. "It's my aunt's newest effigy—not the real Lady Leith."

"As anyone can see, who's not half blind," snarled Williard, pulling himself together and casting a blighting glare at his sister.

With comprehension came rage. Mrs. Maitland turned on Diccon, shrilling, "Oh! How horrid you are! You deliberately tried to frighten me!"

"A shameful and dastardly trick to play on a helpless lady," roared Williard.

"Nonsense," said Diccon coolly. "I regret the lady was frightened, but it was an accident."

"If you would be so kind as to—get off my lap, ma'am?" ventured Sir Lionel.

Williard pulled the widow up, and Diccon left the cart and helped Sir Lionel to his feet.

"It wasn't the Major's fault, sir," quavered Arthur, clutching his "pistol" and looking very scared. "We was just playing Highwayman, but—"

Williard boomed, "I hold you responsible for your son's deplorable conduct, Warrington! And you had best pray my sister ain't seriously hurt! As for you, Major, dash it all, I'd think a grown man could find something more worthwhile to do with his spare time than to play games with children!"

"We differ," drawled Diccon.

"By grab!" exclaimed Mr. Williard's groom who had been watching Diccon narrowly. "I thought I reckernized you! We was in the same company at Waterloo. D'you remember me, Sergeant?"

Marietta's eyes flashed to Diccon's expressionless face.

Fanny, who had come to stand close to her, murmured, *"Sergeant?"*

Innes Williard gave a bark of laughter. *"Sergeant,* is it? I *knew* you were no officer! Lie your way out of this, fellow!"

Ignoring him, Diccon put out his hand. "Of course I remember you, Skipton. I'm glad to see you survived. Not many from our company did."

The groom drew back, eyeing his employer uneasily. "Beg pardon, sir. Wasn't me place to have spoke up."

"You did well," said Williard, grinning broadly. "Now I'd like to hear what our pseudo major has to say for himself."

Marietta said, "I am sure we all honour any gentleman who fought in that terrible battle. Regardless of his rank. But instead of standing about talking, we must get my father home, Maj—er, Mr.—"

"Major is correct, ma'am," said Diccon, his smile awakening tiny laugh-lines at the corners of his eyes.

" 'Ware deception, Miss Marietta," jeered Williard, helping Mrs. Maitland to mount up. "I fancy he'll claim a battlefield commission."

"Are you subject to such flights of fancy?" Diccon raised his brows. "From sergeant to—major? Egad! It's clear to see you've never served in the army!" He turned to Sir Lionel. "You must go home in the carriage, sir. You've taken a nasty spill."

Sir Lionel's eyes turned longingly to Orpheus. "But, I—"

Marietta took his arm. "This way, Papa," she said firmly, leading him towards the coach.

"I want our physician to look at you, Isolde." Williard raised his voice and called vindictively, "And you'll be hearing from me, Warrington. In more ways than one, I promise you!"

❧

Sir Lionel sat in his favourite chair in the book room and stared at the empty hearth, pondering Fate. Marietta had gone upstairs to put Arthur down for his nap; Dova was in the withdrawing room, fussing over her decapitated "friend"; Fanny was setting out luncheon, and Diccon was at the stables attending to his hack. So, as usual, here sat the head of the house, deserted; with no one to confide in, or offer him sympathy. It had been thus, ever since his darling Elsa died. Trying to cope, all alone. And life was so deuced full of traps. It was clear that Innes Williard meant to be difficult over that unfortunate wager. And very likely Diccon would march back in here, claiming that confounded brute of a horse had a strained hock, or some such thing. Lord knows, he'd meant no harm when he'd taken the stallion out for a little jaunt, but—

The faintest silvery sound alerted him, and he looked up to find the Major—or whatever he was—standing beside his chair.

"By George!" he exclaimed. "You tread softly, man! I didn't

hear a sound till your spur jingled. You don't mean to ride out again after luncheon?"

"No. Before, sir. I rather think I've outstayed my welcome."

"Fiddlesticks! Now sit down, do! Never think I care whether you're a major or a private! You keep m'cellar well-stocked and I'd be a fool not to comprehend that in your line of work small—ah, deceptions, are sometimes a necessity. Truth is, I owe you an apology for borrowing your hack without asking permission."

Settling into the chair indicated, Diccon said, "No harm done, though I seldom allow anyone to ride Orpheus. He's a tricky brute to manage."

"Speaking of which," put in Marietta, coming into the room, ginger jar in hand. "However did you manage to double our Chinese Funds, Papa?"

Diccon, who had stood when she entered, acquired an apprehensive expression and edged towards the door.

Mystified, Sir Lionel said, "How's that again?"

"What is twelve from forty-two?" she asked, stepping in front of Diccon and looking up at him enquiringly.

"I—er—," he mumbled.

She nodded. "Too difficult, sir?"

"If you can't deduct twelve from forty-two, you ain't even a sergeant," said Sir Lionel, laughing. "It's thirty of course, m'dear. What else?"

"Sixty-five, apparently." She flung out an arm to bar the door. "Oh, no, you shan't escape, sir! Papa, I believe we have caught Major Diccon with his fingers in the ginger jar!"

Sir Lionel was much shocked, and leaning forward in his chair, protested, "That's not an accusation to be made lightly, Marietta!"

"You shall be the judge," she decreed. "And pending the verdict the accused may not leave the court-room! Sit—down—sir!"

She advanced determinedly, and Diccon retreated and half-fell into a chair while declaring that he knew nothing of Chinese Funds.

"It is what we call the ready cash we keep in our Chinese ginger jar," she said. "The case is, Papa, that I tallied up the funds last night and arrived at a total of forty-two guineas. I took out twelve with which to shop and pay some bills today. But when I put back the change just now, the jar was much heavier. It now holds sixty-five guineas, twopence three farthings!"

Sir Lionel frowned. "I really see no cause to discuss such matters in front of our guest. Perhaps your aunt—"

"Aunty Dova had borrowed ten shillings, not added a groat. So—unless you made a deposit, Papa . . . ?"

He shook his head, and they both turned and looked at the accused.

Diccon said, "This is ridiculous. How could I know of your secret vault?"

"Because you move like a shadow," said Marietta, "and likely saw one of us open the jar at some time or other."

"By Gad, sir," exclaimed Sir Lionel. "If you fancy we charge our guests for their accommodations, I don't scruple to say I am affronted!"

"I think I am the one to be affronted," said Diccon, rallying. "You accuse and judge me with not a shred of proof. Doubtless Miss Marietta was tired when she took her reckoning last night and made a small error. I will tell you that I do not make a habit of spying on my friends, nor do I interfere in their financial matters. However, you remind me of an obligation. I must pay the apothecary for his services, and will insist that you give me his reckoning."

This resulted in a heated argument that was terminated when Mrs. Cordova came and called them to luncheon. Not in the least anxious to question such a fortuitous windfall, Sir Lionel at once made a show of formally escorting his sister-in-law to the dining room. Diccon lost no time in emulating his example and offered his arm to Marietta. Taking it, she looked up at him. His eyes slid away from hers, guiltily. She leaned nearer and said with a twinkle, "I think you are very sly, Major. No wonder you were in such a hurry to escape us."

Relieved, he answered, "Unfortunately, I really must leave, Miss Warrington. You have been more than good, but I've business—er, matters to be dealt with. I—er, I was rather hoping I might tempt you to ride down to the manor with me."

She glanced out of the window. They were already well into autumn; there would not be many more of these golden afternoons. "I wish I could," she said as they walked into the corridor. "But I was out all the morning, and there is so much mending waiting to be done."

"And lots of grey and rainy days in which to accomplish it," he argued. "Please come. You must grant me a favour, you know, since you so cruelly accused me of playing—er, the spy."

She glanced up at him in mild surprise. He was evidently becoming more at ease with her and his pale eyes were suddenly lit with sparkling glints of laughter. Belatedly, it occurred to her that he was a very attractive man. "If I owe you anything, sir," she said, "it is my thanks for your patience with Arthur. I know bachelor gentlemen do not much care to be pestered by small boys."

"Very true. That rascal is rapidly ruining my reputation in the district! So you see, ma'am, you have no choice. You must protect me from his cunning blandishments, for I am putty in his hands!"

She laughed. "I will come on one condition—that you permit me to ride your magnificent grey."

Watching them from the dining room, Mrs. Cordova enquired, "Do you two mean to join us today?"

❧

Orpheus balked at the unfamiliar side-saddle, and, evidently feeling that he had been sufficiently put upon today, made a bared-teeth grab at Diccon's hand. His reward was a sharp rap on the nose and a reprimand in the tone that he knew meant business. However, Diccon began to unbuckle the girths and said apologetically that he should never have entertained the notion that the stallion could be ridden by a lady.

Indignant, Marietta protested, "But you agreed! Besides, I am not an inexperienced rider. Come, sir, you must give me the benefit of the doubt!"

Diccon hesitated, Marietta coaxed, and, unable to resist, he at length tossed her into the saddle while Bridger kept a firm hand on the bit.

As if chastened, Orpheus started off meekly, and they rode side-by-side down the slope, Diccon keeping his borrowed mare close to the stallion, ready to intervene if the different balance angered the high-strung animal.

The meadow grasses tossed to a light breeze, the air was warm, and beyond Lanterns the blue waters of the Channel glittered as if spread with diamonds.

Marietta exclaimed happily, "What a perfect afternoon!"

"Perfect, indeed," agreed Diccon, watching her. An enchanting smile was turned to him. He thought, 'Lord, but she's a lovely little thing!' and managed to say more or less sensibly, "But you would rather be in Town, I think?"

"Sometimes, yes. I miss the home where I was born, the social whirl, our friends." Her smile became rueful. "Rather more than some miss me, I fear. There is something to be said for being reduced to—to a lower standard of living. Only your real friends still come to call."

"And the false friends you are better off without. Were you deeply disillusioned, ma'am?"

"In a few instances. For the rest, I was fairly sure of the reaction I could expect. Oh, dear! Does that sound dreadfully harsh and cynical?"

He shrugged. "Sensible, rather. To put humanity on a pedestal is to invite disaster."

"Yes. We all have our failings. And however we try to hide them, I think most people are not deceived." She added with a chuckle, "I could wish they were!"

"On the other hand, some people have so many good points that without a few failings they'd be nigh unbearable."

She glanced at him in time to see him turning his head away. "I suppose you think I was fishing for that compliment," she said mischievously.

"Were you? My apologies. In point of fact, I was referring to myself."

That won a laugh. She said, "It certainly might apply to your horse, sir. He has a silken gait. My own favourite mount—" She broke off, suffering a pang as she thought of her loved little white mare.

"You had to leave her in Town, did you?" he asked, eager to chase the shadow from her eyes. "Shall you try to buy her back when you return?"

Marietta stared at him.

He said innocently, "Well, you do plan to restore your fortunes, do you not?"

"Do you mean by wedding one of the fabulously rich princes and potentates lining up before my father's front door?"

"Just so. Do but ally your beauty to a positive outlook and you will be a wealthy young matron in no time, comfortably restored to a Curzon Street palace, and a position as leader of London Society."

"What a picture you paint!" she said merrily. "Thank you for it. That would answer my father's dream, Fanny could have a proper London Season, and I could meet all my friends again."

"Is that what you would like?"

Was it what she would like? She pondered for a moment, and he watched her and marvelled at how charming was the change from gaiety to gravity.

She said then, "For my family—yes. But—do you know, I would miss this place. It is so peaceful and beautiful. Even poor old Lanterns."

"You're not repelled by the manor, then?"

"No, indeed. I feel sure it was once a happy home. Though

I'll own I'd not dare be alone there. Even in the daylight. How can you be so brave as to stay after dark?"

His lips quirked. "Nerves of steel. Poor Mr. Fox shares your fears though, and demands that I hold his hoof once the sun goes down."

"No, be serious. Have you never witnessed strange lights at night time? Or seen the—the—"

"The ghosts? Oh, yes."

"Good gracious! Or are you teasing again? There have been so many stories and Aunty Dova says there must be some fire behind all that smoke."

"I expect she does." He pursed his lips. "I haven't told anyone this, Miss Marietta, but there is a knight in black armour who trots along the corridors at midnight, howling, and slicing about him with a great war axe, and—"

"I wouldn't think a knight in full armour, carrying a war axe, could 'trot' anywhere without his horse," she put in, her eyes mirthful.

"Ah, but ghostly axes likely don't weigh much. And besides, if what one reads about the times is truth, they were a sturdy lot."

"Hmm. Why does he howl and slice about?"

"From what I can gather his admired lady ran off with a wandering minstrel, and the knight longed to—er, do him in."

"If the knight was so bloody-minded, she probably made a wise choice."

"More likely she regretted it. Life with a wandering minstrel must have had its drawbacks."

"Unless she was a music-lover."

He looked at her sharply. "Are you, ma'am?"

"Oh, yes. Indeed I am! Isn't everybody?"

A grim expression drove the smile from his eyes. He said a clipped, "No, Miss Warrington. Most decidedly not!"

They had by now reached the courtyard at Lanterns. Diccon dismounted, looped the reins over a post, and reached up to lift Marietta down.

As she leaned to him, Orpheus, who had endured to that moment, lost his temper and shot stiff-legged into the air.

Marietta became the second Warrington to be hurled from the stallion's back. She gave a shocked cry, but then was caught and held firmly. "Thank heaven!" she exclaimed breathlessly. "You . . . were . . ." The words faded. His arms crushed her close. His head was bent above her. She knew now what Fanny had meant by her remark that when he looked at her his eyes were far from cold, for they glowed as if lit with silver flame. She was neither afraid nor angry. That scorching light was replaced by a deep tenderness. For a breathless moment she thought he was going to declare himself. Instead, his eyes became veiled. He set her down, and asked with quiet courtesy if she was all right. "I should never have let you ride the silly brute."

"I enjoyed every moment," she argued, shaken, but trying to match his poised control. "Still, I am very glad you were so quick to catch me, Major. No, do not unsaddle him. I cannot stay."

"I know. It was good of you to come. But you will ride the mare home, ma'am."

There was a set to his jaw that told her it would be pointless to object. Not that she intended to do so. In fact, his sternly protective air brought her an odd sense of comfort. This man guarded those he cherished. She experienced a fleeting sense of envy for the lady who would become his wife.

He exchanged the saddles with swift, practised hands and asked if she would care for a cup of tea or a glass of ratafia before starting back. "I could bring it out to you," he added, bowing to the proprieties.

Curious, she asked, "Do you really have ratafia?"

His eyes danced but he replied gravely, "Let us say I could lay my hands on some."

"Oh, how silly of me! I quite forgot your—er, trade."

He put a finger on his lips. "Careful, Miss Warrington. The walls have ears and you'd not want— What is it?"

Gazing at the house she felt chilled and said, "I would have sworn . . . Oh, I expect I am being silly, but—I am sure some-one was watching us from that upstairs window!"

He scanned the house narrowly. "Did he wear armour, ma'am?"

"No, and I wish you will not make light of it. I *saw* him!"

"Then it is likely just some poor Waterloo veteran starving politely. Now, if you will mount up, Miss Warrington, I—"

"I shall do no such thing! What if it is a—a thief, or a real highwayman? No, do not be brave and noble. I know you mean to investigate, and I'll not leave until you're sure all is well."

He looked down at her with the whimsical half-smile that she was coming to like so well. "I'll have your promise," he said, "that if you should hear an uproar, or if I'm not back in five min-utes, you will ride *ventre à terre* for the dower house."

She nodded, and watched as he avoided the drawbridge, sprinting lightly across the moat to the main entrance. He paused there for a second. A pistol, long and gleaming, ap-peared in one hand. The door opened, and he seemed to melt into the inner shadows. It occurred to her that he'd made not a sound.

The instant he entered the house, Diccon sensed that some-one was there. It was an instinct that had served him well in the past and that he never ignored. He stood behind the door, unmoving, waiting for his eyes to adjust to the dimness. If there was more than one intruder, which was very likely, they must not be in this room, or they'd have attacked when he was sil-houetted against the light. He drifted across the hall to the main staircase, alert, tense, one finger hovering over the hair trigger of the pistol.

The faintest creak.

He stood motionless, looking up.

Someone was moving along the balcony. He shouldn't have let Marietta come here. If this intruder was Ti Chiu . . . ! He glanced swiftly behind him, but the entrance hall was empty.

Aiming steadily, he called, "One more step and I fire!"

The response was immediate and indignant. "Hoot, toot!

And is this the thanks I get for being tossed aboot on that mis-errrrable ship forever and a day?"

"Mac!" Diccon released the hammer with respectful caution and ran up the stairs to grip the hand of his valet/groom/general factotum. "Welcome back! Tell me quickly, is it done? Nobody knows?"

"Aye, 'tis as ye wished, though in a court o'law I'll swear I had nae hand in the wicked business, ye ken?"

"I know, you old curmudgeon. And I do thank you! Man alive, but I'm glad you're home at last!"

"Home is it?" grumbled the Scot. "A fine home this is! Are ye aware ye've had callers? When I came in the kitchen door, a body ran oot the front. And y'r pairsonal belongings hae been rummaged and mauled aboot something shameful! Come and see fer yer ain self."

Accompanying him, Diccon muttered frowningly, "Likely just a tramp."

"Hah!" MacDougall opened the door to the vast bedchamber. Light flooded in at the windows, revealing the chaos wrought by ruthless hands. "Dinna be telling me ye left it in this state," said the Scot, and turning to face his employer in the bright room, he gasped, "Whisht mon! Ye're something changed!"

"Oh—a slight accident, but—"

"I'm thinking there's more changed than that! I've nae seen that look in y'r eyes since—"

"Well never mind that," said Diccon, his face rather red, "Let's see what the varmint made off with, and you can tell me about Italy. But be quick. There's a lady waiting."

"Is there then?" said his man smugly. "I'd a wee bit thought there might be!"

The moments dragged past and with each one Marietta became more tense and apprehensive. Surely, five minutes had gone by?

There had been no uproar, in fact she'd heard nothing in the least ominous, yet the very silence seemed to throb with menace. She kept her eyes fixed on that great front door. It still stood partly open, the afternoon sunlight slanting in to paint a bright bar across the inner darkness. He should be back by now. If all was well he'd not leave her standing here for so long, worrying. She began to creep forward, as if drawn to that open door yet ready at the least sign or sound of danger to run, as she'd promised.

But when the sound came she halted and stood very still, transfixed. It was the last sound she would have expected; the mellow strains of a violin, masterfully played. Astonished, she began to move forward again, and the music grew louder, swelling into a soaring and proud melody. She was so intrigued that she paid no attention to the hoofbeats until they were directly behind her. With a yelp of fright, she whirled around.

Orpheus tossed his head at her and walked on past, ears forward, hooves thudding hollowly on the ironbound planks of the drawbridge.

Marietta drew a sobbing breath of relief and closed her eyes for an instant, a hand pressed to her galloping heart. When she looked up, the big grey was half-way up the steps, peering into the hall. She hurried forward as the melody rose to a crescendo and died away. Diccon came to the door, replacing a violin in its case and watching her with a diffident smile.

She clapped her hands with genuine admiration, and he bowed, then patted the grey's neck as the big horse nuzzled him. "I told you he follows a tune," he said, propping the violin case against the wall.

"So you did! And how splendidly you play, Major! When did you learn such skills? And why did you never mention it? And how could you have been so horrid as to leave me worrying here all this time without so much as calling to me that everything was all right?" Anxious again, she asked, "It is—isn't it?"

He took up Orpheus' reins and they began to follow the moat

along the north wing. "To answer your last question first, Miss Warrington, you were perfectly right. There was someone inside the house."

"And you stayed to chat, did you? With whom, pray? The lady?"

She had a brief impression of utter stillness, then he said, "Actually, she is rather difficult to converse with, since she carries her head in a bucket. However—"

"Wretch!" she said with her lilting laugh. "Next you will say you've had a chat with Saladin!"

"Oh, several chats. He won't tell me where it is, if that's what you mean. The fellow's a real marplot."

"Then you know the legend of the jewelled picture?"

"But of course. Why do you suppose I stay here?"

"Well, to say truth, I thought it was handy to the beach and your free-trading friends. Now, will you answer my other questions, or do you mean to fob me off on that subject also?"

He smiled at her use of the cant term. "My grandfather was an accomplished violinist. He began to teach me when I was three years old."

"Surely that was very early. Was it hard for you?"

"No. It was my greatest joy. Grandpapa had a small violin made for me. In fact I still have it, just in case someday I may teach my own son—" He broke off abruptly, the steely look returning to his eyes.

"You play splendidly. You must know I mean to demand that you play for us at the dower house. Unless—" She hesitated and added with care, "Am I intruding on very personal ground? If so, I beg pardon."

At once his expression lightened. "How could I be anything but pleased? Amateur musicians love a captive audience, you know."

"Your performance just now did not sound in the least amateurish. How is the piece called?"

" 'The Honourable.' I wrote it for Sir John Moore, who was

one of the most truly honourable gentlemen I have ever known."

Marietta stopped walking and put an impulsive hand on his arm. "*You* composed that beautiful music?"

He nodded, her admiration causing his lean cheeks to flush with pleasure.

"But—how wonderful! What a great gift! Is *that* why you stay here, all alone? To concentrate on your composing? What else have you written? Oh, I must hear it all!"

"I'm afraid you have, ma'am. At least, that is my only concert piece."

Bewildered, she said, "But—why? How could you have thrown away such talent in exchange for a military life? You should have studied with a famous composer, or at some great school of music, like—like that university in . . . in Paris is it?"

"Can you mean the Sorbonne, perhaps?"

"Yes, that's the place."

Briefly, his long fingers covered the small hand on his arm. He said huskily, "How kind you are. Thank you. That was my dream, certainly. But—life has a way of rearranging dreams, alas." He paused, as if again viewing a past only he could see, then he said brightly, "Do not be thinking me a failure, however. A few friends are willing to let me play for them now and then. Mr. Fox doesn't mind, and Orpheus is a true afficionado." His eyes met hers. He said with a little hesitancy, "If I dare believe that my music has pleased you, then I have scored a—a true triumph."

"It has indeed pleased me, Major. Now, do you mean to tell me who was inside the manor?"

Gazing down at her, he muttered, "What? Oh! My man has returned. MacDougall is my good friend as well as my servant. You must come and meet him. He's going to fetch tea into the garden for us."

Amused by his proprietary air, she said, "That would be nice, but I wonder what Lord Temple and Cloud would think of us trespassing on his property like this?"

"Oh, I doubt he would object."

"Easy to say, sir. But suppose he should come riding in this very moment? Then what would you say?"

"I would likely be speechless with astonishment. To the best of my knowledge no peer of the realm has set foot on the place for more than a decade."

"He has been abroad, so I was told. But I should warn you that he is back in London and likely to come down here very soon."

"Really?" He looked at her thoughtfully, then asked, "Will this suit for our tea party, ma'am?"

A blanket had been spread on the weedy turf that once had been lawns, and a sturdy, rather dour-looking man, probably in his late forties and very neat in a dark brown habit, was setting a laden tray on a stool.

"Oh, lovely," said Marietta, undaunted by thick mugs, a tin teapot, and a chipped plate piled with bread and butter.

Diccon said wryly, "Far from a fashionable party, I'm afraid. But I think you'll find the tea worthwhile."

"However illegal," she murmured. "But never fear, I have lived in Sussex long enough to ask no questions."

"In which case you may enjoy your tea with a clear conscience. Over here, Mac! I must make you known to Miss Marietta Warrington. Micah MacDougall, ma'am. Sir Lionel Warrington and his family are leasing the dower house, Mac. And you had best set me straight on something since you know all the *ton* gossip. Is Lord Temple and Cloud in London?"

Having jerked a stiff bow to the young beauty who smiled at him so charmingly, MacDougall directed a level stare at his master. "Tae the best o' my knowledge, Major, he isnae."

Marietta said, "If he has left Town it must be all the more likely he means to come here, no?"

"Nae, Miss Warrington. I fancy Lanterns willnae see Lord Temple and Cloud again. I'll tend tae the hacks, sir." A curt bow and the Scot strode away.

Marietta sat on the blanket and looked after him curiously.

"I wonder how he could possibly know that. Servant hall gossip?"

"Undoubtedly. It spreads like wildfire and is usually infallible."

Perhaps it was, she thought, yet it did not match what Sir Gavin Coville and his son had said.

Diccon sat beside her and she poured the tea, spread damson jam on a thick slice of bread and butter, and, perhaps because she was out in the clear sunlit air, found both exceptionally delicious. The moments flew while they chatted easily, discovering a shared love of children and music, the paintings of that rather odd but brilliant gentleman, Joseph Turner, and a difference of opinion over the prospect of a steamship ever crossing the Atlantic Ocean without sails, which Marietta thought unlikely and Diccon was sure would be accomplished within a few years. After a short companionable silence, she asked if he really was at Lanterns to try and find the legendary *Sigh of Saladin*, and what he knew of it.

"Not a great deal," he admitted. "You may be sure I'd be delighted to find the pretty thing, but what I was able to learn is very likely one part fact and ninety-nine parts fiction. When you consider how rumours fly around London Town and are embellished and enlarged upon in only a few hours, you can imagine how a tale would become distorted over six centuries."

"But legend says that it is a picture comprised entirely of gems and framed in solid gold—true?"

He nodded. "Supposedly captured from under Saladin's nose by Lord Simon Cloud during the Third Crusade, brought to Lanterns, and then lost again while the manor was under attack by the French. Some stories have it that Saladin himself sent emissaries here to try and retrieve it."

Refilling his cup, she said, "With his great wealth, I wonder that the sultan would have gone to so much trouble over one small picture."

"Because it was a national treasure, ma'am. Entrusted to his keeping. He was reputed to be a proud and honourable gentleman and counted it a shameful blot on his character that he had failed his trust. That is why they named it *The Sigh of Saladin*, you see."

She finished her tea and was quiet for a little while, drowsily content, thinking of the mighty sultan and the treasure he had lost. She roused when Diccon waved a bee from her hair. "I wonder," she said, "if it will ever be found."

"If it is, the finder will be a very wealthy man. And his children and grandchildren after him, I'd guess." He added with a grin, "If he's not murdered for it! Only find an object of great beauty and you also find an army of cut-throats ready to take it away."

"You *had* to spoil the romance! And I must get home, Major." Smiling, she reached out and he sprang up to help her to her feet. She asked, "Are you sure you won't stay with us for another few days? You cannot be very comfortable here."

He thanked her, but said that MacDougall could make a frozen ditch comfortable, and that he had work that must be done. He insisted on riding back with her, however. She said little on the return journey, and he suspected she was thinking of the lost *Sigh of Saladin*.

Actually, Marietta's thoughts were on Sir Gavin Coville and his son. If their suspicions were true and Temple and Cloud really did mean to come to Lanterns, Major Diccon could very well be in great trouble. To trespass in a peer's home would be punishable by transportation, at least. And if his lordship should discover Diccon's smuggling activities, the death penalty would certainly be imposed. She stole a glance at the man beside her. He rode with lithe ease and appeared to be relaxed but she experienced again the sense of leashed power. In his business he had undoubtedly learned how to take care of himself. Yves had said that the Major "should have been dead many times" but always survived. She hoped fervently that his luck would continue.

They rode into the stableyard at the dower house and Diccon swung from the saddle, and walked around to lift her down.

A familiar voice called her name. Marietta's heart gave a little leap and she turned to see Blake Coville stride across the yard to greet her.

His eager look faded into an almost ludicrous disbelief. Staring at Diccon, he cried, "*You!* I thought you were still at your friend's convent!"

Turning in bewilderment, Marietta saw that Diccon's head was high, and on his face the forbidding hauteur she had seen when first they met. He said icily, "I am very sure you did!"

"You are—acquainted?" asked Marietta.

"To my sorrow, ma'am," said Diccon. "I suppose I should have—"

"Allow me to present my step-brother," shouted Coville with fierce hostility. "The *ig*noble Mallory Diccon Paisley, Lord Temple and Cloud!"

CHAPTER VIII

It seemed to Marietta that for an instant everything was as if frozen. The mellow sunlight was as bright, the sky as deeply blue, while they all stood like so many statues: Coville slightly crouching, his face distorted with passion; Diccon straight and proud, his eyes meeting her shocked gaze steadily; Aunty Dova, who had come out onto the back step, smiling an empty smile.

Finding her voice somehow, Marietta said threadily, "It's not true! It cannot be true! You couldn't . . . you *wouldn't* lie to us like that."

"Oh, would he not!" Striding to face his step-brother Coville demanded, "Where is she, you merciless rogue? What have you done with Lady Pamela?"

Ignoring him, Diccon said, "Miss Warrington, I have not lied to you, I only—"

"Attend me, damn you!" shouted Coville.

Diccon's eyes narrowed and turned on him, glinting oddly. He said with soft but ineffable menace, "You had best hope I do not."

Coville drew back a little, then, to Marietta's astonishment, turned and ran past Mrs. Cordova and into the house.

"He has gone to get his courage," said Diccon contemptuously. "Miss Warrington, if I did not tell you everything about myself, it was—"

She felt betrayed and foolish, and deeply hurt, and she interrupted, "It was *deliberate* deception from the start! You knew very well who I was and where we lived!"

"No."

"You said your name was Diccon."

"So it is. Your father did not give me time to finish my introduction, and—"

"You neglected to add the rest of it! Why? To amuse yourself? You stayed in our home, pretending to be a poverty-stricken free-trader, and all the while knowing you *own* this house! Did you enjoy laughing at us? Was that a *very* funny joke, Major? Ah, but I forget, your rank is only another of your lies! Mr. Williard's groom named you sergeant, and I was so trustingly stupid as to believe—"

"No!" He caught her by the arms and said desperately, "Listen! Marietta, you *must* listen! I've been—"

She wrenched free. "Do not *dare* to touch me! Will you deny telling me this *very afternoon* that no peer had visited Lanterns for many years?"

"No, but—"

"Do you deny that your ancestral title is Lord Temple and Cloud?"

His lips tightened. He said stormily, "If you will stop firing off accusations at me, and listen for—"

"Stand away from him, ma'am!"

Mrs. Cordova had gone. Blake Coville stood alone on the steps, a long-barrelled duelling pistol aimed steadily at Diccon's back.

Horrified, Marietta cried, "Don't! Oh, for pity's sake—do *not*!"

Without so much as a glance at Coville, Diccon said, "Never fear, Miss Marietta, it's just so much bravado. He'd not dare shoot me."

"Do not refine on that," said Coville grittily. "If you don't tell me what you've done with Lady Pamela, I'll be more than justified to—"

"To shoot me in the back? And before ladies?" Diccon swung around and began to walk slowly towards that deadly muzzle. "You're very free with your unproven accusations. Now try if you've the gumption to shoot an unarmed man while you look him in the eye!"

Coville set his teeth and took aim.

Watching his face, her breath held in check, Marietta suddenly ran forward and threw herself between the two men.

Startled, Coville's grip tightened instinctively.

Diccon threw Marietta aside even as the shot fragmented the silence. The ball burned a hole through his sleeve. With a leap he was atop the steps. His left hand smashed the pistol from Coville's grasp; his right, in a hard backhanded swipe, sent the man sprawling. "Murderous carrion!" he snarled, and ran to help Marietta to her feet, then grip her shoulders and shake her hard. Through his teeth, he said, "Do not—*ever*—do such a stupid thing again! Are you all right?"

Shocked and enraged, her voice was shrill as she answered, "No thanks to your silly heroics! Accusing *me* of stupidity, when *you* walked straight at a loaded gun! If ever I heard of such—"

"What a'God's name are you about?" Sir Lionel burst from the kitchen followed by his sister-in-law and a white-faced Fanny. "Fighting before ladies? Have you *quite* forgot your manners, gentlemen?"

Running to throw her arms about her sister, Fanny asked, "Are you hurt, dearest?"

Marietta shook her head, but clung to her, trembling from the reaction.

Over-riding Diccon's attempt to respond, Sir Lionel shouted, "I will ask that you leave my house at once, Major!"

Coville picked himself up and said, "You'd best have a care, sir, or his lordship might revoke your lease."

Sir Lionel stared at him.

Mrs. Cordova danced down the steps and sang in her shrill wavering voice, "Our Diccon is a baron; an old name and proud. Our Diccon, brother dear, is Lord Temple and Cloud."

"Wh-what . . . ?" gasped Sir Lionel, his eyes goggling.

"And his lordship is just leaving," said Marietta.

Diccon scanned her scornful face and, without another word, mounted up and rode from the yard.

<hr/>

I never trusted him," declared Fanny with vehemence. "Never!"

Marietta, who was already tired of that remark, said nothing.

"That is because you are afraid of him," said Mrs. Cordova, knowingly. "You have something of me in you, my love. You can sense the danger of the man."

A small fire had been lit in the drawing room and the three ladies were gathered around the hearth. Blake Coville and Sir Lionel were still in the dining room, lingering over their wine and cheese. Coville had blamed his loss of control on his anxieties for Lady Pamela Coville, and admitted shamefacedly that he should never have brought the pistol outside with ladies present. He had not meant to shoot, he insisted, but the hair-trigger needed only the slightest pressure and when Marietta had run in front of him, the shock had caused his grip to tighten just sufficiently to make it fire. He knew his conduct had been reprehensible and could easily have resulted in a tragedy. The very thought unmanned him, and he'd apologized so humbly to Marietta that tears had come into his eyes. He had been forgiven and invited to stay for dinner, an invitation he'd accepted gladly.

Marietta had been petted and praised, becoming quite the heroine of the deadly incident. In private she was congratulated because Mr. Coville had returned apparently as enamoured of her as before. But, although her nerves were calmer now, she felt depressed and unhappy. Her aunt's words irked her, and she said, "Why either of you should be afraid of the Major, I cannot think. He deceived us certainly, and told the most dreadful untruths, which is past forgiving. But I won't believe he meant us harm."

"He harmed Arthur," said Fanny stubbornly.

"You know that was unintentional, and he has since made the boy very happy. Indeed, what we are to tell the little fellow, I do not know. He'll miss Diccon so."

Mrs. Cordova nodded. "Yes, he will. You can't deny that, Fan."

"Perhaps not," said Fanny. "But I'm very glad Mr. Coville is here again, so that Etta can put the wicked creature out of her mind."

"The 'wicked creature,' " said Marietta, "probably saved my life this afternoon! Had he not pushed me aside when Mr. Coville fired, I might very well have been hit."

Fanny had been unaware of that fact. Dismayed, she exclaimed, "Then I owe him an apology, and my most fervent thanks. But—oh, dear! I still cannot like a man who has kidnapped his poor mama."

Marietta said, "I don't believe for a minute that he has done such a thing!"

"Then you believe that Sir Gavin and Blake Coville are lying?"

"Say, rather, that I think they must be mistaken."

Fanny sighed, and said dubiously, "But consider all the fibs the Major has told us, and how skillfully he evades an issue if he doesn't wish to answer."

"Evasions, yes," admitted Marietta. "He has many faults, I admit. I'll just not believe that murder is among them. Don't you agree, Aunty?"

Mrs. Cordova pursed her lips, leaned to whisper in "Captain Cameron's" ear, then said gravely, "I have no doubts at all, my love. He has killed. Oh, yes. Our noble landlord has killed!"

"Aunty!" cried Marietta, taken aback. "I thought you liked him!"

"But I do, child! I like him very well. Only Fan is perfectly right to be afraid of him. We all should be. He is a very dangerous man—even as his step-brother told us!"

Y e've got three bullet holes in ye, aside from that musket ball you hauled around in your back for yearrrs!" MacDougall's accent was very broad as he slammed a plate of perfectly cooked eggs and juicy pink slices of ham onto the kitchen table. "Ye've been knifed and beaten and had a great rogue horse trrrample ye half tae death—" As if to emphasize this unhappy inventory a bowl of buttered toast and a pot of jam joined the plate. He turned to the coffee pot that was hissing fragrantly on the hob. "And for—what?" he demanded, snatching it up. "What hae ye tae show fer all that meeserrrry? Is there never tae be an end of thumbing yer nose at Fate?"

Diccon reached for the damson jam, his thoughts on a certain idyllic tea party. "What would you suggest?" he asked absently.

"I'd suggest," growled MacDougall, dashing coffee into a mug, "that ye turrrn yer back on the whole ungrrrrateful parcel of 'em! May they rot! I'd suggest," he went on, thrusting the steaming mug in front of his employer, "that we go back tae Toon, kick yon parrrasites oot o' your fine hoosie, and that ye take your place in Society as is your rrright and bounden—"

"You know how I feel on that subject," interrupted Diccon, an edge of impatience to his voice. "As for the town house, my hands are tied. I cannot prove my right to it without leaving myself open to immediate arrest."

"Which I warned ye would be the case," said the Scot grimly. "So what are we tae do, then? Wait here for the Swiss and his mountain tae come and slaughter us? They know ye're here, mon! That thieving varmint who brrroke in here was Monteil's spy, else why was nothing taken?"

"Probably because you interrupted him before he'd the chance. No, Mac," Diccon waved his fork to cut off MacDougall's indignant response. "I mean to stay here. Lanterns is my heritage and it's been abandoned and neglected for too long.

I can all but hear my ancestors demanding that I restore it. This is a beautiful spot—"

"And a beauty up the hill," muttered MacDougall under his breath.

Ignoring that shot, Diccon went on, "—And I intend to make the manor beautiful also."

MacDougall dared to say with heavy sarcasm, "Planning on spending a deal o' the rrrready, are ye, sir?"

"Of which I have very little, is that what you mean, damn your impudence?"

"Och aweigh, I'll own I shouldna hae' said it," mumbled the Scot repentantly. "There's times, just noo and then, ye mind, when I'm drrrriven tae forgetting me place. I ask y'r pardon, my—"

"Do not *dare* throw that blasted title at me! And as for your 'place'—you need not be acting the part of a humble servant, for once!"

MacDougall looked injured, and maintained a stiff silence while slamming dishes about, and Diccon returned his attention to his breakfast.

But they had been together for a long time. On a few occasions they had fought side-by-side, and if the Scot had not been allowed to accompany Diccon on his more desperate adventures, he'd never failed to rush to his bedside when he was hurt or ill. After the manner of old family retainers, MacDougall exercised the right to a little judicious bullying. Sometimes, more than a little. But no one knew better than Diccon that his courage never wavered and his loyalty was beyond question. Which presented a problem. He'd been an eighteen-year-old ensign and the Scot twice his age when the man had become his batman. So Mac was now past fifty. He was still hale and hearty, but this particular kettle of fish was liable to be very nasty.

"Besides," he said, holding out his mug to be refilled. "Business may—er, pick up."

"*Business!*" snorted MacDougall, wielding the coffee pot.

Diccon said quietly, "Because I choose the rural life is not to say you must. You prefer Town, Mac, and I know many gentlemen who'd be more than glad of your services. Do but say the word, and I'll send off some letters at once."

MacDougall, who had stood watching him from under frowning brows, drew in his breath with an audible hiss, banged down the coffee pot, and stamped from the room without a word.

Diccon could all but hear the skirl of Highland pipes accompanying that regal exit. "Phew!" he muttered.

The Scot had likely guessed why he would never leave here, and just as likely thought him all about in his head. He sighed. Which he was. Who'd ever have suspected that the long perilous years would culminate in his coming to his own estate and finding the lady who might well have been fashioned from his dreams? Or that Fate would be so unkind as to give her some quite logical reasons to despise and distrust him? That she'd not been snapped up by some fellow in Town did but prove what a silly, empty-headed lot they were. But at any day a sensible man of wealth and position might come along and see her sweetness and courage and beauty. And, worshipping her, would be able to offer all that she deserved. Which was, he thought miserably, as it should be.

These past two days had been dreary stretches of emptiness. He missed her so much that it was a continuing ache in his heart. And he missed the boy also. He'd not gone near the dower house, but he had looked that way often. Very often. And he'd caught not so much as a glimpse of Mrs. Gillespie, or the tail of Friar Tuck. Of course, it had rained most of the time, the greyness adding to his gloom. He'd kept busy, inspecting the house and grounds, and making plans for repairs, but he could not banish Marietta from his thoughts. What was she doing at this very moment? Helping Mrs. Cordova replace "Dora Leith's" head? Singing in her soft pretty voice as she dusted or polished? Worrying over those damnable bills? Did she ever think of him at all? And if he did come into her mind, was he remembered with disgust or—

"What ye mean!" snarled MacDougall, erupting into the kitchen red-faced and wrathful, "is that ye're packing me off oot o' harm's way, as ye've done before and before! Ye think tae sit here alone, eating your hearrrt oot for the bonnie lassie up yon, and waiting for Monteil and his mountain tae come and put a perrriod tae ye!"

"Devil take you, Mac!" exclaimed Diccon, starting up guiltily, "I—"

"Well, I'll nae have it, d'ye hear?" roared his man, banging a clenched fist on the table and causing all the dishes to jump. "If ye mean tae be such a muckle fool as tae bide in this god-forsaken glummery, then I'll bide too, so dinna be trying tae be rrrid o' the MacDougall!" And with another soundless skirl of the pipes he marched out, pausing before he slammed the door behind him to add a provocative, "Your lorrrdship!"

Diccon shook his head and shrugged into his coat. He'd tried. "Thimblewit," he muttered fondly, and went out to visit his less belligerent four-legged friends.

The sky was mantled with heavy grey clouds but the rain had eased to a drizzle. Orpheus was grazing in the deep grass of the paddock behind the stables. He cantered to the fence to exchange greetings with his master, then went off at full gallop, tail and mane flying. The little donkey was indulging his morning sulks in a corner of the old barn where the roof was still intact. Diccon went into the stall and handed over the letter that Mac had brought from the village post office yesterday, and Mr. Fox closed his eyes and digested it with appreciation. Taking up the currycomb, Diccon went to work, chatting with the animal as was his habit.

"I hope you are taking note of what you're chewing. It's from Smollet. He has another little bit of business for me, and I'll tell you frankly, I don't like the smell of it. I sometimes think I missed my calling. I should have followed a respectable trade. Been a parson or a diplomatist or some such—"

A trill interrupted him. Mr. Fox snorted and peered at the ginger-and-white intruder that was wrapping itself about his master's boots.

"Well, well," said Diccon, putting the comb on the rail and

picking up the visitor. "I thought pussycats didn't like rain."

Friar Tuck purred and rubbed his whiskers against the fingers that scratched so competently behind his ear.

"Why did you run 'way?" enquired a small, accusing voice.

Diccon turned to confront a bedraggled outlaw. One did not advise 'Robin of Sherwood' that his tunic was soaked or that his feather was sagging. "I expect Miss Marietta told you why," he evaded cautiously.

"Friends don't go 'way an' not say g'bye, even if they do got work to do," said Robin. "I missed you."

"I'm very sorry, old fellow, and I'm glad you came to see me. If it's allowed."

"Outlaws does things what's not 'lowed. That's why they're called outlaws. 'Sides, Aunty Dova keeps forgetting her part. Yest'day she was 'sposed to be Queen Guin'vere an' she started being Merlin instead. What good is that?"

"I'm sure she tried. But we mustn't worry your—your family. I'd better take you back."

The small face fell.

"Soon," Diccon added quickly. "But we'll have some hot chocolate first, if you don't mind. I'm rather cold. And we never did finish our hold-up, did we?"

"No. An' you said you'd got some d'livers for The Dancing Master."

"So I did! And I still have them. Come along, and I'll deliver them now. Or perhaps you could be The Dancing Master on the way home."

Arthur thought about it, but said with proper integrity that he didn't have the highwayman's mask.

"Oh, I think we can make one," said Diccon.

"What about Friar Tuck? I 'spect he'd like some milk."

"We'll steal some for him from the Lord of the Larder."

"A'right." A small hand slipped trustingly into his own. "Is he a terr'ble genie sort of lord?"

"Dreadful! With a great fierce voice and big boots that make the floors shake."

Arthur sighed contentedly. "Good. I *knowed* you'd make everything all right, Sir G'waine."

To love and be loved, thought Diccon, did not make life easier.

MacDougall's scolding was reserved for private moments with his employer, and he was all polite deference as he hung Robin Hood's tunic before the kitchen stove, wrapped the boy in a blanket, set out a dish of milk for Friar Tuck, and prepared the hot chocolate. He saw nothing untoward in Arthur's awed eyes and subdued behavior and would have been surprised to know that the boy thought him very fierce indeed.

They had a merry visit. Diccon could not in honour ask the questions he yearned to have answered, but Arthur chattered on gaily, so that he did learn something of the activities of his beloved. She was always busy it seemed, and thought "a lot of big thoughts" because when people spoke to her she didn't sometimes answer. The Widow Maitland had called and gone down to Papa's workroom, but had started screaming.

Diccon exchanged a surprised glance with MacDougall. "Do you know why?"

Arthur said solemnly that the widow had tried out his father's new invention without permission and—here, he lapsed into shrieks of laughter—"It got caught in her hair!"

Diccon could picture the scene and joined in the boy's mirth, and MacDougall warmed to Arthur to such an extent that he went off and returned with his bagpipes. When the first wailing howls rang out, Arthur's hand sought out Diccon's in terror, but the Scot was a notable piper, and the impromptu concert ended with them all marching from end to end of the great manor, with Diccon playing his violin and Arthur 'drumming' on a bucket. They made, as the boy said exuberantly, "A jolly good noise!"

It was past time to take the child home, and, very aware of a small and drooping lower lip, Diccon told MacDougall to saddle Orpheus. He thought it would be a treat for the boy to ride in front of his saddle, but Arthur tugged at his sleeve and put in a request that they walk. "To ride would take quicker," he said.

It was still drizzling when they set out, Arthur swamped in a seaman's jacket that Diccon wore when on a voyage with Yves and his crew, and Friar Tuck cleaning one paw on the back step and paying not the slightest attention to their departure. Arthur was busily occupied with keeping the sleeves under control, but between bursts of hilarity he imparted the news that Mrs. Gillespie had gone to a fair at Lewes and had seen a giant; that Mrs. Maitland had visited the great Madame Olympias and had been very cross because of something she'd been told; and that Mr. Coville was always at the dower house. "I 'spect you know that, though," he added. "Oh, there goes Friar Tuck! Look at him run!"

Diccon glanced at the cat which flashed past and up the slope at a great rate of speed. "Why would I know that Mr. Coville was there?" he asked.

" 'Cause he comed down here to see you, a'course. Is you coming back, Diccon? He can't play, you know. He just talks to Etta and to Fanny."

So Coville had visited Lanterns. Looking for Lady Pamela no doubt, thought Diccon with a grim smile. If so, it had been a covert search; certainly, he'd not come to the front door.

". . . do you?" asked Arthur.

"Er—your pardon? Do I—what?"

"Like him. I don't. He's always patting me on the head an' telling me to 'run along like a good boy.' An' he smiles a lot, but he doesn't laugh. Not even when Friar Tuck chased a mouse all round the kitchen 'fore dinner las' night, an' Aunty Dova an' Fan screamed an' screamed. Papa an' me, we laughed."

"I expect you did, you rascal. What about Miss Marietta? Did she laugh?"

"Yes, but she opened the back door an' Friar an' the mouse runned out. Mr. Coville just smiled. Papa likes him. I heared him tell Aunty Dova he's a fine fellow. An' Fanny says he's very han'some an' that he's payin' Etta interest, or something."

Diccon scowled, but said quietly, " 'Fixing his interest,' perhaps?"

"I dunno. Oh, here comes Etta now. I found Sir G'waine, Etta!"

Marietta was walking down the hill towards them, her cloak billowing in the wind. Diccon's heart convulsed painfully. He halted, watching her. The wind had blown her hair into a tangle and painted a becoming glow on her cheeks; raindrops sparkled on her dainty nose, and she looked predictably cross. But she had come herself, not sent Lem Bridger or Mrs. Gillespie to fetch Arthur home.

Longing to see those stern lips curve into her enchanting smile, he said, "Good morning, ma'am. I was just bringing him home."

"Yes." There was no smile and after a brief cold glance, she avoided his eyes. "Thank you."

"This is Major Diccon's seafarin' jacket," said Arthur importantly. "Isn't it fine, Etta?"

"It was very kind of the Major to let you borrow it, dear. But I brought your coat, so you must give it back now."

"Let me wear it home, Etta. Please do. I want to show Papa, an' Sir G'waine can take it back when—"

"No, dear. Major Diccon is very busy, and Papa told you not to come to Lanterns any more. You disobeyed him, after you promised to do as he said. That was naughty."

He said rebelliously, "I crossed my fingers, so it wasn't a real live promise. An' 'sides, he's not busy, are you, Sir G'waine? He likes me to go there, an' so does Mr. Fox an' the Lord of the Larder, an'—"

Marietta blinked. "Who?"

"MacDougall," supplied Diccon.

"Oh."

"An' he played the pipes, an' I drummed, an' Diccon played his fiddle, an' we marched all 'round the house!" Arthur jumped up and down in his enthusiasm, shouting, "It was such *fun*, Etta!"

Marietta watched him fondly, marvelling that this was the same child who had for the past two days been so listless and silent. The hurt look of bewilderment and loss was banished from his face now. He was a happy little boy again, bursting with energy and enthusiasm. How perverse was Fate that her little brother should have taken such a liking to this treacherous individual, and that so ruthless and deceitful a man would spare the time to be kind to a child he scarcely knew. And how could she, loving the boy so much, fail to be grateful to *anyone* who had given him such joy? She said smilingly, "It sounds lovely, dear. That was kind in you, Major. Even so, you will understand that he must obey my father."

"Yes, of course. You see, old fellow, we cannot always do what we want to." Diccon met Marietta's eyes and said, "Even if we want it more than—more than anything in the world. And an honourable gentleman doesn't break his promise, young Warrington."

"I 'spose not." Arthur looked crushed, then said brightly, "Thass all right, Sir G'waine. You can come an' see *me*. Can't he, Etta?" He tugged at Diccon's hand. "I'm not too busy. Come now, an' after lunch you can tell me one of your stories 'bout—"

"I'm afraid I won't be able to do that. For a while. But—"

"You're goin' 'way!" Arthur peered up at the tall man in new anxiety. "Don't go, Major. Please don't go 'way. You're my bes' friend, an—" His voice broke. He said scratchily, "Can't I come an' see Mr. Fox, even?"

Diccon touched the tumbled curls and looked regretfully at the tearful little face.

Marietta thought miserably, 'Oh, if only he was a different kind of man! Someone Arthur could really look up to and respect!' But "if onlys" paid no toll, and smothering a sigh, she reached out. "Come, dearest."

Arthur turned on her, his eyes gemmed with tears. "It's your fault!" he sobbed. "You taked 'way Harry Rogers, an' Spotty Bill, an' the milkman, an' now I've found a new bes' friend you're making him go 'way too. You don't *want* me to have friends! I don't—I don't love you . . . no more!"

Diccon said sharply, "Arthur! You mustn't—"

But the boy was gone, running madly towards the dower house, the jacket sleeves flapping and his sobs echoing after him.

Distressed, Marietta said, "Now see what you have done!"

"Yes. I'm very sorry. I didn't dream—"

Turning on him, she interrupted, "What? That you might become fond of him?"

"That he would become fond of me. I suppose I should have sent him away, but—" He gave a rueful shrug.

"Only think, my lord. Had you told a few truths instead of very many untruths, this could have been averted!"

She looked vexed, but she was talking to him, and she made no move to follow her brother. He said, "Perhaps, it could have been averted had you not been so willing to believe ill of me."

Her little chin tossed upward. "How should I not believe what you yourself admitted, sir?"

"That I am Lord Temple and Cloud, for instance?"

"Among other things—yes."

"No."

She stared at him. "But, you said—"

"Your pardon, ma'am. You asked if that was my ancestral title. It is. The thing is, you see, that I don't want it."

Her eyes widened and the rosy lips formed a pretty 'O.' She echoed in astonishment, "You won't use—the title? Good gracious! Why ever not?"

He shrugged. "Pride, I suppose you might say. I like to earn my honours. No, really, Miss Marietta, why on earth should I expect other men—men probably more deserving than I—to bow and scrape and call me 'my lord' because of something my grandfather-several-greats-removed did? I won my military rank on my own merits, but—"

Recovering her wits, she interrupted, "Which is what, exactly? Sergeant? Or major? Or is it perhaps sergeant-major?" And fearing that she might again be judging him too harshly, she asked quickly, "You were not really promoted at Waterloo?"

"No, Miss Marietta. I was awarded my majority in 1813."

"I suppose you will claim that you have renounced that, also."

"I'll own I've almost lost it a few times. But my demotion at Waterloo was—er, a matter of expedience."

Intrigued, she asked, "Are you allowed to speak of it?"

He hesitated. "Yes, if you will keep it to yourself, ma'am."

She nodded, and to his delight raised no objection as he began to walk up the slope beside her.

"There was a clever thief about Town," he explained, "who specialized in safes and strong-boxes. My superiors had reason to believe that during his illicit pursuits he had come upon some particularly vital information. The robbery was not reported by the victims, but he'd been identified and was hunted. He had no idea of the importance of what he had seen, or why he was so relentlessly pursued, and when an attempt was made on his life he became very frightened and hid himself in Rifle Green. We never dreamed then that Bonaparte would really strike, and I was sent in to try and smoke out our man, as it were. But I'd never have managed it as an officer."

"And so became a sergeant. I see. And were you able to 'smoke him out' before the battle?"

"Fortunately, I was. During the battle."

The empty look had come into his eyes at that memory, and seeing it, Marietta said, "There is a story there, I think."

"Yes, ma'am. Perhaps you will permit that I tell it to you—sometime?"

He sounded so hopeful. Almost, she was lured into a smile, but then she remembered, and said hurriedly, "I had prefer that you tell me—" And she paused, for she had no real right to demand information about a family matter.

Diccon watched the swiftly changing play of emotion on the face that had become for him the epitome of feminine beauty. "You want to know if I have really murdered my mother."

Her eyes shot to his with an eagerness that both angered him and warmed his heart. He said grimly, "I see my dear step-brother has been spreading his vitriol."

Marietta frowned. "Mr. Coville is understandably anxious for the lady."

He gave a shout of bitter laughter. "Oh, understandably! Good grief, madam, can you really believe that of me?"

He had stopped walking. She stopped also, and searching his face, said hesitantly, "I can believe that if someone were spreading such untruths about my brother, he would call them out in an instant!"

"Then—you know them for untruths? Marietta," he stepped closer to her, "is that what you're saying?"

That dreadful silver flame was in his eyes again, frightening her yet making her heart thunder with excitement. She said, "How can I *know* anything except—except that you do not deny it?"

He caught her hand and drew her closer, demanding huskily, "Can you look into my eyes and judge me capable of such a thing? Can you?"

She tried to steel herself against the tenderness that was so clear to see, but her attempt to break away was feeble in the extreme. It was all wrong, she thought in desperation. Blake should be looking at her in this unnerving way. Blake should be the one to make her heart pound so violently. He was the man who could provide for her family. Not this man of mystery who was so enigmatic and intense about things, and who lacked Blake's looks and light-hearted charm. Yet Diccon had shown unexpected depths of kindness, and of a strength that would be such a bulwark against the world for the lucky lady who— She thought, 'Good gracious!' and struggling to hold on to common sense, heard again Coville's sombre words, "He is the most dangerous man I have ever known."

"Even if I did not believe it," she said, turning her head away, "so long as you do not speak up, my family must have doubts. Who are we to believe? Sir Gavin and Mr. Coville have been most kind to us. Why would they lie about such a dreadful thing? Why even tell us of it? We are not long-time friends."

He relaxed his hold on her hand. "But you live very close to Lanterns, Miss Marietta. I'll warrant my step-father desired you to keep him informed of what goes on at the manor."

It was true. Walking on slowly, she said, "But if they wanted to watch Lanterns, why would they have leased us the dower house in the first place? Why not stay there themselves?"

"Probably because I had not at that time loomed as a threat on their horizon."

Shocked, she said, "How do you constitute a threat? Sir Gavin is a very wealthy gentleman, and—" She bit her lip and did not finish the sentence.

"And Lanterns is a ruin and I am very far from being wealthy?" He nodded. "Quite. And I forget my manners. It is very bad form to slander members of one's own family behind their backs. Therefore, ma'am, I must say no more, and can only beg you to believe that as God be my judge I never have, and never will, I pray, harm a lady."

Troubled, she was silent.

He touched her hand tentatively, and she stopped once more and faced him.

"Will you trust me, ma'am? May I be permitted to see the dauntless Outlaw of Sherwood Forest again? And . . . and your—very lovely—self?"

Marietta hesitated. Surely, no man could meet her eyes so steadily, so worshipfully, and be a liar and a murderer? And dear little Arthur loved him so.

"Please?" he murmured.

"I shall have to speak with my father. I think I can persuade him to allow my brother to come down and see you, even if he will not permit you to come to—" She laughed suddenly. "How silly of me! It is, after all, your own house!"

"Not by the law of the land, Miss Marietta. The lease is signed. For its duration, Sir Lionel is the legal owner. But—I thank you for allowing me to hope."

He took her hand and bowed over it with courtly grace.

And went away dizzy with triumph, for she had smiled at him.

Chapter IX

"I'll tell you what it is." Sir Lionel stamped into the kitchen scattering mud from his boots and rain-drops from the capes of his driving coat. "That stream is more like a river than—"

"Papa! My dumplings!" squealed Fanny.

"Eh?" He paused to stare at her.

She bent protectively over her bowl of dough. "You're dripping all over them."

"Oh. Sorry, Fan." He sniffed. "Jove, that smells good! Stew for lunch? Stew's common, so Dale says. But to my mind, it's always good on a rainy day."

Marietta came to help him out of his coat. "Did you find what you needed in Eastbourne, sir?"

"I did." He dug an elbow in her rib and winked like a mischievous schoolboy. "And won't your aunt be surprised!"

Standing at the stove and prodding a reluctant prospective dumpling from the spoon while watching her father expectantly, Fanny asked, "What kind of surprise, Papa?"

"It missed the pot!" exclaimed Marietta. "Shoo! Go away, Friar Tuck!"

Mrs. Cordova hurried into the kitchen, having kicked off her pattens in the scullery but with her voluminous cloak scattering even more raindrops. "Such a dreadful time I had with that wretched Maitland woman," she wailed. "And I have— Why are we feeding raw dumplings to Friar Tuck?"

"Be dashed if the stupid animal ain't lapping it up," said Sir Lionel, intrigued.

"Then he must go out, for he will be sick." Mrs. Cordova flung off her cloak revealing Madame Olympias' spangled wrapper beneath it. "Come, puss!"

"Why must Friar Tuck be thrown out in the rain?" protested Arthur, joining the group.

"Because your sister will persist in giving him scraps," said Mrs. Cordova, ejecting the annoyed Friar. "And I will tell you, Warrington, that your would-be lady is extreme irked, so you may expect her brother to come demanding payment at his first opportunity."

"Oh, egad!" moaned Sir Lionel, sweeping her discarded cloak from a chair and clutching it as he sat down. "What have you done now?"

"I have done nothing." She retrieved the cloak and shook it out, drawing a howl from her inundated brother-in-law and another shriek from Fanny. "Madame Olympias, however, has saved you from matrimony. For the moment, at least."

"Did the widow arrange for a reading?" asked Marietta. "I wonder she did not come here to see you, Papa. Whatever did you tell her, Aunty?"

"Madame Olympias looked into the Mystical Window Through Time—" said Mrs. Cordova with dignity.

"You mean that silly little crystal ball," scoffed Sir Lionel.

"—And told her that she will never be Lady Lionel Warrington," she went on, ignoring him. "I quite thought," she added musingly, "that she was going to strangle me."

Cheered, he said, "By Jove, now that was well done!"

Arthur tugged at Marietta's skirt and hissed, "Has you asked him about Major Diccon?"

"What about that—that lying renegade?" demanded Sir Lionel, his eyes sparking.

Arthur looked scared and went outside mumbling that he

was going to see if Friar Tuck had gone into the barn.

Following him to the door, Mrs. Cordova called, "Take an umbrella!" then moaned as the boy ran across the side yard carrying a closed umbrella.

"Well? Did our smuggling peer dare show his face at my door?" asked Sir Lionel.

"On his own property?" said Marietta demurely.

"Dash it all, girl," he snorted. "Why must you defend the rogue? If I thought—"

"Marietta Paisley, Baroness Temple and Cloud," trilled Mrs. Cordova. "It has a ring, Warrington. You cannot deny it has a ring."

"Not if he refuses the title," Fanny pointed out. "Oh, dear! Where ever is my lid?"

"And not the ring of gold," said Sir Lionel. "Yes, you will say that sounds vulgar, but if he is not pockets-to-let why would he have abducted his mama?"

"I must have the lid, or the dumplings will be ruined," wailed Fanny, searching.

"He did *not* abduct the lady," said Marietta, carrying a jug of milk from the pantry.

"He told you that?" asked her father.

"Yes. I asked him if the rumours speak truth, and he gave me his solemn oath that he has never harmed a lady in his life."

"Evasion number ninety-three," muttered Fanny.

Marietta frowned, then said, "Oh—Aunty has your saucepan-lid, Fan."

"His solemn oath?" Sir Lionel pursed his lips. "Hmm."

Fanny attempted to appropriate the large iron lid that Mrs. Cordova held and was gazing at dreamily. "Aunty Dova? May I have my lid please?"

"Oh dear, oh dear!" sighed Mrs. Cordova, relinquishing it. " 'Double, double, toil and trouble.' "

"Is that so?" growled Sir Lionel, linking this remark with Major Diccon's questionable character. "Well, I'm not surprised."

Fanny hurried to put the lid over her stew, then turned to scan her aunt uneasily.

Also recognizing the signs, Marietta asked, "What else did you see in your Mystical Window, Aunty?"

Mrs. Cordova gave her a tragic look. " 'Something wicked this way comes.' "

"Is it the widow?" cried Sir Lionel, with the air of a cornered rabbit.

"I must warn his lordship," muttered Mrs. Cordova worriedly.

"Egad!" exclaimed Sir Lionel. "Is she after him too? He's too young for her, by more'n a decade I'd think."

Marietta entered this fragmented conversation to ask sharply, "Which lordship?"

It was a question not destined to be answered. From the side yard came a clattering of hooves, and an exuberant shout of "House, ho!"

For an instant nobody moved. Then they heard Arthur scream, *"Eric!"*

"By George!" exclaimed Sir Lionel, springing up. "The boy's home!"

The back door burst open. Eric Warrington, a tall, good-looking young man with abundant chestnut hair and a pair of merry blue eyes, hurried in to be embraced, kissed, slapped on the back, and welcomed with an outpouring of love and joy. As usual, the heir brought with him a vibrant aura of energy and enthusiasm so that the household seemed stirred to a new excitement. Arthur was swept to his brother's shoulder. All the ladies were pronounced diamonds of the first water, Sir Lionel was "looking very fit," and Eric announced that he had "squeaked away from Cambridge" to attend to a pressing matter of business. Yes, this was a new coat, and they would like to see his new jacket, the tails were more sloping now, and most fellows wore pantaloons these days. But never mind about all that, they must come outside and see something. "And," he said with glowing pride, "one or two little surprises."

In the yard a large surprise awaited. Lem Bridger was admiring a team of matched bays harnessed to a neat and fast-looking closed chaise. They all stared, struck to silence.

Marietta was first to recover her voice. "What a dashing coach. Have you hired it, dear?"

"No such thing! It's mine! Ain't it splendid? Do come and see!"

Bewildered, they gathered in the rain to admire the coachwork, the springs, the large wheels, the luxurious red-and-white interior, thick rugs, and fat squabs. "Tooled it down here myself," said Eric, ignoring their astounded expressions and adding with a fine nonchalance, "But I mean to take on a servant who will also be my coachman. How do you like the hacks, sir? Bought them off a poor fellow who had a beastly run of luck at the tables and has the tipstaffs after him."

Agreeing that the team was also splendid, Sir Lionel asked uneasily, "On tick, m'boy?"

"No, sir! I owe not a groat. It's all paid for! And only see what we have here!"

The rug was folded back to reveal a pile of gaily wrapped parcels. "For all of you," cried Eric, beaming. "Come, help me carry them. See to the team, please, Lem. You've some real bloodstock to care for again! The thing is," he went on gaily, handing out parcels to be carried to the house, "I had the most fabulous piece of luck on a race between Galen Hilby and Freddy Foster. You likely heard of it. I chanced to have some inside knowledge, and risked every penny of my summer earnings. And I won! Oh, I can scarce wait to show you what I've brought! Hurry and let's get out of the rain!"

Following the others to the steps, laden, Marietta said happily, "How glad I am that this is not the 'something wicked' you spoke of, Aunty."

Mrs. Cordova, who doted on her eldest nephew said, "And I, my love. Bless his heart, he fairly radiates *joie de vivre*. But we must keep our wits about us, Etta, for the wickedness is coming. Oh, yes. It surely is coming!"

Marietta hummed softly as she stood before the cheval-glass in her bedchamber and surveyed her reflection. The white taffeta gown trimmed with pink embroidery fit perfectly, and the bell-shaped skirt was in the very latest style. She added the matching pink manteau; lined with white silk, it fell to her ankles and had wide pink ribbons to be tied in a bow at one shoulder. Taking up the dainty circular fan of white lace with gold sticks, she fanned herself gently. "You look very fine, Miss Warrington of Warrington Hall," she advised, with a curtsy to the mirror. There were elbow-length white gloves also, and a beautifully embroidered reticule. She touched the reticule with one fingertip and sat on the bed, gazing at it.

The day had been almost like Christmas-time. Over luncheon Eric had answered their eager questions about friends and the famous in London. Afterwards, he had presented his gifts, and enjoyed their excitement. Fanny had been radiant, promenading around the drawing room displaying her exquisite shawl of Norwich silk and the pearl necklace and matching ear-rings and bracelet. There had been a hat of the very latest curly brimmed style, and a fine new tool set for Papa; Arthur had been rendered speechless with delight by a large box of toy soldiers and an hussar's uniform, complete with a plumed helmet; Aunty Dova had declared she was ready to swoon with joy when Eric presented her with a lilac silk parasol trimmed with black lace, and a most fetching lilac bonnet over which three large feathers waved proudly.

At dinner, when Arthur was in bed, Eric had told them more about his wonderful wager, and had thrilled them with a description of the horse race which sounded to have been rather a desperate affair. Later, in the drawing room, he'd regaled them with amusing anecdotes about University life and had made them all laugh by describing the plight of the hapless students cramming for their examinations and of his noble forbearance when they were "so stupid as to defy belief." Clearly, he had much to discuss with his father, and very soon after tea the ladies had gone up to bed to admire their various treasures in private.

It had been a long and eventful day, and Marietta was sleepy, but she did not change into her night rail, crossing instead to open the casement and look into the darkness. The air was cold and it was raining steadily. She knelt in the window-seat and leaned out a little so as to feel raindrops on her cheeks. Her windows faced south and she thought to see a little light far down the slope, near the cliffs. It would seem that Major Mallory Diccon Paisley was still up. Her thoughts drifted to their encounter this morning; the firm clasp of his hand; the light eyes that could be so cold or so tender or suddenly take on that devastating glow. The memory made her shiver.

The curtains billowed.

Eric said softly, "Small wonder you're cold. Are you wits to let, my best of sisters?"

He closed the door, and she pulled the casement shut then ran to hug him and thank him once more for her "lovely finery."

"It becomes you," he said with a fond smile. "I'm glad you modelled it for me. Did you know I meant to come up to talk?"

"I thought you might, as you were used to do." She took off the manteau and laid it on the bed carefully, then sat beside him at the empty hearth. "It's so wonderful to have you home again, dearest. I suppose we must not hope that you mean to stay for long?"

"No, I cannot. But long enough to give you what I really came for." He said boyishly, "Close your eyes and put out your hands."

Obeying, she protested, "Not another present? You've given me too much al—" The feel of what now reposed in her cupped hands silenced her. She opened her eyes and stared at a thick pile of banknotes. Looking into her brother's solemn face wonderingly, she faltered, "Why—there must be . . ."

"A hundred pounds," he said with an emphatic nod. "And there'll be more, Etta, I promise you! I would have given it to

Papa, only—well, where money's concerned, I'd sooner you were the one to dole out the dibs."

She gazed down at the notes she held. There would be enough now to pay the many bills she'd had to shuffle about, and to complete the tuition fees for Arnold. To be given such a sum was providential, but— "I—I don't know what to say. You are so good." And with a searching glance at him, "How can there be more? Surely, wagering must be extreme risky business?"

He laughed, took the notes and went to put them on her dressing table. "I knew that was coming. My Etta. Always the sensible one, yet you manage to look so pretty that a fellow would never guess you'd a brain in your head." Sitting down again, he pulled his chair closer. "No, I do not mean to gamble anymore. I've been offered a chance to make a good deal of money handling the investments of several gentlemen. You know I was always quick at arithmetic. I've a little capital left from my wager, and soon I'll be able to invest on my own account."

Impressed, she said, "It sounds a wonderful opportunity for such a young man. But what of your studies? Shall you continue at Cambridge?"

"For a while." He looked thoughtful. "Till I am more sure of where I stand.

Marietta said intuitively, "You're worried. There's something wrong with all this, I can feel it! Dearest, if there's a danger—"

"Of course there's danger. There's always risk where large amounts are involved." As though her words had irritated him, he jumped up and paced to the window and stood there, gazing broodingly into the rainy darkness. When he spoke it was in a harsh voice she scarcely recognized. "Did you ever think how I felt, Etta? To see my father whistle our fortune down the wind? To watch our home, our carriages, our horses—everything! swept away. To lounge in the calm detachment of University life, doing nothing to help, whilst you were reduced to living down here in poverty, scrubbing and slaving, with no servants, no social life at all!" Returning to stand with his back to the hearth he gave an impatient gesture that silenced Marietta's attempt to respond. "I know how brave you are, and that you will tell me it's not so bad here. But do you think I don't see your pretty hands? Look at them, Etta! Work-roughened, the nails broken. Do you remember that ode Vespa writ for you, called 'Lovely Hands That Hold my Heart'? What would he think could he see them now?"

Marietta promptly hid the offending articles by sitting on them. She well remembered Jack Vespa, who had adored her. One of Wellington's dashing captains, his grand sense of humour and a courageous ability to pull himself up again however Fate crushed him had made him her dearest friend and most favoured suitor. She had not, she believed, ever known the mystical elation of being 'in love,' but she had loved Jack and would probably have been quite content to marry him. However, his countless offers for her hand had been sternly rejected by Papa on the grounds that he could not support her in the manner to which she was accustomed. She stifled a sigh. Poor Jack. He would have been even less able to support the whole family!

"And our beautiful little sister," continued Eric. "With so much promise. Toiling over that stove like some hapless kitchen-maid, instead of having a proper Season and making the brilliant match she deserves! Gad! It fairly makes my blood boil!"

"Yes, because you are so good, and you love us and want to help. I honour you for that, dear. But you have only to look about Town to see fine old families brought to ruin. Sad as it is, such tragedies happen every day. I won't pretend it was not rather—terrible—at the time, or that I don't miss our lovely home and the jolly life we were used to lead. But only think how fortunate we are. This is such a lovely place, and by exercising caution with our funds—"

"Funds?" He snorted disgustedly, "What funds? You had to sell nearly everything we owned to pay my father's debts."

"But I've been able to put a little in the bank, and you have worked so hard to help with school expenses, and Aunty Dova does quite well with her readings."

"You mean she hornswoggles the gullible into paying for her flim-flams and fancies! That's called charlatanism, Etta!"

"No, no! Never say so! Truly, she has a gift!"

"Aye! The gift of losing herself in delusion. Even as my father loses himself in his foolish inventions and leaves to you the task of struggling with the bills and somehow managing to keep us afloat!"

Distraught, she sprang up and ran to throw her arms around him. "Do not! Oh, Eric, you must not say such things! You know how Mama's death broke his heart and his spirit. But he loves us, my dear one, and we shall never be loved in just that same way by anyone else."

"I know." He sighed and kissed her, and, still holding her, asked gently, "And does he keep out of mischief, Etta? I stopped at the Seven Seas before I came home, and I heard some talk of a widow with ambitions in his direction. The lady must not be of very good *ton,* for I gather she has a brother who has boasted that he holds some sort of note from my father. Is it truth?"

"Oh, dear." She sat down again. "I'd not realized the gossip-mongers had it. That *wretched* Mr. Williard! I admit Papa is— is not always very wise, but—"

"A masterpiece of understatement! Gaming again, is he? My God! And I have not the authority to stop him! Do you wonder that I search for a way to help? I mean to see you all back in Town, Etta. In our own home, if possible. And one way or another I'll do it, by heaven but I will!"

He looked so determined. 'He has grown up,' she thought, 'and I never noticed—never dreamed he was so bitter!' She said, "Not if it means taking risks, I beg you! Besides, I have some news also. I've an admirer, brother dear! Three, in fact! One is rich and handsome. One is rich and—and not so handsome. And one is poor and nice-looking."

He straddled the dressing table bench and grinned at her, once again her youthful, fun-loving brother. "And you mean to accept the rich and handsome one, do you? Is he the one you care for, love? Or is it a matter of expedience?"

She blushed and said shyly, "Well, to say truth he hasn't offered yet. But if he does, our problems will be over, and you won't have to worry about restoring our fortunes."

"Jolly good! Who is this young money-bags?"

"His name is Blake Coville."

"Sir Gavin Coville's heir?" His eyebrows lifted and he whistled softly. "Well, well! I've seen him about Town. He's quite the non-pareil, but—lots of handkerchiefs have been dropped for that one, Etta. 'Twould be a real feather in your cap if you could snare him. Does he call on you down here?"

"Yes. Quite often. We hired this house from Sir Gavin's steward, you will recall."

"So we did. I'd forgot. The owner's Lord Temple and Cloud, though, is he not? I wonder you haven't set your cap in that direction. Or is he a loathesome old reprobate who lurks and leers amid his ruins?"

Marietta looked at her hands. "No, dearest. He's not a loathesome old reprobate."

The tinkling of the little bell hanging over the door awoke Diccon. As always he was fully alert the instant he opened his eyes. Something had disturbed the long cord he'd strung from the old wing all the way to his bedchamber. Perhaps Friar Tuck was paying a nocturnal visit. Perhaps an enterprising rat had called. Or perhaps the rat was of the two-legged variety. And although he'd been dubbed "a revolutionary," he was sufficiently conservative to prefer to be aware of the identity of guests; especially those who arrived, uninvited, in the middle of the night. Flinging back the covers, he pulled on his breeches, snatched his new flint-lock pistol from the bedside table, and hurried into the corridor. It was very dark save for the glow of the broad candle on the landing, and he raced towards that flame, the floorboards icy cold against his bare feet. Unless this was one of Imre Monteil's assassins it was unlikely that the intruder would come into the new wing, but he paused at the top of the stairs, ears straining and eyes narrowed against the gloom. There was no slightest movement, and not a sound other than the occasional flurries of the wind.

The treads of the stairs were prone to creaks, but there was a quicker method. He slid soundlessly down the banister rail and was across the great hall running to the door leading to the old wing. It was shut. He set the hair trigger on the pistol that Tathum and Egg had made for him, then lifted the latch and eased the door open. The hinges, newly oiled, did not betray him. Moving with the soundless speed for which, in some circles, he was renowned, he was inside, down the steps, and had flattened himself against the wall. It was doubtful if the glow from the 'new' stairwell would have been seen when he opened the door, but he again paused, listening intently. He heard nothing, but his keen sense of smell detected the faintest hint of difference in the air; the acrid scent that signalled the presence of an oil lamp where there should be none. So his suspicions were justified. He moved on, progressing more cautiously here, feeling his way over the debris but swearing in soft anguish as he stubbed his bare toe on a fallen chunk of masonry. He sensed rather than saw that he'd reached the original great hall. At the far end a gleam of light came and went at the top of the stairs above the minstrel gallery. Someone, he thought grimly, was searching for *The Sigh of Saladin*; someone who was undeterred by ghostly rumours or the tales of mysterious lights and wailings.

Faint as it was, the glow helped him to avoid the few pieces of furniture. He crept up the stairs, passed the minstrel gallery, and climbed to the first floor. Now the light was moving about in one of the upper rooms. This was the lantern he'd smelled, and the fact that the beam was narrowed must mean the intruder was aware that the new wing of the manor was occupied. He heard an odd, smothered sort of snuffling, as of some large beast rooting about. A familiar sound. His foot touched something small that rolled across the floor. The noise was barely perceptible but at once the lantern was extinguished and the darkness became absolute.

There was a thudding of boots, a grunting, a sense that something vast was rushing at him. There was no time to shout a warning. He fired blindly, the retort shattering the silence. A howl rang out, terrifying in its depth and fury. He was caught up in a mighty grip and swept off his feet. The arms about him tightened savagely, driving the air from his lungs. Struggling frantically to break free before his ribs were crushed, he managed to strike out with the pistol and felt it connect hard. A bestial roar and he was hurled aside. He crashed against the wall with stunning force. From a long way off Arthur's voice echoed in his ears. "Mrs. Gillespie seed a giant at the fair in Lewes." His last conscious thought was a disgusted, 'Stupid! Stupid. . . .'

⚜

The morning dawned bright and sunny with a brisk wind stirring the trees. Mrs. Gillespie arrived punctually for once and started work on the windows. Eric took his sire and Arthur out for a drive in his new chaise. Mrs. Cordova went about in a preoccupied manner and when spoken to responded only by singing to herself and shaking her head glumly. Fanny commandeered Marietta to help pick blackberries and the sisters went off into the woods with their baskets.

Fanny was light-hearted and full of excitement over Eric's arrival and his good fortune. It was especially wonderful, she said blithely, for little Arthur to have one of his brothers at home, and how kind of Eric to promise he would make up for their long separation by spending as much time as possible with the boy. Much as she loved Eric, Marietta was under no illusions. Her eldest brother's promises, always well meant, had a tendency to be forgotten as soon as they were uttered, and at this particular time he had so many concerns on his mind. She said nothing to dampen Fanny's sunny mood, however, and they spent a merry hour gathering the ripe berries until the worn strap on Marietta's sandal snapped, hampering her efforts. The thick blanket of pine needles and leaves underfoot seemed soft enough, until she tried walking on it barefoot. They used Fanny's hair ribbon as an impromptu strap, but it proved a poor substitute and at length Marietta reluctantly gave up. Eric's sweet tooth had offered Fanny the chance to express her gratitude for the gifts he'd brought her, and she was dismayed to find they had not nearly enough berries for the two pies she hoped to bake. They solved the problem by emptying their collection into one basket which Marietta carried off towards home while Fanny continued to pick.

They had come farther than Marietta realized. Very soon her sandal became such a nuisance that she took it off again and trod cautiously through the sun-dappled woods, wishing she'd thought to wear her pattens. The air was fragrant with the scents of damp earth and wildflowers; an occasional gust of wind rustled the branches sending sparkling little showers of droplets from the leaves, and except for the merry chirping of the birds it was so peaceful that she was sorry to leave the canopy of the trees.

The sun was warmer now, but the thick meadow grasses were still damp. Limping along, she gave a yelp as she trod on something sharp. A fallen tree-trunk offered temporary seating and she put down her basket and investigated the damage. She had evidently stepped on a broken branch and quite a large splinter had driven into her heel. With a quick glance around, she removed her stocking. The splinter proved stubborn and hurtful; working at it carefully, she was breathless when she at last managed to extricate it and she exclaimed triumphantly, "Go away, you vicious beast!"

"Alas," drawled a deep voice. "Once again I am *de trop*."

Marietta's heart gave a leap, her head shot up and her bare

foot was whipped under her skirt. She was embarrassed to realize that she'd been too engrossed to be concerned with propriety, and her cheeks were hot when she stammered, "Oh! M-Major Diccon! I had stepped on a splinter you see, and—" She checked. He was riding Orpheus and he came up and dismounted with a marked lack of his usual ease. He was pale, there was a livid bruise down his left temple and he limped slightly. "My goodness!" she exclaimed, standing. "Not more of the work of the Warringtons I hope?"

He shook his head. "An uninvited caller. Nothing serious, I promise you. Is your splinter dealt with, Miss Marietta? May Orpheus carry you home?"

Her foot was sore, the dower house was out of sight, and it would be a long and uncomfortable walk. She said, "Oh yes, if you please. I would be most grateful. In a moment. If you would be so good as to first turn around?"

He grinned and presented his back to her. Marietta replaced her stocking and the broken sandal and sat down again, inviting him to join her. "Are you in a hurry? Or could we rest for a little while? It's such a lovely morning."

He assured her that he had "all the time in the world," and sat beside her, lowering himself cautiously. "You have been blackberrying, I see."

"Yes, with Fanny. But my sandal broke, so I left her to do the rest of the work. My brother is come home from Cambridge laden with gifts for us all. . . ." For just an instant her eyes became troubled, then her bright smile dawned and she went on: "Eric loves sweets, so Fanny's going to bake some pies. I'll allow you to share some of these berries if you tell me about your 'uninvited caller.' "

She offered the basket. Its dark harvest gleamed richly and temptingly, and Diccon accepted the bribe at once. He gave her a light-hearted version of the attack, dismissing his injuries as "just a few scrapes logically come by as a result of not pausing to wake Mac before charging the enemy."

Undeceived, she said with a concern that delighted him, "It

does not look like 'just a few scrapes' to me. You make it all sound of little consequence whereas it was more likely a desperate struggle. How fortunate that you were able to drive him off!"

He smiled wryly. "I wish I could say I'd put the fellow to ignominious flight, ma'am, but after he tossed me at the wall I was in no case to defeat a cockroach."

She paused in the act of popping a blackberry into her mouth and stared at him. "You mean he pushed you against the wall?"

"No, ma'am. I mean he objected when I gave him a whack with my pistol, and he quite literally took me up and threw me aside."

She blinked. It didn't sound very heroic. "If you had a pistol why ever did you not shoot the nasty creature?"

"I did. I think I hit him, in fact. It was too dark to see."

Envisioning Lanterns' gloom, even by daylight, she revised her earlier opinion. "You should never have gone after him alone and in the dark. And how very odd it is that anyone could hope to find a lost treasure at night time! I suppose there is no chance of your recognizing him if you saw him again?"

He said slowly, "That's why I was riding over to see you. Arthur mentioned that your Mrs. Gillespie had gone to a fair at Lewes, and I wanted to talk to her about it. Did she come today, ma'am?"

"Yes, and she'll be glad to tell you about the fair. She could speak of nothing else last time she came."

"Arthur said she saw a—giant?"

"So she claimed. He quite frightened her. I thought she meant he was part of a side-show, but she said he was just walking about and everyone was staring because he was enormous and of extreme strange appearance."

His lips tightened. "Did the lady say that her giant was from the Orient?"

"That is what she thought, but—My heavens! Diccon! You do not suspect he was your intruder?"

"I think it more than possible, yes. He had great strength, and if he's the man I suspect, we've met before. It would explain why he was obliged to do his searching under cover of darkness, for he's instantly recognizable and not the type who could venture abroad unnoticed." He frowned, thinking that if Imre Monteil had heard of the legend he'd be the very man to lust after *The Sigh of Saladin*. In which case last night's break-in might have no connection with— He glanced up. Marietta looked frightened. He said quickly, "That's probably the sum and substance of it. A thief after a treasure that likely doesn't exist, and who poses no danger to you or your family."

"But considerable danger to you?"

He shrugged. "Fore-warned is fore-armed. Speaking of which, forgive me, but—why has your brother's arrival upset you?"

His eyes, which had been abstracted, were now piercingly intent. Dismayed, she thought, 'How could he possibly know?' and she protested, "Really, Major! Why ever should you think such a thing? It makes me very happy to welcome Eric home. If I seem a little excited, it is—"

"No." His long fingers closed over her hand. "Please do not freeze me, Miss Marietta. I am aware that I have no right to intrude in your affairs. I can only say that nothing would give me greater joy than—than to serve you in any way possible. If I were able to—" He bit off that useless wish, and amended, "I have nothing to offer you but my friendship; and that I offer with all my heart. If you are ever distressed and need someone to just talk with perhaps, or—or if I could be of help, you have but to call."

She knew by now that his nature was proud, yet he had spoken so earnestly, so humbly, and he sat there with devotion plainly written on his bruised face, both hands holding hers as if he took some ancient oath of fealty. With an odd ache of the heart she realized that here was love; implied even if it could not be uttered. Here was a strong shoulder to lean on; a confidante when she so badly needed one. Her eyes blurred and she had to turn away, so moved that she could say nothing for a moment.

To Diccon, her silence and her averted face were ominous. Likely, he had made a proper fool of himself, and she was trying not to laugh at him. 'Clumsy idiot!' he thought, and retreated behind his customary sauvity, saying with a smile, "Jupiter, what a speech! My friends would never believe it. You must think me a proper windy-wallets."

"Don't spoil it!" Marietta dabbed furtively at her tearful eyes. "I think it quite—quite the nicest thing that was ever said to me."

"You do?"

"I do. Thank you, my—friend. You are, of course, perfectly right. If you will be so kind as to let me sit in front of your saddle you can carry me home, and along the way I will tell you, in strictest confidence, what is worrying me. You can be very wise and knowing, and say I am being a silly widgeon and making mountains out of mole-hills."

He chuckled and said he thought he was a reasonably brave man, but would never dare tell any lady that she was a silly widgeon. Because of the stallion's uncertain temper, he swung into the saddle first and held the horse steady while Marietta used the tree-trunk as a mounting block. In no time he had settled her before him. He reined Orpheus to a walk and kept one arm about Marietta's slender waist, joying in the feel of her clasped so close against him, breathing the sweet fragrance of her, listening as she told him of her beloved but headstrong brother, and her fears for his sake.

By the time they approached the dower house quite a lot of the blackberries had vanished and so had the few lingering doubts Marietta had entertained. Diccon had a way of making her feel that he was not only deeply interested in what she had to say, but that he respected her opinions. It was a courtesy she seldom received from gentlemen. Papa and his friends tended to exchange indulgent smiles when she dared air her views on events, and invariably she would be told not to trouble her "pretty little head" with such deep subjects. Even Blake, who showed such partiality towards her, didn't seem to have much interest in her remarks, and on one or two occasions had changed the subject so abruptly that she'd been convinced he hadn't heard a word she said.

When she finished her account, Diccon said gravely that in his view Eric Warrington was to be commended for striving to help his family. "However," he added, "he does seem to be venturing into deep water at a rather young age. I think your concern is justified and far from widgeon-ish."

She turned and looked at him searchingly. "What must I do? If I try to advise him he'll just say I'm being a nag and spoiling his triumphs. Should I speak to Papa about it?"

Having formed a very good idea of her father's mental acuity, he advised against such a step. "You don't want your brother to think you're going behind his back. On the other hand, I agree that a sensitive young fellow might balk at accepting advice from his sister. I wonder if he would come down and meet me? I might be able to find out a little more about the scheme and drop a friendly hint if it sounds at all smoky."

She was delighted by this suggestion. Eric, she said, was exceedingly fond of Arthur, and when he knew how kind Diccon had been to the boy he would certainly want to go down to Lanterns and meet him.

They parted at the lodge gates. Dazzled by her smile, Diccon watched Marietta pick her way cautiously up to the house. She paused on the terrace to wave to him. He returned the wave, then reined Orpheus around to the south once more.

He rode down the hill slowly, reliving their moments together, dreaming foolish dreams. But he must not indulge such thoughts. With an effort he forced himself to stop mooning like a lovesick boy and use his mind to some purpose. He pondered what she'd said and tried not to be influenced either by his love for her, or by cynicism. If Eric Warrington was a financial genius everything might be perfectly legal and above-board, and what a blessing that would be to his family. On the other hand, there was no denying that for a young fellow to have come by such a large amount and so quickly, sounded somewhat havey-cavey.

Plagued by unease, he relaxed his grip on the reins and allowed Orpheus to spring into a thundering gallop.

CHAPTER X

acDougall ran to take the bridle when Diccon rode into the courtyard at Lanterns. There was a frantic look in the Scot's eyes, an expression so foreign to the usually phlegmatic individual that Diccon stared at him in astonishment and, dismounting, asked, "What is it?"

"I'd nae bargained for this, y'ken," gabbled MacDougall, his accent so thick as to be barely understandable. "A muckle bonnie brrrawl has the MacDougall fecht wi' a musket or a dag i' his clout, but bogles and goblins and witches, bonnie though they may be, isna whaur I'll bide, mon! I'll nae . . ." The words faded as he led Orpheus away, shaking his head.

"I suppose you know what you said, Mac." Shaking his own head, Diccon muttered, "Be damned if I do!"

He crossed the bridge, entered the house by the front door, and wandered along the corridor his thoughts still on the lovely Marietta. "My friend," she'd said, with such a warm smile. And how sweetly trusting she had looked while telling him of Eric Warrington's grandiose plans. He pushed open the door to the kitchen which was at present the most habitable room in the manor. He'd have to see what—

A soft chuckle, and the door slammed shut behind him.

Whirling about, pistol in hand, he gasped, "Gad, ma'am! Never do that!"

Emma Cordova spread her skirts wide and sank into a low curtsy. "As you command, my lord."

"I am not—" he began, restoring the pistol to his pocket.

"—What you seem," she finished, and curtsied again.

He grunted and pulled out a chair for her. "Is anyone?"

" 'Something wicked this way comes,' " she quoted. "If I thought 'twas you, Temple and Cloud. . . ." She leaned forward, arms on the table, peering up at him.

"My name is Mallory Diccon Paisley. A mouthful, I agree. So most people simply call me Major Diccon." His unexpectedly endearing smile chased the grimness from his eyes. "And what would you do, ma'am? Inform against me as a free-trader?"

"Oh, no. I would kill you."

She spoke matter-of-factly, but his smile died and he stood staring down at her. "By Jove, I believe you would make a try at it."

"I love my family. And what I see in your eyes tells me—"

"That I am the evil coming this way?"

"Very possibly. In spite of how much you love her."

He stiffened, then turned away to open a cupboard. "May I offer you a glass of ratafia, ma'am?"

"Only if you have nothing livelier. Ah. You are exceeding attractive when you smile, which you know, of course. Yes, the Madeira will do nicely, thank you." She sipped the wine he handed her and watched as he poured himself a glass and pulled a chair closer. "You don't bother to deny it, do you, Major?"

He said blandly, "Deny what is the threat I pose? I've not the benefit of your Mystical Window Through Time, ma'am. Perhaps you will tell me."

"That's not what I meant, as you are well aware. I suppose 'twould be a waste of my time to try to wring a plain answer from you, and as I know the truth at all events I won't make the effort. As to the other"—Mrs. Cordova sighed heavily—"it is very confused just now and difficult to understand. But I must warn you because there is trouble and danger, and a visitor who seems to threaten you, and . . ."

"And—ma'am?"

In a sudden and disconcerting shift of mood she giggled and said coquettishly, "And this is excellent wine, sir. I will take a teensy bit more, if you please. Thank you. I do hope there has been a great tragedy in your life? Oh, dear. Now I've made you spill the wine!"

Slightly breathless, he said, "You've a way of catching a man offstride, Mrs. Cordova."

"Good. Has there been? I don't mean the war or anything connected with your—er, occupation."

In the act of taking up his glass again his hand stilled for an instant. Then he said expressionlessly, "When I was eighteen."

To his astonishment she choked on her wine, sprang up, and began to pace round and round the table, wringing her hands and wailing. "Oh, no, no, no! Too long ago! Then, it will be here! It will be here!"

He was silent, watching her, wondering if she was quite sane or if she really did possess clairvoyant powers. Fortune-tellers, mediums, mystics were very popular nowadays and although he'd always viewed matters of the occult with scepticism he knew several people of fine intellect whose decisions were influenced by the advice of their astrologers.

Mrs. Cordova halted before him, clasped hands pressed to her mouth, her big dark eyes fixed upon him with such drama as to be ludicrous, yet he felt no inclination to laugh, and asked gravely, "Do you say that this visitor will be responsible for a tragedy?"

She nodded.

"Here at Lanterns? Or at the dower house?"

"There you are," she wailed, throwing her arms wide. "Which? I only know that dark clouds are all about us. The Mystical Window warns of a most dreadful threat. But it makes no sense, do you see? For sometimes it seems to come from far away, and sometimes is here. *Here!* And how can that be? Unless . . ."

He said quietly, "Unless I am the threat."

"Oh, I hope not. I really do. Perhaps it is that I'm not reading the warning properly, but I felt I must tell you, just in case. So many tangled threads. And death hovering . . . so *horribly*! And everything will be changed!" She moaned distractedly. "Oh dear, oh *dear*!"

He stood and took her hands and led her to the chair again. "Now, now. Do not be so troubled. I thank you for coming down here to warn me. But—your visitor may already have arrived, ma'am, in which case you worry for nothing."

She looked at him dubiously, and he poured a little more wine in her glass and told her about his uninvited late-night caller.

"He must have been a big fellow to toss you about," she said, looking somewhat cheered.

"His height is not exceptional, but he's almost as broad as he is tall and of incredible strength."

"You saw that much—at night? Or is it that you have met him before?"

"I've met him before, and certainly he has no love for me. But in this instance I think he was simply looking for *The Sigh of Saladin*. And that may be the danger you were warned of, ma'am: that unscrupulous men are hunting for the supposed treasure."

"Hmm. This very strong man who attacked you. Is he English?"

"He is Chinese. And his master is a Swiss. There, you see? They are from far away, yet they are here."

She gave a sigh of relief. "Praise heaven, then that would explain it!"

"It would indeed, and it is nothing that would bring trouble upon your brother's household, so you may be at ease."

"Ye-es." She sprang up in her abrupt fashion and trotted to the door. "And I must be off."

Diccon offered to drive her up the hill, but she declined, saying that she liked to walk. He accompanied her across the draw-bridge, and when they reached the north end of the manor she stopped and reached up to pat his cheek. "Such a kind smile," she said. "Poor boy. What a terrible grief to have lost your lady so young. The young feel things so very intensely."

Once again his breath was snatched away. He gasped, "You—you heard about it?"

"No. But it was a simple puzzle to solve, after all. I did know that you had been devoted to your papa, but he died when you were eleven, I believe, and you said your tragedy occurred when you were eighteen. At that time you had already left home. Your mother was still living, so the only other cause of such grief would be a lady." Her brow wrinkled. "It might, I suppose, have been a beloved sister, or aunt. But—it wasn't, so now you will think me very clever, no? And you will pay heed to my warnings. Be very careful, 'plain and simple, Major Diccon.' You are neither plain nor simple, and I know you have lived with danger for most of your days. I fear you, my dear. But I like you. And I would purely loathe to discover that we have arrived at the wrong solution to what my Mystical Window is trying to tell me."

A beaming smile, a little pat on the arm, and she was gone, but Diccon still stood there watching as she walked with quick, bouncy steps up the slope and across the meadow.

MacDougall emerged from the barn and wandered over to join him. "Whisht! She's well away. It's demented she is, puir lady."

Diccon said thoughtfully, "Or very wise, Mac. Either way, I think you and I must do what we can to make Lanterns more secure. I've a feeling that we've not seen the last of unexpected visitors."

Oh, a famous fellow, I agree. I always liked George." Sitting beside Eric Warrington in the withdrawing room, Blake Coville was quite aware of the admiration in the younger man's eyes, and although he longed to terminate this conversation he added graciously, "In fact, I helped him get out of England two years ago."

"Did you, by Jove! How famous! I never even saw Brummell. Did you know him, Papa?"

"Not well," said Sir Lionel. "One encountered him at various functions, of course. But I have never been an admirer of the Carlton House set, and Brummell seemed to me a very cold fish. Etta liked him, though, didn't you, my love?"

"He was very kind to me," said Marietta, "when he might easily have snubbed me. And that is how we judge people really, don't you think? Less by what men say of them than by how they treat us personally."

Coville had come here this afternoon hoping for a private chat with Marietta. Unfortunately, young Warrington had driven in only moments after he arrived. Now he was properly trapped and would likely be subjected to a half-hour of dull small talk before he could decently escape, without ever having spent a moment alone with her. All it wanted was for the lunatic aunt to appear! He conjured up a rather tight smile and said, "I hope that gentle tolerance will not be extended to my step-brother. I have been trying to hint your sister away from him, Warrington, but Miss Marietta is of a trusting nature, and he has a smooth tongue and I fear has managed to deceive her."

Indignant, Marietta protested, "I think you are saying I am gullible, which is not the case! I broached the subject with Major Diccon and he gave me his word of honour that he has not harmed his mama!"

Coville said with an edge to his voice, "Easy said, ma'am, when he has no honour!" Eric looked shocked, and Coville added, "My apologies for speaking plainly. I've good reason for anger, Mr. Warrington, as your father could tell you."

"Just so," said Sir Lionel. "And now is as good a time as any. Perhaps Mr. Coville will excuse us for a few minutes while you lend me a helping hand downstairs. I've a small problem with my new invention."

Coville stood at once and said he would be on his way, but Sir Lionel insisted he remain and take tea with them. "Fanny will brew up a pot for us," he said jovially. "In the meantime, I feel sure Marietta would enjoy to take a stroll around the gardens now that the weather is so pleasant. Ain't that right, m'dear?"

Once again embarrassed by her father's sledgehammer tactics, Marietta had no choice but to agree. Fanny tried not altogether successfully to hide her amusement and went into the kitchen to prepare the tea tray, while Sir Lionel took his son down to the basement.

On the stairs Eric said uneasily, "Perhaps I should go and fetch Aunty Dova. Surely it's not proper for Etta to be alone with Coville?"

"What, in our own garden? Never be so prim, boy. Coville cannot very well pay court to your sister whilst we all sit and gawk at him, now can he? And I promise you he's a damn sight finer catch for her than is that penniless and reluctant peer down the hill."

"Jove! There's no chance of that, is there, sir? Fanny says he is a bad man and that he very probably murdered his mama and hid her body in the old barn." Reassured by his father's hoot of laughter, he went on, "Yes, well, I must say it sounds like so much fustian to me, because if it were true Bow Street would have him safely locked up in Newgate."

"So Marietta holds. Sir Gavin claims he hasn't called in the law because he don't want scandal, but . . ." Sir Lionel shrugged. "Who knows? Temple and Cloud struck me as a reasonable enough man at first, but he's up to his ears in smuggling at the very least."

"You never mean it! A *peer*—free-trading?"

"A peer who won't use his title, which of itself is a sure sign he must be short of a sheet."

"Yes, indeed! Does he appear deranged?"

"No, no. Quite a fine-looking chap, in a manly way. One of

those strong and silent types. Your aunt says there's an air of the panther about him." Sir Lionel chuckled. "Emma and her fancies!"

"Is it truth that he was at Waterloo, sir?"

"So he says, and I'll own I'd not care to have his glove in my face! He'd be a man to reckon with. Hand me down that tub of glue, there's a good lad."

Obliging, Eric said thoughtfully, "I know Fanny is afraid of him, but Etta and Aunty Dova seem to like him. I wonder why."

"Because they're women, of course. Show them an upstanding gentleman of character, and they'll toss their pretty shoulders and forget him. But let them suspect a man is dangerous and with a touch of mystery about him, and they flock about him like so many moths round a flame. Aye, you may smile, m'boy, but I've seen it before and I don't want to find Etta fluttering around that particular flame! No future in it. Now, you'd best run upstairs, and make sure Fan don't volunteer to keep her sister company and drive poor Coville demented!"

Oh, I think the guv'nor was grateful enough," said Eric, riding beside Marietta early next morning. "But he didn't like my having given the funds into your capable hands."

Marietta sighed ruefully. "Poor dear Papa. I only hope he may not begin to resent my interference."

"Interference be dashed! Now don't let him break your shins—I mean, borrow from the reserves, Etta! You ain't betrothed to Coville yet. Er—are you?"

She laughed. "Foolish boy. As if I'd not have told you. Certainly Papa would have made the announcement if Mr. Coville had asked for my hand."

"From the way he behaved yesterday afternoon, I thought he was about to do so. He seemed exceeding anxious to be alone with you. When I peeped outside he was talking to you most animatedly. Wanted to find out about our background, I'll warrant?"

Marietta watched the clouds that were massing to the north-east, and said slowly, "When first we met he said he intended to ask me lots of questions about myself. But most of the time he only talks about himself or wants to know whether I have been down to Lanterns." And she thought, 'Just as Diccon said he would.'

"He's likely worried for his step-mama. I wonder you didn't send him to Madame Olympias."

"You very much dislike Aunty Dova's—hobby, don't you, Eric?"

"Of course I do. I suppose the whole County must know their local fortune-teller is really my aunt! What a come-down!"

"Oh, I hope they do not! You should only see how she dresses when she goes to the caravan! The wig, and all the paint on her face, and the funny accent she uses. I promise you it would be hard to recognize her and I think it simply would not occur to most people that a gentlewoman would do anything so outra-geous. Besides, she listens to their troubles very kindly, and they really do value the advice she gives them."

"Do they indeed! I shall go down and consult her myself. She can look into her crystal ball and tell me if there really is a trea-sure."

Marietta laughed. "Have a care, brother dear. Madame Olympias would be more likely to read your palm and find out all about your jaunts in London."

Eric's grin vanished. He snapped, "How did you know I was in Town?"

" 'Miles Cameron' told her. Isn't it extraordinary that she— Eric? You're not angry?"

"No. Of course not, you silly widgeon." His brilliant smile chased away that sudden look of rage. "But I think I'd best not let her read my palm. My reputation would be—Jupiter! Who the devil is that?"

Marietta turned and saw a great grey horse galloping across the meadows at breakneck speed. "Oh, that's Major Diccon!" She waved. "I think he has not seen us."

"He has now; see, he's turning."

"He'll have to swing south to cross the stone bridge."

"Devil he will! He means to jump the stream!"

Alarmed, she cried, "No! He cannot, it's too wide! Oh, heavens! He has Arthur up before him! Wave him off, Eric!"

"Too late. There he goes. Oh, jolly well done! Gad, but he can ride!"

Orpheus came thundering up, then slowed and approached them with mincing decorum.

"Etta! Eric!" screamed Arthur, his face flushed and his eyes blazing with excitement. "Did you see? Sir G'waine an' me jumped over the moon! Like the cow! Wasn't it fine?"

"A fine risk to take with my brother up before you," scolded Marietta.

Diccon said blandly, "Oh, I felt perfectly safe in the company of the dauntless Lancelot, ma'am."

Noting the smile on the man's fine-drawn face and the sparkle in his sister's eyes, it occurred to Eric that Mr. Blake Coville had better make haste with his wooing.

"He says I mayn't try it till I get a horse like Awful," said Arthur. "He says a man must know his mount 'fore—"

"Major Diccon says," Marietta corrected. "Not 'he.' You must allow me to present my brother, Major. Eric, this is Major Mallory Diccon Paisley."

"Temple and Cloud, eh?" said Eric, reaching out eagerly for the handshake. "Very glad to meet you, sir. Jove, but that's a splendid horse."

"Yes, he's a fine fellow." Diccon patted the stallion's smooth neck. "I'm told you've a nice team of matched bays."

Eric blushed with pleasure but gave a man-of-the-world shrug. "Oh, pretty fair. They're good goers, but not in the same class with your animal. Is he really called Awful?"

"Orpheus."

"And he is musical." Marietta glanced at Diccon and added with meaning, "You must give my brother a demonstration, Major."

"It would be my pleasure. Now, if you dare enter my wicked castle, Warrington. I've a fearsome reputation, you know."

Eric grinned, but Arthur, who had been gainfully employed in tying a knot in Orpheus' mane, said confidently, "I'm coming, too!" Diccon gave him a stern look and he added, "If y'please, sir."

"That's much better," said Marietta. "But it's time for your lessons, young man."

The boy's lower lip thrust out rebelliously.

Eric said, "Beastly luck, child, but I only take educated pirates out rowing."

Arthur's eyes became very round. " 'S afternoon?"

"This afternoon."

"You promise?"

Eric put a hand over his heart. "A sacred vow."

"And you can ride home with me," bribed Marietta. "Can we manage that, Eric?"

Warrington dismounted, handed his reins to Diccon and lifted Arthur to Marietta's saddle. Settling his brother into place, he murmured *sotto voce*, "He don't sound demented to me."

"Who's 'mented?" asked Arthur, loud and clear.

Marietta closed her eyes and moaned softly.

⚜

It could be jolly fine if you restored it," said Eric, walking back through the new wing beside Diccon. "Assuming you enjoy country life, of course. Thank you for showing me around."

"I'm glad you like the old place. I take it you don't enjoy country life? Perhaps you're eager to get back to University?"

"Devil I am! The country's all right. For a day or two. But school—ugh! It's damnable. Didn't you find it so, sir?"

Beginning to feel like Methuseleh, Diccon said, "Sometimes. But to have a degree in your pocket can be most helpful to your career. Depending upon what you mean to do with your life, of course."

"So everyone says. Did you win a fellowship, sir?"

"Oh, don't look to me for your example. Not if you expect to wind up with plenty of lettuce in your bowl!"

"Well, that's just it, you see. Even if I were to cram night and day it would take another two years to finish. I'm a fair scholar, but to say truth, I've no interest in the business. And my family needs help now!"

Diccon thought of a spanking new coach and thoroughbred team, and the coat that was as if moulded to Warrington's shoulders and proclaimed the costly genius of Weston. He kept his scepticism to himself and opened the kitchen door to wave his guest inside. "I haven't started any repairs yet, and there's not much in the way of usable furniture. I'm afraid this is the most presentable room in which to entertain you, but if you can stay for a glass of cognac I'd be glad of some intelligent company."

Flattered by such an invitation from a man whom he had recognized at once as a regular "top o' the trees" Eric accepted eagerly. When he was settled at the table with a glass of most excellent brandy, Diccon sat opposite and granted his request to be told about *The Sigh of Saladin* and the ghosts said to haunt the manor. Then, with skilled expertise he guided the conversation to Sir Lionel and his family. The brandy was velvety smooth, the kitchen warm, and the Major's interest gratifying. Drowsily content, Eric relaxed, and quite soon the floodgates opened.

Diccon listened to a wistful account of their grand house in London and of the life that had been "so very different" to their present circumstances, which were obviously regarded as deplorable. "Fanny was too young to have gone out into Society very much," said Eric. "And she don't miss Town. But it has been devilish hard on Etta, though she's a good girl and don't cry over spilt milk. My father hoped she would make a splendid match and rescue us all, but—buried out here . . ." He shrugged resignedly.

"You cannot hide a diamond of the first water for very long, and Sussex is scarcely in the middle of the Gobi Desert. Miss Marietta will assuredly make a splendid match. I only hope it may be a happy one." Diccon became aware that he had spoken sharply and that Warrington was staring at him. "I think it admirable that you mean to help your family," he went on in a milder tone. "But it's rather a tall order for a young fellow, isn't it? At your age I had all I could do to provide for myself."

"Not much lettuce to be made in the Army, I fancy?"

"Even when they remember to pay me—which they seldom do! Luckily," Diccon met Eric's gaze and said with a grin, "I have other—ah, irons in the fire."

"So I've heard. And if this brandy's a sample I imagine you make more at your illicit career than at your public one!"

"Well, there's always money to be made. Provided one's willing to take the risk. But I don't recommend such unlawful activities to a young sprig like you, and I'll be grateful do you keep mine to yourself."

It seemed to Eric that there was just a touch of condescension in the other man's attitude. Irked, he reacted with the boastfulness of youth. "Never fear, sir. I'm told you refuse your title, whereby one gathers you also have no love for our present ridiculous form of government." Lowering his voice, he leaned forward. "I'll admit to you that I've set more than my toe outside the law. And more than once!"

Diccon chuckled. "So your generous gifts to your family weren't paid for by a lucky wager. What a slyboots to have fobbed your sister off with some tale of grandiose investments! I knew it was unlikely, at your age. Rum running, eh?"

"Not so!" exclaimed Eric, indignantly. "Bigger game, sir! I"—a swift glance at the door—"I am a—a sort of courier. An exceeding high paid courier, I might add. For a group of influential gentlemen."

Diccon's eyes were veiled, but his lips twitched and one of his brows arched upward ironically.

Touched on the raw, Eric flared, "You think I brag, and that gentlemen would not trust weighty matters to the care of a man of two and twenty! Well, that is *exactly* why I am hired! Because I look younger than I am." He laughed suddenly. "You should only see the rig I wear when I'm sailing! I look like nothing so much as an underpaid apprentice clerk. How I laugh to myself when the Riding Officers don't so much as glance my way! If they did but know what—" He broke off. He'd said more than he intended, and finished rather lamely, "You'd not credit the amount of secrecy and spying that goes on in the world of industry."

"Is that so? Well, I expect you're old enough to know what you're about, and whether the risks you run are justified. For my part, I'm of a mind to marry and settle down." Diccon sighed, and said ruefully, "I'll have to give up smuggling then, of course. A gentleman cannot take the chance of bringing shame to his loved ones."

Eric frowned into his wineglass and said nothing.

"I can't tell you how much I have enjoyed meeting your family," Diccon went on, his eyes very keen under the thick brows. "They've been most kind to me. I really envy you your young brother. He's an engaging little scamp. You're his idol, and it's plain to see that he'll take you for his model in life."

Lifting his head, Warrington searched the lean features and found only a friendly smile. "Yes," he said, setting down his glass. "Well, I must be getting home. Good day, sir, and thank you for your hospitality."

Outside, the skies had darkened, the air was very still and the clouds had the yellowish tinge that warned of a thunderstorm. Eric Warrington rode up the hill slowly, in a marked departure from his customary neck or nothing pace. The smuggled brandy was potent stuff and his head felt just a touch fuzzy. But it was not the effect of the wine that brought the uneasiness to his spirits. He wondered if he'd said too much to a man he really scarcely knew. He heard again a deep voice that said, ". . . he'll take you for his model in life." It did little to lighten his mood.

Diccon stood on the drawbridge and watched him out of sight. Deep in thought, he wandered around to the barn, kicking a pebble before him. Mac had gone back into the house and the barn was dim and quiet, the air heavy with the scents of hay and animals. He came to a halt and gazed blankly at an empty stall. Then he drove a clenched fist at a post and said an explosive "Damn!"

* * *

The storm, which had been threatening all day, broke in full fury shortly after four o'clock. Jocelyn Vaughan pulled the top cape of his riding coat higher about his throat, ducked his head against the teeming rain and urged his horse to a gallop. He'd glimpsed the chimneys from the top of the hill and thought it would be a short ride to the manor, but the distance was deceiving and by the time he approached the closed lodge gates he was soaked. The little lodge was unoccupied and he had no intention of dismounting to open the gates. The tall grey gelding cleared the hedge neatly and cantered along the short drivepath to the terrace steps.

Even through the downpour Vaughan could see that it was a much smaller house than he'd envisioned, and in better repair. Urged on by a deafening peal of thunder, he dismounted, secured the reins to a post, and ran up the steps and across the terrace.

There was no sound from within, and not a single candle brightened the windows. "Hello!" he shouted, pounding on the door. "Are you asleep again, you lazy varmint? Wakey, wakey!"

Rushing into the kitchen with her arms full of damp washing, Fanny heard the shouting and the repeated blows on the front door. "Oh, rats!" she panted. "Go away, whoever you are!"

The pounding was redoubled and an irate roar advised that if the door wasn't opened instantly there would be bloody murder done.

Mrs. Gillespie had gone home early with one of her

"headaches," and Marietta was striving frantically to rescue the rest of the laundry. Papa and Eric had driven off somewhere in the new coach, which left to Fanny the task of dealing with this violent caller. She deposited her load on the kitchen table and hurried across the withdrawing room, prepared for battle. Lightning flashed as she entered the hall. The front door was being pushed open. A gauntletted hand came into view and that irate male voice shouted, "Where the devil are you, traitor? Guard yourself! I'm coming in!"

Fanny's impassioned retort froze on her tongue. Into her mind came Marietta's story of the intruder who had broken into Lanterns and so brutally attacked Diccon. This was very likely the same creature. Having failed at the manor he'd decided to search the dower house! She started to back away. Terrified by the slow opening of the door, she fled into the drawing room. There was no time for a further retreat. Fortunately, they'd not yet lit candles and the room was quite dim. She sank onto the sofa next to "Mrs. Hughes-Dering" and did her best to resemble a dummy.

Jocelyn Vaughan stepped into a spacious but gloomy entrance hall. He peered about curiously, his eyes still dazzled from that brilliant lightning flash. Directly opposite, heavy draperies were tied back on each side of an archway giving onto a corridor. He went over to the archway and saw a flight of stairs at some distance to his left, several rooms to his right, and, facing him, a partly open door. It was chill and deathly quiet. He took off his hat and shook it, sending water spraying from the brim. 'Grim sort of place,' he thought, and howled, "Hello? Did everybody die?"

Aside from another peal of thunder there was no response. He crossed the corridor, pushed the door wider, and looked into a large drawing room. He was considerably put out to find upon entering this shadowed chamber that several people were present, all of whom saw fit to ignore him. "Good day," he said stiffly. "Your butler must not have heard me at the door."

Silence. Not a word, not a movement.

"All dead, are you?" he enquired with heavy sarcasm.

The complete lack of any reaction was peculiar, to say the least. They were so unnaturally still. Uneasy now, he moved forward and addressed the military man seated by the empty hearth. "Are you asleep, sir? Have I broke into the wrong house? I'm here to . . . see . . ." The eyes were open, however, their fixed, glassy-eyed stare was unnerving. Vaughan, who was no stranger to death and had himself almost succumbed to wounds sustained at the Battle of Quatre Bras, recoiled, the hair on the back of his neck lifting. He held his breath, put out a hand and gave the man's shoulder a tentative shake. There was no angry protest, no resistance at all. Slowly, the soldier slumped to the side.

"Jupiter!" yelped Vaughan, horrified.

He touched the arm of one of three ladies seated on a sofa, and the large dowager sagged slightly. The lady to her left sagged more than slightly, her head lolling in a most horrid fashion.

"What a . . . ghastly . . . thing!" he whispered, breaking into a sweat. His hand shook as he reached for the slender girl on the far end. A piercing shriek rang out and his hand was knocked aside. His heart jumped into his throat. With a terrified shout he fairly leapt back. The young woman sprang to her feet. The poor creature's mind must have cracked, he thought dazedly, for in such a place of horror she was laughing hysterically.

Desperate, he looked about. Three roses in a crystal vase were displayed on a round occasional table. He snatched up the vase, removed the roses and flung the water in the face of the convulsed girl. Her laughter was cut off. She stood rigid and gasping, her eyes (which, sadly, were very pretty) wide with shock, and water dripping down her nose.

"Ooo-oh!" she gulped.

"My poor little soul," said Vaughan kindly, setting the vase aside and putting a consoling arm about her tiny waist.

"*Monster!*" she shrieked, swinging one damp but efficient hand into cracking contact with his cheek. "How—*dare*—you!"

"What—on earth?" Another lady, very wet and dishevelled and wrapped in a large apron, hurried to join them.

"Don't look!" cried Vaughan, flinging up a gallantly protecting hand. "It's horrid! Is your master still alive?"

Marietta's lower lip sagged, and Fanny stared at this (astonishingly handsome) young lunatic speechlessly.

"There has been a most frightful tragedy," said Vaughan, drawing his handkerchief and wiping his pallid brow. "This poor demented maid appears to be the only survivor! We shall have to call in the authorities at once. Are you the housekeeper? Or is there someone who can—"

"Survivor . . . of what?" asked Marietta, bewildered.

"Mass murder in the drawing room," spluttered Fanny.

"Oh, dear me! Another visitor! The Mystical Window Through Time was right again!" A startling figure came in from the front hall and peered up into Vaughan's face. "So you have this way come," she remarked. "But you don't look very wicked."

He was unable to return the compliment and gazed at her, stunned. A tangle of wet hair was plastered to her forehead, thick face paint was running, giving her a most ghoulish appearance, and a voluminous cloak sagged, drenched, about her.

A small boy clad in what appeared to be chain mail, and with a most odd helmet on his head came clanking down the stairs accompanied by a large ginger cat that flashed across the dining room and launched itself into the visitor's arms.

"I knowed he wouldn't keep his promise," the child wailed. "I'll split his wishbone!"

Vaughan whispered, "Oh . . . my . . . God!"

Fanny could not contain herself, and laughed till she cried.

hen the explanations and introductions had been made Vaughan was invited to stay for tea. In the absence of their groom he took his mount to the barn and tended to its needs with the swift efficiency learned by all those who had been members of the Duke of Wellington's dauntless cavalry.

When he returned to the house the younger ladies and the pile of washing had disappeared somewhere. Mrs. Cordova was in the kitchen and offered a curtsy so deep and flourishing that he was taken aback, but with the paint removed from her face, she looked far less frightening. Despite her odd appearance he was astonished to find a lady of Quality working in the kitchen, but there was no doubt that this was a very unconventional household. Mrs. Cordova seemed not at all disconcerted by his presence but bustled about making preparations for tea, and chattering endlessly about his uncle, John Moulton, of whom she spoke very highly. Enquiring after Lord John's bride, Lady Salia, she smiled nostalgically at the tea strainer, and murmured, "She was of the gypsies, I know, but such a beautiful creature." Before he could comment, she burst into song. "She has healing hands of green. But through my window she's not seen!"

He had not the faintest notion of how one responded to such odd behaviour and was murmuring a feeble, "How—ah, nice," when to his great relief Miss Warrington reappeared and ushered him into the drawing room. She had changed for dinner and he thought her very pretty in a white gown trimmed with red velvet. A moment later her sister arrived, and his breath was snatched away. In a gown of primrose and gold, with a golden fillet threaded charmingly through her dark curls, Miss Fanny was so dazzling that he was scarcely able to respond properly when Mrs. Cordova left them, saying she had to "make some necessary repairs."

"You must think me a proper cloth-head," said Vaughan, taking the cup of tea Fanny offered. "I can only plead that I should have recognized Miss Warrington at once save that the light was rather dim, and—er—"

"And one sees what one expects to see," said Marietta, adding a log to the now merrily blazing fire. "You could not have expected to see me here, and considering the way I was dressed I'm not surprised that you were confused."

Miss Fanny's big hazel eyes laughed into his as she proffered milk and sugar. A dimple flickered at the corner of her mouth reminding him that he was staring again and had not replied to her sister's remark. He said hurriedly, "You are very kind, Miss Warrington. I'll confess I'd not known you had removed from Town."

"We have suffered reverses, you see," explained Fanny in a frank, unspoiled way that he thought enchanting. "We lost our own home and in fact this house is only leased."

"I would never have guessed," he declared staunchly. "Leased homes are so often rather stark, whereas this is perfectly charming." And indeed, now that the candles were lit and firelight warmed the room, it was very different. So different that had he been offered the choice of any mansion in the land at that moment, he would have wanted to be nowhere else.

"It is a nice house," said Marietta, taking a seat nearby. "But I can appreciate what a great shock it was for you to come upon my aunt's—er, 'friends' in a darkened room in the middle of a thunderstorm."

"Oh, a very great shock," said Fanny demurely.

He grinned. "You had a jolly time laughing at my consternation, Miss Fanny. If I had suffered a heart seizure, you'd have been sorry!"

"How could I help but laugh?" she countered. "You looked so funny, and clearly feared you'd wandered into a mad-house."

"And indeed we would have been very sorry," said Marietta, quite aware of the becoming blush on her sister's cheeks and the mischievous sparkle in her eyes. "I promise you the figures were not made with the intent of alarming people, but to console my aunt. She misses her friends, you see."

Fanny said, "I expect you think it odd that she pretends they're really here, chatting with her."

It seemed to him excessively odd but he said heartily, "Now that I see them in a better light I have to say the likenesses are remarkable. Miles Cameron especially. You'll have to make a change though; Miles was promoted. And about time!"

This news was received with delight. "He's a charming gentleman," said Marietta. "A close friend of your cousin, Lord St. Clair, unless I mistake it. Were you all at Waterloo?"

"Lucian and Miles were. I was knocked down at Quatre Bras, so can't claim the distinction of having survived the big battle." He paused, a far-away look creeping into his dark eyes.

Marietta was reminded of just that same haunted expression in Diccon's eyes when he'd spoken of Waterloo.

Fanny said earnestly, "I think most people think of Quatre Bras as being a part of the battle. You may be sure we are all very proud of the men who fought for us so bravely."

Touched, Vaughan flushed and stammered that although his own participation had been minimal, there were countless splendid fellows who deserved such accolades.

"No such thing!" Mrs. Cordova surged into the room clad in an impressive purple gown and a turban in which a single rather threadbare feather soared skyward. "Lucian St. Clair never tires of telling people that you saved his life," she went on, "and very nearly lost your own in the process. One cannot like a braggart, but false modesty is tiresome."

Vaughan had stood politely when she entered. Red as fire, he wished the floor might open under him, and said with an embarrassed laugh that it was hard to know where one began and the other left off. And maligning the cousin who was as close to him as a brother, he added, "Besides, St. Clair is a very frippery fellow, ma'am. I'm not eager to go about claiming responsibility for his continued existence!"

Viscount Lucian St. Clair's exploits had won him widespread admiration, and at this they all laughed.

Fanny said, "I am going to guess that is why you are in the neighbourhood. Lord Temple and Cloud was also at Waterloo, and is a friend of yours."

Grateful for this change of subject, Vaughan sat down again. He had not met Temple and Cloud, he said. "I intruded on you so rudely because I thought this was a manor called Lanterns. Am I very far off?"

"About two miles," said Fanny, puzzled.

"You are on the Lanterns estate," explained Marietta, passing a dish of warm scones. "But this is the dower house."

"Do you mean to call on Lord Temple and Cloud?" asked Fanny.

In the act of reaching for a scone, Vaughan paused, looking at her curiously. "No, ma'am. Should I?"

Marietta said, "I understood you to say you had mistaken this house for the manor. I believe there is no one else there, unless perhaps you are calling on Micah MacDougall."

Relieved, Vaughan exclaimed, "Oh, good! If Mac's there, Diccon must be somewhere nearby." The scone was light as a feather, and he was about to compliment the cook when he saw their exchange of glances. At once apprehensive, he said, "Something is wrong, I collect. Never say Diccon has met with another accident."

"Oh, several," said Fanny.

Watching him over the rim of her teacup, Mrs. Cordova said, "That disturbs you. Are you close friends?"

"I think not," Fanny interpolated. "When Mr. Vaughan arrived he called the Major a traitor."

Vaughan said tersely, "Your pardon, ma'am, but I said 'trader,' not 'traitor.' And we are indeed friends. Is he badly hurt this time?"

Marietta answered, "Fortunately, not," and hid her surprise that even his friends did not know of Diccon's title.

Less tactful, Fanny exclaimed, "But if you are his friend you surely must know that Diccon Paisley *is* Lord Temple and Cloud?"

Vaughan stared at her speechlessly. Then laughter gleamed in his eyes. He said, "Miss Warrington, I think someone has been hoaxing you."

Mrs. Cordova sighed. "I fear you are right, Mr. Vaughan. On more counts than one."

❦

Of all the chawbacons!" exclaimed Vaughan stretching his cold hands to the kitchen stove at Lanterns. "How could you not have expected it would pass to you? After your great-uncle's death surely you realized it was a possibility?"

Diccon tilted his chair backward, settled his spurred heels on the kitchen table, and regarded his friend drowsily. "With one great-uncle, one uncle, and two cousins between me and the title, why should I suspect that illness would claim two, the war another, and a hunting accident the last?"

"Even so, anyone who turns down a proud and ancient title such as yours should be placed under strong restraint!"

"Did you gallop all the way from Town to give me that unwanted opinion? Or have you joined the ranks of treasure hunters?"

"Treasure?" Vaughan sat straighter. "What treasure? I demand that you tell me at once!"

Diccon groaned and appealed to MacDougall, who was busied with potatoes at the sink. "I can't bear it. You tell him, Mac."

The Scot obliged, inserting several pithy opinions of his own which made Vaughan chuckle and Diccon swear. When the tale was told however, Vaughan's eyes were alight with enthusiasm. "What a jolly good hunt we'll have! Is that why you're here, Major, sir?"

"Oh, no," said Diccon mildly. "I came to murder my mama so as to get my hands on my inheritance. Past time, wouldn't you say?"

MacDougall threw down the potato and waved his hands in the air, muttering a furious burst of Gaelic at the ceiling.

Vaughan watched Diccon uncertainly, then laughed. "Long past time. I'll keep your ghoulish secret provided you do not give me the room in which the poor lady is buried 'neath the floorboards."

Diccon's rare and brilliant grin was slanted at him. "You'd be better advised to go back to Greenwings, Joss. Ti Chiu is fouling our good Sussex air."

"Ah," said Vaughan, sobering. "So you know."

"Did you come to warn me?"

"I did. How did you find out?"

"He found me. Broke in here a few nights back and we had a slight tussle."

More Gaelic rumbled from the direction of the sink.

"And you're alive?" said Vaughan, incredulous. "I thought you looked a shade wrung out, but the great lout must be losing his power. Last time we encountered him he levelled . . . how many of us?"

"Six, or was it seven? But I think he came here only for *The Sigh of Saladin*, not for me. If he'd recognized me . . . ." He shrugged.

"It would be a case of '*de mortius nil nisi bonum*,' " said Vaughan lightly. "So you want to run me off from a jolly good adventure! Blister it, Diccon! That you have survived to the ripe old age of three and thirty astounds me, but the fact that you're six years my senior don't make you my grand-papa, so stop being a marplot!"

"My good idiot, in the spring we spoiled Imre Monteil's scheme to make off with a fortune in stolen *objets d'art*. We extricated his chosen lady, who is—"

"Who is to become Mrs. Valentine Montclair next month. I brought your invitation, by the way."

Diccon's eyes brightened. "Did you, by Jove! That's good news! Which doesn't alter what I was saying. Between us, we ruined and infuriated a very dangerous man, and he swore vengeance on—"

"On all of us. After you let him get away!"

"*I* let him—" Diccon swung his feet down from the table and said indignantly, "Devil take you, Vaughan! I did my damnedest to—" He checked, glared, then said reluctantly, "Well, I suppose you're in the right of it. I did. The more reason—"

"For me to tuck my tail 'twixt my legs and scamper off, eh? What good would that do? After they dealt with you, they'd come after me, sure as check! There's safety in numbers, my tulip." Vaughan raised a silencing hand as Diccon started to speak, and added airily, "Besides which, I've a far more compelling reason to stay at your tumble-down ancestral pile."

Diccon knew that dreamy look. Incredulous, he shook his head. "So soon? Ye Gods! Can I believe it? You've found another 'one and only'!"

"I've found the *only* one, rather. Oh, I know you're not in the petticoat line, but how can you live so near to the exquisite Miss Warrington and not have noticed how glorious she is?"

For a moment Diccon watched him levelly and in silence. Then he said quietly, "She is much admired."

"Admired! She should be besieged by men who would adore her! Worship her! Be honest now—have ever you seen such a beautiful lady?"

"Once. A long time ago."

Remorseful, Vaughan exclaimed, "Gad, what a clumsy clod

I am! My apologies, old fellow! I shall say no more about it."

Diccon gave a dismissive gesture, and there came a muffled grunt from the sink.

Typically, Vaughan was able to control his exuberance for only a moment, then he burst out: "But having loved, you can understand how I feel, can't you? Those sparkling eyes. The shapeliness of her. The pretty way she has with her little laugh, and her soft voice. Can you wonder that I took one glance—well, very few—and was enchanted? She is a fairy-tale princess, personified!"

Diccon wandered over to push more wood into the stove, then stood gazing down at it.

Very quiet now, MacDougall turned from the sink and watched him.

"Do you mean to court her?" asked Diccon.

"I mean to win her! And I shall! Uncle John and Salia will adore her, don't you agree?"

"Yes."

"And she will love Greenwings, surely?"

"It's a beautiful old place."

Vaughan glanced at his friend's broad shoulders uneasily. "You have reservations, I think. Oh, Jupiter! Is she bespoken? Have I formidable competition? I'd the strongest feeling that she was as much affected as I."

Diccon's fist clenched hard. "Of course you have competition," he said harshly, turning to face the dismayed younger man. "You saw her beauty and her gentleness. Did you also have time to consider her courage? Did you stop to think how hard it has been for a gently bred-up girl to be reduced to living in near poverty? To have to juggle duns and try to outmanoeuvre an irresponsible brother and a foolish spendthrift father? I think her greatest fear is that she may not be able to keep them all together, but thus far she has contrived, and managed also to keep a cheerful spirit and not go about bemoaning her lot. She is as valiant as she is beautiful, and she deserves the best, Joss. The man to claim her must offer her comfort and a release from worry and care. And above all—undying love and constancy."

Astonished, Vaughan exclaimed, "Be dashed! Who'd have suspected a fire-eater like you to spare a thought for such things? I'm glad you approve. At least . . ." His brow wrinkled suddenly. "I think you approve. Was that a low lance you just hurled? About—constancy? I may have fancied myself in love a time or two, but—"

"Or a dozen!"

A frosty note came into Vaughan's voice. "You have a list, perhaps?"

"Devil I do! But from what I've heard there was a beauty in Spain—something to do with a bullfighter, I think St. Clair said. And several other 'one and onlys' whilst you were in the cavalry. Then came the beauty Rich Saxon eventually married—"

"Felicity Russell," said Vaughan, grim-lipped now, and coming to his feet to stand very straight, as though in a tribunal. "And Alicia Wyckham, whom I would have wed, only she changed her mind. I know now that I gave my heart to not one of those lovely creatures. Nor did any of them suffer at my hands, I promise you. Can you claim as much?"

The flush drained from Diccon's face leaving him very pale. For a moment the guards were down and his eyes betrayed him. He ducked his head and turned away. "No," he said in a hoarse half-whisper. "You are—perfectly right and—"

But Vaughan had seen that stricken look, and with a muffled exclamation he sprang to clap an arm about the other man's shoulders. "I had no right at all! I'm a hasty-tempered, brawling maggot-wit and don't deserve my friends. You know my faults and naturally fear for the lady . . . and—" Glancing past Diccon, he encountered MacDougall's eyes. The Scot, he knew, had always liked him, and the glare that was scorched at him now struck like a physical blow and shocked him into belated comprehension.

He drew back, and looking at Diccon's averted face, demanded, "All right. Let's have cards on the table. Who else courts the lady?"

Diccon sat down and said wearily, "Among others, my step-brother, Blake Coville."

"Deuce take it! Is that make-bait lurking about here?"

"Yes. And about her. And there are a couple of other fellows. Neither fit to wipe her shoes, but one has money. Her father favours Coville." He gave a short and bitter laugh. "Thinks he's plump in the pockets."

"Ain't he?"

"He was. But he's a gamester. I suspect he's under the hatches. I doubt Sir Gavin knows that. At all events," he forced a smile, "you are the most eligible bachelor, Joss. I wish you—the best of luck."

"You lying rogue!" growled Vaughan. "You do nothing of the sort! You love her yourself!"

Diccon linked his hands between his knees and stared down at them, saying nothing.

MacDougall growled and strode forward, the long paring knife glittering in his hand.

"And your Scottish humbug knew it!" accused Vaughan bitterly. "Are you going to let him slit my gizzard with that potato peeler, Diccon?"

"Don't be a fool. He wouldn't dream of it."

"Aye. I would, that," argued MacDougall his aspect fiercer than ever. "Sooner than let this pretty stripling come 'twixt yersel' and the lassie!"

Vaughan uttered a strangled howl. His face flaming with rage, he leapt at the Scot. "Damn you! How *dare* you call me—"

MacDougall sprang to meet him, the knife flying upward.

In a lithe uncoiling, Diccon was between them. A twist and a heave, and Vaughan hurtled across the table and took it down with him. Diccon's fingers clamped around the Scot's wrist. "Drop it!"

All the fierce pride of his fighting clan was in MacDougall's blazing eyes. The grip around his wrist tightened inexorably, but he would not release the blade. Diccon said softly, "Please, Mac." A smile crept into his eyes and he added, "He can't help it, you know. I think the poor cawker was born in a volcano."

MacDougall had never been able to resist that half-smile. He grunted, and the knife clattered to the floor. "It's yersel' means tae step aside wi'oot a fecht, then, is it?"

"I've never had the right to address Miss Warrington, much less fight for her hand."

"Mon, ye addrrress her every time ye look at her!"

Vaughan crawled back into view, and peered blearily over the edge of the table. "That was a deuced fine . . . toss, Major, sir," he panted. "Where'd you—where'd you learn it?"

"From one of Claude Sanguinet's Lascar cut-throats in Dinan." Diccon helped him to his feet. "My apologies. But I don't have many friends. Can't afford to have them killing each other."

Dour and silent, MacDougall righted the table.

Diccon steered Vaughan into a chair and asked, "Do you mean to call me out, Joss?"

Vaughan sighed heavily. "I rather suspect we're at Point Non-Plus. I can't in honour court my friend's chosen lady."

Diccon looked down at him and knew that here was a man worthy in every respect to marry his beloved. Young, thoroughly decent, courageous, handsome, and with a large fortune. The urge to strangle him was strong, which was pure dog-in-the-manger selfishness. It was not impossible for Vaughan to have formed an immediate and lasting attachment. If he himself really loved her—and Lord, how he loved her!—he should be rejoicing at her opportunity to make what everyone would consider a brilliant match.

He was, he discovered, incapable of such saintly behaviour, and it was as much as he could do to admit, "My own case is quite hopeless, Joss, else I promise you I'd fight for her every step of the way. But—if I must lose her, I couldn't wish to lose to a better man."

"Thank you kindly," said Vaughan acidly. "But I've no wish to win by default." He frowned. "Of course, you are a—er, a touch old for her, and that might—"

"Nine yearrrs isnae a major gulf," growled MacDougall.

"Nine? Why, if she's a day over nineteen, I'll—"

"*What?*" gasped Diccon, his head jerking up.

"Hoot-toot! 'Tis Miss *Fanny* is the laddie's one and only!" howled MacDougall.

Vaughan stammered, "Eh? You never supposed—?"

"You said 'Miss Warrington,' you block! Marietta's the elder."

"Oh. But you argued that she's so beautiful, and I thought surely—"

"So she is, deuce take you! What—are you quite blind?"

"Well, I—er, I—" To each man his own vision, thought Vaughan, and said with rare tact, "I suppose once my eyes had rested on Miss Fanny, I simply didn't see anyone else!"

MacDougall was at his elbow with a beaming grin, a mug, and a bottle of cognac. "Will ye no sluice some o' this over yer ivories, Lieutenant?"

"By George, but I will!" said Vaughan.

"We all will!" With not a twinge of saintly regret that Marietta had just lost a splendid suitor, Diccon raised his mug. "A toast to your good fortune in having found your true 'one and only,' Joss. And may your courtship prosper!"

"And yours also," said Vaughan. They drank again and he exclaimed, "Hi! I've had a thought!"

MacDougall lifted his glass willingly. "Losh, but we'll drink tae *that!*"

"No—seriously," said Vaughan. "If I win my lovely lady, *your* lovely lady won't be obliged to marry for convenience, Diccon! Don't you see? I'm perfectly able to support the family! And you needn't tell me you're too destitute to be an acceptable *parti!* You may not claim your title, but you've a fine old name, and I seem to recall your mentioning once that you've a sizeable inheritance from your grandmama, to say nothing of all that back pay still owing you! And only look at this splendid estate. Oh, I know it's been let go to seed, but if you was to turn it into a producing farm it would likely support you comfortably. There! Our troubles are over!"

"If the lassies will hae either of ye," qualified MacDougall.

"Of course they will," said Vaughan. "How could they refuse such a dashing pair? I'll own I never expected to have a rascally free-trader for a brother-in-law, but barring that complication, there's nought to stand in our way! Here's to love and a pair of betrothals!"

Diccon echoed the toast heartily. The threatened barrier between them had disappeared, which was certainly a cause for rejoicing, and not for the world would he throw a shadow over Vaughan's happiness. But there were still formidable obstacles in his own path. Firstly, of course, was the tragedy of his mama; and then, even if Vaughan was accepted and the financial security of the Warringtons assured, Marietta might not want Diccon Paisley for her husband. Furthermore, the menace of the Swiss and his mighty killing machine, Ti Chiu, remained, and Sir Gavin and Blake Coville had to be reckoned with. The final and most potentially deadly threat was the newly arrived letter now residing in his pocket. But perhaps he was borrowing trouble. More than likely his suspicions were completely unjust. They had better be unfounded, by heaven! They *must* be!

If you was to ask me, miss," said Mrs. South, leaning over the counter of her tiny haberdashery and post office and speaking in a hushed voice, "that queer foreign lady takes advantage, expecting you to collect her mail!"

Marietta had walked to Cloud Village on this cool morning to buy knitting wool and some buttons for Fanny's new evening gown. She took up the two letters addressed to Madame Olympias in care of Sir Lionel Warrington, and gave Mrs. South the three letters to be sent off. She could not but feel deceitful when she replied excusingly that Madame Olympias paid a generous rent in exchange for being allowed to leave her caravan on dower house property. "All we really do in return is keep an eye on the caravan and pick up her letters and messages."

"Aye, but it's an imposition, if I may be so bold as to say it. What's more, with all the open land round here, I don't see why that there caravan has to be on Lanterns' property!"

"Why, Madame Olympias has to leave it somewhere safe, you know. She is in Town most of the time."

"Even so, there's something very strange about that Madame, if you was to ask me. No one never sees her come. No one never sees her go. And *where* do she come *from* or go *to?* Aha! There you are then, ain'tcha! On top of my boy disappearing of hisself like that, I mean! I wouldn't be surprised if—"

To Marietta's relief Mrs. South's surprise was forgotten when Blake Coville came in, ducking his curly head as he entered the little shop and brightening it with his easy, assured charm. He dazzled Mrs. South with a smile, and bowed to Marietta. He had chanced to catch sight of her as he was driving through the village, he said, and nothing would do but that he take her home.

The sky was acquiring a whitish look and the wind was a little more chill than she'd expected, and her shawl too light to provide much warmth. Marietta accepted Coville's offer gladly, and made a mental note that some story must be conjured up to shield her aunt from a suspicion of witchcraft.

He carried out her small parcels and handed her into the stylish curricle. "What luck to have captured you!" he said with an air of triumph.

"Lucky for me, certainly. I thought you had gone back to Town, so that Sir Gavin could meet with the—er, sheikh, did you say?"

He threw the warm rug over her knees, swung into the curricle and took up the reins a small villager had held for him. "Correct, ma'am." Tossing a coin to the child, he guided his team along the cobbled street. "I could scarce wait to get back here. Dare I hope you missed me? You were in my thoughts every—"

"Oh! Do have a care!" she exclaimed.

He had driven to where the street widened outside the Seven Seas tavern and turned his team neatly but at a pace that caused a sturdy man in smock and gaiters to jump for his life.

"Look before you leap!" shouted Coville laughingly. "Egad, Miss Marietta, how do you bear this bucolic wilderness? The dim-witted yokels alone would drive me berserk!"

"That particular dim-wit is Jed Westmere. He was near blinded by a mine blast at the Battle of Badajoz, and probably did not expect anyone to be driving on a narrow street at such a rate!"

"Oh, dear!" He gave her a quizzical look. "Then I beg his pardon. Come now, lovely one, do not pinch at me when I've missed you so." She still looked stern and he added cajolingly, "I've brought you a little surprise from the metropolis."

Marietta glanced at the small package he placed on the seat between them, and realized that her feelings for Blake Coville had undergone a subtle change. She felt vaguely disloyal to be in the curricle beside him because, charming as he may be, he was Diccon's enemy.

"Come now, open it," he urged. "You're never going to forbid that I give you a very small token of my—regard?"

His eyes were full of laughter, the high crowned hat was set at a jaunty angle on his thick hair, and his coat emphasized the breadth of those fine shoulders. He was undeniably a very handsome man, and the eyes of every female they passed followed him admiringly. 'Which he knows,' thought Marietta. But after all, he would be a fool not to know it. And, besides, she was not betrothed, and was under obligation to no one. Impatient with herself she took up the little box and unwrapped it.

The brooch was of gold filigree around a central oval on which was painted a picture of old London Bridge, as seen from the river. The detail was extraordinary for such a miniature work and Marietta exclaimed, "How lovely it is! Oh, but I cannot accept, Mr. Coville. You are too kind, but you must know it would not be—"

"Now pray do not say it would not be proper! You will note it is a poor gift really, for I chose with care and there are no jewels, and the gold is likely brass! Furthermore, it is a used piece that I came upon in Town and hoped might not offend."

"Poor gift, indeed! It is an antique and I suspect valuable! And as for the gold being brass—" She broke off, for he was watching her with a broad grin. "Oh, but you are teasing me. No, sir, truly I am most grateful, but—"

"You must consider me a poor friend if so simple a gift cannot be accepted. Have I offended, Miss Marietta? Or is it, perhaps, that my step-brother has been turning you against us? He is very cunning and can twist truths to suit—"

"Please stop, Mr. Coville! Major Paisley has been very kind to us and—"

"Whereas I am *unkind* and too evil to dare present a little gift?"

"No! I did not mean that at all, but—"

"If you will not accept the brooch, ma'am, what else am I to believe? I had hoped you were beginning to think of me as— more than a friend. In spite of the depth of my own feelings, I've taken care not to move too fast, but you must know what my intentions are."

Suddenly, her mouth was dry. Again, she searched his face. The boyish grin had vanished. He looked sad, and she knew she had hurt him. So he really meant to offer for her. That was surely the highest tribute a man could pay a lady. It was what she had hoped for, wasn't it? Papa would be ecstatic with joy. Any sensible maiden would at this point lower her lashes and tremble and flutter her fan while stammering shyly that she did not know what he meant, so that he would be obliged to declare himself. She heard herself saying instead, "How could I think you either unkind or evil, when you and Sir Gavin have been our good friends? I promise you that Major Diccon Paisley does not speak of your quarrel. Certainly, I do not wish to distress you. The brooch is delightful and I will accept it most gratefully."

He gave a whoop of triumph. "Splendid! And you will wear

it? Not take it home and hide it away in your jewel box?"

She laughed. "I will put it on now, if you wish."

He did wish, and drew the team to a halt while she pinned the brooch to her shawl. "There," she said, turning for his appraisal. "Does it look nice?"

His admiring gaze was not on the brooch but on her smiling face. He said huskily, "No. It looks fairly breathtaking!"

CHAPTER XII

em Bridger climbed down from the box of the old coach and handed Madame Olympias out. "Coming on to rain, marm," he said in his crisp London voice. "What time shall I call for you?"

"Oh, dear! I don't know!" She scanned peaceful meadows and the rich loom of the encircling woodland, and murmured, "What a bother this is! Were we followed, do you think?"

"I don't, marm. Likely we might be on the way back, for Miss Marietta's right, and folks is curious, no use denying. They want to see where I go to meet up with Madame's coach."

Mrs. Cordova sighed. It was all Isolde Maitland's fault. The wretched woman had cornered Fanny after Church and demanded to know how Madame Olympias arrived at Lanterns, and where she came from. Fanny's inventive mind had not failed her. Madame, she'd said, had been born a gypsy but had married into a noble house. Sadly, the family had fallen upon bad times, and when she was left a widow, Madame had found herself very short of funds. She had resumed her occupation of telling fortunes, but in the strictest secrecy, for, however impoverished, her late husband's family was proud and would be horrified if they discovered the source of her income. To preserve her secret she occasionally borrowed her sister-in-law's coach, but instructed the coachman to set her down at some distance from Lanterns. Sometimes, she would walk through the woods to her caravan. Sometimes, she would send a message asking that Bridger call for her at this or that hedge tavern. After Mrs. South's remarks, Marietta had thought it necessary to reinforce this tale, and Bridger had driven out in the coach this morning with Madame Olympias hiding under the seat. Once they were sure they were not followed, he'd detoured into a wooded area and when he drove out again Madame Olympias had been "picked up" and was conveyed to her caravan.

She consulted the letters in her reticule. "I've Miss Deerhurst coming at half past eleven," she said. "A Monsieur Gistel at one; he's new and by his writing I think an elderly gentleman. Then there's old Mrs. Middlewich. And I'd not put it past Isolde Maitland to call without an appointment! You'd better come at four o'clock, Bridger."

The coachman nodded, carried a well-supplied picnic hamper into the caravan, and went away.

As soon as she was inside, Madame Olympias brightened. This cosy little place was all her own; she felt stronger here and quite sure of her powers. When she lit the solitary lamp she saw that The Mystical Window Through Time was dusty. She wiped it off with the soft piece of flannel she kept for dusting, but the crystal looked no clearer and she peered at it uneasily. If it refused to cooperate she might have a troublesome time with her new client, this Monsieur Gistel. She wound her little clock and put it on the bookcase, then sat in the impressive bishop's chair, rested her elbows on the round table, and prepared her mind to receive her clients.

Miss Deerhurst arrived punctually, as always. A tall, stringy, twittery spinster, she lived with her uncle in a fine house outside Eastbourne that had been promised to her if she cared for the gentleman for the balance of his lifetime. A good cook and a meticulous housekeeper, she was keeping her part of the bargain, but she mistrusted her crochety old uncle and had confessed that she was often sleepless at night, dreading the prospect of what would become of her when he went to his reward. It would be nice if there was something encouraging to tell the poor woman, but thus far the only indications were that the house would be left elsewhere and Miss Deerhurst's future would not be bright. No point in telling her that. Time enough for sorrow when the blow fell. Therefore, Madame Olympias listened patiently to her fears, told her some entirely spurious stories of ladies she'd known in similar circumstances upon whom Fortune had smiled, and after consulting the Mystical Window Through Time, sent Miss Deerhurst home twittering with excitement because of the 'stranger' who would soon appear to change her life.

There was now plenty of time for a leisurely luncheon, but the rumble of carriage wheels and a shrill female voice announced the arrival of the Widow Maitland, even as Madame Olympias had anticipated.

"I care not if you've other appointments," announced the unscheduled client, sweeping into the caravan with a rustle of petticoats and a snap of her hard dark eyes. "They must wait! I was most displeased with my last sitting. At the rates you charge, Madame, one is entitled to expect satisfactory results. No! I do not wish to hear excuses! You were not, I am assured, concentrating properly, or else your Mystical Window was clouded or something. It certainly looks murky now," she added snidely as she seated herself across the table. "Most murky! And you need not bother with all your Jupiter in the ascendants, or Moon in transportation, or such fustian. I am not easily gulled, I promise you. I expect to be married within the year, and I wish to know if it is truth that the gentleman in question may soon be rescued from his financial, er—embarrassments."

'The horrid woman is afraid Lionel will slip through her clutches if one of the girls marries well,' thought Madame. "'Ave I not tell you at your last consult this gentleman is not for you?" she purred, slipping a hit in under the widow's guard.

Mrs. Maitland scowled. "You told me almost nothing! I require more details. Look into your Mystical Window if you please, and tell me by what means this change in his finances is to be accomplished."

Madame Olympias first demanded her fee, plus the amount the widow had neglected to pay after her previous visit.

Mrs. Maitland quivered with rage, but fumbled in her reticule and tossed the coins onto the table.

'Two guineas wrest from the miserly clutch-fist,' thought Madame Olympias gleefully. However, she really tried to give value for her fees and she concentrated upon her Mystical Window. It was still clouded, which was worrisome, but she said with high drama that she saw nothing worthwhile in Mrs. Maitland's present romantic interest. "A male is in your future, but yes. Another gentleman. This male, he is not. For this male there is much trouble." To her inner dismay the last sentence came involuntarily.

Abandoning her interest in "this male" Mrs. Maitland demanded to know more of the other "gentleman" and Madame Olympias painted a glowing if unidentifiable portrait of good looks allied to rank and fortune so that her client finally departed with far less antagonism.

As the door closed Mrs. Cordova sighed with relief, but the unscheduled consultation had taken almost an hour and there was little time now for anything but a hasty nibble at her bread and butter and sliced cold pork. She was sipping a glass of milk when the caravan rocked. A cow or some large animal must have brushed against the steps. Glass in hand, she went over to pull aside the window curtain and peep out. She stared, transfixed. A very tall individual was sauntering towards the steps watching a groom who, although not above average height, seemed to her to be gigantic. Immensely broad, with chunky legs and long powerful arms, his features were of an Oriental cast and as if hewn from solid rock; the mouth a narrow slit and the eyes deep-set and almost hidden under the heavy overhanging brow. He had evidently circled the caravan, and he approached the tall man and appeared to make a brief report. His employer nodded and the groom turned and strolled towards the carriage that waited in the shadow of the trees.

Emma Cordova flew back to her little table and whisked her

lunch from sight, wondering with considerable indignation whatever this Frenchman had expected that he must be so cautious. To be ambushed by gypsies, perhaps? To be set upon and robbed by a gang of thieves of which she was the ringleader?

In response to a firm knock she called harshly, "Be pleased to enter."

He came in, stooping so as not to bang his head on the lintel. Straightening, he said in perfect English, "Henri Gistel, madame. I am expected, no?"

The smile that curved the full red lips was not reflected in a pair of very dark eyes that were strangely dull and devoid of expression. He removed his hat politely, revealing lank black hair that emphasized the extreme pallor of his long, narrow face. His demeanour was respectful and mannerly, his garments of excellent fabric and superb tailoring. He seated himself in the opposite chair and Mrs. Cordova's resentment was forgotten. She sensed power, and a threat that caused her heart to flutter. Struggling against a strong compulsion to run away, she stammered, "I regret, Monsieur Gistel, but my crystal it—er, is today clouded. In fairness I—I will postpone your appointment."

His smile did not waver, nor did he make any attempt to rise but instead began to strip off his gloves. "Perhaps Madame would be more comfortable did we converse in French?"

It was blandly said, but his eyes mocked her. "Madame is comfortable," she lied defiantly. "You make the other appointment, yes?"

"But—no, ma'am. I have no time to waste. Your crystal seems clear enough. Perhaps you did not look closely."

She forced her reluctant gaze to The Mystical Window Through Time. It was clear and gleaming. By the very force of his presence this strange man had enhanced her psychic abilities.

The chink of coins broke through her astonishment. Monsieur Gistel had placed five guineas on the table, one after another in a straight line. 'Five guineas!' she thought, and said, "Monsieur is also, I have think, a psychic."

He shook his head. "I was a priest at one time. I am now many things, and at present an art collector. But I will admit to a deep interest in mysticism. You are rumoured to possess a genuine gift, Madame. That is what brought me to you."

And five guineas was five guineas! "Do you desire that I look into the past, Monsieur? Or is it your future that—"

An impatient gesture silenced her. He folded his hands on the table. They were well-manicured hands and so white that the black hairs stood out in sharp relief. Leaning forward, his eyes seemed to bore into hers. "I am interested in a certain work of art called *The Sigh of Saladin*. I wish to know if, in fact, it exists."

She bent over the crystal for fear that she might betray her excitement. She had at least part of the answer to his question. If she could discover some more he might even add to his already enormous largesse.

She gazed deep and deeper, the minutes ticking away while Monsieur Gistel waited in a tense and obviously hungry silence. Never had the crystal seemed so clear. "Ah," she intoned in her best mystical voice. "I see a knight . . . a knight in armour. From long ago. He comes home bearing a gift for his bride. It is . . . *magnifique!*"

"Then it really does exist! Can you see it? Where is it now?"

"I see a small picture wrought in . . . in gold and gems. Very old and dirty. But beautiful still. It is there . . . at the manor house."

"Ah!" he said eagerly. "You mean Lanterns, yes? Well, go on, go on! Whereabouts, exactly?"

Another interval of peering silently. She said, "Many have search. For centuries they seek. But no one has found. It . . . stands up straight. And it is with . . . music. Alas, it is fading. I can no longer see."

She spoke truly. The bright clarity of the crystal had faded. Monsieur Gistel continued to question her, but she replied erratically, for now there was in the depths of her Mystical Window a swirling mist that came very seldom and was invariably of great significance. She held her breath, hoping she was to be given the location of the treasure. Instead, she caught a glimpse of something that had nothing to do with the legendary *Sigh of Saladin*. The vision was brief but quite clear, and it made her very frightened indeed.

❧

Did it work?" Diccon raced up the stairs and into the northernmost bedchamber and the table that had been set before the open window.

Vaughan turned, his eyes alight with triumph. "See for yourself!"

A broad-based candle lay on its side in a tray that had been the breastplate of a suit of armour. The flame was extinguished but a thin spiral of smoke hung on the air.

Diccon gave a whoop and clapped Vaughan on the back. "Did it stay lit until after it landed?"

"Yes. I blew it out. Not much doubt that it will ignite the powder, but we'll have to take care not to use too much. Don't want to burn down your—"

"Why are you playin' with the candle?"

The two men turned quickly.

The Scourge of the Spanish Main watched them from the doorway, the skull-and-crossbones drooping in one hand and a forlorn expression in his blue eyes.

"Well, if it isn't Captain Detestable Dag," said Diccon with a flourishing bow. "Lieutenant Vaughan told me you were going off to scourge a few seas. Did you sink any merchantmen?"

"We din't go. Eric forgot."

The resignation in the small face caused the two men to exchange a quick glance.

Arthur asked, "What're you doing, Sir G'waine?"

"Building a signal."

"Why?"

Vaughan said, "If thieves should come Major Diccon might need help, and since he—"

"Diccon wouldn't need no help with thieves! He'd kill 'em all dead!"

His dark eyes twinkling, Vaughan said, "Don't doubt it a bit."

"The thing is," said Diccon with a smile, "if there was a— er, gang of the bounders, Detestable, even I might need help."

"*Even* you!" snorted Vaughan.

"Oh," said Arthur dubiously. "Well, how's a candle goin' to help you?"

Diccon lifted the small impromptu shelf they'd fashioned on top of the table. "You see how the front of the shelf folds down unless I hold it up?"

"Yes. Why has it got that long piece of string tied to it?"

"Because," Vaughan fed the string over a rough frame they'd erected across the desk and pulled it tight and the shelf was held securely in place.

Diccon put the candle on top. "The string goes all the way downstairs and we tie it around that big cauldron in the kitchen. So long as it stays tight, the shelf stays up. But if someone bad should break in, we'd only have to lift the cauldron or cut the string and the shelf would fold down, dropping the candle onto the pan. Do you see?"

Arthur knit his brows. "It wouldn't make 'nuff noise to fright a thief, I don't think."

"Quite right," said Diccon. "Only we'll have a thin line of black powder under the shelf, leading to the far end of the table."

"Oh. So when the candle falls down, it sets light to the pow-der? If it's just a thin line it still won't make much of a bang, Diccon."

"No," agreed Vaughan. "But those will."

Arthur looked at the collection of intriguing packets on the window end of the table, and his eyes became very wide indeed. "*Fireworks?*"

Diccon nodded. "Fireworks."

"An' the powder will catch 'em alight?"

Vaughan said laughingly, "We certainly hope so. If they all

go shooting out of the window, they'll be seen for miles and people will come to help."

"Ooooh! Diccon, can we—"

"I'm afraid not, old fellow. But we'll have a show on Guy Fawkes' Day, how's that?"

Arthur's face fell. "It's in November. An' it's a long way from now."

Diccon knew that Vaughan's plans for the day had included taking Fanny for a drive. His eyes asked a question. Vaughan nodded and said, "You're not forgetting that your doctor prescribed sea air? Why don't you get to it? Mac can help me set that fallen block into the wall downstairs and there'll still be time for my—er, activities."

"Thanks, Joss. Well, Detestable, will you take me along in your galleon?"

His answer was a shout of joy and a crushing hug, and down to the beach they marched, hand in hand.

Diccon was relegated to the rank of Bo'sun and when the Detestable Dag was safely aboard, he bent to his oars and, obeying the command of the Scourge of the Seven Seas, sang heartily,

> No matter your rank, you'll walk the plank
> If you drift across our bow!
> So stay well clear of the buccaneer
> Who's taken The Brotherhood's vow!

Joining the chorus in a piercing scream, Captain Detestable waved the skull-and-crossbones flag with one hand while clinging to the side of the rowing boat with the other.

> Sing Ho for the Jolly Roger flag!
> Sing Ho for the Spanish Main!
> Daring and bold is Detestable Dag
> You'll not see his like again!
> Yo . . . Ho!
> No never his like again!

Pleased with their efforts, they laughed together, and Captain Detestable exclaimed, "Oh, jolly good, Bo'sun!"

The wind was rising, and the rowing boat plunged into a trough. Diccon slanted a glance at the lowering clouds.

Whether or not it is designated a "galleon" a small boat in choppy seas can play havoc with the strongest stomach, but although Arthur gripped the side tightly, his eyes were bright with excitement. What great fun it would be, he said, if they should be shipwrecked. On a desert island.

"Great fun," agreed Diccon solemnly. "But I don't think there is one nearby."

"Then let's go to one far-by!"

Diccon chuckled, but Arthur's face clouded. "He'd be sorry then," he muttered. " 'Specially if we wasn't found for days 'n days!"

In an attempt to alleviate that hurt, Diccon said, "If truth be told I suspect your brother saw weather blowing up and had enough sense to stay on dry land."

"Then he could've taked me with him in the new coach." Arthur scowled. "He told Etta he'd got to meet someone 'portant, but he din't even say g'bye to me when he drove out. He'd forgot."

"Well *we'd* best not forget we're out here looking for a prize. Keep your eyes open, Skipper!"

They sighted sails on the horizon and gave chase, but the cowardly East Indiaman fled before them. A large piece of floating driftwood became a Portuguese pirate frigate and they gave her a broadside, then boarded her and had just sent several members of her villainous crew on a stroll along the legendary "plank" when the bow of the rowing boat drove through a wave and a cloud of icy spray soaked them both. Arthur shrieked exuberantly. Shaking salt water from his eyes, Diccon gasped, "Whew! I'll be for it when Miss Marietta discovers I took you out in heavy weather!"

"She won't mind. She's a good sport. D'you think she's pretty, Bo'sun?"

A brief pause, then, "Aye, Cap'n. I do. Hold tight now, we must turn about and make a run for our home port!"

Arthur had to use both hands to hang on this time, but he showed no sign of fear and when the boat was on a more even keel once more he shouted, "Mr. Williard wants her for a wife. Would he be my uncle then?"

"No, old fellow. Your brother-in-law."

Indignant, Arthur exclaimed, "I don't want him for a brother 'law!" He considered, looking glum, then asked, "I 'spect *you* wouldn't like to have Etta for a wife, would you? She's nice. For a girl, you know."

Again, Diccon did not at once reply, then he said rather breathlessly, "Miss Marietta is—very nice. And I would."

"Oh. Well, are you goin' to?"

"I'm—afraid not. Here comes another big one!"

The big one successfully negotiated they headed in to the calmer waters of the little cove and Arthur persisted, "Why not? Etta likes you better'n that old Mr. Williard. 'Sides, if you had her for a wife you wouldn't go 'way, would you?"

Touched by this betraying question, Diccon smiled down into the small wet face, and the boy beamed back, then shouted, "There she is!"

Marietta was walking down the sands of the cove, her cloak flying in the wind.

"Caught red-handed!" said Diccon, his heart giving its customary leap at the sight of her.

Arthur teased, "You'll be for it now, Bo'sun!" He waved, and howled, "Here we are, Etta!"

Shipping the oars Diccon jumped over the side and began to haul the boat up the beach. Marietta ran to help, then had to back away from an incoming wave. "Oh, for a pair of your hip boots," she said, laughingly.

Arthur waved the skull-and-crossbones as Diccon lifted him over the side. "Ladies don't wear hip boots! You'd look funny, Etta. I'm Cap'n Detes'ble Dag and we been pirates and we singed—sung, a pirate song. Very loud. Bo'sun Diccon can't sing, but he's a good row-er. Are you cross? Is he 'for it'?"

"He will be if you take a chill! You're soaked through!"

"Run all the way up to the manor," urged Diccon. "Please, Captain Detestable. For my sake!"

"Oh, all right!" Arthur started off, then turned back. "Is you goin' to ask her now?"

Marietta turned to look at Diccon curiously.

He felt his face burn, and said gruffly, "I'll let you know when I do. Off with you, brat, and tell the Lord of the Larder to get you warm and dry and find something for you to eat!"

Chuckling, the boy trotted off.

Diccon hauled the boat higher up the beach. "I'm sorry he got wet. I'd not expected weather to blow up so fast, though Lord knows I should have. This coast is famous for that very thing."

Marietta seized the starboard side and tugged mightily. "I suppose my brother charmed you into overriding your better judgment."

"Well, he— Oh, have a care!"

She had tripped on her cloak, and he sprang to lift her as she tumbled to the sand.

"What a fumble-fingers I am," she said, sitting up and tidying her skirts, her heart warmed because of the anxiety in his eyes. "No—don't say it was your fault and that you should never have taken Arthur out on the water in such weather. It was more than kind, and you cannot know how grateful I am. The poor child was so disappointed when Eric had to leave."

Diccon knelt there, drinking in her loveliness so close beside him. His voice a caress, he said, "You must know how fond I am of the boy. He's a grand little fellow."

"Yes, he is, but I'm afraid he has taken you over and you must not let him impose on— Oh, dear!" she exclaimed, interrupting herself. "And here I am come to impose once again, and ask if you were able to talk with Eric. He said nothing of his visit to you, save that he covets Orpheus."

"He's not the only one. Yes, we had a chat. Rather brief, unfortunately. I tried to drop a few hints, but he doesn't know me

yet, after all, and I've no wish to seem too avuncular. Too soon."
She looked at him sharply, and he added a fast, "I think he's
rather shy of this awesome old chap."

"Yes." She said ruefully, "He's awfully young, even for two
and twenty. It seems to me that I was older at that age."

"But that, of course, was very long ago."

"Wretch!" She laughed. "I suppose we all look back and
think how much wiser we were than those who came after us.
But—he is just a boy, Diccon. And very dear to me. You will
try again? Please?"

He said softly, "How could I deny such a very . . . poor old
lady?"

The silver light was in his eyes. A tremor shook her. His lips,
which could be so stern, were curved to a smile of such tenderness that she was suddenly desperate to feel them on her own.
Breathlessly, she waited.

Diccon had felt her tremble. Her lovely face seemed to him
to glow. He reached out and drew her closer and she did not resist. Her eyes were so soft, her lips slightly parted. Enchanted,
he bowed his head and leaned towards them.

A gust of wind sent her cloak flying. Through a golden haze
he saw something glitter on her shawl. And the cold knifeblade
of reality slashed through and destroyed that magical moment.

Marietta saw his face change, and she pulled back, belatedly
embarrassed by such a shocking lapse of propriety. How could
she have allowed herself to lounge about on a public beach all
but embraced in a man's arms? A comparative stranger, really,
who was—who was staring at her bosom! Her hand went up instinctively to pull her cloak closed. His move was faster.
Shocked, she shrank away, but his fingers had grasped the pin
on her shawl.

In a harsh voice she scarcely recognized he demanded,
"Where did you get this?"

"It was a gift. Let go at once, sir!"

Narrowed and grim, his eyes lifted to search her face. Marietta started up and he released the brooch and helped her to

stand. He said coldly, "Blake Coville gave it to you."

It was a statement rather than a question. Irritated, she said, "Is there some reason why I should not accept a gift from a friend? I think it is none of your affair, Major. Besides, how can you know who gave it me?"

He walked beside her towards the cliff path and answered, "It belonged to my mother."

With a gasp, she halted and turned to face him. "Your— mother? But—but why on earth . . . ? Oh! I *knew* I should not have accepted it!" She tried to unfasten the brooch. "You shall have it back!"

"No. He gave it to you. If you wish to return it, return it to him."

"Well, I will—if I can get the wretch— I mean, if I can get it off. The clasp is caught in my shawl. Oh, why *ever* would Mr. Coville have been so gauche as to give me a piece of jewellery belonging to another lady?"

"Probably in the hope that I would see it, and be plagued by guilt," he said dryly.

She looked up at him. The wind tossed his thick unruly hair about and where the spray had dampened it small curls had plastered themselves against his brow. His head was held high, his mouth tight, and with the darkening clouds behind him he looked stern and formidable. She was reminded of a painting she'd once seen depicting a Roman centurion preparing to lead his men into mortal combat; there was the same hawk look, the same fierce intensity. For some reason she felt a pang of fear.

Not looking at her, he said, "You're wondering if I told you the truth, or if I am as guilty as the Covilles say."

She hesitated. "You said very little of it. Have I the right to ask for the whole story?"

"No." His gaze lowered and softened. "If I told you, it would make you an accessory, do you see? I'd not put you in that position."

Appalled, she faltered, "An accessory to—what? Are you— are you saying—"

He put one long finger across her lips. "Whatever you may think—whatever may happen, will you believe that one most unworthy man cares very much about your happiness?"

She did believe and for an instant she was both grateful and comforted, but his previous remark haunted her and she said, "You're frightening me. And you're evading again. Diccon—can't you at least—"

"Etta? Etta . . . ?"

Mrs. Cordova waved urgently from the top of the cliff. She was obviously agitated, and Marietta hurried to the narrow path, Diccon's supporting hand at her elbow.

"Aunty Dova? What is it? Is Papa—?"

"Your father is well." Mrs. Cordova clutched her arm as they reached the top. "I must talk to you. Something has happened. I knew—" She glanced at the silent man and moaned softly. "I *knew!*"

Alarmed, Marietta asked, "Knew what, dearest? Is Fanny ill? Or—"

"No, no! And Mr. Vaughan, the very nicest boy, is so devoted. . . . Only— Oh dear, oh dear! Come quickly, my love! I'll explain in the carriage. Yes, I made Bridger drive me down. This horrid wind! And that awful pastry man! And Mrs. Maitland again. But—we must *talk* Etta!" She glanced at Diccon, who had drawn back. "Not here! *Privately!*"

"Very well. But I must go and fetch Arthur, he got soaked in the boat and is drying off in—"

"He must wait! Etta, Etta! You do not listen, child! I said *privately!*"

Diccon came up to assist the ladies into the carriage. "I'll bring him to you, ma'am. He's likely bamboozled Mac out of a piece of cake. I'll have him home before dark, I promise."

Marietta thanked him gratefully. He slammed the door and the coach jerked and rattled on its way. The wind was blustering in the trees. She thought absently that it was a good thing he'd not taken the boat very far out. How radiant little Arthur had been. Captain—what had Diccon named him? Detestable

Dag, that was it. She smiled fondly. So much of his time he'd given the child; so much of joy. The coach rocked to a sudden gust. The shrubs beside the drive were whipped apart revealing the man who stood among them. She jerked her head around in time to see Diccon gesture violently. The man plunged into the trees.

"You're not listening to me, Etta," said Mrs. Cordova plaintively. "Now what is it?"

"There was a man hiding in the bushes! A boy, rather. It was Sam South. And I'm sure Diccon knew he was there!"

"Then Mrs. South was right, and her boy was at Lanterns! I am not surprised! Oh, Etta! We have been dreadfully deceived! I was right, the good Lord aid us! We are in the most frightful trouble!"

❧

Jocelyn Vaughan tilted the kitchen chair to a precarious angle and smiled dreamily at the ceiling. He had taken his supper at the dower house and returned to Lanterns late in the evening in an apparent haze of bliss. Busily occupied with the letter he was writing, Diccon paused to slant an oblique glance at him.

"My mind is made up!" declared Vaughan. "Fate, or that roseate little nude who flits about loosing off his arrows, has dealt me a lifetime leveller, and I've not the slightest quarrel with the rascal!"

"Hmm," grunted Diccon, his quill pen scratching across the page.

"None," said Vaughan. "She is the perfect lady for me. I knew it, you know, the instant I looked at her."

"Really? I thought at first glance you took her for a dummy."

MacDougall, who sat by the stove polishing Diccon's riding boots, chuckled and said, "A flush hit, y'ken!"

"Yes, and d'you know why?" Vaughan straightened his chair, narrowly avoided knocking over the branch of candles, and retaliated indignantly, "He's jealous! I found the lady of my heart and mean to offer for her with no backing and filling, whereas he sits and glowers and grieves, and does nothing to claim his own love!"

At this Diccon lowered his pen and lifted his head. "Mean to offer for her? What—after a courtship of less than a week? You've maggots in your loft! It's too soon, you silly clod!"

"I let no grass grow under my feet, if that's what you mean. Strike while the iron is hot and all that kind of thing. Don't you agree, Mac?"

"Och aweigh, it makes no never mind; a wench is a wench, forbye. But ma fither used tae say 'love that's soonest hot is soonest cold.' "

"Well, of all the marplots! Miss Fanny is *not* a wench and I'll thank you to watch your tongue, MacDougall! As for you, Major, sir—"

"Gad, and the child is off again." Diccon sighed.

Vaughan's eyes flashed. Standing, he said bleakly, "I'm not a child! I don't want that rascally step-brother of yours for my brother-in-law! And if you mean to let him snatch your lady from under your nose because you lack the gumption to offer—"

Diccon interrupted quietly, "I cannot offer, Joss. You know my feelings on that score."

"Do I? Does anyone—ever—know your true feelings? Oh, you may freeze me, but I'll give you my opinion regardless: with or without a fortune you're a fool not to make a try for the lady. Fanny told me she thinks her sister is half-way in love with you already."

Diccon stared at him. "She never did."

" 'Pon my word! And I think it also. Wake up, man! Don't throw away—"

"Will you stop?" Diccon sprang to his feet and said in a sudden fury, "D'you think I don't know how lovely and dear and desirable she is? D'you think that having found her at last, I *want* to lose her? I'd begun to think I had a chance. But now—I've racked my brain trying to find a way through this bog, but there *is* no way! For the love of God—leave me be!" And with a distraught gesture, he was gone, leaving the door wide behind him as he stamped out into the rainy night.

The two he left behind, looked at each other. After a minute Vaughan rose and went to the door.

MacDougall said pleadingly, "Ye're never after deserrrting him the noo? Mon, he needs ye!"

Vaughan closed the door. "No, I'm not leaving." He straddled the chair Diccon had left and asked, "What is it, Mac? Has something happened that I don't know about?"

"If it has, I dinna ken what it is. A letter came, is all."

"We've been in some pretty tight corners and he's always been a step ahead of everyone else in knowing what to do next. I thought we were friends, Mac, but sometimes I feel that I really don't know him at all."

"He has precious few friends. Since the lassie died." The Scot shrugged. "He lost his family, his music, and then his love. And he but eighteen summers! He put up a wall, y'ken, and let very few come close again till Miss Marietta levelled his wall wi' one glance o' her bonnie eyes. He lost once, and blamed himself—which was fustian, y'ken! But I think—" MacDougall hesitated, embarrassed by such a speech, then finished gruffly, "I think he dared not love again through all these yearrrs. If he loses Miss Marietta . . ."

"He'll build another wall," said Vaughan.

"Aye. And I'm thinking it'll nae come doon this time. It's a lonely life he'll lead behind that wall, Misterrr Vaughan. Nae life at all for a mon wi' sae generous a heartt and sae deep a love for wee bairns."

"No." Vaughan was quiet for a while, then he stood and said, "I'll have to help him, Mac. Whether he wants it or not, I'll have to stop him retreating behind his blasted wall!"

ith typical autumnal inconstancy the morning dawned sunny and bright, the skies blue and innocent of anything more menacing than fluffy white clouds. For Mr. Blake Coville however, reading the letter that had been placed on his breakfast tray, the clouds might have been as dark as those that had carried yesterday's storm. His appetite ruined, he stared, haggard-eyed, at those few deadly lines:

Blake Coville, Esq.,
Care of Lord Dale
Downsdale Park
Near Seaford
Sussex

Sir:

The extension on your loan expired at the end of August. The collateral you put up has now been forfeited, and if the balance is not paid in full by October 15th, we shall have no recourse but to apply to Sir Gavin Coville for redress.

We regret the necessity for such a procedure but it is

our belief that we have been more than patient in this matter.

We expect to hear from you by return post.

Yrs. etc.,

Benjamin Kagel

The signature was one to strike terror into the hearts of countless London beaux who had lived too high and resorted to a moneylender in the belief that just a small loan could be easily repaid next quarter-day. For Coville, crippling rates of interest, plus the conviction that one good win at turf or tables would rescue him, had brought him to within a hairsbreadth of ruin. If Sir Gavin discovered that not only was his entire allowance encumbered, but that Lady Pamela's famous Paisley Emeralds were paste, he would be disowned. Not for an instant, knowing his father's unforgiving nature, did he doubt this terrible consequence of his folly. Indeed, it was quite possible that his sire would stand by, unmoved, while he was cast into Newgate Prison.

Fighting the panic that made him break out in a cold sweat, he bit at one fingernail and stared at the toast on his tray. If only Papa had moved faster in the matter of that arrogant heathen sheikh and *The Sigh of Saladin*! If only he himself had been able to locate the confounded article! But there was nought to be served by lying here fretting. He'd go over to the Lanterns dower house. The Warrington chit knew more than she'd admitted, he was sure. Lord knows, she should. She seemed to spend most of her waking moments hanging about his curst step-brother. Perhaps she counted on his finding the treasure. Perhaps he already had!

Swearing, Coville snatched at the bell-rope and tugged it imperatively.

✤

Marietta had expected to be in the village for a very short time, but after delivering the flowers to the small and ancient church she stopped at Mrs. South's shop to pick up the mail. It appeared that half the village population was gathered around outside, or had squeezed inside, full of excitement because young Samuel South had returned "from the dead."

It was as much as Marietta could do to get through the door, but once inside there was no getting out again until she'd been regaled with the story that she'd already heard three times, at least. Samuel, it seemed, had been captured by a press gang and delivered to a merchant ship. After some adventures "on the High Seas" which became more hair-raising with each retelling, the vessel had returned to the Pool of London. He'd managed to escape and had at last made his way home. Sam was in the shop, grinning from ear to ear, thoroughly enjoying his notoriety. He looked bronzed and the picture of health, far from the ill-used and starving victim of a brutal ship's captain. Marietta was reminded that when the tale had reached Sir Lionel's ears he'd dismissed it as poppycock, saying that if the boy had been aboard ship at all it was likely a free-trader's ketch, and that he'd gone willingly, in search of adventure. Whereupon, of course, she had seized the opportunity to remark that another of the crimes laid at Diccon's door could be dismissed.

Having exclaimed properly and congratulated Samuel's proud parent on his safe return, Marietta succeeded at last in claiming her letters. She went outside to find Bridger looking irritated because he'd been obliged to walk the team several times around the village while waiting for her. She wouldn't have taken the carriage at all save that there had been such a great armful of flowers to be delivered, but the wind was rising now and she was glad enough to climb inside and settle back against the worn squabs.

One of Aunty Dova's spangles sparkled on the seat beside her. She took it up absently, thinking of the little lady and of the terrible warning she claimed to have seen in her Mystical Window Through Time. The picture of Eric flying for his life with dragoons close on his heels was frightening indeed. It was also nonsensical.

Eric had always been the soul of honour. Some years ago when one of his school friends had been caught cheating, he'd been horrified and quite cast down because someone he liked had done so shocking a thing. Even as a very small boy he'd always played fair—when he played. She smiled faintly. Actually, he'd not much cared for competitive sports, his interest tending to wane so that he would soon wander off and find some less taxing activity. He'd once engaged in a fiery discussion with Papa on the subject of politics and it had become clear that he had only scorn for the present government. But that was not alarming, for most young men seemed to enjoy railing against established order. The memory of his sudden affluence brought a worried frown. But although she could not like his leaving the university and venturing into the risky world of finance, it would scarcely bring the military after him.

Impatient with her worries, she picked up the mail and glanced through it. A bill from the haberdashers in Eastbourne. Another from *The Times*—a luxury Papa refused to forego. A letter— She stared with a qualm of unease at her own name inscribed in Eric's familiar scrawl. She had supposed him to be on his way home. If he was writing, it must mean that he was delayed. She broke the seal hurriedly.

My dearest Etta:

This will come as a shock, but I cannot spare the time to be tactful.

I sensed that you doubted my tale of handling the investments of wealthy gentlemen. You were right, love. Have you heard the term "industrial espionage"? That is what I am doing, Etta. I am at present entrusted with the details of a new kind of fuel for lamps. It's in the experimental stage, and, as you may guess, is guarded jealously. I am to deliver a copy of the formula to a German competitor. Are you much shocked? I hope not.

However, it is against the law. And I have been found out. I don't think they know my identity, as yet, but although I dodge about Town there are Runners hard after me.

I must get out of the country, and thanks to you I think I know how to manage this. I write to warn you to be on your guard if any Runner or Constable should come poking around.

Don't despise me, dearest and best beloved of sisters. I have done what seemed best for us. I can but pray I have not disgraced you. If things go well I will escape this beastly net and come to you with all speed. Meanwhile, be careful, and try to think lovingly of

Yr. ever devoted brother,
Eric

⚜

Ignatius, Lord Dale, ate alone in the Downsdale Park breakfast parlour, which was just as well, for despite the pale sunlight that beamed in through the windows he was not in the best of humours. The information that Mr. Blake Coville had taken himself off for an early ride did not distress him. One would be as well pleased, he thought, if that young pest would take himself back to Town and remain there. His sire had been a tiresome enough guest, with his studied elegance and grave know-it-all demeanour, but at least Sir Gavin hadn't set the maids in an uproar and caused the usually placid housekeeper to fly into the boughs and carry tales to Lady Dale.

Leaving the breakfast parlour, his lordship wandered down the corridor, frowning because the expected packet had still not arrived. It was an ugly business that should have been nipped in the bud long ago. Not a bit of use old Smollet holding him to blame because that damned ass had eaten the original report. If the London people were so anxious, they should have sent a rider down here at the gallop with the replacement pages.

He opened the door to his study. This room was inviolate, even to his own family, for although it was not generally known, the stout, snobbish, and far from impressive baron also possessed a keen diplomatic sense and often dealt with matters vital to the security of the nation. Lost in thought, he stepped onto the thick rug, looked up, and stiffened in outraged astonishment. He could move fast at need, and his hand flashed to a cabinet drawer and emerged gripping a small pistol. Aiming it steadily at the tall man who was engrossed in the papers on his big desk, he said, "How the devil you broke in here, sir, I don't know. But—" He broke off, glowering as the intruder turned to face him. "You! Gathering more snacks for your confounded donkey, perchance? I caught you fairly this time, you treacherous scoundrel! You may consider yourself under arrest!"

⚜

More flour! More flour!" said Fanny, glancing up from shelling peas to check on her unlikely assistant baker.

Swathed in a large white apron, with a dab of flour on the end of his nose, Vaughan raised two hands covered in sticky dough and surveyed them with revulsion. It had looked so easy when he'd arrived and found Miss Fanny kneading her bread. She'd dismissed his pleas to go for a walk on this beautiful morning, saying the bread must be "set to rise" before she could leave. Watching her in fascination, he'd begged to be allowed to "have a turn," and she'd agreed, saying with amusement what fun it would be to have "a dashing aristocrat" toiling in her kitchen.

Now, he spread his doughy fingers and reached for the flour bin, only to have her jump up and run to use a scoop to sprinkle the board.

"You can go on, now," she advised, returning to her chair.

"How much longer?"

"Until it's smooth, of course," she said, dimples flashing.

"But every time it's smooth, you say it's got to have blisters."

"So it does. I'll tell you when it's ready." She glanced at him from under her lashes and said, "Perhaps my sister will come back by then, and you'll be able to have your chat without bothering to take me for a walk first."

"Jove," he exclaimed, glancing to the windows apprehensively. "If Miss Marietta's coming back I'd best get cleaned up."

A tiny frown wrinkled Fanny's brow. Lost in love, she had been counting the minutes till he arrived, and it had been a little hurtful when his first request had been to see Marietta. He had asked twice how long it would be before Bridger drove her home from Cloud Village, and while kneading the dough he had lapsed into profound silences as though considering some weighty problem.

She said, "If you are so anxious to be ready for Marietta, by all means leave that, Mr. Vaughan. I had not meant to delay you, and I can finish the kneading while you wash your hands." She was sure he would realize she was quizzing him and would respond with some of the light-hearted banter that sprang up so comfortably between them. Vaughan, however, was preoccupied, and without comment began to take off his apron.

There had been only one adoring look from him today, and that very brief. Perhaps his affections were not as deeply engaged as she'd dared to dream. He was, after all, a brilliant prize on the Marriage Mart, who could walk into Almack's and take his pick from the cream of the current crop of highly born damsels. What a contrast was Miss Fanny Warrington, who never had been and probably never would be presented to Society. Marietta, on the other hand, had been presented, was beautiful, and didn't make gauche remarks or become impatient with the perplexing creatures called gentlemen. It was not remarkable that once having met her, Blake Coville had never even noticed her little sister. Now it would seem that Jocelyn Vaughan, who had noticed and had stolen her heart away, was also turning his beloved but fickle eyes towards Marietta.

She said rather tartly, "I collect your thoughts are far from bread dough, Mr. Vaughan." And with sad double entendre, "Or did the game lose its appeal once you'd tried it?"

He smiled absently, wondering just how to ease into the subject with Miss Marietta. "I fancy I'm just unskilled is all. You ladies are far better at such tasks."

"Is your cook at Greenwings a female, sir?"

"Good heavens, no! My uncle would faint at the very thought! Our chef is a Frenchman. Quite a famous fellow, in fact."

"Really? Had I known I would have been quite in a quake when setting my poor culinary efforts before you."

The curl of her lip escaped him. He was, he knew, ill-equipped for the role of deus ex machina; God forbid he should worsen a tricky situation. Diccon was such a confoundedly private sort of man; not the type to take kindly to interference, however well-meant. Him and his confounded walls! Why was Fanny looking so put about? Whoops! He must not have answered her! He said quickly, "Oh no. I think it is remarkable how well you do; all things considered. Diccon told me, in fact, that he enjoyed some jolly good meals whilst he stayed here."

'All—things—*considered?*' Love or no love, at this her little chin lifted dangerously. "Is that so?"

"I promise you. He likes plain cooking. Which is surprising when you think that he's travelled about the world a great deal."

Fanny drew a deep breath, then purred, "Indeed? Then, as a 'plain cook' I may consider myself flattered, is that what you say, Mr. Vaughan?"

"Oh, absolutely. Ah, here comes Bridger with the carriage. At last!" All unaware of the daggers that were being hurled his way from a very pretty pair of hazel eyes, Vaughan dried his hands and shrugged into his coat.

"Good morning, Miss Marietta! I've been waiting for you—"

"With the greatest impatience, dearest," put in Fanny, smiling so broadly that all her little teeth were on view. She hurled a damp piece of linen at the much abused dough and, ignoring the fact that it missed and flew into the flour bin, said to her bewildered sister, "Thank goodness you are come to rescue the poor man. He has been bored to distraction in my company. I shall go down and help Papa and leave you in peace. Together. Good day, sir."

I fear I annoyed her." Vaughan sighed and held the back gate open.

Hiding her frustration, Marietta walked through. Eric's letter had left her emotions in a turmoil and she'd intended to at once seek out Aunty Dova, but Vaughan had clearly been waiting for some time and she could scarcely refuse to talk to him. She liked Jocelyn Vaughan. His admiration of Fanny had been apparent from the start, and she had begun to entertain great hopes, for she thought he would be a devoted and responsible husband. She said gravely, "Why, my sister did seem a trifle put about, and she usually has the most sunny disposition."

"With an occasional storm," he said ruefully.

"Do you not care for a lady with spirit? Fanny can fire up, I'll admit, and she can be rather blunt, at times. But her bad humours are very brief and she is always contrite afterwards."

He smiled. "It is what one most likes about her. There's no posturing and fluttering with Miss Fanny. She's the most lovely, feminine little thing, but it's straight from the shoulder with her. The man to win her will have to be prepared to defend his opinions, but he'll know few dull moments, I think."

"You like my little sister very well, I see. In which case I cannot but wonder what you found to quarrel about."

"To say truth, I don't really know, ma'am. I was helping— that is to say, she let me have a shot at kneading the dough, and—"

"I thought so." Smiling, she drew him to a halt and faced him, using her handkerchief to remove the flour from his straight nose and not dreaming that from a distance this innocent task could look like an embrace. "Did you drop the dough, or do something dreadful? She is very proud of her cookery."

They walked on through the meadow towards the little humpbacked bridge that crossed the stream, and he said laughingly, "No, no! Acquit me of such a crime! We got along famously on the cooking front. Then, we were talking about Diccon, and—"

"Ah," said Marietta.

Vaughan glanced at her sharply. "She don't like him. Dare I ask why?"

Marietta hesitated and chose her words with care. "During this past week you've had some chats with my aunt, Mr. Vaughan. Perhaps Diccon has told you of Madame Olympias?"

"No. But I heard talk of her in the village. They say she's very mysterious. I'd like to try for an appointment with the lady. Since she keeps her caravan on your land, I thought you might . . ." His honest eyes widened. "Oh, egad! Never say Mrs. Cordova is . . . ?"

She said with quiet dignity, "I wouldn't say it except to a very close friend. We keep it as secret as possible, of course."

He flushed with pleasure. "I'll not breathe a word to a soul, I swear it. Is your aunt really clairvoyant, Miss Marietta?"

"Oh, yes. Sometimes, rather frighteningly so."

"How jolly splendid! But—I don't quite see what that has to do with Diccon."

"It is that to an extent Fanny takes after Aunty Dova and she is sometimes able to—to sense things about people. She is—it sounds foolish, but she is extreme afraid of the Major."

"The devil, you say! Oh, I beg pardon! But—he's a perfect gentleman, I promise you. How ever has he managed to frighten her?"

"I'm not sure. I don't know that she herself is sure. I think it is just something instinctive. She adores Arthur, and I had hoped that Major Diccon's affection for him would have won her over."

"But it hasn't?"

Marietta looked troubled, and Vaughan said earnestly, "You don't share her prejudices, do you, ma'am? They're quite unjustified. I know he seems a touch haughty and reserved at times, but—well, he's had a beast of a life."

"I gather it has been full of violence. What a pity that he gave up his music. He has such great talent, do not you think?"

"He didn't give it up, Miss Marietta." Vaughan hesitated then overcame his dislike of gossip and launched his "Rescue Diccon" campaign. "I don't know all the details," he began. "He never speaks of his family, as you probably know."

"He did tell me that his grandfather was a fine musician, and that he was taught to play the violin as a very young child."

He nodded. "His father also was a music lover, but he died very suddenly when Diccon was about eleven years old. Mrs. Paisley was shattered by her loss, and quite unable to cope with the world. You may know that she was married again a year later."

"Yes. To Sir Gavin Coville."

"It was a disaster. At least, insofar as Diccon was concerned. Sir Gavin took him in dislike. Probably, it was mutual. Sir Gavin is a stern disciplinarian, very set in his notions, and Diccon I don't doubt was stubbornly resistant to the new order of things. One of Sir Gavin's first commands was that his step-son no longer waste his time on so unmanly a pursuit as music."

"Unmanly!" she exclaimed indignantly. "Why, most gentlemen today play some kind of musical instrument!"

"Quite so. The tricky thing was that Diccon had made some sort of deathbed vow to his father that he'd continue his musical studies. But of course, he had no power to defy Coville."

"I think it disgraceful that Sir Gavin should have forced him to break such a vow! From what I know of Major Diccon, he would certainly have stood up to such tyranny."

"He did. But he was only twelve years old. His violin was taken, smashed, and burned before his eyes."

"Oh, poor boy," she said sympathetically. "Could not his mama help?"

"The lady was frail and very timid, I collect, and would do nothing her husband disapproved of. Luckily, Diccon was away at school much of the year. It was while he was still at Eton that he met and fell in love with a most beautiful girl. My aunt knew her and held that it was a real Romeo and Juliet sort of romance. Both so young, you know, and so hopelessly attached."

They had reached the bridge and by mutual consent they halted. Marietta gazed out across meadows and woodland to where the chimneys of Lanterns were backed by the sparkle and shimmer of the Channel. Her thoughts were on Diccon and his young life that had been so tragically different from her own. It was not at all proper, of course, for Vaughan to be discussing his friend's family history, which was probably why he was silent and looked so uncomfortable. But she wished he would say more, and she prompted, "Why—hopelessly?"

"Eh? Oh, well, Sir Gavin had already chosen Diccon's prospective bride. A rather starched-up young damsel from a powerful and wealthy house. Grace, Diccon's own choice, had everything he wanted in his wife. She was the daughter of a corn-chandler. A good family. Well-to-do, but not great wealth or lands. Sir Gavin straitly forbade the match. Diccon defied him and said they'd be married anyway. Sir Gavin went to Grace's father. The gentleman was proud, and was enraged to think his daughter should be judged unacceptable."

"So he also forbade the match?"

"Absolutely. Grace was heartbroken. Diccon was furious. And unfortunately there was no possibility that if they waited a few years their marriage would have been permitted."

"How sad. So that was what brought about the breach with his family?"

"The real breach came when he turned eighteen. Grace was a year younger. She had gone into a decline when she was forbidden to see him and her health suffered. Diccon was desperate, I suppose. At all events, they slipped away one night and made a dash for Gretna. Very bad form, of course. But understandable in the circumstances."

"So they were married?"

"Never got there, ma'am. It was winter, and they were caught in a blizzard and snowed in. Sir Gavin came up with them at some little hedge tavern, and dragged Diccon back to Town by force."

"Good heavens! What about the girl?"

"From all I can gather, they left her there. You can imagine the state of mind she came to. A frail, gentle girl who had never been away from her home unchaperoned; knowing she was disgraced, and likely with no funds." He paused, looking very grim. "Thing is—the poor creature tried to follow them on foot. Someone should have stopped her from going out in such weather. As it was, she became lost."

Marietta gasped and turned to face him. "Oh! Never say they didn't find her?"

"They did, but too late, I'm afraid. She'd evidently stopped to rest. Worst thing you can do in a snowstorm. The poor girl just got too cold, d'you see? Shocking tragedy. There was quite a fuss, but it was all hushed up, so my aunt said."

"How perfectly *dreadful*! No wonder Diccon loathes the Covilles! Whatever did he do?"

"Went berserk, according to servant hall gossip. Da— er, dashed near strangled Sir Gavin, then raged out of the house and swore he'd never come back. He went into the military and worked his way up. Volunteered for the sort of suicidal missions most fellows pray they'll escape. It's miraculous that he's survived this long. Had a charmed life, I suppose you might say."

Appalled by the sad tale, Marietta was briefly silent, then she said in vexation, "And now what must he do but venture into the stormy waters of free-trading! Of all the shatter-brained things!"

'So that's it,' thought Vaughan. Clearly, the lady was interested in Diccon, but she believed him to be a rascally rum-runner. He said earnestly, "Oh, but that was all part of it, do you see, ma'am?"

She looked at him, puzzled. "You never mean to say he is a smuggler for the Army?"

"Supplying the brass with premium port?" Vaughan thought

of General Smollet, and laughed. "I'd not be surprised! No—seriously, Miss Marietta, there's no end to the roles he's had to play in smoking out criminals and conspiracies. He's done some truly grand things for England; most so secret they're not made public. It's a hazardous occupation to say the least, and he has paid dearly for his successes. His life is at risk, even now, because he bested an international gang of art thieves early this year. As usual, the authorities ignored his warnings till it was nigh too late to save the day. That's usually the way of it. You'd think Whitehall would be grateful, but they begrudge giving him any credit. Half the time they don't even pay him! Were he in a regular regiment he'd be covered with honours and awards, but these poor Intelligence fellows are—"

At this, Marietta caught his arm. He was startled to see that her face was paper white, her eyes wide and frightened.

She said gaspingly, "Do you say he . . . that Diccon is . . . an Intelligence Officer?"

"Why, yes, ma'am. About the best of the lot. My apologies if I alarmed you. It's a dangerous game, but he knows his business, never fear." Encouraged by such a display of caring, he said, "He means to leave the service now, I think. Ready to—er, settle down and—and become the—ah, family man." He glanced at her from the corners of his eyes. She was very still, as if overwhelmed. He went on, "In fact, I believe he has found the lady he hopes will consent to be his—er, bride."

Marietta scarcely heard him. So Diccon had not become a free-trader in an attempt to augment his Army pay. Major Diccon Paisley was, in fact, a professional spy! An extreme clever spy. 'There's no end to the roles he's had to play in smoking out criminals.' She experienced a pang of intense pain. He had played a role for *her*!

Persevering, Vaughan said, "I'm very sure that the lady who weds him will find him a most devoted and—and—"

A distant, shrill screaming fractured the quiet.

Turning her head to stare back towards the dower house, Marietta thought, 'Fanny!'

Vaughan was already running down the hill.

She picked up her skirts and followed.

⚜

Papa was in a scratchy temper, probably because Eric had not returned from Town last night as he'd promised. Leaving the basement, Fanny winked away tears, but fought the inclination to go up to her room and indulge in a good cry. Instead, she set the bread dough to rise, and tidied the kitchen. That occupation caused her to think of Vaughan's clumsy efforts, which made her smile sadly. The gentleman *had* seemed vastly preoccupied, but perhaps she had been too quick to find an explanation for his behaviour. He might, after all, have wanted to talk to Marietta about his fondness for Miss Fanny Warrington. Or about Marietta's relationship with Major Diccon. Or—oh, any number of things. Her sunny nature reasserted itself and she decided that she'd been a great silly, taking offence at nothing.

It was very quiet in the house this morning. Aunty Dova was up at her caravan again. She seemed in a glum mood of late, poor dear. Perhaps the rheumatism was troubling her. There was plenty of work to be done. The terrace should be swept and the brasses polished. But . . . the sun slid golden invitations through the kitchen windows. Such a lovely morning, and there was half an hour to spare before the bread must be punched down again.

She exchanged her apron for a sun-bonnet and collected a small basket from the scullery. She would need some mint for dinner and there was a nice patch growing wild down by the stream; there'd be just enough time to gather some.

She left by the front door. Heaven forbid that Mr. Jocelyn Vaughan and her sister should think she was following them! A pleasant breeze was fluttering the tree branches and the sun was warm. Setting off towards the stream, she saw Arthur coming up the hill from the direction of Lanterns astride the little donkey called Mr. Fox. She waved to him, but he didn't see her and she went on in search of the mint. The patch was just past the copse of beeches. Approaching the trees, she heard a male voice.

"Eric?" she called. "Is that you, dear?"

A pause, the sound of a smothered hiccup, and Blake Coville sauntered from the trees. "Now here's a sight to gladden the heart of a lonely gen'leman," he said, smiling at her. "And with more lively conversation than my hack offers."

He seemed very flushed. He must, she thought, be embarrassed because she'd overheard him talking to his horse. "I would certainly hope so, sir," she said, returning his smile. "Are you come to see my sister? She will be back soon, I'm sure."

"Saw her," he said rather indistinctly, and hiccuped again. "She was with Vaughan. Very much with him." He laughed in a way she could not quite like, and added, "I d'cided to wait for her here where it's cooler, though I doubt she'll come back soon. But only see what a kind Fate has sent me; another goddess to br-brighten my day. Whither away, pretty little bird?"

Fanny admired his lazy charm and good looks, but the glitter in his eyes this morning made her uneasy. Clearly, he was annoyed because he'd seen Marietta walking with Jocelyn Vaughan. She said lightly, "Oh, I'm out on the hunt for fresh mint, Mr. Coville. There's a nice patch on the bank nearby."

"Ah, yes. I think I saw some. Back this way, m'dear." He stretched out a hand, evidently forgetting he held something, which fell to the ground. Snatching up the small flask, he reeled a little as he stood straight, and said, "Come. I'll help you find't."

Inexperienced she may be, but Fanny was no fool and to venture into a copse of trees with a gentleman who was in a fair way to being intoxicated would be both improper and the height of folly. She stepped back, half turning from him. "Thank you, Mr. Coville, but—"

"Surely you know me well 'nough t'call me Blake, lovely little thing that you are."

His voice was at her ear. So was his breath. He was indeed intoxicated. And at this hour of the morning!

She moved away from him. "You should not address me in such fashion, sir. Now, if you will be so kind as to—"

He caught her wrist and jerked her to him. "But it is for you to be kind, pretty one." He held her close and bent to her lips.

"How *dare* you!" she panted, struggling furiously.

"Don't be such li'l prude. You think I've not seen you watch me? Come—why grudge a kiss or two?" One of his hands was fumbling with her bodice. He said thickly, "Y'r sister was cuddling with Vaughan in broad d-daylight so there's no call for you to play Miss Prim."

She gave a squeal of rage. "You lie! And you smell like a brewery! Oooh! Let me go—at once!" To emphasize her demand, she kicked his shin hard. Had she been wearing only her light sandals the effect might have been slight. Luckily, however, knowing she would be on muddy ground she had put on her wooden pattens. Coville yelped and his hold on her loosened just sufficiently for her to wrench free.

His face contorted. She knew fear and wondered why she had ever thought him handsome and gallant. He snarled, "You'll pay for that wi' more'n a—"

Over his shoulder, she saw rescue coming, and flung herself aside.

Mr. Fox's nature was whimsical and he liked to play practical jokes. His lowered head struck Mr. Blake Coville squarely in the back and propelled him head-first into the stream.

Arthur slid from the little donkey's back as the involuntary bather soared from the water, spluttering and dashing the hair from his eyes. Mr. Fox brayed raucously, his upper lip curling back in what could only be a grin. Convulsed with laughter, brother and sister clung together.

Blake Coville had cultivated an air of cool elegance and was not in fact given to acts of violence. He was, however, plagued by worry and great stress, and the one thing he had never been able to endure was to be made to look ridiculous. Snarling profanities, he plunged towards the bank.

Fanny saw his face. She grasped Arthur's hand and began to run. Frightened now, the little boy tripped, and as she dragged him to his feet, the infuriated man was upon them.

"Think it's funny, do you?" he raged, and seized the child's other arm.

"Ow!" cried Arthur.

Fanny uttered a shriek and began to flail her little basket at Coville's head.

His temper was out of control. "Laugh at this, you little doxy!" he growled, and with a hard shove sent her staggering to her knees.

Mr. Fox brayed distressfully and hung down his head.

With a wrathful cry, Arthur ran at Coville and rained small fists at his leg. "A gen'elman don't hit a lady! You're *bad!*"

Coville caught him by the hair. "Curst brat, I'll teach you—"

"No lessons today, thank you." Vaughan's pistol cracked across the enraged man's wrist, causing him to howl and snatch his numbed fingers from Arthur's hair.

Coville turned to meet this new attack. What he met was Vaughan's left fist which connected harshly with one eye. In the next second, his chin received Vaughan's famous right. Sprawling, drenched, knowing he'd have a black eye and that he was very likely ruined, Coville almost sobbed, "Damn you . . . Vaughan! You'll—you'll rue this."

Vaughan ignored him. "Are you all right, Miss Fanny?"

She was torn between the need to tell Coville exactly what he was, and another need. She chose the latter and leaned weakly against Vaughan. "Oh, Jocelyn."

"My dearest girl," he said huskily, his ready arm supporting her.

Coville clambered to his feet and started to reel towards the trees where his horse was tethered.

Arthur said in a tremulous voice, "That bad man hit Fanny, Etta!"

"I saw him, love." Hurrying up, Marietta pulled him to her.

"My father will call on you, Mr. Coville. Meanwhile, do not—ever—set foot on our property!"

"*Your* property?" Over his shoulder Coville cried shrilly, "You've ambitions to become Lady Temple and Cloud, have you? Much good will it do you to throw out lures to Diccon Paisley! That filthy, murdering bas—"

Vaughan strode purposefully towards him.

Abandoning the last shreds of honour, Blake Coville ran away.

CHAPTER XIV

V aughan escorted the sisters back to the dower house and broke the news to their father. At first incredulous, Sir Lionel then flew into a passion. Only with the greatest difficulty was Vaughan able to dissuade him from ordering up the carriage and starting for Downsdale Park, to confront Blake Coville, horsewhip in hand. He himself, said Vaughan firmly, claimed the right to settle accounts with Coville. This interesting attitude did much to restore Sir Lionel's spirits. His elder daughter may have lost her chance to make a brilliant match, but it would seem that little Fanny might yet save the day. He said he would have to consider the matter, and Vaughan tactfully departed leaving his love to the care of her aunt and sister while Sir Lionel penned an infuriated note to Blake Coville and another to Sir Gavin in London.

Fanny, meanwhile, was cherished and comforted, taken to her bedchamber, and made to lie down. She was quite willing to rest, and grateful for all the attention, but was perfectly cheerful. Coville's behaviour she mentioned briefly and with disgust. Her interest centered upon Jocelyn Vaughan. His heroism, his good looks, his unassuming manners, his courtesy, were unexcelled. He was the kindest of men, the bravest of men, in short—the epitome of manly perfection.

Mrs. Cordova managed to break in on this ecstatic inventory and shaking her head observed fondly that Fanny lacked sensibility. "Your tongue runs on wheels, Miss! Your poor sister is more upset, I vow. Go and lie down on your bed for a while, Etta. Sweet child, you are shaking like a leaf!"

Marietta needed little persuasion. As she closed the door she heard Fanny murmur, "Poor Etta! I forgot how disappointed she must be in Mr. Coville!"

But it was not Blake Coville's disgraceful conduct that had brought the despair to her eyes. When she reached the privacy of her room she sank onto the bed, staring blindly at the window, as grief-stricken as Fanny was elated. Diccon Paisley was an Intelligence Officer! How lightly Vaughan had relayed that news, and how horribly everything had at once fallen into place. She could hear him declaring so humbly that he had nothing to offer her but his friendship, and managing to imply that he yearned for much more. 'Nothing would give me greater joy than to serve you. . . . If you are ever distressed and need someone to talk with. . . .' Words that had warmed her heart because like a stupid she'd believed them to be sincere. But they weren't sincere at all. They were instead cunning and full of guile.

She had reached out to Diccon gratefully. Like a gullible idiot she had *confided* in him! Had she been completely blind? From the very beginning he had told lie upon lie! Small wonder he had been so eager to conceal his real identity! Small wonder he'd claimed to be a penniless free-trader! He had not come here to restore Lanterns. Rather, he was a cold and calculating spy, slithering about his terrible business, managing glibly to talk his way out of whatever shadow of truth might compromise his plan while he hunted his prey. He had even stooped to use Arthur to inveigle himself into her affections and win her confidence.

He had succeeded on both counts, far more thoroughly than he could know. And as a result there was a deep ache in her heart; the cruel hurt of loss and betrayal. The tears came then; a storm of wracking sobs she had to stifle in her pillows and that left her weak and exhausted. Wearily, she went to the washstand to bathe her reddened eyes.

He was clever—Jocelyn had said he was 'one of the best.' But she would fight him. Somehow, she must circumvent his scheming deceit. Above all, her adored Eric must be rescued. It was terrible to know that he had broken the law, but in a way the difference was slight; Eric was an industrial spy, Diccon was a government spy. Diccon spied for pay, whereas Eric had meant only to help his family.

She sighed miserably, and wished love had not come to her, since it brought such pain and disillusionment. Well, love and grief must be shut out now, and forgotten. Her only thought must be to—somehow—find a way to outwit the cunning Major.

Mrs. Cordova answered Diccon's knock, but instead of admitting him, she stepped out onto the terrace, closing the door behind her.

He asked anxiously, "Is she— Are the young ladies all right? Dale's head groom said there'd been trouble here."

She spread the skirts of her evening gown and began to hum softly. "So you were at Downsdale Park, were you, my lord? Some—urgent business, perhaps?"

"Yes." Her persistent use of his title was a minor irritant. Ignoring it, he repeated, "Is Miss Marietta—"

"The pastry man had urgent business as well," she said inexplicably. "I sent him to Lanterns. You've seen him already, I'd not be surprised."

Gritting his teeth, he fought for patience. "I've seen no 'pastry man,' nor do I know what—"

"He looks like pastry," she clarified. "Uncooked, you know. With black currants for eyes." Diccon tensed, and she giggled. "Ah, yes. You do know, don't you, Major? Beware! He's an evil—"

Marietta opened the front door. "Aunty? Who is it?"

She was pale and there was a strained expression in her eyes, but she appeared to be unharmed and with a great surge of relief Diccon reached out to her. "Thank God, you're all right!"

How terrified he looked. She thought bitterly, 'Such a clever one!' and made herself take his hand. "Quite all right, I thank you. Do come in."

He held her hand tightly as he stepped into the front hall.

Mrs. Cordova skipped past them and went up the stairs, chanting softly to herself.

Searching Marietta's face, Diccon said, "I came as soon as I heard."

"Oh dear. Has it spread about already?" Making no attempt to reclaim her hand, she said ruefully, "I'd hoped we could avoid a scandal. Do you know what happened?"

"Only that your sister was molested. I have no details."

Briefly and without drama she provided the details.

When she finished he was tight-lipped and his eyes glinted anger. He said tersely, "Dammitall! I should have warned him off!"

She smiled faintly at this proprietary attitude. "Why? Does he make a habit of attacking young ladies when he's in his cups?"

"Drunk, was he? Something has set him off, then. He's afraid of his father and has had to repress his true feelings for years. Sometimes, if he's under a lot of strain his control snaps, and when it does he's capable of anything. My dear, I am so very sorry. I feel responsible. Was Miss Fanny much hurt?"

'My dear?' How could he? How *could* he? She struggled against showing her revulsion, and said, "You are in no way responsible, and you did try to warn me, so pray do not blame yourself. Fanny is bruised, but more angry than frightened."

It seemed to him that her eyes were rather too bright and that the becoming colour in her cheeks had been applied, which was not her usual habit. Enraged, he thought, 'That filthy blackguard properly frightened her!' He asked, "Did Joss see it?"

"Yes. And handled the matter deedily."

'They'll go out, then,' thought Diccon. He said, "Blake has ruined himself, and he need not count on his sire to stand by him. The least hint of scandal sends Sir Gavin straight into the boughs, and there's no doubt this tale will be all over Town by morning."

She started to lead him towards the withdrawing room, but he declined her invitation to stay for dinner, saying he would not intrude on them at such a time. "Please give your father and Miss Fanny my sympathy and good wishes. I'll call tomorrow, if I may." As if in an afterthought, he asked, "Does your brother know of the business?"

He meant Eric, the viper! She answered guile with guile. "Yes. Arthur saw it all. Did I neglect to mention that when Coville struck my sister, Arthur sprang to her defence and gave him quite a pummelling."

"Did he, by Jove! My compliments to the rascal! He came down to return Mr. Fox, but I was away, unfortunately."

"He wanted to see you, but he was rather worn out, poor dear, so I put him to bed early."

They walked out onto the front terrace. The sun was low in the sky, throwing a warm pink glow over the land, softening the lines of the house, and turning the clouds to scoops of pink sherbet. Diccon, however, was oblivious to all beauty save the one who walked beside him. Hating this, he said, "Coville must be called to account, you know, ma'am. I fancy Joss will— Or, perhaps your brother Eric has insisted on that right?"

Marietta's hand clenched hard. He fished adroitly did Diccon Paisley of the Intelligence Service! "I think I had better not answer you, sir. Duelling is unlawful. And despite your—illicit activities, you are still a soldier, no?"

She had spoken lightly, but it was an evasion. And if she felt it necessary to evade . . . 'Damn!' he thought, and replied, "Officially, I'm on leave at the moment, Miss Marietta. And to say truth, I'm—I'm very seriously considering leaving the Army and settling down."

This, of course, was said to lull any fears she might have. "At Lanterns?" she asked demurely. "Would it not be too quiet here for you?"

"I've had my fill of action."

He was watching her narrowly. He must not suspect how bitterly she despised him. She forced her lips to smile and said, "You must have led such an exciting life."

"Interesting, certainly. I've seen a good deal of the world; met a lot of fascinating people. Not to mention some dashed tricky, ugly customers."

"Such as this individual Mr. Vaughan spoke of? Monsieur Monteil?"

He drew a breath and wondered what else Joss had told her. "Yes. Your aunt says he visited Madame Olympias. It seems he covets *The Sigh of Saladin.* Among other things."

"Is that surprising? A great many people would like to find it. But if it is really priceless I shouldn't think there was much to be gained by stealing it. Surely, nobody would dare buy it?"

"Imre Monteil is not motivated by money, ma'am. He's extreme wealthy. Made a fortune in munitions. He likes to acquire lovely things, with or without the owner's consent. And he has a deep hatred for England."

"Have you reported him? I suppose you are obliged to— to—"

"Try and lay him by the heels? Actually, it is the duty of any citizen to arrest a criminal, Miss Marietta. I'll own I'm surprised he'd dare return to England. I had no idea he was spinning his webs again."

"You make it sound as if he is interested in more than your treasure."

"He's an evil man with a finger in many pies. If *The Sigh of Saladin* exists it certainly would draw him like a magnet. It's ironic really that the legends of my family should cause our paths to cross again. Oh well, I must hope that others will deal with him." He said repentantly, "And only look at me keeping you standing here, as though you hadn't enough to worry about tonight! Your pardon, ma'am. I'll take myself off and let you get back to your family. Good night."

He bowed, offered a slight military salute, and walked briskly to the gate where Orpheus was tethered.

The sun was lower now, the skies a deep crimson. Watching his tall, erect figure silhouetted against that glow, it seemed to Marietta as though he walked into fire. And despite her efforts, once again, her eyes were dimmed with tears.

Could any lady look lovelier than Marietta had looked just now, her pretty silken gown bathed in the sunset glow, and with a glow of affection in her sweet eyes? How very dear she was. And how unworthy he was. What would she think if she knew the contents of General Smollet's latest letter? How would she feel if she knew of his conversation with Lord Ignatius Dale?

Diccon sighed heavily and reined Orpheus to a walk. Gazing blindly at the rippling scarlet ribbon the sun painted across the waves, he reflected that neither Dale nor Smollet had named names. Nor had he. His suspicions were no more than that, and he clung desperately to the hope that he was levelling his lance at a dragon which existed only in his imagination.

Eric Warrington was weak, perhaps; selfish and a braggart, certainly. But lots of fine men had overcome youthful follies and gone on to carve distinguished careers for themselves. He flinched to the recollection of that slurred voice—"I've set more than my toe outside the law. . . . I am an exceeding high paid courier. . . . If the Riding Officers knew . . ." Lord above! How much more incriminating could it be?

And, of all men, why must it be *her* brother? His perfect lady. His pure and brave and beautiful love. The thought of the misery that might lie ahead for her was wrenching. His chances of winning her had always been slight, but that made her no less precious, no less to be protected from hurt. If only he could spare her. If only it didn't all tie together so damnably!

Reaching Lanterns he dismounted, unsaddled Orpheus and turned him out in the paddock. The skies were darkening as he walked across the courtyard, but Mac had not yet lit the candles and the house was silent.

He stepped inside. Instead of the smells of dinner, he breathed the faint cloying scent that was used by only one man of his acquaintance. Quicksilver in his reaction he sprang away from the dark figure that lunged at him. The pistol he always carried whipped into one hand, his dagger into the other.

A club flailed at him, but he was well-versed in the art of close combat and the weapon whispered through his hair.

"I want him *alive*, remember!" The howled warning carried a slight accent, and Diccon's identification of Imre Monteil was verified even as he vaulted the kitchen table to avoid a slashing knife blade.

A big man, a chair swung high, sent it hurtling at his face. He dodged, but one of the legs raked across his cheekbone, narrowly missing his eye. He leapt and kicked out savagely in the French style and a wailing cry sounded as he ducked under a flying club and his dagger struck down the man who aimed it.

"Are you all slugs?" shouted Monteil furiously. "*Sapristi!* You're four to one! Finish it!"

One of his henchmen snatched up an iron skillet and flailed it at Diccon. It was solidly heavy, and would have broken his skull had it landed squarely. He dropped to his knees, the skillet whizzed over his head, and he fired. His opposition was reduced to two, plus Monteil.

The confidence of the Swiss waned. Cursing, he pulled a duelling pistol from his pocket and stepped from the corner where he'd watched what should have been an easy victory. Diccon was up and launched himself before Monteil had the chance to steady his aim. The duelling pistol barked shatteringly. The shot grazed Diccon's forearm. He hurled his own pistol at an advancing ruffian and in a continuing blur of movement his dagger was at Monteil's throat, his free hand twisting the man's arm up behind him.

"Stay back," he shouted. "In the name of the King, I arrest this man!"

His battered assailants eyed each other uneasily, then moved closer, like a pack of wolves circling a solitary but dangerous prey.

"Do as he says," ordered Monteil with surprising calm.

Dragging his captive with him, Diccon began to edge towards the stove and the heavy iron cauldron. Mac had not appeared, nor had he set off the signal, which meant that Monteil's juggernaut, Ti Chiu, might be lurking about. The varmint he'd shot was crawling to his feet. Reinforcements were badly needed.

Monteil said, "My dear friend Claude Sanguinet is dead thanks to the connivings of you and your friends. You have interfered with my plans too many times to be pardoned. Yet I cannot but admire you, Major. You are a fighting machine *par excellence*. England treats you shabbily. Work for me, and you will be treated very well indeed."

"Don't be absurd."

"I was afraid you would answer so," said Monteil with a sigh.

The man with the cut arm stood between Diccon and the cauldron that anchored the cord to their distress signal. "Move!" snapped Diccon, and, scowling, the bully backed away.

Diccon snatched blindly for the cauldron, but his hand grazed the hot stove and for a fraction of a second his attention shifted.

From behind came something that blurred past his eyes. He was jerked back and a crushing weight was across his throat.

He heard howls of triumph and a soft snuffling chuckle. Ti Chiu! He struck out with his dagger and that animal-like chuckle became a blood-freezing growl. His hand was seized and twisted so that the dagger fell from his numbed fingers.

Unable to draw breath, he clawed desperately at the mighty arm that was strangling him. His lungs were bursting . . . his ears rang . . . he could no longer see. . . . Abruptly, the stranglehold was gone. He sagged helplessly, gulping in air, groping blindly at the table for support. Barely conscious, he heard echoing voices, but his dazed eyes were focusing again and they focused on a heavy iron cauldron. If he could but reach it without attracting their attention. . . . He allowed himself to sway and sink to his knees, his left hand swinging out apparently helplessly to send the cauldron crashing down. He thought a pained but exultant, 'Excelsior!'

Monteil was saying something. ". . . not propose, my dear Diccon, to search the vastness of your Lanterns . . . cooperation by far the most advisable."

They were hauling him to his feet and supporting him roughly. Something wet and cold slapped at his face. He blinked, and Monteil's soulless eyes were peering at him. The razor-sharp tip of his own dagger was tapped on his chin. "I believe you heard me," purred Monteil. "*Certainement* you know what it is that I desire. And you know that I get what I want. One way—or another. Why not tell me now? I know you are a brave man. I respect this. There is not the need to prove it further."

Diccon looked around blearily. Five of the hounds. And Ti Chiu counted for another five. The odds would have been dim with the mighty Chinese alone. He said hoarsely, "What have you . . . done with my . . . man?"

Monteil gave a deprecating gesture. "This, it is of *peu d'importance*. Where is *The Sigh of Saladin?*"

"If I knew," croaked Diccon, "d'you think I'd still be in this mouldering ruin? I don't even know if—if it's fact or . . . fiction."

A shadow hove up before him, and he realized they'd lit a branch of candles.

Ti Chiu's deep rumble sounded. "The Runner lies."

One of the ruffians gave a gasp. "He's a *Runner*? Gawd!"

Monteil said conversationally, "You possess, I have before remarked it, beautiful hands, Major. Ti Chiu will start there, I think. One finger at a time."

The great paw of the Chinese giant stretched out.

Diccon said, "Dammit, I *told* you! I *don't know* where it is!"

Ti Chiu chuckled and seized his wrist, forcing him to his knees again.

Even as he went down there was a loud explosion, then a series of sharp retorts. Vivid flashes lit the room. Ti Chiu released Diccon and quailed against the wall with a yowl of guilt and fear.

"*Nom de Dieu!*" gasped Monteil.

The back door was wrenched open and a liveried groom ran in. "Someone's sent up a buncha rockets upstairs, Monsewer! Some sorta signal. Be seen fer miles, I reckon! There'll be troopers here, on the double!"

Monteil unleashed a burst of French and Italian profanity. His men began to edge for the doors with muttered comments about Runners and The Law.

Recovering himself, the Chinese towered over Diccon. "Ti Chiu he will break this for honourable master. Then we go. Very quick."

"No. I'm not ready to leave England yet, fool. He's a peer now. If they don't find him the whole countryside will be up. We'll deal with him, but this is not the time, and I've other plans."

Looking down at Diccon, Monteil's thin mouth curved into a smile although his eyes were as cold and dead as ever. "When you did battle with my dear friend Parnell Sanguinet," he said softly, "your comrade Harry Redmond stole Parnell's lady for himself. Your fight with Claude Sanguinet resulted in Mitchell Redmond finding his bride. This past spring I admired a pretty widow on the Longhills estate in—"

"Didn't get your wish that time, did you?" said Diccon recklessly.

Monteil's smile faded into a deadly glare. Ti Chiu grunted and stepped forward. A pulse throbbed beside Monteil's left eye, but he raised a delaying hand and said softly, "Another overdue debt. But my point is that you, my fine soldier"—he bent suddenly, and wrenched Diccon's head back—"never seem to—how is it you say?—end up with the girl. You are not, perhaps, a strikingly handsome man. Nor, however, are you plain. Indeed, the fair sex would find you attractive, I think." The knife in his hand glittered, and Diccon prepared to try and defend himself against the sudden slash that would disfigure or blind him. "You are still a young man," went on Monteil gently. "You should be, to use one of your crude English expressions, setting up your nursery. I wonder if you may have, at last, found a lady whom *you* . . . desire for your wife?"

Diccon was suddenly icy cold.

The groom announced urgently, "Riders coming, monsewer!"

"Go, then," snapped Monteil without turning. "And you may take these bumbling clods with you! Except for Ti Chiu. It would be so easy for me to destroy you, my dear Diccon," he went on. "But I am granting you a little time to think about *The Sigh of Saladin*. And to put a price on your—future. *Adieu*. We will talk again."

A moment later the kitchen was empty save for the man who sagged against the wall, massaging his bruised wrist and staring blankly at the overturned table.

⚜

It worked!" exclaimed Jocelyn Vaughan, jubilant as he hurried back into the kitchen, a branch of candles in one hand. "Poor old Whinyates would have rejoiced! The whole blasted sky lit up! I'll not be surprised if half the county comes in at the gallop." He inspected the graze across Diccon's cheekbone that Lem Bridger was tending. "You had a close call, old fellow. Dash it all, I told you it was a risky business to stay down here with murderous treasure hunters lurking about! You must hire some guards!"

Diccon asked, "How's Mac?"

"Tucked into bed. He lost a tooth, which he says he can ill afford, and there's a lump the size of a duck egg on his head. But he'll do. His whole concern is for you. I wonder those bastards didn't put a period to you before they turned tail and ran."

"I suspect the notion that I was from Bow Street threw them into a flutter."

Vaughan laughed. "If I know you, they took some damage along."

Diccon flinched away from Bridger's hands and the groom exclaimed, "That's an ugly bruise on your throat, sir."

Vaughan sobered and asked, "Ti Chiu again?"

Diccon nodded.

"I'll stay here tonight, sir, if it's your wish," volunteered Bridger. "I've brought my blunderbuss. It's old, but worth twenty pistols in a scrap. I know Sir Lionel would be willing. He'd've come himself but he was afraid to leave the ladies all alone."

Diccon thanked him but refused the offer and sent the groom back to the dower house with instructions to be on guard. Bridger's eyes grew round, and he left.

There came a clatter of hooves outside.

Vaughan strode to the window. "By George! It's Williard and half the village! And here comes— Be dashed if it ain't *Dale* with most of his people by the look of it!"

Diccon said, "We discovered we've some mutual acquaintances."

Vaughan stared, then hurried to the back door.

In this time of open flame for heat and lighting, all men rallied to aid their neighbours against the terrible threat of fire, and soon the courtyard was crowded, waggonloads of villagers augmenting the stream of carriages, curricles, and riders.

Mr. Innes Williard, in full evening dress, was incensed to realize that his dinner had been interrupted so that he might come to the aid of the common vagrant who was trespassing at Lanterns. He uttered a scathing denunciation of rascally demobilized soldiers who went about vandalizing private properties.

Ignatius, Lord Dale, was his usual haughty self. After a narrow-eyed scan of Diccon he said, "I thought we were coming to help put out a fire. Are you all right, Temple and Cloud?"

Mr. Williard's jaw dropped ludicrously. A spreading incredulous silence became an enthusiastic welcome for the returned lord of the manor. Diccon was one of their own; Sussex born even if he'd not had the sense to spend much time in his home county, and the anticipated disaster became a minor celebration. There were shouts of anger when he told of a greedy and unprincipled gang of thieves, hunting for the fabled treasure that, in his personal opinion, did not exist. Vaughan took several of the more curious upstairs to inspect their improvised alarm, and, in accordance with custom, the volunteer firefighters were offered ale and whatever the larder could provide.

It was two hours before the last waggonload of cheerfully singing villagers drove out. Innes Williard took his leave, saying irritably that it was beyond him to know why people found it necessary to conceal their true identities, for such deceits led to nothing but "needless embarrassments." Diccon, who was very tired, ignored his comments, but expressed with quiet courtesy his thanks for Williard's help.

A few minutes later, he walked outside with Lord Dale to offer another small speech of appreciation to his lordship and his retainers. Watching from the doorway as the two men shook hands, Vaughan heard Dale say solemnly, "Have a care, Paisley. The Swiss is not likely to give up and may well be involved in the other matter!"

Vaughan went back into the kitchen and gathered up the bone of a joint, a small hunk of cheese, and an empty bottle of pickled onions.

Diccon came in and sprawled on a chair with a sigh of exhaustion.

"They wiped out our rations," said Vaughan.

Diccon yawned. "You'll be able to take breakfast at the dower house. I fancy you're first oars with Miss Fanny, after your heroic rescue." Vaughan threw a heel of bread at him, and he laughed and asked, "No, seriously, how does the poor lady go on?"

"Very well. She's a resilient little soul. I vow she was more inclined to shoot Coville than to swoon!" He smiled fondly. "I could talk of her forever. But I'll restrain myself, for you look properly wrung out, old fellow. What an ordeal! You must fairly ache for your bed."

"I'm too tired to climb the stairs. Besides, I have something to say to you, and I want to know what happened when you went after Coville."

"Nothing." Vaughan's expression hardened. "The swine has gone to earth somewhere, but I'll come up with him, never fear."

"I wish you joy of him. Now you may ask the questions that are burning your tongue."

"Thank you, Major, sir. I'll not trouble you with many." Straddling a chair Vaughan asked, "Firstly, why did you tell Bridger to be on guard at the dower house?"

Diccon frowned. "Monteil left me with a veiled threat. He's deduced I have a—a fondness for the Warringtons."

Aghast, Vaughan said, "Good Lord! You never think he means to take revenge on you by striking at them? He would! Dammitall, he's without conscience!"

"I agree. One or other of us must always be up there." Diccon drew a hand across his eyes wearily. "You'd best get on with your questions before I fall asleep."

"Yes. Well, you were at Downsdale Park when Miss Fanny was attacked. Why? I thought old Dale blamed you for letting Mr. Fox eat his letters?"

"He did. I got them back for him."

"How the deuce could you do that?"

"Quite simply. Young Sam South fancied some adventure, so he's been leading the free-trading life with our Yves. When he landed a few days ago I sent him off to the Horse Guards for copies of Dale's letters."

"The . . . *Horse Guards? Dale?* Oh, you quiz me! The man's a high-in-the-instep bird-brain!"

"So I thought till Smollet wrote that Dale's a power behind the Whitehall scene, and an authority on international espionage."

"The devil you say! Then the papers Mr. Fox gobbled up were—"

"Were of rather vital importance." Diccon sighed. "Finished?"

"Almost. What did Dale mean just now when he spoke of 'the other matter'?"

Diccon stared at the fire. "You've quick ears, friend."

"And you don't mean to tell me, I see. Or is it that you cannot tell me?"

"Both," lied Diccon. He stood and stretched. "I'm for bed."

"One more thing, please. Of a different nature. I've spoken to Sir Lionel, and I'm now an approved suitor. But I want Fanny to have a London Season. She's—" His colour rose as Diccon slanted a raised-eyebrows glance his way and he said defensively, "Well, she's seen nothing of the world, you know."

"And you want to give her a chance to look over the competition? Noble. She's a beauty, Joss. You're a good man, but she'll be besieged. You're taking quite a risk."

"I dare to hope the risk is small. My last question is—if I win her—dare I also hope I'll have you for a brother-in-law?"

Diccon was on the edge of exhaustion, his bruises throbbed, and Imre Monteil's threat hung always at the edges of his mind. "How many times must I tell you?" he said with a flare of irritation. "No! I *cannot*!"

Vaughan stood, and faced him. "Is the reason that you 'cannot' connected to the disappearance of your mama?"

"Yes. Now—let me be!"

He started to the door.

Vaughan said, "Then what has Smollet to do with it?"

Diccon paused, swore, and walked on.

Vaughan took three quick strides and stood with his back against the door. "Your pardon, but I must know."

His fists clenching, Diccon stared at him, then laughed stridently. "What's this? The gallant cavalry officer galloping to the rescue again? History repeats itself, doesn't it, Lieutenant? Always the same! You glorious fellows in your scarlet and gold!

Sabres drawn, dashing in where only the brave dare go! While men like me creep and crawl about, peeping and spying and sniffing out traps and potential disasters! A sorry crew, and earning only sneers, or—"

Vaughan's hand cracked across his mouth like a pistol shot, cutting off the bitter words.

Diccon gasped and stood rocking on his heels, staring in bewilderment at the handsome, honest face.

Vaughan said gently, "Sorry, old lad. You were becoming a trifle shrill."

A trifle shrill.

Suddenly, Diccon was just too tired to struggle anymore. He sank into the nearest chair and buried his face in his hands.

After a minute Vaughan bent over him and offered a glass of cognac. "Here. You need it. You're worn to the bone, and I shouldn't have—"

"No. You shouldn't." Diccon lifted the glass with a hand that shook. "But you have." He took a generous sample of the wine. "And perhaps you've the right, at that. It's in the Bible."

Puzzled, Vaughan went to the shelf that housed the few books Diccon had brought here. The Bible was very old and most beautifully illustrated. He took it down, and opened it and a letter fell out.

Diccon said sardonically, "I thought that a fairly safe hiding place."

Vaughan flushed. "If you suspect I've been searching Lanterns for your personal correspondence, you may go to the devil!"

"No. But I knew you'd recognize the writing if you saw the direction. Like a sentimental idiot I wanted to spare you, when it's likely better that you should be forewarned."

Vaughan turned the letter over. He did recognize the writing, and said apprehensively, "Smollet!"

Diccon nodded. "General Sir Nevin's latest communique. Read it. As you said, you must know."

Vaughan unfolded the page, read swiftly, turned paper white, and closed his eyes. "Dear God! Diccon—you *cannot* connect Eric Warrington with this?"

"You appear to have done so—without the slightest delay."

"Smollet says, 'Any young fellow from the Sussex area who is suddenly and unaccountably plump in the pockets.' There might be many such."

"Who are believed to affect disguises on frequent journeys to Europe? It fits, Joss."

"But—but this is *treason*, man! D'you realize? No, it *must* be coincidental. Some other fellow."

Diccon lit a candle. "You'll never know how I pray that is so. Good night, Joss."

Vaughan read the letter again, then ran into the corridor. "Wait! What are you going to do?"

With ineffable weariness Diccon started up the stairs. "Have a look at poor Mac."

"Yes, of course. But—you know what I mean."

"What can I do? Wait. Hope old Nevin's following the wrong scent, as you said."

"And—heaven forbid!—if he's right?"

"Pray that I'm not the fellow who has to . . . deal with it."

"But—but you're on sick leave! They can't ask you—"

Clinging to the banister rail Diccon turned and looked down at him. "Whitehall wouldn't let me off that easily. Nor would my conscience."

"But—"

"Whether I'm on sick leave or not, I'm a military officer. I've taken a solemn oath to serve my country." Diccon shrugged, and went on up the stairs. "Besides," he added bitterly, "I cannot stomach traitors."

CHAPTER XV

The news of the attack at Lanterns had frightened all three ladies at the dower house, and Marietta was scarcely able to conceal her panic. All her bitter resentment of Diccon's duplicity was swept away by the fear that he had been hurt, and she was beside herself with anxiety until Bridger returned and assured them that "his lordship" was safe. Later, Vaughan came back, to give them a detailed report. He seemed more elated over the splendid fight Diccon had put up than dismayed by the event itself. Worn out, Marietta went up to bed soon after he left again. She passed a miserable night, despising her weakness because, knowing the threat Diccon posed, fearing him and wanting to hate him, she could not stop loving him.

In the morning she awoke feeling wrung out from lack of sleep, and her nerves were on edge when at eleven o'clock she ushered a distinguished caller into the book room. Her heart had convulsed with fright when she saw the military uniform, but there was only one sergeant riding escort and the General seemed a pleasant, fatherly sort of man. He had made Sir Lionel's acquaintance at the home of Lord Kingston Leith, he said, and since he was in the neighbourhood had thought he'd pay a courtesy call. She knew her father would have wished to be denied, but she did not dare deny this particular caller.

Fanny was in the workroom watching Sir Lionel struggle

with his new invention, a long track from which hung several strands of thin wire, and was enquiring as to the name and purpose of this device.

"It's called a Riser," he said. "And its purpose is— Ah, hello, Etta. Has someone come? I thought I heard the doorbell. Not Eric, I suppose?"

"It is a military gentleman, sir." She gave him the calling card.

"General Sir Nevin Smollet." He said frowningly, "Never heard of the fella."

"He says he met you at Lord Leith's house. He's short and square-ish, rather gruff and formidable-looking, but very courteous."

"Hmm. I fancy he's come to find out what we know about last night's disgraceful fiasco down at the manor. He'd do better to call on Temple and Cloud—or Major Paisley, as he calls himself. Sure he ain't mistaken this for Lanterns?"

She assured him that this was not the case, and he stamped his way up the stairs grumbling that what with lecherous London beaux, murderous thieves, exploding rockets, and the County turned topsy-turvy, a man's privacy was doomed.

Watching her sister, Fanny asked, "What is it, dear? Are you grieving because Blake Coville showed his true colours?"

"Good gracious, no! I am only thankful your gallant Jocelyn was at hand. Do you expect he will call today?"

"But, of course," said Fanny pertly. "He is anxious to talk to Eric, you know."

Marietta dropped the pliers she'd taken up absently. "Why?"

Startled, Fanny said, "Why, to tell him he wishes to fix his interest with me, I expect." She took Marietta's hand, searching her face anxiously. "Etta—there is something! Do you think I can't tell when you are worrying? Is it that you do not approve of Jocelyn?"

"Of course I approve, you goose! He is exactly the type of man I prayed you would find." Fanny looked unconvinced, so

Marietta said, "I'll admit I was most shocked by Mr. Coville's disgraceful behaviour."

"I know you favoured him, dearest. I'm so sorry you were disillusioned. It seems wrong that I should be so very happy while you are sad. But—oh, Etta, it is perfectly glorious to be in love!"

Marietta hugged her. "And it is glorious to see you so happy. Besides, I am not sad. Though I'll own I am somewhat surprised, because Mr. Vaughan does not appear to be a poor professor or an artist, and though he most certainly has a brain in his head, he does not go about quoting from the Greek or Latin, so—"

"Wretch!" cried Fanny, won to a laugh. "I never said such things!"

"Oh, yes you did!"

"Then I must have done so when I was very young and foolish! Jocelyn Vaughan is all I could ever wish for in a husband, so do not be reminding me of my nonsense. No, really, Etta," with sudden shyness, Fanny said, "I just marvel that I could be so lucky."

"You deserve it, love. And I think Mr. Vaughan is a very lucky man to have won your heart. Now I must go and find Arthur. I hope he hasn't wandered off to Lanterns again."

They walked up the stairs together and Fanny asked, "Why? I thought you had quite forgiven Major Diccon. In fact, you were so worried about him last night that I was convinced you had become rather fond of him."

So she had been that obvious. She said slowly, "And if I had, would you be pleased? Or are you still afraid of him?"

"Oh—I'm just a silly. Jocelyn thinks very highly of him, and he could not like a bad man, I am sure. Only look at the time! Half past eleven already! Jocelyn will be here at any minute! I must go and change my gown!"

Lost in thought, Marietta wandered along the corridor. Fanny had avoided her eyes and had answered her question in a flustered way. She did still fear Diccon. And her fears were all too well justified. If she did but know— But she must not know. Nothing must be allowed to shadow her happiness. Looking up, she gave a shocked gasp. Her aunt knelt on the floor outside the parlour, peeping through the keyhole.

"Aunty!" she hissed, hurrying forward.

Mrs. Cordova flapped an arm urgently and responded with a marked lack of contrition, "Ssshh! I can't hear!"

Marietta crept closer and was able to discern male voices. They sounded very serious and there was no cheerful laughter.

Her aunt turned a stricken face and reached out for assistance. Helping her to her feet, Marietta whispered, "Are you acquainted with the General?"

"No, no. Nor is your father, I am assured."

"But General Smollet said—"

Trotting to the kitchen beside her, Mrs. Cordova gasped out, "You can believe not one word any general tells you, my love!" She sank into a chair and flapped a handkerchief at her heated countenance. "It is just as I feared! The General touched very briefly on that ugly business last night. It was all too clear that what he really came for was to warn your father to be on the lookout for any gentleman in the vicinity who has suddenly come into money."

Marietta sank to her knees beside the chair and clutched at her aunt's free hand. "Did he . . . did he n-name any names?"

"From what I could hear, they are hard after a young man who has eluded them thus far. Smollet said"—Mrs. Cordova's eyes were dark with apprehension—"he said if your papa suspects anyone—*anyone*—he should report it at once."

Marietta's lips felt stiff. She gulped, "To—to whom?"

"He said that luckily one of his finest men is in the area. A man with an impressive record of unmasking . . . tr-traitors!" The last word was an anguished wail.

Marietta closed her eyes and bowed her head against the chair arm. "The man with the 'impressive record' being Major Diccon Paisley."

"Yes." Mrs. Cordova's clasp tightened on her niece's fingers and she moaned, "*Traitors!* Oh . . . Etta! *Whatever* are we to do? If Diccon catches him—"

Marietta summoned a smile. "He hasn't caught him yet, love. And my brother may have been very naughty, but it *isn't* treason! We know that! We'll think of something, never fear."

The General's visit was short. Sir Lionel imparted over luncheon that Smollet was a good enough fellow and that he would have invited him to stay and join them, "but he's a grim sort of old boy, y'know. Full of worries about some traitor or other. I told him I've a musket loaded and ready, and if a cur of that sort comes in range I'll know how to deal with him!"

When the meal was over Mrs. Cordova decided to go up to her caravan, and was not deterred when Sir Lionel said he would be unable to spare Bridger this afternoon. She felt quite safe in walking to the caravan, she said, as no one was likely to stand about spying on her in the pouring rain.

Despite the weather, Vaughan borrowed Diccon's handsome closed carriage and came to whisk Fanny off for a drive.

Arthur had taken his luncheon early, as usual. He'd eaten sparingly and gone up to his room to play. Preoccupied with her anxieties, Marietta didn't realize until the house was quiet again how long the boy had been gone. His nature was much too affectionate for him to enjoy solitude. Suspecting that he'd fallen asleep, she went in search of him and was half-way up the stairs when the most terrifying thought occurred to her. In her trusting idiocy she had sent Eric to meet Diccon. And in his letter Eric had written: "I must get out of the country, and thanks to you I think I know how I can manage this." She'd assumed he meant that their occupancy of a home that was so close to the Channel would be useful to him. But suppose he intended to seek help from the man he believed her to like and to trust? What if Eric turned to Diccon the free-trader for an escape from the law, little knowing that Diccon *was* the law? Her knees felt weak. She clung to the stair railing and to her nerves, and she prayed.

She had regained her composure, outwardly at least, by the

time she walked into the room Arthur shared with Arnold when Arnold was at home for the holidays. The little boy was curled up in the windowseat with Friar Tuck beside him, watching the raindrops race each other down the pane. He accepted an offer to be read to, but with a marked lack of enthusiasm. He seemed subdued and there were few of his usual interruptions. Concerned, she stayed with him for a time, reading, then drawing. They were playing raindrop races on the window-pane when there came the busy sounds of hammering. "It must be Papa and Bridger," she said lightly. "I expect they're making a surprise for us. Shall we go downstairs and see?"

He shrugged apathetically. "If you like."

"What would *you* like? Something to eat, perhaps?"

Another shrug. Staring at Friar Tuck, who had fallen asleep on the book, he answered, "It doesn't matter."

She felt his forehead. It was cool. "Do you feel well, dearest?"

"Yes. Thank you."

"Is something troubling you?"

"No."

Desperate, she asked, "Did you want to go and see Major Diccon?"

He stroked Friar Tuck's fur forward between his ears, giving the cat what he called "The Snake Head," and concentrating on this endeavour, muttered, "Aunty Dova says I'm not to go there no more."

So that was it. But in her own opinion the pretence must be kept up, at least until Eric was safely away. She offered to walk to Lanterns with him, but he said apathetically that he didn't want to go out, adding an unprecedented, "It's too wet."

Giving up, she took him with her and went downstairs to help with dinner.

The skies were darkening and the drawing room was shadowy. Sir Lionel and Bridger were tidying up tools and carrying ladders out to the barn.

"Time for tea, eh?" said Sir Lionel hopefully, and over his

shoulder added, "Now—don't *touch* nothing, Etta! It's a surprise. For your aunt."

Bridger chuckled.

"And don't *tell* her!" called Sir Lionel.

Mrs. Cordova joined them for tea, and was agog to learn about the surprise, but Sir Lionel insisted it must wait until they were all here. An hour passed before Vaughan and Fanny came into the house with a flurry of laughter and raindrops. They had driven as far as Lewes, and had purchased a bottle of cognac that made Sir Lionel's eyes gleam; some pastries that Vaughan said loyally were not to be compared with Fanny's cookery; and a marzipan soldier for Arthur. The little boy brightened and was promised he should have some after supper, but by the time he was taken up to bed, declared himself tired and said he would save the treat for tomorrow.

Marietta went downstairs and told her aunt that she feared her brother might be sickening for something. She had little time to worry about it however, for Sir Lionel was clearly eager to show them his latest invention, and announced they would be given a showing after dinner.

The evening was cool so a fine fire was lit, and, with only two small branches of candles burning and the rain pattering against the windows, the drawing room was cosy and inviting when they all were assembled there. Beaming with suppressed excitement, Sir Lionel directed each of them to a specific chair, and was about to begin his demonstration when they heard a carriage pull up outside.

Mrs. Cordova went in search of an umbrella.

"Oh—no!" wailed Sir Lionel, exasperated. "Only a noddi-cock would venture out on such a night!"

His worst fears were borne out. Holding an armful of cloaks, Marietta showed three evening callers into the room. With smothered giggles, Mrs. Cordova appropriated the damp garments and carried them off to be hung up to dry. Mr. Innes Williard was glorious in formal evening dress and knee breeches but wore a glum look that said he was here against his will. Mrs. Isolde Maitland was clad in an ornate gown of purple satin with a profusion of frills and little bows on the bodice and sleeves and an overskirt of silver lace. Under a vulgarly large and wide-spreading diamond necklace her bosom was very much on display. She fluttered her fan coyly at Sir Lionel's aghast face, and presented her mother to the company. Rustling in stiff forest green bombasine Mrs. Crosbie Williard was small, thin, and waspish. She was clearly on the far side of sixty but her auburn hair was suspiciously untouched by grey. Her faded brown eyes were still keen, however, and darted about, birdlike, as if determined to miss nothing.

The guests were comfortably settled and at once Mrs. Maitland directed the conversation to the topic that seemed uppermost on everyone's mind today: the disgraceful invasion of Lanterns by armed criminals, and the return of Lord Temple and Cloud to the neighbourhood. With high drama she announced that her nerves were "completely overset" by the realization that the countryside "fairly swarmed with thieves and murderers"! Her brother said testily that he hoped the gentlemen of Sussex were able to deal with such riffraff, whereupon Mrs. Crosbie Williard retorted dryly that she very much doubted it. Her daughter's laugh shrilled out, and Marietta and Fanny retreated to the kitchen to assemble refreshments.

"Papa is furious." Fanny giggled, setting biscuits on a serving plate.

Marietta put the kettle on the hob and said innocently, "Why? Because his Isolde is flirting with Jocelyn?"

Fanny squeaked and had to muffle her laughter. "Is it not hilarious? Between her eyelashes and her fan he'll be lucky to avoid the pneumonia!"

Both eyelashes and fan were at top speed when Marietta carried a laden tray into the drawing room, and Mrs. Cordova, who had slipped into the room and sat on the far end of the sofa, was watching the widow's gyrations in fascination.

They had come through "a veritable deluge" declared Mrs.

Maitland, and her "little heart" had fairly fluttered because the stream was so high and the bridge so very old. One wondered that Temple and Cloud did not build a new one.

Fixing Innes Williard with a resentful stare Sir Lionel said that *he* wondered they had ventured out on such a stormy night.

"I, for one, didn't want to come," stated Mrs. Crosbie Williard baldly. "It's hard enough for a frail and elderly lady to get about, let alone climbing in and out of carriages in the middle of a flood!"

"Not my intention," grunted Williard, darting an irked glance at his sister.

"Oh, but we *had* to, dear sir," gushed Mrs. Maitland. "Now, Mama, did I not tell you it would be well worth your while? You visit us so seldom and you've never seen anything like these— oddities, you must own." She fluttered her fan and her eyelashes in the general direction of the sofa.

"Can't see 'em now hardly, it's so dim in here," grunted Innes Williard. "You practicing economies with candles, Warrington? Advisable, I don't doubt."

His mother, who had been staring at the effigies, barked, "That's a fair dummy on the end. Looks more lifelike than the rest of 'em!"

Mrs. Maitland screamed, "Mama! You naughty thing! That is Mrs. Cordova!"

Vaughan turned away and was grateful for the dim light.

Innes Williard, grinning from ear to ear, explained that his mother was inclined to be deaf and likely had not heard the introductions.

Sir Lionel could be frosty when he chose. He said that he believed his sister-in-law had not been present at that time, and with great formality rectified the omission.

To Vaughan's utter delight, Mrs. Cordova rose, swept into a stately curtsey, then held out her skirts and waltzed about the room singing somewhat inaccurately, " 'Like untuned golden strings some women are, Which long time lie untouched, will harshly jar.' "

"Mad," sniffed Mrs. Crosbie Williard in an audible aside to her son.

Fanny began to hand around cups and saucers. One look at her love's brimming eyes was almost her undoing, and she moved on hastily.

Mrs. Maitland said with sugary cajoling, "Now you must own how clever the likenesses are, dearest Mama."

"I'll own it's one way of filling a room with company, if you've no worthwhile acquaintances," her mother observed with no sugar at all.

Undaunted, Mrs. Maitland tittered, requested more milk in her tea and said, "Speaking of filling a room with company, I had thought Mr. Blake Coville might be here. Do you expect him to call, Sir Lionel?"

"No, madam," said Sir Lionel frowningly. "I do not."

"Such firmness." The widow opened her eyes at him admiringly. "I don't blame you, of course. I suppose it was inevitable that he would fall from grace." She sipped her tea, watched Marietta over the rim of her cup and purred, "Now that Temple and Cloud has returned to the neighbourhood. . . . Though rumour says *he* has not a feather to fly with."

Williard had the grace to be embarrassed by his sister's behaviour, and he snorted, "Rumour! Blasted area fairly hums with rumours!"

"Yes, indeed." Not one to miss an opportunity, Mrs. Maitland added, "I myself am a victim—as are you, Sir Lionel! Indeed," she hid behind her fan and said roguishly, "our names are . . . linked, I fear."

Sir Lionel threw an agonized glance at Marietta.

"Were I you, ma'am," put in Mrs. Cordova with unexpected clarity, "I'd give not a thought to such nonsense. I'm very sure my brother pays no heed to gabblemongers!"

Vaughan caught his breath.

For an instant the room was very still.

Sir Lionel stood nervously, and retreating from this dangerous conversation went to the credenza at the side of the room and began to rattle glasses about.

Flushed, and her eyes glittering wrath, Mrs. Maitland sat up poker stiff and snapped, "There are some very unkind people about, dear Mrs. Cordova. For instance, there are those who believe that this silly Madame Olympias, who pretends to be a clairvoyant is no other than—"

Her venom was stilled by a sudden bellowing clap of thunder.

Mrs. Cordova sprang to her feet and said dramatically, "Beware! The spirits walk tonight!"

This impressive proclamation was followed at once by a strange high-pitched squealing sound. Padding across the room en route to the kitchen, Friar Tuck arched his back and hissed at the ceiling.

Fanny reached for Vaughan's hand nervously.

In the act of refilling Innes Williard's cup, Marietta stared in astonishment at the sofa.

"Mrs. Hughes-Dering" was moving! As she watched, spellbound, and heedless of the tea that overflowed both cup and saucer, the arm of the large figure lifted slowly.

Mrs. Cordova said, "Awwk!" and slumped into an armchair, staring in a mixture of delight and consternation.

Friar Tuck's stomach brushed the floorboards as he departed in a flash of ginger-and-white fur.

Fanny uttered a shocked squeal. Holding her hand firmly Vaughan felt the hair lift on the back of his neck.

Had it been broad daylight the effect might have been less spectacular, but in the dimly lit room with thunder rumbling outside, the sight of that plump arm lifting to point, it seemed, at Mrs. Maitland, was awe-inspiring.

The widow uttered a piercing scream. Her "frail and elderly" mama wasted no time on such outbursts and was already bolting for the front door at a rate many a young athlete might have envied. In full cry, the widow followed.

Mrs. Hughes-Dering's arm sank down again to land in an ungainly position that somehow emphasized the bizarre quality of the scene.

Sir Lionel stammered apologetically, "No—wait. I wish you will not—"

"My *cloak*!" shrieked his admirer with little of admiration. "Don't stand there like a lump, Innes! Get us out of this accursed house! We'll wait on the terrace!"

"Yes, but—" said Mr. Williard, regaining some of his colour.

Marietta dropped the teapot and ran to collect the cloaks.

Vaughan, who had come to his feet when Mrs. Crosbie Williard launched into her sprint, gulped, "I'll call up the carriage," and went nobly (and tearfully) into the rain.

Five minutes later the Williard carriage departed at speed, the surprised coachman having been ordered to spring his horses no matter the state of the muddy drive-path.

Inside, Mrs. Cordova, who had been anxiously restoring her "friend," looked up with a tangled length of wire in her hand. "Lio-nel . . . ? Did you hide this wire behind the bell pull?"

He sighed dejectedly. "What a disappointment. They were all supposed to move! That was my surprise for you, Emma. Another failure, alas."

He won little sympathy. In fact, between bursts of hilarity, the others didn't appear to consider it a failure at all.

❧

"Friar Tuck was very scared," said Arthur, caressing the cat who was curled up on the bed beside him. "I 'spect it was the thunder. He's frighted of thunder, but I only heard one banger. Was there lots? Why am I let have my breakfast in bed when it's not my birthday?"

Setting the tray across his lap, Marietta said, "There were a few smaller peals, and something else happened which startled him a little. Papa and Lieutenant Vaughan are mending it now so that you can see it too. But it's a surprise and not quite ready, so Papa doesn't want you to come downstairs just yet."

He asked hopefully, "Is the surprise about Eric? Has Eric comed home?"

"No, dear. But he will come very soon, I'm sure."

"Can I go outdoors and wait for him?"

"After you've seen the surprise, perhaps. In fact . . ." She hesitated, then said, "I've something I must show him before he talks to anyone else. If you should see him first, would you tell him that? It's—a secret, and a very important secret."

"Sort of like the secret orders the Staff Officers carried for the Duke at Waterloo?"

"Yes, dear. Just like that."

He was impressed and agreed to relay the secret message, provided he could wear a blue coat. "Staff Officers wear blue coats y'know."

Luckily, Marietta was able to unearth a faded blue velvet coat from Arnold's press. It was too big, but with the aid of a belt and turned up sleeves it would serve. She left Arthur eating his porridge and sliced peach and explaining to Friar Tuck that he knew all about Staff Officers 'cause a friend of Aunty Dova's had married with a lord whose son had been one. "His name's Colonel Leith," he said, "an' he's very fine, an' taller than . . ."

The sentence went unfinished, which Marietta put down to the charms of peach and porridge.

It had rained steadily all night and this morning a strong wind drove flurries of drops against the windows and set the barn door to banging. Marietta washed the tea-stained tablecloth and hung it over the clotheshorse in a corner of the warm kitchen. Fanny was gathering ingredients for a seed cake, and when the repairs to the "risers" were completed she sent Vaughan out to the barn to collect eggs. He hurried in with a piece of sacking over his dark head and announced that he had "liberated" ten eggs and that the rain seemed to have set in for a long stay.

When Marietta went upstairs to fetch Arthur, Vaughan

said, "You look very grave, Miss Fanny. I saw how you watched your sister; do you think she grieves because of Coville's behaviour?"

"No." Fanny cracked an egg and emptied it into the bowl then stood staring down at the two pieces of shell in her hands. "I believe she had already realized he was—well, not the man we thought him." She sighed. "Etta has been so good, Jocelyn. You cannot know how hard she has worked, taking care of us, handling all the details that Papa— I mean . . ."

"Yes," he said understandingly. "I know what you mean. In a sense Miss Marietta has mothered you all."

She smiled up at him. "You do understand. It is exactly that." She blushed and said shyly, "Thanks to Etta I am so very happy. But I want her to be happy also, and she is not. I *know* she's worrying. And it must be very bad, because she can usually hide her worries from us all." She reached for another egg. "I do wish I knew what was troubling her."

Vaughan concentrated on folding his piece of sacking, and said nothing.

Marietta slipped quietly out of the front door and into the grey and misty morning. Leaves and grasses drooped soddenly and large drops fell from the eaves, but the rain had eased to a drizzle. Arthur was nowhere in sight. She pulled the hood over her hair and started around the far side of the house, avoiding the kitchen area. There was no need to disturb Fanny and her devoted assistant cook. As she'd expected, apart from two ducks who waddled about unperturbed by the damp, the back gardens were deserted. Arthur had probably crept out and gone towards the London Road to wait for Eric. She drew her cloak tighter and started off, keeping to the trees so as not to be seen from the house.

Her pattens were in the scullery and rather than go in and claim them she'd come out in half-boots that were soon thoroughly soaked. She trod carefully and paused several times to peer about through the misted air, hoping to catch a glimpse of a small solitary figure. She was almost to the bridge when she saw a flash in the copse of beeches by the stream. Perhaps Arthur had put on his chain mail before venturing into the rain.

Relieved, she hurried forward, only to stop abruptly. The figure she came upon was solitary but far from small.

For the barest instant her heart leapt, and she had to repress a strong compulsion to run to him. But then came the pain of comprehension; the glint of light had come from a spyglass, trained at the moment on the distant London Road. He was up here waiting in the rain with remorseless patience; hoping for a sight of his quarry. Crushed by despair, she had to blink away tears.

As though he had sensed her presence Diccon swung around. He whispered her name, and there came that blaze of joy in his eyes; the silver blaze that wrought such havoc with her foolish heart.

Somehow she kept her voice calm. "Good morning, Major." She glanced pointedly at the spyglass in his hand. "I'd not realized you were one of those people who have an interest in birds."

He looked bewildered, then said with a wry smile, "The creatures I watch for, Miss Marietta are, unhappily, birds of prey."

"The same species that visited you last night?" She had noted at once the ugly graze across his cheekbone and said with instinctive sympathy, "They marked you, I see. I— We were very anxious for you." His eyes lit up again, and she went on quickly, "Lieutenant Vaughan said there was quite a battle and that you were able to defeat them all except for that terrible Chinese man."

He smiled. "Vaughan exaggerates, as usual. As for Ti Chiu, I must own I was quite outclassed, but I'll excuse my defeat by claiming that it would take a troop of heavy dragoons to subdue that ugly customer."

"Then that is just what should be done. You are an Army officer, why have you not called for reinforcements to arrest him? You said he and his master were in the country illegally."

"So they are, ma'am. And to say truth I did send out a call for help. Unfortunately, the local troopers have been occupied with another matter which causes my attempted robbery to appear comparatively insignificant."

She said with real indignation, "I cannot think that the attempted murder of an English peer could be judged insignificant!"

"I hope that no murder will ever be judged so, Miss Marietta. Only—the other matter, you see, involves our national security."

She was suddenly very cold. "Oh."

Concerned, he said, "You're shivering. And small wonder. Those little boots were not intended for walking in the rain. May I escort you home?"

What he meant was, "May I come and see what is going on at the dower house?" But Vaughan was there, of course, to report to him. With another pang of misery she thought, 'Oh, heavens! Is that why Jocelyn courts little Fanny?'

Diccon's hand was on her arm. Scanning her face anxiously, he asked, "What is it? I thought we had agreed that if you were troubled you would come to me?"

How could he look at her with such tenderness and be so treacherous? Truly the officers of the Intelligence Service were a breed apart! But she would not be taken in this time; she would be as deceitful as he.

And so she smiled up at him and said, "Well, I am with you, am I not? My trouble is that Arthur has gone off again and I can't find him. I thought perhaps he had run away to London, or come to you. Have you seen him?"

"No, and I would have done if he left after eight o'clock. Are you sure he's not in the house—or the barn, perhaps?"

"He wasn't in his room. He's been rather downcast these past few days, so I thought . . ." She shrugged. "No doubt you're right. I'll go home and look more thoroughly."

He folded the glass. "I'll come with you."

"No. Really, there is not the need. It is just a short walk, and—"

"And I could wish you do not walk out alone, ma'am."

He looked stern, and like a ray of light it came to her that he might not have been setting a trap for Eric after all. That he might have been standing here in the rain hour after hour because he feared that the ruthless treasure seekers might next break into the dower house. Her heart leapt with joy and she said, "But surely you don't really think this Monsieur Monteil and his henchmen mean to invade our home?"

It was exactly what he feared, but not for the world would he frighten her. He'd given Joss strict instructions to alert Sir Lionel and Bridger to the threat without alarming the ladies. He said, "Oh, no. Why would they? If *The Sigh of Saladin* had been hidden in the dower house it would have been discovered centuries ago."

Joy faded. "Yes," she said quietly. "Of course."

CHAPTER XVI

Realizing that she may have betrayed herself, Marietta tried to remedy matters by chattering gaily all the way back to the dower house, making Diccon laugh with her description of Sir Lionel's disappointing new invention. And because she suspected he would know of it anyway and think it odd if she failed to mention it, she said casually, "Oh, and we've been visited by an Army General. He warned Papa to be on the look out for "some traitorous gentleman" who might journey through the area. It seemed rather a pointless warning," she added with a little laugh. "How does one recognize a traitor? Would he wear all black, perhaps? Or ride in a very fast coach and four with the words 'I Am A Traitor' inscribed on the panels?"

Diccon thought regretfully that she would have no trouble recognizing this particular fugitive, but years of concealing his true feelings stood him in good stead and as they approached the house he managed a smile and said that all traitors were known to sport very large black whiskers and go armed to the teeth with sword and dagger and at least one pistol. "Indeed, you'll recognize him at a glance, for he'll scarce be able to stagger about under all that weight!"

He was rewarded by her infectious chuckle and an invitation to come inside for a cup of tea. Longing to accept, he declined politely, on the grounds that he must get back to his "post."

His "post" being the hill from which he could watch the London Road, thought Marietta. The road along which Eric would very likely come. She had never pleaded for the company of any gentleman, but she swallowed her pride and coaxed, "No, must you go? Surely you can spare us a few minutes?"

For a second he looked down at her, his expression enigmatic, then he asked, "Has Sir Lionel forgiven me, then?"

With all her other worries Marietta had quite forgotten her father's wrath at Diccon's deception, and she hesitated.

He said, "I thought not. But I thank you for the invitation. I'll go back to the bridge and turn my glass this way. If you don't find the boy, please wave to me from the upstairs balcony, and I'll come down and help search for him."

"But wouldn't it be easier if you waited here? It likely won't take me very long to find him if he's in the house or the barn."

He agreed, but pointed out that he had no wish for Sir Lionel to see him lurking about the house. Marietta could think of no more reasons to delay him, and had no recourse but to thank him for his concern and leave him there.

Diccon stood at the end of the back lawn and watched her follow the path that led past the west end of the house and around to the barnyard. How graceful was her walk; how proudly she held her lovely head. And there could be no doubt now: she knew. He had been too long schooled to read people's faces not to recognize the fear she'd tried so hard to hide. She was afraid of *him*! What a bitter irony when he loved her so dearly. But her fear meant that she knew about Eric's guilt, and suspected he was hunting her brother.

If she could but know how he dreaded that Eric Warrington might come this way, or of how passionately he prayed that her traitorous brother would be taken long before he set foot on Lanterns soil. To watch her valiant effort to appear light-hearted had wrung his heart, and he'd longed to take her in his arms and cherish and comfort her. But he shrank from admitting his involvement while there was still the possibility that the wretched Eric would be caught in Town, or anywhere but here. If not, if

Fate levelled the ultimate challenge and he was the man who must send her loved brother to shameful and hideous public execution . . . His shoulders slumped. Anguished, he turned away, thinking, 'Lord, *please*. Don't make it be me! Don't let me be the one to break her heart!'

He looked up and found Mrs. Cordova standing only a few paces distant, watching him. There was compassion in her round face, and he knew the bland mask he showed the world had slipped. For the first time in years he was unable to reclaim it, and without a word strode rapidly across the meadow.

❧

Marietta's search of the barn and sheds having proven fruitless she went back into the house and climbed to Arthur's room hoping he might have returned. Once again unsuccessful, she went through the other first-floor rooms and was about to go downstairs and see if he was in the cellar when she heard a faint sound behind her. Friar Tuck emerged from the passage leading to the attic stairs, his claws making little clickings on the boards. At the sight of her he feigned terror; his back arched and with tail bushed out and ears back he scampered along the corridor and thundered down the stairs, headed kitchenwards, no doubt.

He had pointed the way for her, and she went very quietly up the narrow attic stairs. The door was slightly ajar. Pushing it wider, she heard a doleful sniff. Arthur sat huddled against the broken rocking horse Eric had promised to repair last year. He looked pathetically small and stricken, head bowed onto drawn-up knees, arms wrapped around them as though holding himself together.

She crept inside, the creaking of the floorboards drowned by a sudden shuddering sob. Sinking to her knees, she waited, watching him, aching for him, wondering if somehow he'd heard about the terrible folly of the brother he'd always idolized. When he at last lifted a reddened and tear-streaked face, she said gently, "My dearest, how can I help?"

He dragged a hand across his eyes and gulped a hoarse, "You can't, Etta. No-nobody can h-help. 'Cept him. An'—an' he won't, 'cause . . ." His voice broke. " 'Cause he's jus' . . . bad!" He reached out, leaning to her, the tears overflowing.

Marietta held him tight, rocking him gently, murmuring words of comfort until the storm of grief eased a little. Stroking his hair, she asked, "How did you know, love? Did you overhear someone speak of it?"

He sniffed and drew back. She gave him her handkerchief and when he'd blown his nose and wiped his eyes he said scratchily, "I *saw* him! I told you. But you wouldn't listen. No one wouldn't!"

Bewildered, she said, "I'm sorry, dear. I don't recall—"

"No, 'cause you din't listen. But I told you! An' you said it wasn't *him*, and that he was just l-living there! An' his name was diff'rent so I thought it wasn't him. An' he was so . . . kind . . . to me. An' he said he never . . . did nothing like that. But—but he *did*, Etta! Mr. Blake said his name's really Temple an' Cloud, so it *was* him! An'-an' . . . Oh, I l-liked him so *much* an' I didn't think I'd ever like someone what . . . what was *wicked*!"

Marietta stared wide-eyed at that small, sorrowful face, and asked in a half-whisper, "What did you see, Arthur? Would you please tell me again? I'll listen hard this time. I promise."

So he told her all about the two men who had carried the muffled figure out to the carriage on that fateful evening. "An' Diccon said that whatever happens *she* mustn't never be found. I *heard* him, Etta!" He clung to her again, and gulped, "It was his own *mama*! How could he be . . . so *bad* when I thought he was so *good*? How *could* he, Etta?"

She soothed him as best she might, but she felt numbed and desolate, and thought miserably, 'How could he indeed!' She took Arthur back to his room and made him lie down and rest and sat beside him, hearing again that loved voice saying, "If I told you, it would make you an accessory, do you see?" Surely, that had been as good as an admission of guilt, but she'd refused to believe evil of him because he had seemed to be brave and decent and honourable.

With a sigh for her gullibility she saw that Arthur had fallen asleep, probably worn out, poor little boy. She pulled the eiderdown over him, closed the curtains, and tiptoed out.

Fanny was scrubbing the kitchen table, and told her that Vaughan had gone down to the workroom to chat with their father, and that Friar Tuck had fairly shot out of the back door when Aunty Dova went to gather some onions. The cat was terrified of thunder and if he'd retreated to his favourite hiding place in the barn it was a sure sign that they were going to have another storm from this very stormy autumn.

The skies were getting darker by the minute and Marietta decided to feed the chickens before the rain really came down. She met her aunt coming out of the barn carrying a basket of onions and carrots, her hair and her cloak flying.

"We're in for some weather," she announced. "Speaking of which, have you and Major Diccon quarrelled? I saw him leave. I think I've never seen such desolation in a man's eyes. He is head over heels in love with you, child. Now why do you smile?"

For a moment Marietta considered sharing the bitter news that Major Mallory Diccon Paisley had almost certainly done away with his parent, but there was no telling what her aunt would do with that information and if it was spread about its possible usefulness would be ended. She said, "Because I believe he loves only his work, and is using us to accomplish his goal."

"No, no. You wrong him, Etta. Poor creature. I cannot but pity him."

Her eyes wide, Marietta said, "But I thought you so feared him? Have you changed your mind?"

"I admire him. And—yes, I fear him. More than ever now, alas."

"Then, what . . . ? Do you think I could use this alleged love he holds for me? I mean, if Eric should come, might Diccon help him—for my sake?"

"I wonder." Mrs. Cordova said thoughtfully, "However he may deny it, there are centuries of tradition behind him. I rather suspect the case would be, 'I could not love thee, dear, so much, Loved I not honour more.' Hurry and come inside, Etta. After all the rain I'm afraid we'll have lots of trees down if this beast of a wind keeps up."

During the night the wind not only kept up, it increased to gale proportions, howling in the chimneys and roaring in from the sea to hurl itself against the house with a force that threatened to tear the roof off.

Morning brought low clouds scudding across leaden skies. The grounds were littered with leaves and broken branches; several tiles had fallen from the roof; and a distant booming spoke of whitecaps crashing against the cliffs. There were occasional lightning flashes and distant growls of thunder. To Marietta's secret relief Eric did not put in an appearance. Nor did either Mrs. Gillespie or Friar Tuck.

⚜

It was a good thing Merlin's hat could be tied on. He wouldn't have risked wearing it in the wind except that a great wizard might have a better chance of finding a runaway cat. Sitting on the root of an oak tree, Arthur pulled the cloak tighter under his chin. Autumn was finishing up. It would be winter soon. Or was winter not till after Christmas? Anyway, his feet were tired. He'd searched the house and the barn and he'd even gone into the henhouse which had made them all beside themselves, and Sir Strut, the big goose who ruled the grounds, had shouted at him. Bridger had said he hadn't seen any cats, but Bridger was cross 'cause water had come through the roof and made a sack of oats wet, and hay had blowed everywhere. Etta had been cross, too, 'cause Mrs. G'lespie hadn't come and how they were to get the wash done, she didn't know. And Aunty Dova had been worried 'bout her caravan and had gone off with Mr. Joss to see if it had been blowed over.

If they hadn't all been so busy, he'd prob'ly never have 'scaped. He was a bit hungry for his breakfast, but he wasn't going back. Not till he found the Friar. And he'd best be getting along, 'cause if they was looking for him a'ready—

A shadow fell across him. He glanced up guiltily and gave a startled gasp. It was the biggest and most unhandsome man he'd ever seen. It was the sort of man you'd pretend to be the wicked giant in a story. Which prob'ly meant it was a good man, 'cause the men you thought were good turned out to be bad, so prob'ly men what looked bad were good men.

He stood up and tried to be tall. "Are you a giant?" he enquired.

A slit appeared in the strange face. Great arms were raised to the sides, hands clenched into great big fists and a great big voice rumbled, "I am Ti Chiu. A mighty warrior."

He had an odd way of talking, with *l*s for *r*s, but p'raps he couldn't help it, so Arthur refrained from pointing out the error. Instead, he raised his small arms to the sides and said in a small growl, "I'm Merlin today. An' I'm a b'ginning warrior."

The slit in Ti Chiu's face became wider. "More like small cockroach than beginning warrior. Why does Merlin sit in rain?"

"I'm *not* a cockroach! I'm looking for my cat. He's a mighty cat. Have you seen him?"

"Your cat—it has a tail?"

" 'Course. All cats have tails!"

"No. In my country, few cats. No tails."

"I don't b'lieve you!"

The slit vanished. The Mighty Warrior stamped closer. "Many men do I kill. Little Cockroach be careful."

"Why? I've got my sword." Glad that he had worn it under the cloak, Arthur drew it and flourished it about.

Ti Chiu threw back his head and uttered a shattering sound that was, hopefully, a laugh.

"If you're not doin' anything much," said Arthur, "I'd 'preciate it if you'd help me find my cat."

"I am doing much. As my master wish. Why does Small Cockroach wear funny hat?"

"It's not funny!" said Arthur, indignantly. "It's a wizard's hat, and you shouldn't be a rudesby!"

The gash grin vanished. The fists stretched out, then clamped shut, and the Mighty Warrior stepped closer. "Do you know," he growled, "what I do to people who make fun?"

Arthur had to tilt his head up to look at him. He was afraid. Just a little bit. But he reminded himself that he was also Robin Hood. And Sir Lancer Lot. And Destes'ble Dag, the Scourge of the Seven Seas. "I'm not making fun," he said stoutly. "An' it's not nice for grown-ups to tell raspers to little boys."

Those great hands shot out. Arthur gulped with fright as he was swept up and held high in the air. Like a snake hissing, Ti Chiu demanded, "What is—rasper? And you be careful, cockroach boy!"

Arthur's heart was beating rather fast. But a true-blue gen'leman did not show fear. Diccon wouldn't. Whatever happened. He took a breath and explained, "It means a fib."

The big hands tightened, and the smile was a terrible thing to see. "If I drop you, stupid cockroach, you know what happen?"

"I'd come down bang, and you're jus' trying to frighten me 'cause big men don't hurt little children. 'Sides, it wouldn't be fair 'cause you did say a fib! It's no use making your eyes go 'way. You did! You said you'd got a master. You're the biggest warrior I ever saw, so how could anyone be your master?"

For a moment he hung there, suspended, looking down into that fearsome scowl. Then he was whirled around, another roaring laugh blasted his eardrums, and he was set down.

"Whee!" he cried. "That was fine! Do it again, please!"

Instead, one mighty paw seized him by the chin, forcing his head up, while the massive face was lowered to within inches of his own. The big man smelled funny, but Arthur decided it would be best not to mention that, either.

"You are lucky like cricket," the deep voice said. "Maybe you so lucky you will grow to be man. You go home, before big wind blow you far across seas." He released his hold so suddenly that Arthur almost fell, then he turned and went stamping off.

"If you were nice, you'd help me find my cat," called Arthur.

But the Mighty Warrior walked on without a backward glance, making a strange rumbling sound as if he was talking to himself.

⁂

No, he's not down here," snorted Sir Lionel irritably, bending over his workbench. " 'Pon my soul, I've a house full of people, but can any of 'em keep an eye on one small boy and allow me to work in peace? No!" A gust caused the door to slam shut, and he exclaimed, "If this wind gets much stronger there'll be no roof over our heads! Speaking of which, that fellow Williard sent his groom round with a dashed impertinent note. Did you hear me send him packing?"

'So that's why he's so testy,' thought Marietta. "No, Papa. I collect that Mrs. Crosbie Williard is still displeased with us."

He grinned. "One good thing to come out of it all is that the old lady has decided your aunt is demented, and her fool of a son says I may forget any aspirations to his sister's hand. Hah! Kind of him, I'm sure! He's decided now to press me for payment of the debt—much good it may do him, for I can't pay monies I don't have. Lucky thing Fanny has attached the affections of young Vaughan. He'll likely—"

A shout, a crash, and a piercing shriek cut off those ignoble sentiments.

They exchanged a startled glance, then Marietta was running to the stairs, her father at her heels.

The entrance hall was empty, but a stranger stepped from the drawing room and smiled at them amiably, despite the pocket pistol he held in one very white hand.

Sir Lionel roared, "Who the *devil* are you, sir?"

Marietta felt icy cold. She did not need the mockingly polite introduction offered by this uninvited caller. With his pal-

· 279 ·

lid skin and jet hair and eyes he could only be the "pastry man" whom Aunty Dova had described to her; the deadly individual who was Diccon's bitter enemy. She heard her father blustering a demand to be told what Monsieur Monteil was doing in his house.

"By all means," said the Swiss with a wave of the pistol, "join us."

Hurrying into the drawing room, Marietta paused, stunned. Jocelyn Vaughan was slumped against the wall with Fanny holding a handkerchief to his forehead. Blood streaked down his cheek, his eyes were closed, and he looked as if he could barely manage to stay on his feet.

Fanny turned a frightened face and half-sobbed, "Papa! Oh, Papa! They hit Joss so cruelly! With—with no warning!"

"Now you must be fair, Miss," purred Monteil. "He would not let us come inside. Most inhospitable. Besides, we have encountered the lieutenant before, and he warrants no kindness from us, eh, Ti Chiu?"

A heart-stopping rumble of a laugh brought a gasped, "Good God!" from Sir Lionel.

Following his goggling stare, Marietta thought, 'My heavens! How did Diccon ever survive a fight with that enormous creature?'

Sir Lionel wet his lips and his voice shook slightly when he asked, "Are you all right, Vaughan?"

"Now there is a singularly stupid question," observed Monteil.

Marietta started towards her sister, but the Swiss threw up a detaining hand. "Stay where you are, pretty lady. I know; it is heartless. But you see, I have only Ti Chiu with me. He is," he added with a chilling smile, "usually sufficient."

Sir Lionel demanded, "Sufficient for what, sir? What the deuce d'you mean by breaking into my house, attacking my guests, bringing—"

"I require information," said Monteil. "You may help the Lieutenant to a chair, Miss."

. 280 .

Fanny guided the sagging Vaughan to a chair, and knelt beside him.

"What information?" asked Sir Lionel. "If you're after that stupid treasure, I don't believe in it!"

"Nonsense," said Monteil. "You have had our friend the Major as a guest. From all I hear he is quite devoted to"—he strolled closer to Marietta—"this lovely lady."

Sir Lionel pulled Marietta behind him. "Do not *dare* look at my daughter in that way, you insolent—"

Grinning broadly, Ti Chiu stepped forward and gave Sir Lionel a shove.

Fanny screamed as her father went flying across the room and crashed into the round table, taking it down with him.

Vaughan struggled to rise, but was helpless.

Infuriated, Marietta's hand flashed out and she slapped Monteil hard. He rocked on his heels. The marks of her fingers began to glow on his pallid cheek. He swore in French, moved fast as a striking snake, and seized her hair, jerking her to him. "It will be my pleasure to gentle Diccon's woman!"

"Don't! Don't!" screamed Fanny.

Astonishingly high-pitched, Ti Chiu's voice rang out in rapid sing-song Chinese.

Monteil paused, glancing at him sharply.

With a look of stark horror on his face the big man was staring fixedly at the effigies on the sofa.

Following his gaze, Monteil pushed Marietta away. "But how interesting," he murmured, and went over to examine Mrs. Cordova's "friends."

In the same high-pitched voice his henchman cried, "No, no! Master must not touch honourable dead!"

"Stupid fool!" Monteil held up "Mrs. Hughes-Dering's" arm and shook it. "They're dummies. Stuffed dolls. Not stuffed people."

Ti Chiu turned his little eyes to Marietta. "These, they were alive?"

Her knees were shaking, but sensing the superstitious nature of the big man, she answered, "Yes. They were once my aunt's friends."

The Chinese drew back. "This evil house. These people they have call up honoured dead. The gods will be angry! We must go, Master."

"So we will, idiot. When they've told me what they know of *The Sigh of Saladin*."

A clap of thunder made them all jump.

Marietta said, "We don't know anything of the treasure, but you can search the house if you wish."

"You are too eager, I think." Monteil's black eyes narrowed. "Who else is here?"

Sir Lionel, who had sunk into a chair, stood again and said, "Only my groom, who is in the barn and would not have heard—"

"Go and call him," snapped Monteil. "Or is there a bell?"

Sir Lionel's mouth opened.

Marietta said quickly, "Yes. Over here. I'll ring it." She started for the bell pull.

"No!" snapped Monteil. "I trust you not an inch, madam. Ti—you may summon another fool to join us."

Vaughan lifted his head painfully and stared at Marietta.

Sir Lionel looked frightened. He said, "No—it doesn't—"

"We'll see," said Monteil, smiling his icy smile. "Move, Ti!"

Ti Chiu seized the bell pull, his big paw encompassing the wire that Sir Lionel had so carefully concealed behind it. He tugged. In fact, he gave several tugs.

Lightning flashed in a lurid blue glare as four of the effigies leapt into the air and jerked about in a crazy dance.

Imre Monteil was a poised and intelligent man, but his jaw dropped at the sight. The effect on his henchman, however, was catastrophic. Ti Chiu gave a shrill scream of terror, released the bell pull, and fled, his charge staggering his master as he galloped madly for the kitchen door.

Vaughan, who had been gathering his strength, threw himself at Monteil's legs and brought the Swiss down. With lightning reaction, Monteil reached for his fallen pistol. Marietta snatched it up, ran back a few paces, and aimed it at him, her face set and determined.

Vaughan had stood. He was very pale, but he held his own pistol and said, "Careful, Miss Warrington. I'll handle this scum!"

"He's a perfect beast, and—" In her fury, Marietta's grip tightened and the pistol went off deafeningly.

Monteil, who had dodged aside, sprang forward and sent Fanny hurtling at Vaughan.

Sir Lionel ran to help his daughter.

His aim blocked, and his eyes losing focus, Vaughan dared not shoot.

Moving very fast, Monteil was in the corridor, across the kitchen, and wrenching the back door open.

Sir Lionel snatched Vaughan's pistol and sprinted in pursuit, but, despite his terror, Ti Chiu had retained sufficient of his wits to have scrambled to the box of Monteil's carriage.

With a crack of the whip and a thunder of hooves, the carriage, Monteil, and his henchman were gone.

❧❦❧

Merlin's hat was all droopy now, and the cloak was awf'ly wet. The wind was nastier, and even great wizards got hungry. But worst of all was the thunder and lightning. Arthur didn't like either. Eric said lightning was more dangerous, but thunder made such a horrid noise. It was lucky he'd found the big tree, 'cause he didn't get quite so much rain on him, but he must've walked hundreds of miles, and although he'd called lots of times, Friar Tuck wouldn't come.

Shivering, he huddled against the tree and decided to go home. Not that he was 'fraid, o'course; not really 'fraid. But the Friar had prob'ly gone home by now, anyway, so he wouldn't be a coward to go an' see. He'd jus' rest his feet a bit, first. . . .

His neck was stiff when he awoke. He hadn't meant to fall

asleep and he got up quickly and started for home. The trouble was that he didn't know this part of the woods. He'd come in here 'cause he'd seen the bushes moving about and something small had gone running off. He'd stopped when he realized it wasn't Friar, but now he couldn't seem to find his way out.

He was beginning to feel quite lonely when at last he emerged from the woods, and he was dismayed to see that the sky was getting to look like lunch-time. The thunder rumbled now and then, but it was a long way off, and the lightning was more like a glow on the clouds, not that horrid zig-zagging dart down the sky. The clouds were awful dark, though, and looked heavy. He'd be glad if they didn't let the rain out till he was home. Wherever home was. If there was someone about, he could ask. But there wasn't. Just him.

He trudged along a rutted lane, with hedges on one side and the woods on the other. Soon, the lane would leave the woods behind and go somewhere, and then he'd be able to see Lanterns and he'd know how to get home. After a while he began to sing his Detestable Dag song, so as not to feel so lonely, but stopped when he heard a horse coming.

"Please, sir," he said eagerly when the horseman drew level, "I'm jus' a little bit lost, an'—" He stopped, and frowned. "Oh. It's you. I don't like you anymore."

"That's not a very nice way to greet a rescue party, you know," said the horseman with a smile. "Come on up, old fellow, and we'll get home just in time for tea."

Never had "tea" sounded so magical.

In another moment rescued and rescuer were riding back into the woods.

CHAPTER XVII

W hy must he do it?" demanded Sir Lionel irascibly as Marietta helped him into his greatcoat. "I tell you what it is, Etta, that child has the wandering itch! It will do him good to lose himself for a little while. He'll find his way home, never fear. He always does, and everyone hereabouts knows him, after all, so there's no danger of his getting really lost. Perhaps this time it will teach him a lesson!" He paused and took her by the shoulders, scanning her face. "Shall you be all right here, my love? You've had a dreadful shock. I'd not go off and leave you alone, but if I send for Constable Davis he'll likely not stir his stumps until the storm passes, and this ugly business must be reported to the authorities at once. Besides, that fool Wantage must come and look at poor Vaughan."

"Yes, of course, Papa. And I shan't be alone. Fanny and Aunty Dova are here, and Joss—Mr. Vaughan—will likely wake up feeling quite restored."

Sir Lionel, who thought that Vaughan had looked extremely ill when Fanny had insisted he go to bed, doubted that remark, but said only that it was very probable and repeated his injunction that Marietta was not to go out searching for Arthur.

She walked to the front door with him. "But, it is half past one and he has been gone since breakfast-time. You know how a storm upsets him!"

"What I know is that he's worried about that confounded cat and won't come back till he's found the creature. If he's not home by the time I get back, I'll lead out a proper search party. I don't want *you* going off and taking cold in the wet. You're a gentle creature and will need a good rest after that ordeal! Promise you'll do as I say."

Nothing would move him. Reluctantly, she gave her promise and waved from the terrace as the coach lurched and splattered its way through the mud. The downpour had eased a little, but the skies were very dark and threatening. Poor Arthur must be very cold and hungry. Unless—

"He's likely gone down to Lanterns, my love." As if reading her mind, Mrs. Cordova watched her from the hall.

"I hope so." Marietta came in and closed the door. "But he would have to be very desperate to go there. He's greatly disillusioned with the Major because"—she broke off in the nick of time and rephrased—"because he was not allowed to help with the rocket signal."

"Perhaps." Her aunt regarded her steadily. "But whatever else he may be, there's no pretence about Diccon's affection for the boy."

Stifling a sigh, Marietta asked, "How does Mr. Vaughan go on?"

"He is asleep, and Fanny is sitting in the corridor keeping vigil. I left the door wide. Most improper, I know. Now I think we all will be better for a cup of tea."

Marietta offered to help in this endeavour, but was ordered to sit and rest while her aunt bustled about preparing the tea and exclaiming over the audacity of Monsieur Monteil.

Listening with half an ear, Marietta's eyes turned often to the leaden skies beyond the rain-dappled windows, and her thoughts turned to Diccon, who had not come when she so needed him. Was that because he'd seen who the uninvited callers were and, despite his ardent promises, had cared only that Eric Warrington was not among them? Or dare she hope that Aunty Dova was in the right of it? Had Arthur indeed gone

down to Lanterns, and was Diccon at this very moment indulging him with cake or whatever the Lord of the Larder could
provide?

Vaughan was still sleeping and Fanny refused to leave him,
so Marietta carried her tea up to her. When she went downstairs
again she found that her aunt had started a fire in the drawing
room, and they took their tea before the hearth together. The
big room was soon warm and cosy, the crackling of the logs mut-
ing the sounds of the storm. The violent episode with Monsieur
Monteil and his monstrous hireling had been more of a strain
than Marietta realized, and she began to feel drowsy. . . .

She awoke with a start when a log fell in half on the grate.
She had slept for an hour, and was alone. Neither her aunt nor
Arthur were to be found, and Fanny had dozed off in the chair
outside Vaughan's room. The storm had increased in strength,
the wind lashing the trees and driving the rain in grey sheets
against the house. Ever more worried about her little brother,
out and alone in such dreadful weather, she peered out of the
kitchen windows. There was no sign of the carriage as yet, but
if Papa had gone on into Eastbourne he could not have returned already. She saw then that a note penned in her aunt's
large printing was propped against the tea-cosy. *I know you
promised your father not to go looking for Arthur, my love, but I did
not. Miles Cameron has told me something I cannot like, so I'm going
to walk down to Lanterns and see if he's there. Arthur, I mean. Don't
worry, I'm taking the umbrella.* There was a postscript: *The umbrella blew inside out, silly thing, so I won't take it. Aunty D.*

Despite her anxieties Marietta had to smile at this, and was
about to go up and show it to Fanny when gloved hands came
from behind to cover her eyes. Her heart leapt into her throat
and she whirled, snatching up the teapot and prepared to use it
as a weapon.

"Hi!" cried Eric, throwing up one hand to fend off her attack. "I know I'm a reprehensible fugitive, but do I deserve such
a welcome from my nearest and—"

He was here! Very wet, but tall and handsome and, whatever else, so dear to her heart. Not until this moment had she realized how overwrought were her nerves. Tears choked her, and she threw herself into his arms.

Eric hugged her, then held her away. "What's all this? My brave girl—weeping? I'm here, love, never fret. I've given the hounds the slip and all's well, at least for—"

"But—it isn't well," she interrupted, dabbing angrily at her eyes. "We've had the most d-dreadful men here, demanding to know where that st-stupid treasure is, and breaking poor Vaughan's head, and knocking Papa d-down, and—"

"What? Where is he?"

"Gone to report it all to—to Constable Davis or the military post, and to fetch—"

Eric stiffened. "Military post?"

"Yes. And we've lost Arthur again. He's been gone since before breakfast, in all this rain and storm, and— Oh, what am I babbling at? Eric, You didn't tell me the truth about your—your employers!"

"I know. I wrote to you. Have you not had my letter?"

"Yes, but a general called on Papa, and he said you'd been engaged in selling *military secrets*, not—not industrial sabotage, as—"

He had paled noticeably and now again interrupted, "A *general?* Who? Not Smollet?"

"Yes. And he warned Papa to be on the look out for—"

"The devil!" He put her aside and striding quickly into the dining room took down the ginger jar. "I have to borrow this, Etta. I'm sorry, but I'll repay. I must get out of England as quick as may be, and—"

Heartsick, she gulped, "It is truth then? You really are . . . a traitor! Oh, Eric!"

"Don't put on such a tragedy face, for Lord's sake!" He thrust the money into his purse and said roughly, "Traitor to whom? A stupid fat Prince who is glutting himself into the grave? Much allegiance I owe Prinny and his crew of sots and spendthrifts!"

"You owe allegiance to England! Would you see us ruled

from Versailles? Or Madrid, perhaps? How could—"

"Have done! I've no time for nonsense!" He pushed past her and stalked across the corridor and into the kitchen saying in that harsh voice that was so strange to her, "My father whistled my future down the wind with his careless gaming. What prospects have I now, save by taking a risk or two? No, don't preach at me, Etta! With luck, I could have restored our fortunes! You were glad enough to take my ill-gotten gains last time I came, but now I'm in the suds a fine thanks I get for my efforts!"

Running after him, she tugged at his sleeve. "Wait! Eric, you know we all love you. Please listen to me! You must not—"

He was already on the back steps, and glancing up the hill exclaimed, "A coach! And coming at the gallop! Damme, but they're hot on my heels!" He gave her a quick kiss. "I'm sorry, Etta. You always were a good girl—"

"Wait! You *must* listen! Don't go to—"

He ran into the rain shouting down her attempts to warn him, and swung into the saddle of the weary horse that was tethered in the lee of the barn. "Don't worry about the brat, he'll come home. My love to all."

Desperate, she ran after him, shrieking, "Don't go to Lanterns! Diccon is an . . ."

But he was gone, thundering down the hill, the skirts of his coat flying, horse and rider silhouetted against the massed black clouds that were lit by occasional flashes of lightning. Standing in the rain, watching that headlong flight, Marietta thought that Aunty Dova would have said this frightful storm was an omen. The contents of the note came into her mind. Aunty was at Lanterns now. If she saw Eric before Diccon did, she might be able to warn him. 'Please God!' she thought fervently, and dashing rain from her eyes, turned back to the house.

The sounds of the team had been muffled by the storm but the carriage was coming at a neck-or-nothing pace and was almost upon her. Mud flew and she retreated to the steps. Bridger, grim-faced and soaked to the skin by the look of him, stared at her from the box. The carriage door was flung open and her father jumped out and hurried to join her.

"Has Eric come?" he asked, following her into the kitchen. His voice was strained, his face drawn, and a look of pained bewilderment was in his eyes.

'He knows,' thought Marietta. "He just left, Papa. He thought you were—"

"Bow Street coming after him?" He threw his hat onto the table and sat down drawing a hand across his eyes wearily. "He's a traitor. My son—a traitor! I couldn't believe at first, but . . . It's as well your dear mama is gone. This would have broke her heart!"

"Yes, Papa. But—"

"You knew, I see. Am I the last to know? Where did we fail him, Etta? I brought us to this nice house. I managed to keep us together, didn't I? He had a better life than thousands of other lads. How could he foul our honour and turn traitor to his own land? Surely— But, enough for that. Did he leave any message for me?"

"His love, Papa. He was only here for a minute or two."

"Would that I'd been here! I'd likely have taken my horsewhip to his sides! The crazy young fool! Dragging our name through the mud! Well, they're hard after him, just as he—as he deserves." Sir Lionel's voice shredded. He said hoarsely, "I collect the best we can hope for is that he gets to France so that we're not subjected to the—the humiliation of a—a public hanging!"

"Yes, sir. I tried to warn him, but he wouldn't listen, and—"

"Warn him of what? That your friend Diccon is a crack Intelligence Officer?"

Her "friend Diccon." Her *beloved*, rather. She flinched a little, but managed to keep her voice steady. "Yes. And that Major Diccon is ordered to take a suspected traitor if he comes this way. I did not dream it was my—my dear brother. Papa, my fear is that Eric will go to Lanterns believing that for my sake Diccon will help him leave the country."

Horror-stricken, Sir Lionel sprang up. "He'll walk into a

trap! You must go, Etta! Get your cloak! Quickly! Quickly! I would go with you save that I must be here if the troopers come. How could you not have told me what Diccon was? When I think of how the lying, deceitful snake wormed his way in here to spy on us, and all the while pretending— But never mind that. He loves you, no doubt of it. He'll do anything you ask! Go to him, Etta. Plead. Beg if you must. For your brother's life! You can't take the coach, else they'll wonder where it is. You'll have to run. Here's my pistol. Take it, and, if you have to, blow the miserable varmint's head off!"

⁂

There was no sign of life when Marietta picked her way across what had once been Lanterns' wide-spreading park. There were fallen branches everywhere and she was shocked to see that the great tree at the south end of the house was down, the roots sticking up starkly against a background of mountainous in-rushing whitecaps. The wind was so strong that it was hard to stand straight, and the booming of surf meeting cliffs shook the ground under her.

The hollow that once had been the moat was a sea of mud and she trod across the stepping stones fighting to hold her balance against the wind that seemed determined to make her fall. The back door wasn't locked, and she entered the scullery with a rush, then leaned back against the door, short of breath. She'd expected that MacDougall would be here, but there was no sign of anyone. Thunder growled as she hurried across the kitchen and along the corridor and lightning painted brief brilliant squares on the flags. Dreading to find the elder of her brothers here, she prayed the younger might be in the old house. She was sure that Aunty Dova was somewhere about, but although she peeped into each of the empty rooms she passed she did not see the lady. The sounds of the storm were much louder in the central single-storey hall, the rain drumming a tattoo on the roof. The heavy door of the south wing stood slightly ajar. She went down the steps slowly and with a heavy heart. This was where she'd waited to ambush Diccon with the music stand. It seemed so long ago. Who would have dreamed then that the tall quiet man would steal her heart and prove to be so treacherous? Or that she would have come here to beg for her brother's life.

The gale drove like a great fist against the house. The floor shook and Marietta gave a gasp as something flew into her eye. Wiping away involuntary tears, she saw that dust was filtering down from the ceiling. The moat and the south end of the drive-path had long since joined the piles of rubble on the beach far below. It was all too possible that the pounding breakers of this fierce storm would undermine the cliffs and bring the whole place tumbling down.

As usual, it was dim and gloomy in this windowless wing and she hurried past the rows of rooms neither seeing nor hearing a sign of life, until she reached the original great hall. She saw a distant glow then, and heard a familiar voice, and her heart sank.

Eric was saying furiously, ". . . inform your military masters about your free-trading! Then where will you be?"

"No worse off than I am now." Diccon's quiet drawl. "I should tell you, Warrington, that free-trading was an integral part of my military activities and helped me deal with several tricky customers."

"Is that what I am to you? A tricky customer? You didn't think that when you were lounging about as my father's guest and pretending to court my trusting sister!"

There was no answer.

Under cover of a great crack of thunder Marietta crept across the long dark room towards the glow of a single candle. She could see Eric now, looking pale and desperate, sitting hand-cuffed to a rail of the stairs that led to the minstrel's gallery and the upper floor. Diccon stood by a massive old table, lighting a lantern, the glow revealing his cold and stern expression.

"If you ever hope to win her," persisted Eric, "you had best give me a chance."

"But you see, I do not hope to win her under any circumstances. And even if I did—"

Eric had seen his sister, and his eyes widened. Ever alert, Diccon jerked around. Marietta heard his faint gasp. Her fingers touched the horrible coldness of the steel in her pocket that seemed to match the icy fear in her heart, but she said gently, "Under *any* circumstances . . . my friend?"

That lance went home. One of his long, sensitive hands clenched hard, but he replied quietly, "Under any circumstances, ma'am."

She walked closer. "Diccon, I beg you. Give him a chance. A five-minute start is all I ask."

"I am sorrier than I can say. But you ask the impossible."

Another step forward, and she pleaded, "You could claim that he stole Orpheus before you could stop him. You said no other horse could touch him."

He shook his head, but a small pulse was beating at his temple, and that betraying fist was very tight.

"Do I mean nothing to you?" she murmured. "I had begun to hope there was more between us than just—friendship. Diccon, dear Diccon—he is my beloved *brother*. I *implore* you—don't send him to a hideous death! It would break my father's heart. And poor little Arthur adores him. Don't destroy my family. Don't hurt me so, my dear, I *beg* you."

He winced at that. He was paler than Eric now, perspiration shone on his brow, and his voice was strained. "You must rest that responsibility on your brother's shoulders, Marietta. I am a serving officer. The oath I took to serve my King and my country did not contain a clause that said I could break it if I was personally affected. Please—please do not ask it of me."

She blinked away tears and did more than ask. She stepped even closer and sank to her knees, stretching up her hands to him while her brother watched, awed and breathless.

Diccon groaned and shrank away. "No! Get up! For mercy's sake, Marietta! Get up!"

She said brokenly, "You must know that I care for you. I

know you loved another lady, my dearest, and—and that you might not have much love left for me, but—"

Anguished, he leaned to her and took her beseeching hands in his cold clasp. "For the love of God! Stop! And try to understand. If I—if I worshipped the ground you walk on. If I thought you the bravest, purest, most beautiful lady I ever saw. If you held my whole heart and soul in these lovely hands—oh, my dearest of the dear—I could *not!*"

She knelt there, gazing up at him with the tears streaking her face and her pretty mouth trembling piteously. "Have you no mercy, Diccon?"

His own eyes dim, he said, "Your brother is a traitor. I can't turn away from that, even if it costs me my every hope of happiness."

"It will, you great fool!" shouted Eric wildly. "Think twice before you throw her love away! To my certain knowledge she has never loved before!"

Diccon's eyes did not leave Marietta. In a strained, hoarse voice he said, "During the war, my closest friend was working behind enemy lines. He was a splendid young fellow—clever, gallant, a man with a brilliant future and—and a fiancée who adored him. He was betrayed by a British traitor. The French took him and they tortured him . . . blinded him. But he would not give away the man he was working with. Me. Because of a conscienceless traitor he died in—the most frightful agony. And because of his unshakeable loyalty and courage I am alive today. I *cannot* do as you ask, my dearest girl. Do you see? I *cannot!*"

Marietta did see. He was right. But no matter what Eric had done she still loved him. She bowed her face into her hands and wept.

Diccon bent to her. "Come. Get up, sweet soul. As soon as Mac returns he'll take you home."

Still on her knees she looked up at him. "Mac is—is not here?"

"He was sent to the barracks to fetch a troop," said Eric

scornfully. "Your would-be suitor hadn't the backbone to take me in himself!"

Diccon said, "My orders were that if I encountered the fugitive I was to keep him under house arrest and send for support. The General feels that there are too many opportunities for ambush hereabouts. Especially with Monteil and his bullies lurking about. And he wants the men your brother works for."

Marietta thought dully, 'So he is alone here!'

Diccon was lifting her. She clung to him and he gazed down at her for a moment, his eyes ineffably tender, ineffably sad.

"Don't just *look* at him!" screamed Eric hysterically. "*Do* something, Etta! Help me!"

She must, of course. She must try. So she said, "I had hoped I would not have to resort to this. But—you leave me no choice, Diccon. You told me once that you have never harmed any lady, least of all your mama." He watched her steadily, but said nothing. She drew a deep breath, and, feeling slightly sick, went on: "We can prove now that you did harm the lady. Or even that you have probably d-done away with the poor soul."

Eric gave a triumphant whoop. "Aha! The biter bit!"

Diccon said without expression, "I would be most interested in knowing how you expect to prove such a thing."

"You were seen." Marietta's voice sounded faint and distant in her own ears. "You and MacDougall wrapped the-the—"

"Corpse?" he supplied with the ironic lift of one eyebrow.

"Yes," she whispered. "You wrapped it in a blanket and put it in a carriage that another man drove off. And you t-told Mac that 'she' must never be found. We-we have a witness."

Diccon stared at her, then said half to himself, "Arthur! The young scamp told me I was a murderer! So *that's* why he attacked me!"

Exultant, Eric howled, "We've got him, by George! Take off these shackles, you blasted hypocrite! Looking down your haughty nose and calling me traitor, and all the while knowing you've murdered your own mother! Jupiter! It defies belief!"

Diccon ignored him, and watching Marietta's drawn face

said gently, "My poor girl. Knowing you, and your high moral code, I can guess how hard it was for you to do this. But—I'm afraid it won't serve."

"Oh, yes it will!" cried Eric. "Only let me go, and you're free. You have my word that Arthur will never speak against you!"

Diccon gave him a contemptuous glance. "And I am to take *your* word? I think not. Besides, Arthur will not speak against me."

"How do you know that?" Eric eyed him suspiciously. "The child is missing, and . . . ! My God! Etta! He's got the poor little fellow!"

"Try not to be so ridiculous," said Diccon. "The boy is too young to give evidence, Marietta. He *cannot* testify against me."

"Untrue! Untrue!" Eric's voice rang shrilly. "Don't listen to him, Etta! He's killed his mama, what's to prevent him doing away with a child who can name him the despicable murderer he is? Make him let me go so that we can find my poor little brother! Don't listen—"

Marietta waved a hand, silencing his raving "No, Eric. He is deeply fond of Arthur. He'd never hurt him."

"But he's eager to hurt me! Does that count for *nothing*? Do you mean to let him drag me to public disgrace and dismemberment and execution? It would kill Papa! You *know* that! *Do* something!"

She smiled wearily. "Yes, I'm afraid I must." She took the pistol from her pocket and levelled it at the man she loved. "I am not an amateur," she said. "I know how to shoot. You must unlock the handcuffs, Diccon."

He looked from the pistol in her delicate hand to her shadowed eyes. How sad she seemed. He said, "Can you reconcile this with your conscience, my dear? It will make you as guilty. You'll have to leave the country, you know."

"Much she cares for this miserable country," cried Eric. "I will take my darling sister to France and she'll live like a queen. Now get these accursed manacles off me!"

The pistol in Marietta's hand was very steady. "Please do as he says."

Diccon nodded, took the key from his pocket, and walked towards Eric. His hand flashed upward. Something glittered briefly and was gone. They heard the faint clink as the key landed far down the dim hall.

Eric uttered a howl of fury. "You miserable bastard! Shoot him, Etta, and run quickly and find that key before—"

A roaring onslaught of wind against stone drowned his words. The house shuddered and the steps to the minstrel gallery creaked and shifted ominously. A cloud of dust and debris rained down from the ceiling, and upstairs something fell with a great thump.

"Hurry!" Eric shouted as the uproar faded. "Do you mean to wait till the troopers come? Or until this horrid old pile slides down the cliff? *Shoot him!* Shoot!"

Marietta's finger tightened around the trigger.

⚜

Sitting amidst the rubble Mrs. Cordova coughed and sputtered and was extremely disillusioned. The Mystical Window Through Time had warned her that something wicked was coming—the horrid pastry man and his accomplice, she'd thought—but it had said nothing about tycoons or hurricanes or whatever they were called, or about walls falling in on the heads of innocent ladies. She blinked tearfully, and wiped dust from her face and eyes. Her hair must be thick with the beastly stuff, and her head hurt quite nastily. She explored with caution, and felt a lump that did not like to be touched. One of these horrid chunks of stone must have struck her.

The thick clouds of dust were settling now, and she saw that a section of the outer wall had collapsed and that she'd actually been quite fortunate, because some of the chunks were really large and she might very easily have been killed. Her right shin seemed to have caught a rap, also. Investigating, she pushed away the slab of stone that had fallen on her leg. Her stocking was torn and the skin was scraped, and she would have a fine

· 297 ·

bruise. It was most unfair. She was trespassing, of course. She'd crept up those very rickety stairs just in time to avoid being caught by Diccon when he'd ridden in. She had wandered about, through small rooms and large, searching for Arthur, and then had been intrigued by the carving of a harp on the chimney-piece of this great chamber that must at one time have been the music room. The wind had made so much noise that she'd had little fear of being discovered, and it was unkind of this piece of stone to have hurt her poor leg when she had been doing nothing wrong.

"Nasty thing!" she exclaimed, kicking the slab in annoyance. She didn't kick very hard, because she had no wish to add a broken toe to her injuries, and she was surprised when the slab shot across the floor. It wasn't very thick, of course, but even a small piece of stone is usually quite heavy. She sat and considered it. "Hmm," she said, and getting up went to give the offending slab an exploratory prod. It looked like a piece of stone, but it couldn't be, because it was—soft! Intrigued, she bent and took it up. It weighed no more than five or six pounds and for some most peculiar reason it had been wrapped up in cloth or sacking. Now, why on earth would anyone want to wrap up a piece of stone? She began to unpeel the wrapping, but the fabric was rotted and thick with dust, and fell apart in her hands. The afternoon was fading fast and the light was dim, but she caught a glimpse of something shiny. Her bright eyes grew round with excitement, and she pulled away the rest of the wrappings paying no heed to the rain blowing in on her, or the shower of dust dislodged by another thunderclap.

"Oh, my!" she whispered, staring down at what she held in reverent hands. "Oh, my goodness, gracious, me!"

Dammitall!" Eric Warrington's frenzied howl cut through the voice of the thunder. "Do not stand there like a statue! It's his life or mine, girl!"

Diccon stepped forward. "Put it down, Marietta."

She was reminded of the way he had walked straight at the pistol when Blake Coville had threatened him. He was not an easy man to intimidate. She would *have* to shoot! She thought achingly, 'Oh, Lord! I love him! I cannot!' But for the sake of Eric and her family, perhaps she could put a ball in his foot, or his leg, or—

"No! Don't shoot!"

Shocked, she glanced aside.

Blake Coville's entrance had been unheard because of the storm. He held a long-barrelled duelling pistol trained on Diccon and he moved quickly to wrest away Marietta's weapon. "My apologies," he said. "But I cannot let you kill my so loved kinsman, m'dear."

Eric groaned with frustration and lowered his head onto his captive arms.

For once caught completely off-guard, Diccon kicked himself mentally, and drawled, "You reserve that privilege for yourself, do you?"

Coville grinned. "To attend your obsequies would not throw me into a decline, dear brother. On the other hand, your friend Smollet would likely make England too hot to hold me, and I've no wish to leave this green and pleasant land."

"More fool you," grunted Eric sourly.

Marietta said, "Blake—help my brother, I beg you."

Coville glanced at Eric. "I might. But first I'm here to bargain for myself." He stepped closer to his step-brother. "I have absolutely no compunction about putting a bullet through your knee, Paisley, and as you know, I'm a crack shot, so abandon any heroic impulses."

Diccon sighed. "We're back to that confounded treasure, are we? I don't know where it is. Not that I'd tell you if I did. Actually, I don't believe it ever existed, but—"

"Yes you do! Blast your eyes, d'you take me for a flat? I know why you're down here! I saw your sketches. You mean to renovate this hideous old pile. And you've not a louis to bless yourself with, so the money's coming from somewhere!"

"If I ever—"

"Be still! I'm not here to *discuss*, dear brother! I'm here to bargain. I have something you value. I'm willing to make a trade."

Diccon's eyes narrowed. "You can have nothing of the slightest interest to me, unless you refer to my mother's emeralds, and—"

"Fool! I got those years ago! I refer to something your so admired lady would give anything to reclaim."

Marietta gasped, "Arthur!"

Incredulous, Diccon said, "You cannot mean you've taken the boy? No—not even *you* would sink so low as to harm a child!"

"I've got him," confirmed Coville, his eyes glinting with triumph. "He's safe. For now. But not for long. No! Stay back or I'll cripple you, Paisley! I have the brat tucked away where he'll never be heard, never be found, I promise you. And nobody—*nobody* else on this earth knows where he is. So if I go away, or if anything should happen to me, he'll starve slowly."

"You *wouldn't*!" cried Marietta, horrified. "He's just a little boy!"

Eric snarled, "Let me free, Paisley, and I'll tend to this carrion!"

Watching Coville, Diccon said, "You've not the backbone to do something like this unless you're properly in the suds. What happened, Blake? The ponies? Or the tables?"

Coville glared at him murderously, then gave a short nervous laugh. "Think you're damned clever, don't you! Well, find a way out of this, Major, sir. I'm sunk deep to the cents-percenters. If I can't make good on my loan, I'm ruined, and you know my doting sire—he'd throw me to the wolves without a second thought. I've nothing to lose, and I haven't much time. Nor has dear little Arthur! So make up your mind, dashing old lordship. The boy—or the treasure!"

tell you, I don't—" Interrupted by the howling wind, Diccon paused, then shouted, "I *don't know!*"

"You *do* know, damn you!" Blake stuck Marietta's pistol into his belt and stepped closer. He looked wild and desperate, his hair wind-blown, his face flushed, hatred for his step-brother glaring in his eyes. "I warn you, I mean to have it! But if I leave here empty-handed, your beloved will never see dear little Arthur again, and you'll be responsible for the deaths of *two* of the lady's brothers." That barb pierced Diccon's icy self-control, seeing which Coville sniggered, "It would appear that you make a habit of bringing death to your women, my lord."

Eyes narrowed and fists clenching, Diccon crouched, and Blake steadied his aim and shouted, "Stay back! If I have to shoot I'll see to it that you suffer as slow an end as the boy will face!"

Eric said, "By God, Coville, you're worse than he is! If anything happens to my brother—"

"You'll do—what? Accuse me from the gallows? Hah! Who'd take the word of a convicted traitor? At all events, nothing could be proven against me without the boy, and since he'll never be found—"

Lightning flashed glaringly, and the immediate thunderclap was echoed by an ear-splitting creak. More debris showered down.

Eric howled, "This curst pile is falling to pieces! I'll be trapped! Get me out, Paisley, or—"

Coville said, "No one leaves here till I have *The Sigh of Saladin* in my hands!"

From the corner of his eye Diccon saw Marietta edging back towards the table. He said with the cool disdain that always infuriated his step-brother, "What a fool you are, Blake. Greedy men have sought that picture for centuries and been unsuccessful. How typical that you would expect me to be able to find it in a few minutes!"

"I *know* you found it, you lying rogue! That fortune-telling gypsy told Imre Monteil that she'd *seen* it, and that it was here at Lanterns! I've no time to waste! Tell me, or—" The floor shuddered and he glanced at the ceiling uneasily.

Marietta had taken up the candle and moved close behind him. He was, as always, immaculately clad, and must have arrived by coach because he wore no overcoat and his clothes were dry. When Marietta applied the flame to the tails of his coat, they caught at once.

"Believe it's upstairs, do you?" purred Diccon. "I'll own it, Blake. You're—ah, getting warm."

Of this, Coville was unpleasantly aware. He could smell something odd, and the light in the room flickered strangely. Warrington gave a shriek of mirth. Looking at him uneasily, Coville sensed that the sudden warmth came from the rear. He glanced down, saw a bright flame, and screamed.

Diccon leapt forward, and smashed the pistol from his hand.

Still screaming and beating wildly at his tails, Coville fled into the rain.

Diccon began, "Well done, Mari—" then was staggered as the floor lurched under him.

There was a growling rumble, whether of thunder or the gale, Marietta could not tell.

On the stairs by the minstrel gallery, clutching something under her cloak, Mrs. Cordova called, "Major! I must tell you— Oh, dear! I rather think your house is falling down!"

"For the love of God, get me out of h
rington.

With a roar that beat at the ea
of the room disappeared and the air
and tumult.

Diccon ran through the thick dust a
down the stairs. "Outside, ma'am!" He se
"Hurry! Hurry! Get her out!"

She said, "But—Eric . . ."

"I'll bring him. Go! Before the whole upper
down!"

"But you haven't the key!"

"*Out!*"

He pushed them towards the front door. This end of th
wing was going to crumble to the beach at any second. Th
was no hope of finding the key in time. He sprinted to the wal.
dim-seen through the gloom, whereon hung the ancient
weapons. Eric's screams rang in his ears as he gripped the handle of a war axe and tore it from the iron brackets that held it.
Succeeding, he was staggered by the weight, and went weaving
back through the dust, praying he could swing the weapon and
that it would not fall apart in the process. When he reached the
stairs to the minstrel gallery, he panted, "Lean—as far back—
as you can!"

Eric obeyed promptly.

With all his strength, Diccon swung the axe. The rail splintered but was driven into its neighbour.

Eric looked up and whispered, "Oh—Lord!"

A hand came over Diccon's shoulder and plucked the axe
away. He knew of only one man who could lift the heavy
weapon with such ease. He whipped around.

Holding the axe in one hand Ti Chiu gave an odd little bow
and said, "Now, two warriors will fight."

Eric began to struggle frantically with the railing that still
trapped him.

"You're mad," said Diccon unequivocally. "This storm

He leapt for his life as the axe came at him in a flying

ou very good warrior!" cried Ti Chiu, his little eyes lit by
tical gleam. "My honour it is shamed because I ran from
beings in other house. For my ancestors I must win honour
k."

"One looby after . . . another . . . !" groaned Eric, striving.

Diccon made a lunge for Blake's fallen pistol. He felt the
whisper of air as the axe flailed an inch from his ear. Laughing,
Ti Chiu kicked the pistol aside. Diccon continued to the wall
and snatched a great two-edged sword from its rack. Even as he
turned, Ti Chiu was upon him, the mighty curving blade
whistling at his throat. He avoided that attack and leapt away
but Ti Chiu swung again. Gripping the heavy sword with both
hands Diccon struck out with all his strength. The air rang to
the shock of steel on steel. Diccon's hands were numbed by the
impact, and he was staggered, but he had turned the axe aside,
and it rammed deep into the beam that served both as end post
for the stair rail and support for the minstrel gallery. Ti Chiu
tore it free and roared something in Chinese, then added, "You
worthy foe, Major!" He lifted the axe high, only to pause as the
gale thundered against what was left of the south wall. With a
deafening creak the minstrel gallery tilted.

Diccon ran to Eric and kicked the splintered rail free.

Eric slid his hands down to the break and shouted, " 'Ware!
'Ware!"

Diccon whirled, dragging the sword up.

Behind him, Eric kicked out hard and Diccon was sent
sprawling.

Ti Chiu grinned and ran forward, the axe swinging up for
the blow that would decapitate his opponent and restore his honourable name.

Eric made a mad dash for safety.

Agile as a cat, Diccon rolled and sprang up. The deadly axe
blade whistled past his shoulder.

A deep growling roar coincided with a sickening heave beneath their feet. With a keening whine of splintering wood the minstrel gallery sagged, sloping downward.

From a long acquaintanceship with unquiet ground Ti Chiu grunted, "Earthquake!" dropped his axe and headed for the door.

Diccon followed. Outside, the power of the gale snatched his breath away. The rain was coming down like a grey wind-whipped curtain. Drenched, Blake Coville sat in a large puddle looking balefully at Marietta, who had evidently retrieved her pistol and held it aimed at his head. Of Ti Chiu there was no sign. Mrs. Cordova was clinging to Eric's arm, obviously imploring him to help.

Marietta said, ". . . tell us where Arthur is, or we'll have you charged with kidnapping—or perhaps, heaven forfend, murder!"

"Without proof?" Coville sneered, "Never!"

"He's right," said Diccon, coming up with them. "He won't tell you, but at least we can make sure that he pays for his crimes." He hauled Coville up by his collar. "I've several scores to settle with you," he said grimly. "And no time to spare, so I'll make this a quicker end than you deserve." Blake struggled frantically to free himself, but with a practised twist Diccon forced his arm up behind him and began to march him towards the cliff edge.

"What are you doing?" cried Blake, his voice squeaking with fright.

"It's an old Cornish custom called being put to the cliff," said Diccon. "And as good a way as I know to rid the world of your worthless self."

Coville fought and kicked, but Diccon had long experience with such tactics, and his captive was borne relentlessly into the teeth of the gale. Even as they approached the cliff edge another section dropped away landing with a force that sent a great plume of water into the air.

Coville shrieked. "I nigh went over! You *want* me dead, curse you!"

Half blinded by the wind and rain, Diccon peered downward. They were at the brink now, and Coville was right except that almost they both had gone over and could very well be swept to their deaths at any second. The earth underfoot was fissured and unstable and far below the angry breakers raced in to explode against the cliffs.

Marietta screamed, "Diccon! You'll fall! Come away, for mercy's sake!"

"Stay back!" he shouted. "This carrion has murdered Arthur. He deserves to die!"

The wind was so strong that he could scarcely walk, but he forced Coville on until the toes of the man's boots were over the edge. "Farewell, dear Blake," he shouted, giving his stepbrother a nudge between the shoulder blades.

"No!" shrieked Coville. "I'll tell! *I'll tell!* For the love of God don't kill me! *Swear* you'll let me go if—"

"Quickly, fool, or you'll be too late!"

Coville sobbed out, "He's in . . . in the priest's hole."

"Under the pantry? Liar! It's empty."

"No, no!" Babbling in his terror, Coville said, "There's another. A smaller one. Under the steps to the minstrel gallery. There's a trapdoor. You—you open it by pushing the bottom step inwards. Now—let me go." He began to cry. "I beg you, br-brother! *Please* let me go!"

Diccon had a mental image of those tilting stairs, and the splintered beam that supported them, and his blood ran cold. With a grating curse he pulled Coville back, and sprinted towards the house.

Marietta flew to seize his arm. "Where? Where?"

"In a priest's hole under the minstrel gallery. Damn him! I'll need help." Running on, he shouted over his shoulder, "Hey! Warrington!"

Eric went to his sister. "Did Coville tell?"

"Yes." Marietta clutched at him as a gust almost swept her from her feet. "He's in a priest's hole hidden under the minstrel gallery."

"Then the poor imp's as good as killed. That whole section was coming down just seconds ago."

Steadying herself against him, Marietta pushed back her flying hair and saw Diccon rush into the old wing. The southwest corner was no more. It would be a miracle if the minstrel gallery in the opposite corner of the hall had not already collapsed. She wrenched at Eric's arm. "Help him, dearest! For mercy's sake. Help Arthur!"

He hesitated, then ran after Diccon.

Once inside, despite the missing corner of the wall there was a measure of relief from the howling gale. The newly created "window" admitted daylight, and faint as it was on this violent afternoon the ancient hall was brighter than it had ever been. Racing to the south end, Diccon paused, aghast. The minstrel gallery had slewed sideways and teetered on the steps. The supporting beam, weakened when Ti Chiu's axe had shorn into it, had snapped in two, and the upper half, still attached, hung like a great splintered lance from the sagging gallery.

Blue arrows of forked lightning lit the scene with a brief bizarre glow. The voice of the following thunder was echoed by a sharper roar, and the gallery jolted downward.

Diccon scrambled over the debris-littered floor and threw himself to his knees at the foot of the stairs. He pushed with all his strength at the base of the bottom step, but there was not the least movement. Probably, the great weight on the stairs had jammed the trapdoor. He glanced around. Warrington stood behind him, gazing with wide scared eyes at the wreckage of the gallery that hung poised above them.

"Give a hand here," Diccon shouted. "Your brother's underneath this lot!"

He saw the gleam of white teeth clamping onto Eric's lower lip, and snarled angrily, "*Move*, confound you! There's not a second to lose and I can't budge the step alone!"

Warrington closed his eyes briefly, then knelt, and reached out to help. Together, they strained and shoved, and at last the bottom of the step gave, and folded inward. Lying flat, Diccon could discern a heavy iron chain, but no sign of a secret chamber. He gripped the cold, rusty links, trying not to hear the grinding screeches from the gallery. The chain moved, but it was stiff, as if caught up somewhere, and the effort was exhausting. He glanced up, dashing sweat from his eyes. "Any sign of—a door?"

Warrington was kneeling, gazing up at the looming bulk of the gallery as if hypnotized, his face white with fear. "It's coming down! We'll all be crushed!"

"Not if we move fast! I think this chain is jammed somehow. Help me, will you?"

Warrington drew back, shaking his head.

Diccon swore and tugged mightily.

A loud crack, and a stair rail snapped, sending shards of wood flying in all directions. Diccon ducked instinctively, heard a choking scream and caught a glimpse of Warrington galloping back across the hall.

The chain gave suddenly and moved smoothly. The floor under Diccon's knees began to jerk open. So the priest's hole was underground. Praise God for that, because if the door had opened from the side in some way it would likely have been blocked by the buckling steps. He heaved at the chain and the opening widened, a stone slab rolling back to reveal a black aperture.

A hoarse, shaking voice arose from the gloom. "I knowed you'd come . . . Sir G'waine! I *knowed* you'd come!"

Peering down into that dark hole Diccon couldn't see the boy. Over the lump in his throat he called, "That's the spirit, comrade! Can you come here?"

A muffled sob. "He . . . he tied me up. He said it was a game, but . . . I don't like it. Please g-get me out."

"Right away! I'm coming—"

An ear-splitting rumble; another rain of debris. Diccon wrapped his arms about his head and lay flat, waiting helplessly for the gallery to smash onto him.

A blinding lightning flash. He still lived!

Arthur quavered, "D-Diccon . . . I'm very frighted. Am I goin' to-to be dead?"

"Not if I can help it," said Diccon through his teeth. He swung down into that black hole, and groped about. "Where are you, old Detestable Dag?"

"Here! Here I am. Oh, D-Diccon, thank you for—"

Chunks of stone and wood cascaded down. The darkness became a ravening greyness. Arthur screamed. Frantic, Diccon cried, "Are you hurt, lad?"

A moment, then came that quavering but dauntless little voice, "Not very . . . bad. What happened? I can feel the wind and—and I'm—getting wet."

"So am I. The wall's dropped off I'm afraid." Diccon could see the boy now, lying on a rough iron bed frame, his small hands and feet tied. 'Poor little devil,' he thought. He indulged a second's blistering evaluation of his step-brother but said lightly, "I think we'd better get out of this."

With a gallantry that wrung his heart the wan little face tried a smile, then the big eyes looked past him and widened. "What's . . . *that?*"

Diccon turned his head. His bones seemed to melt. The gallery was directly above now, the broken beam hanging from it like a splintered battering ram. As he gazed numbly, it lunged downward.

He grabbed the child. "Don't worry about that mess up there. I'm going to push you through now. I'll come after you, but don't wait for me. Roll as far away as you can."

He had swung the boy high when the floor heaved upward, knocking him off his feet. Arthur was torn from his arms. Sound was a continuing roar and more and heavier debris rained down, several chunks striking him. Sure that this was death, he scarcely felt their impact and strove desperately to reach the boy. He was unable to move. Something very heavy was across his legs. The priest's hole was filled with bellowing wind that was blowing the dust away. Blinking dazedly he saw that the entire south wall was no more. Part of the ceiling of the priest's hole had been ripped off and the opening where the trapdoor had been was bigger now. The minstrel gallery still hung over them, leaning at a crazy angle. It was much closer, but at least the stairs were holding the weight. There was enough space left that he could hoist the boy through, if he could get up, but the severed supporting beam was poised above, as if aimed straight at them. His mouth felt dry. He knew that Arthur watched him and his shouted enquiry elicited a trembling and barely audible, "I'm . . . all right."

He wouldn't be all right for long, thought Diccon grimly. Investigating, he found that a plank, probably from the floor of the gallery, had fallen across his legs. It shouldn't be this heavy. He tried to lift it, but it gave not an inch, and then he realized that the end was buried under what had been the slab of the trapdoor. He tried again, exerting all his strength until the blood roared in his ears and his eyes dimmed. But it was useless. Panting, he rested for a second.

"Oh, Diccon! Oh, *Diccon*! You can't *move* it! Is that tree coming . . . down on me?"

The beam was inching closer. Inexorably, inevitably, it would fall and crush them. How infuriating that he'd come so close to getting the boy to safety, only to—

"*Diccon?* Where are you? Diccon?" Marietta's dear voice.

"Down here," he wheezed. "Don't come too near."

He heard running footsteps, and then her sudden appalled cry.

"Arthur's here," he shouted.

She peeped in at them. He saw stark terror in her eyes, and called, "I'm afraid I'm not much use. Can you—get help?"

She wasted not an instant but nodded and was gone. And watching the slow advance of that murderous beam, he knew the help would have to be very fast and very sure.

"If ever I saw a man so in the habit of getting himself into tight spots!" Jocelyn Vaughan, pale and ill-looking, was gazing down at him.

He managed a grin. "Stand there another minute or two, and you'll be pushed in here with me, you block!"

"Mac's coming with the troopers. We've signalled him to charge." Vaughan disappeared.

There followed shouts and a scrambling noise. Then another outburst of shouts; angry now, half lost in a roll of thunder, but definitely angry. He thought in exasperation, 'Of all times to get into a brawl!'

"Sir G'waine . . . ?"

"Yes, Detestable?"

"When I get to heaven . . . will I see my mama?"

He couldn't answer at once, then said huskily, "If the lady is watching you now, she must be very proud." He stretched out and was able to touch the cold cheek. "Courage, Sir Lancelot."

"I'm awful glad you're with me, Sir—" The words ended in a shriek.

Diccon jerked his head around. The jagged end of the beam was sliding straight down; not at him, but at Arthur.

He shouted, "No! Damn you! *No!*" and in a burst of rage dragged himself onto his side, threw his left arm across that terrified little face, and took tight hold of the iron bed frame now lying on its side behind the boy. "Turn your head the other way, lad! *Turn your head!*"

Arthur's face whipped to the side.

Peering about desperately for something to use as a brace, Diccon was momentarily unable to breathe as the beam grazed past his face and jolted onto his outstretched arm. With an effort of will that left him drenched with perspiration he managed not to cry out and to keep his hold on the bed frame.

He heard Marietta's voice from a great distance, raised in a gasping scream, "It's fallen through the trap! Oh, my dear God! We must hold it, Joss! We *must!* Oh, *why* don't they come?"

Vaughan called breathlessly, "Hang . . . on, Trader! We're holding it . . . back, best . . . we can."

So that was why it hadn't smashed through bone and sinew.

His love and his friend were fighting for them. God grant the help came fast.

A deep and familiar rumble. His heart sank. 'Not now, Ti Chiu! Have some sense . . . can't fight you now!'

Vaughan roared, "Get the hell away from there, you great . . . Ow!"

The pressure increased savagely. Gritting his teeth, Diccon hung on to the iron frame and consciousness.

"You are down there, Small Cockroach?"

"Come to . . . gloat . . . have you?" panted Diccon.

Arthur sobbed, "It's me, Mighty . . . Warrior."

A deep, amused chuckle.

Her voice shrill with grief and hysteria, Marietta exclaimed, "You *wicked*—evil great *brute*! Go away and let us try to—"

The beam slid again. Diccon heard a soft, sickening crack and could not keep back a cry of anguish.

Arthur gulped, "You're bl-bleeding all over me, Sir G'waine! Oh, Etta! *Help* him! *Please*, Etta!"

"You just wait, Cockroach," growled Ti Chiu.

Lightning glared, throwing the tiny room into sharp relief, but to Diccon the details were blurred and indistinct. He couldn't endure this hideous agony much longer. . . . Something in his arm had broken, that was sure . . . but he mustn't let go. If he could just hang on till Mac came with the troopers. . . . Just long enough to keep the boy from being crushed. 'Please God . . . don't let me fail him!' Hang on. . . . Must hang on. . . .

❦

My name is Avebury." The voice was cool and businesslike, the face, with its ruddy cheeks and splendid side-whiskers, more suited to a country squire than to a doctor. But the hand that dabbed a cool rag at Diccon's face was gentle, and the grey eyes were kind. "From what they tell me, you've done magnificently," he went on. "I'm afraid we're going to have to make you a trifle uncomfortable for a little while, but I expect you're accustomed to us doctor-chaps."

Diccon blinked at him and wondered why he was in his former room in the dower house, and how he'd come here. He had a very vague recollection of being lifted, and of Joss complaining that no one would guess he weighed so much, but that was all. His left arm hurt horribly and with pain came memory. He asked in a voice that sounded far away, "How . . . ?"

"A jolly great Chinese fella held the beam back, so they tell me, till your friends got you out."

"The boy?"

"Is bruised and shaken, poor little lad. And won't leave your door. Ah, the arm pains you, of course. I'm very sorry, but . . ."

"But you're going to . . . amputate."

Avebury nodded gravely. "It's quite hopelessly shattered. I thought you might want to talk to, er—someone, before we get started."

Diccon felt a chill of fear. "You mean, I may want to say my farewells? Don't . . . hide your teeth, Avebury."

That brought a faintly admiring smile. "You're a soldier. You know the rules of the game. You're in fine condition, but you've had a great shock and lost a lot of blood, and now, unfortunately, I must—put you through the wringer again."

"Yes. What are my chances?"

The doctor hesitated.

Startled, Diccon said, "As bad as that? I want the truth, please."

Avebury said reluctantly, "I'd guess—about seventy-thirty."

"Against? I see." He took a deep, steadying breath. "In that case—you're right, sir, and . . . I thank you. There are things I want to say. I'd like to see Miss Warrington for a minute."

The doctor nodded, and went out.

Diccon closed his eyes wearily. Seventy-thirty. Arthur was safe, thank God! And he meant to beat those odds. But he wondered in a detached fashion how he would play his violin with one hand.

There was a gentle fragrance on the air. He looked up. Marietta sat beside the bed, smiling down at him. Her eyes were red, and her lips trembled a little. She said, "I wonder if you can imagine how much—"

He lifted his right hand, and found it quite an effort. "Yes, but it's not necessary. You know how I feel . . . about the boy. Eric?"

She flinched and blinked tears away. "He—ran. I doubt we shall see him again. And knowing him, I doubt he will ever forgive himself. Papa is—is hit hard, I'm afraid. Diccon—"

He lifted his right hand again, and it was caught in her quick vital clasp. He said, "There is something I must explain. I really haven't—" He broke off, holding his breath and praying.

Marietta bathed the white, haggard face, and fought against weeping. When his eyes opened he looked dazed, and she lifted his good hand and pressed a kiss on it. "You need not now—or ever—explain anything to me," she said huskily. "You are—are the bravest of the brave, and I shall always—"

"I must tell you."

His voice was weaker and once again she was pierced by the lance of terror. "Whatever you wish, my very dear."

"I want you to know that—that I really didn't—kill my mama. But I did . . . steal her. I could be hung or—or transported for kidnapping, do you see?"

She bathed his face tenderly. "I think I have always known that if you did such a thing, it was for a good reason."

To speak was a great effort, but he persisted doggedly. "Sir Gavin forged my mother's signature and—and took my inheritance from—from my grandmama. My mother found out. He was afraid she'd tell her friends, so he kept her isolated and . . . told everyone she was mad. He hired doctors to . . . treat her. Terrible treatments that nigh killed her. We'd never been very close, but . . . she is my mother. She was able to smuggle a letter to me, pleading most piteously that . . . I come and rescue her away, but . . ." He closed his eyes.

Marietta said gently, "Poor lady. How dreadful. Now please

do not talk anymore. I can guess what happened. He was her husband, her next of kin, so legally your hands were tied."

"Yes. He simply cannot bear any scandal, so he wanted to have her legally"—he sighed—"legally declared insane."

"It was splendid of you to take such a risk. I'm sure you have her safe and happy somewhere, but you are tired, my love. Do not—"

"In Italy," he muttered. "But I am still liable to . . . prosecution if he ever . . . should press charges. I wanted you to know, in case. . . . I'd like you not . . . not to think too badly of me."

Dr. Avebury came in. "I'm afraid I must ask you to leave now, Miss Warrington."

She looked up at him, her face tear-streaked and full of dread.

He smiled, and patted her shoulder. "There's a young gentleman in the corridor who needs you."

She bent over Diccon and kissed him full on the mouth. "God be with you, my brave one," she said.

ut—yesterday you said he came through the surgery splendidly." Holding Fanny's hand tightly and sitting very close beside her on the drawing room sofa, Marietta asked anxiously, "Is it a relapse? He *is*—oh *please* say he is going to live."

Dr. Avebury pursed his lips. "Temple and Cloud, or Major Diccon as you call him, has kept himself very fit. But he is no more immortal than the rest of us, my dear ma'am. For the system to suffer such a shock, and relatively soon after the other surgery is—um—a risky business."

Marietta started to shake, and Fanny put an arm about her. "Now, dearest, don't fly into the dismals. Dr. Avebury hasn't said Diccon is failing."

"No," whispered Marietta, the tears very close. "But—oh, Fan! I don't think I could bear it if—"

"And I don't like it when people put words in my mouth," scolded the doctor gently. "As I told Sir Lionel, we have to expect the Major's condition to worsen before it improves. I'll not sugar coat matters; for a week or so he's going to have a nasty time of it. But I have installed a competent nurse, and with you charming ladies pampering him, I don't see how he can help but make a recovery. Just don't expect too much, too soon." He saw tears beading Marietta's lashes, and came to his feet. "Enough of my blathering." He took her hand. "Keep him in your prayers, Miss Warrington. It's the best remedy I know."

Marietta said something in a scratchy, unintelligible voice, and the doctor turned to shake hands with Sir Lionel. "You must be very grateful that your little son was spared to you, sir."

"Yes." Sir Lionel's smile was wan. "I am, of course. Only . . . I have another son, you see."

Marietta exchanged a quick glance with Fanny, and Vaughan frowned. The doctor decided there were murky waters here, and took his leave, promising to call in the morning.

His prognosis proved all too accurate. Diccon's life became a dreary ordeal in which his only escape from pain was to plunge into a dark world of searing heat and the re-living of the most nightmarish episodes of his past. His moments of full consciousness were plagued by fears of life with one arm, and his mind seemed determined to conjure up every possible difficulty that might face him. Longing to see Marietta, he dreaded to see her eyes full of pity. Loving her with every breath, he shrank from the thought that she might consent to be his wife only out of a sense of obligation. He knew from experience that such anxieties would not help him, but was too weak to overcome them.

After a long and exhausting period of hopeless confusion he roused to the awareness that he was very ill indeed, and to a sense of indignation. What was left of his arm was aching fiercely, his head pounded, he felt as if he was on fire, and as though he were not sufficiently miserable, something was tickling his nose. He lacked the strength to brush away whatever so tormented him, but managed to open his eyes. The room was dark except for a shaded lamp that provided a soft circle of light at the foot of the bed. Someone was sitting there, reading. Closer at hand, two big green eyes stared into his own.

He said in a croaking voice that shocked him, "Get your whiskers off . . . my nose, Friar!"

A pair of disembodied hands came to take up the cat. Mrs. Cordova scolded, "Oh, you wretched creature! How did you—"

"Please." Diccon sighed. "Don't take him away."

"Of course, my dear," she said gently, restoring the miscreant to the bed. "Whatever you wish."

Not finding a hand on one side, Friar Tuck sought out the other. It failed to bestow the caress that was his due, but he was an accommodating animal. He squirmed and nudged and wriggled until the fingers, if they did not exactly stroke him, at least curved around his back. It would do, he decided, and snuggling closer, began to purr.

Diccon smiled faintly, and fell asleep.

❧

Sitting gingerly on the side of the bed, Vaughan was heartened by the fact that Diccon had improved sufficiently to ask questions. "Tuesday," he answered. "Or to be more exact, eight days since you decided to play the hero."

Feeble but indignant, Diccon said, "Damn you, Joss! What a wretched thing to say! Had you been in my shoes you'd have done exactly the same!"

Today there was a tinge of colour in the drawn face, and although it was all too clear that the poor fellow was still miserably uncomfortable, his spirit was evidently undimmed. Vaughan said slowly. "I hope I would. The thing is, you *did*, and never think people are going to let you forget it. Your lady, especially."

Diccon closed his eyes. Vaughan thought he slept again and was preparing to creep out when his friend asked, "Did Ti Chiu come and help? Or did I dream it?"

"He came. As nearly as we can work it all out, Monsieur Imre Monteil's one-man brigade met young Arthur while the boy was searching for Friar Tuck, and took a liking to him. Ti Chiu showed fear when he ran away from Mrs. Cordova's flying "friends," and by his standards his honour was besmirched. To restore it he must defeat in battle someone he respected. Odd reasoning, I grant you. But in the long run it saved you and the boy. He was the only man could have held up that damnable beam long enough for us to get to you."

"What you mean is that you risked your neck to crawl in there and haul us out. And you've the unmitigated"—Diccon shifted restlessly—"unmitigated gall to name me a—"

"You see?" interposed Vaughan hurriedly. "You're hurting yourself and if I cause you to fall into a fever again my life won't be worth living, so behave, or I'm off."

"Aye, aye, sir. But I'll thank you, just the same, Joss. No, don't go—please!"

"All right, all right! Don't fly into the boughs. Two more questions, is all though, I warn you."

"What about Ti Chiu? Any more sign of him?"

"No. When he trundled off he appeared to think his honour was restored. Smollet's had men combing the entire area and patrolling the coast. Monteil's nobody's fool, and likely took ship from some lonely spot in the west country."

"How has Sir Lionel taken all this? I don't think he's dropped in to chat."

Vaughan hesitated. Luckily, before he was obliged to answer, Diccon fell asleep again.

❧

Marietta awoke when Vaughan shook her gently. She had sat down in the kitchen for a moment, and dozed off. She sprang up with a frightened gasp. "What is it? Is he worse again? Is—"

Vaughan smiled and put a finger across her lips. "He's going on much better, so Avebury tells us. Smollet has come. He's in the withdrawing room with Sir Lionel. I thought you might want to see him."

"Yes. Yes, of course." She said nervously, "I must run upstairs and tidy my hair. You're sure Diccon is all right?"

"Your aunt and the nurse are with him." Vaughan's eyes twinkled. "Mrs. Cordova tells me that someone is coming. No, don't start worrying again. She didn't say it was someone wicked."

She reached out impulsively. "Joss, you've been such a tower of strength through this terrible time. I don't know how we would have gone on without you!"

"I'm glad." He pressed a kiss on her hand. "Because I don't mean to give you the chance to try."

She gave him a misty smile, then hurried away.

Fanny came in from the scullery, and went to Vaughan, and he slipped an arm about her. She said, "It's been almost two weeks. Has he said anything?"

"No. I've thrown out a few hints and he either pretends to go to sleep, or changes the subject. I'm afraid . . ." He frowned.

Fanny said indignantly, "I'm not! He adores her. You know he does!"

"Oh, yes. And I know him. He has a fierce pride, Fan. Coville stole his inheritance and even if that could be proved, the lying bounder would doubtless claim that it all went on medical costs for Lady Pamela. All Diccon has left is a good deal of back pay and this estate. And now, he's lost an arm."

"Poor dear man. But he's taken it so bravely. Not a trace of despair or self-pity."

"No. But he probably regards himself as a considerably less than excellent matrimonial prospect."

"What stuff! He saved my dear brother's life! Marietta could not wish for a finer husband! Besides, he cannot be penniless, surely? He must have had a fine return from his free-trading activities?"

"All of which went to pay for his mother's care and her little house in Italy. That's the only reason he went back into the trade, you know. To provide for her."

Mrs. Cordova danced in from the dining room. "You must come! You must come! General Smollet has something to tell us!" She danced out again, singing, " 'Love makes those young whom age doth chill, And whom he finds young, keeps young still.' "

Curious, Vaughan and Fanny followed her.

In the drawing room, the stocky little general stood with his back to the fire, a glass of Madeira in his hand. A thin, blushful lady of middle age sat in an armchair peeping curiously at the effigies. Sir Lionel, very proud and haughty of aspect, presented Vaughan and Fanny to Miss Deerhurst, who blushed fierily and twittered some incoherent half sentences.

Smollet wrung Vaughan's hand. "I hear you pulled Major Paisley out of that hell-hole. It was well done, Lieutenant!"

"Thank you, sir. I couldn't have done it without that rascally Chinese colossus."

"Possibly not, but you did splendidly, just the same." The General turned to bow over Marietta's hand as she hurried to join them. "Ah, we've met before, ma'am. Am I correct in believing you are betrothed to Paisley? He's a dashed lucky man if that's the case."

From the corner of her eye Marietta saw her father's irritated scowl. Before he could comment, her chin lifted and she answered, "I fear you are a little previous, General. But I hope very soon to confirm your belief."

Smollet blinked and looked somewhat taken aback, but Miss Deerhurst dabbed a handkerchief at her eyes and murmured, "Oh, how very affecting!"

The General's expression softened as he looked at her. "I think you are unaware of my relationship to this lady," he said. "I am very proud to announce that she is soon to become my wife."

There was an outburst of surprise and congratulations. The ladies pressed in upon the even more blushful Miss Deerhurst, who twittered happily. The General jerked his head to Vaughan, and the two men slipped out.

Beaming, Mrs. Cordova said, "Is it not romantic? And—*we* are responsible, my dears!"

Marietta asked, "How so, Aunt?"

"Why it was my clever brother here who recommended to the General that he lodge at Beachy House in Eastbourne. The proprietor chances to be a friend of Miss Deerhurst, and—"

"And we met at her gate in a most dreadful thunderstorm," interposed Miss Deerhurst excitedly. "We have had such a horrid wet summer this year, have we not? I slipped on a leaf and was rather shaken, and the General was so kind. He carried me to my house, and my uncle invited him to dinner."

"Miss Deerhurst is an exceptional cook," put in Mrs. Cordova merrily.

"Well, yes, I am, if I say so—" The newly betrothed lady paused, and asked in bewilderment, "But how could you know that, ma'am?"

Her eyes dancing, Fanny said mischievously, "Yes. How could you, Aunty?"

Unabashed, Mrs. Cordova said, "Madame Olympias told me."

"Oh! Do you consult that wonderful lady, also?" Her eyes alight, Miss Deerhurst said, "She *told* me that this was going to happen! She said a gentleman was going to come who would change my life, and he has, oh but, truly, he *has*! To think that she would know! She looked into her Magical Window—"

"Mystical Window," corrected Mrs. Cordova absently.

"Yes, that's right. Her Mystical Window Through Time, and—she *knew*! Isn't it marvellous? She must be indeed a very great mystic!"

All earnest admiration, the newly betrothed lady was rather offended when Sir Lionel gave a whoop of laughter.

❧

Diccon had been permitted to sit up in a chair on this late autumn afternoon. The mellow sunlight slanted across the room and illumined the voucher in his hand. He blinked at it speechlessly.

Watching him in amusement, General Smollet said, "Too bright in here, is it?"

Diccon looked up at him uncertainly. "If I seem dazzled,

General, it's because I think there's been a mistake made. I'm more than grateful for my back pay, but—Jove! It doesn't amount to this, surely?"

"Interest," said the General with a bland smile, drawing a chair closer. "If ever a man deserved compensation, you do. Prinny's well aware of your devoted service to your country, and of how often your life was at risk while your warnings were ridiculed. This is his doing."

"With your prompting, eh, sir? To say thank you, seems inadequate."

"I accept it, just the same. Now, are you going to wish me happy? The old war horse settling down at last, is that what you're thinking? You're right. I've never had a lady to care for me; to give a tinker's damn whether I lived or died, or see that my neckcloths were clean, or my cook capable. And what a run of cooks I've suffered from, Diccon!" He patted his ample middle and declared, "Indeed, it's a wonder I'm not a wraith! Well, I've found a lady who must be the best cook in the world! And who has a kind and gentle disposition. Oh, she's not one of your beauties, I suppose, but then, neither am I!"

Diccon put out his hand, and as it was taken and wrung strongly, he said, "Then you have indeed my heartiest congratulations, sir!"

"Thank you. I think we shall deal well together. Now, what of you? There's a stunningly beautiful girl downstairs who is ready and eager to be your wife unless I mistake it. Why do you back and fill? Don't care for the lady?"

Diccon stared unseeingly at the bank draft in his hand. "She is grateful, sir, because I was able to help her little brother."

"What matter her motives? She's a diamond of the first water! Were I you, I'd strike while the iron is hot, and before she has time to think on it! Why not?"

Diccon said slowly, "Perhaps, because . . . she *is* a diamond of the first water, sir."

Stamping down the stairs a few minutes later, Smollet

paused, glaring at the inoffensive front door until Marietta's lovely face came into his field of vision.

She smiled up at him. "I like your lady, sir."

"What it is," he grumbled, "he's too full of pride!"

Startled, she asked, "Who, sir? Diccon?"

"Aye, Diccon." He continued down the stairs to seize her hand and declare fiercely, "But England will never cease to need such prideful fools. Or to find them, I pray God! I've recommended his promotion to Lieutenant Colonel. He's a rare human being. And stubborn as his donkey!"

❧

Towards the end of October there came, as if to make amends for the storms of the past, a season of warm, sunlit days, brilliant sunsets, and brisk, clear evenings. Diccon was allowed to go outside, and on a golden afternoon lay on many pillows in a garden chaise as he had done once before, and watched the graceful movements of Marietta's hand as she sat beside him busied with her sewing.

She said with a smile, "How very nice it is to see you looking comfortable and contented. Did Yves bring good news?"

"He brought a letter from my mama."

"Is she happy in her new home?"

"Very happy. And, thank heaven, she sounds far more at ease in her mind."

"Poor lady. She must be very grateful to you."

"So she says."

Marietta resumed her sewing. "Gratitude," she said, with an oblique glance at him, "is good for people. I mean, it is only right to be grateful for—good deeds. Such as yours, for instance."

A pause. Then he pointed out, "You made a knot."

"Yes." She tucked her needle into the shirt she was repairing, and folded her hands. "It was a nice place for one. As I was saying, gratitude is—"

"Good for people," he drawled. "But a poor substitute for love."

"It is rude to interrupt," she said sternly. "And anyone who could mistake the one for the other must be quite blind."

"My thoughts exactly. It would be almost as bad as—as confusing pity with love."

She gritted her teeth. "Mallory Diccon Paisley—"

"Lord Temple and Cloud," he prompted, his lips twitching.

"Do not try to change the subject."

"I thought we'd exhausted it. Do you like the future Lady Smollet?"

"She is very kind, and will be just the wife for him, and as you know very well—"

"No, ma'am. Your pardon, but I've never met the lady."

"—As you know very well," she persisted, fixing him with a steady stare, "we all are grateful to you. And there is not a bit of use your pretending to fall asleep, for you look perfectly able to take Orpheus out for a gallop!"

He said with a smile. "My thanks to all of you for your gratitude. You did mean *all* of you, did you not?"

He meant Papa, of course, who was crushingly polite to this man to whom he owed so much. With an inward sigh she took up her sewing again. "My father would have been heartbroken if we had lost Arthur. And Eric is—is safe away."

"No thanks to me. Had I been willing to abandon my principles, he would not have to live away from England."

It was a painful subject, even now. She poked her needle at the shirt and said slowly, "He brought it on himself, and I suppose, sooner or later, he would have been caught at all events."

"Hmm. And Sir Lionel shares those sentiments, does he?"

"You are being horrid." Again, she met his eyes, and said softly, "And I am four and twenty, Diccon, and told you once before how I feel about—"

He interrupted hurriedly, "You must indeed think me horrid, if you fancy that I would be so gauche as to enquire about a lady's age! Did I tell you, by the bye, that your father has been so kind as to volunteer to create several devices whereby I'll not be such a burden to, er—my friends? A little stand, for instance, so that if I wish to read in bed I won't have to hold the book, and small wheels for my chair which will make it easier to pull it up to table. He's working now on a neck-cloth, already tied, that will—"

"Be useful for people to strangle you with?" She sprang up, her eyes flashing, and leant over him in such a rage that he shrank back and threw up his hand as a shield.

"Don't hit me! I'm a frail invalid, and—"

"Do you suppose that anyone who loved you would not be eager to help with small difficulties? Do you seek to paint yourself as so helpless and infirm that I must run from you in horror, only because you lost your forearm while most gallantly saving my brother's life? Must you be so confoundedly proud that you will reject any—"

"*Marietta!*" Mrs. Cordova approached, a large tray in her hands, formally spread with an embroidered cloth and holding several glasses. "You *swore!* How very naughty."

"And at a helpless invalid," confirmed Diccon reproachfully. "And now, only look, Miss Marietta is gnashing her teeth at me!"

"So she is! Goodness, child, that front one has a crack in it!"

Marietta gave a yelp and started to run in search of a mirror, then stopped as she heard their laughter. "Aunty, you great tease! If you had but heard him, you'd have gnashed at him too."

"At my time of life, one does not dare take such chances. I have brought some lemonade instead." Mrs. Cordova handed out glasses, then sat in the chair, clutching her tray. "Sit down do, Etta. I can recover from your naughty language, but I would purely dislike to see you fall over. You can't have my place but Diccon can spare you a little room, can you not, dear boy?"

He agreed readily, and Marietta settled herself on the end of the chaise. "Though why you should think my balance so impaired, Aunty Dova, that I would fall—"

"Stop prattling, child. Now Diccon, I have something to say. I would have said it long since, save that I didn't want to upset you whilst you were so ill."

He looked at her warily, wondering if his stubborn adherence to his moral code was to be flung at him again.

"You may recall that when we were in your house during that dreadful storm," she began, "I warned you that it was going to fall down. And it did, so I was right. At least the south end of it did. You shall have to see about having the cliff shorn up—" She frowned, and muttered, "Is that the word? Or should it be 'shored' up? Well—whatever—"

"Aunty," inserted Marietta, her eyes on Diccon's set face, "Shall we not talk about that? I think it would be better if—"

"Do you, child? Very well, we'll make it 'shored.' However, my point is that your house fell on me, Diccon, whilst I was upstairs, which was not very nice. It knocked me down. Well, part of the wall did."

"Good Lord, ma'am! I had no notion! I am very sorry. If it has resulted in an injury you must see Avebury when next he—"

"Hush, hush! Close your nice lips! Oh, *why* will no one let me speak, when I have waited so long and been so patient? There—that's better. The thing is that, as usual, I was right. For I said it was with music, you see. The Mystical Window Through Time never lets me down. Or very seldom. Of course, there was that time when it said Mr. Beck's mare had been naughty with Lord Dale's black stallion. . . . What an uproar that caused! You'll remember, Etta? And what Mr. Beck said about Madame— Well, never mind! The thing is, Diccon, that"—she handed him the flat parcel that had been underneath the tray cloth—"this also fell on my, er—limb."

He set down his glass of lemonade, and unfolded the wrappings. He was slow and clumsy about it, but although Marietta yearned to help him, she wisely made no attempt to do so.

Succeeding at length, he became perfectly white, his hand

shook convulsively, and he whispered, "Oh . . . Jupiter!"

The sunlight awoke a thousand dancing fires from the small but exquisite Eastern lady who stood between two trees, all depicted in sparkling jewels, and enclosed by a magnificently carven gold frame.

The glass fell from Marietta's hand. Awed, she murmured, "So—so it really does exist, after all! Oh, how *beautiful* it is!"

Mrs. Cordova cried triumphantly, "*The Sigh of Saladin!* Your troubles are over, Diccon! It is worth a king's ransom."

Gazing with dazzled eyes at that ages old work of art, he thought she was very probably in the right of it.

❧

The following evening there was a small celebration at the dower house. Young Samuel South was pressed into service in the kitchen, and Mrs. Gillespie arrived looking neat and sober and in a high state of excitement when she found that she was to assist MacDougall at table.

Among the guests were Lord and Lady Dale, and a very stiff Innes Williard and his sister. General Sir Nevin Smollet was accompanied by his prospective bride, the lady blushing furiously at each introduction but looking surprisingly attractive in a stylish evening gown of fawn brocade. Jocelyn Vaughan was dashing in regimental evening dress, and Diccon, also in his regimentals with his left sleeve pinned up, looked romantically haggard and won many admiring and sympathetic glances which reduced him to a state of abject cowardice. Marietta, a vision in pale green satin, stayed close beside him, and since he clung to her hand in a panic when the subject of Arthur's rescue came up—as it frequently did—everyone present formed an accurate opinion of the state of affairs between them.

The Sigh of Saladin was prominently displayed on the drawing room mantelpiece, and Sir Lionel, in an expansive mood, lost no opportunity to draw it to the attention of each arriving guest and seemed never to tire of relating its history.

Drifting to Diccon's side when the gentlemen rejoined the ladies after dinner, Vaughan murmured, "I do believe you've won back the old boy's favour, Major, sir."

Diccon repressed his own cynical thoughts on that subject, and said, "I told you I didn't want the picture displayed tonight."

"I relayed your message to Sir Lionel and was advised not to be a marplot, and that we mustn't deny our neighbours a chance to rejoice in your good luck."

"His tongue runs on wheels! The news will sweep the county by morning, and we've precious little in the way of guards here, you know."

"You're right, by George! I shall go at once and get a pistol!"

Luckily, the weapon was not required. The guests were genuinely awed by the work of art, and, with the exception of Mr. Williard and Mrs. Maitland, appeared delighted that such good fortune had come to Diccon.

"You deserve to be rewarded, be dashed if you don't," said Dale.

General Smollet laughed and, with a wink at Marietta, said that he rather suspected Major Paisley would win a fair reward.

Diccon appeared not to have heard.

Lying awake that night, Marietta watched the shifting shadows of the tree branches that the moonlight cast on her curtains and thought of the love that had come to her, and the power and wonder of it. She had found a gentleman she could not only love, but could honour and respect—a man to whom her children could look for inspiration and guidance.

But there would be no children if she could not overcome his foolish pride. Heaven knows she'd hinted him often enough. But now that he was suddenly wealthy, how could she manoeuvre him into offering without it seeming that she was one of those horridly pushing ladies who pursued wealth?

She thought, 'Oh, heavens! And he has a title, as well! He'll think I'm just like the Widow Maitland!' She moaned into the darkness.

⁂

I got questions," said Arthur, standing by his sister's bed with Friar Tuck sagging over his arm playing "dead cat."

Marietta yawned and opened one eye. "What is the time?"

He trotted round to the clock on her bedside table and imparted doubtfully. "It's gone past nine o'clock."

"All right, love." Marietta sat up and stretched. You may climb on and ask your questions."

They climbed on and without beating about the bush Arthur demanded, "When is Diccon goin' to be my brother 'law?"

"Who told you he was?"

"He said he'd like you for a wife, and I wish you'd hurry up, Etta. I heared Mrs. Maitland say he's full o' juice an' can take his pick now."

'Horrid cat!' thought Marietta.

"An' Lem says that means Diccon's rich an' lots of ladies want him. You're nice, but there's not many men like Sir G'waine, you know. He's not *pretty* han'some like Mr. Blake, but he looks like a man ought to. An' I like him lots. An' I want him for my brother 'law, so please stir your stumps, Etta."

"Well, I never did!" she gasped, astounded. "Wherever did you learn such terms?"

"Oh—here an' there," he said airily. "But when is you goin' to tell him yes you'll marriage him?"

She sighed. "Whenever he asks me, dearest. But you see, he hasn't."

"Oh. Well that's all right. You ask him."

She smiled forlornly. "I can't. At least, ladies aren't supposed to."

"Do you got to be a lady? I'll bet the Widow Maitland would ask him!"

· 331 ·

Marietta laughed. "You may be right at that. But—well, you see, there are reasons why I cannot."

"Oh. Well then, *make* him ask you."

"How, you little rogue?"

He frowned, and thought for a moment. And then he told her.

CHAPTER XX

"T"he Regent has allowed his crest to be used on the coat of arms of the Literary Fund," imparted Marietta, reading *The Spectator* aloud as she sat beside Diccon in the sunny garden.

Arthur, who was busily engaged in driving Friar Tuck mad by dangling a long peacock feather just above his nose, asked, "What's that?"

"Probably an association to promote the teaching of reading," answered Diccon drowsily. "That should cheer up poor Byron."

Marietta said, "I'm sure it would. But I believe the Literary Fund was established to help financially distressed authors. Prinny has always supported it, and now he's arranged a Charter of Incorporation for—"

"I tell you he does not wish to receive you! And that you would dare show your face here, sir, is past belief!" Sir Lionel's outraged tones caused Marietta to stop reading and look up anxiously.

Shading his eyes against the sunlight, Diccon also looked up and swore under his breath.

His step-father, elegant as always, marched across the lawn, waving aside Sir Lionel's objections. He was accompanied by a tall Eastern gentleman clad in a richly ornamented knee-length coat, satin trousers, high riding boots, and a flowing burnous.

Three other Arabs followed, all similarly but more plainly garbed, all tall and formidable of appearance, their wide-swinging cloaks revealing the great curving blades of scimitars.

"Oh!" exclaimed Marietta, springing up in anger and indignation.

Sir Gavin stopped beside Diccon's chaise, and said importantly, "As you see, sir, my step-son has been gravely injured, which will explain why he does not rise to greet—"

Very obviously venerated by his companions, the tall Arab silenced Coville with a gesture, then his hand moved in a graceful salaam and he spoke in a deep voice and perfect English. "Have I the honour to address Lord Temple and Cloud? My title is long and of no importance. You may call me Ibrahim."

Diccon scanned the proud, finely etched face, the high-arched nose, the piercing eyes, and ruthless mouth, and came to his feet. He bowed slightly but with respect. "You may call me Major Paisley, my lord."

The Arab smiled. "You know me?"

"I believe your title is Sheikh al-Balad. Will you be seated, sir?"

Coville sprang to pull up Marietta's chair.

The sheikh said, "But I think the beautiful lady occupied this. Unless, perhaps, she is to leave us?" The thin lips smiled, but the hard, dark eyes left no doubt of his meaning.

Marietta felt a twinge of fear but said defiantly, "The lady is staying, my lord. But by all means take the chair. I will sit beside Major Paisley."

Sir Gavin, who had intended to share the chaise, frowned and murmured, "This is a matter for gentlemen, Paisley."

Turning to him, Diccon said acidly, "Then you had best retire, sir."

Coville flushed scarlet.

The sheikh's dark face was lit by a very brief flash of white teeth.

"May I present Miss Warrington, and—" Diccon glanced down, but Arthur and Friar Tuck had fled.

Marietta was accorded a polite but less flourishing salaam, and the sheikh sat down, his men at once stepping close behind the chair.

No sooner were they seated than Sir Gavin said, "Sheikh Ibrahim has come here to—"

The sheikh turned his head and looked at him and he floundered into silence.

"I am told that you have found an object that was stolen from my family," said the sheikh uncompromisingly.

"I believe such things are called spoils of war," countered Diccon.

The Arab's thin lips curled. "Not in all circumstances, Major. But—no doubt you are aware of the circumstances?"

Sir Lionel said in exasperation, "It happened over six hundred years ago! How could *anyone* be aware of the circumstances?"

The sheikh regarded him as though he were a very strange insect then returned his attention to Diccon. "You are aware, perhaps, Major, that your ancestor, Simon, Lord Cloud, was wounded in battle and carried into the home of Salah ud-Din, sultan of Egypt, to recuperate?"

"I am aware only that Lord Cloud returned to England with *The Sigh of Saladin*," said Diccon coolly.

"Which he stole while an honoured guest!"

"How do we know that?" demanded Sir Lionel, bristling. "Eh? How? And what difference does it make after all this time? Poppycock!"

Ignoring him, as he ignored Coville, the sheikh's dark gaze never left Diccon's face. "*The Sigh of Saladin* did not belong to my ancestor. It was a national treasure, considered sacred by my people. It was entrusted to the protection of Salah ud-Din during the fighting. Naturally, he did not expect a man whose life he had saved to rob him. He was deeply grieved and felt he had betrayed his trust. To the end of his days he mourned the loss."

"War is war, sir," said Coville with a regretful shrug. "But I am sure that when Major Paisley hears your offer—"

"So you are prepared to make an offer?" said Diccon.

"But of course." Sheikh Ibrahim's smile was touched with contempt. "We know the way of the western world. You invade and slaughter and destroy in the name of God, and steal in the name of greed. So—" He spread his hands. "It is a national treasure; what can I do? I am prepared to make an offer."

"And a most generous—" began Sir Gavin.

Diccon interrupted curtly, "Then we had best have the object here for you to inspect, my lord. So that you may be sure the greedy westerners are not trying to foist off a poor imitation on you." He turned to Marietta. "Would you be so kind, Miss Warrington?"

"I'll come with you," volunteered Sir Lionel hurriedly, and went off beside her, talking earnestly, snatches of his remarks drifting back to them: ". . . heathen savages . . . ," and ". . . all a bunch of crafty horse traders."

"I have seen your house, Major," said the sheikh, apparently not having heard the words which had brought a flush of embarrassment to Diccon's thin face. "Do you really intend to rebuild? A costly venture, I suspect."

Diccon nodded. "Too costly for my purse at the moment, my lord."

"Ah. You—also—hope to realize a long-cherished dream. Is that—" He broke off, staring.

There came a clanking sound. Sir Lancelot advanced, helmet firmly set, lance in one hand and sword in the other. Friar Tuck attacked the end of the lance and the knight tripped. One of the sheikh's guards chuckled, and was the recipient of a glare from his master that wiped the mirth from his face.

Arthur marched to take up his stand beside Diccon and face the enemy with fierce determination.

Diccon said, "My lord, this is Master Arthur Warrington. Arthur, make your bow to Sheikh Ibrahim."

Arthur managed a jerky bow.

The sheikh stood and offered his gracious salaam. "For a moment," he said, "I had thought I faced your legendary Sir Lancelot."

Arthur beamed his approval. "That's right, sir! He got me right, Diccon!"

Sitting down again, the sheikh asked, "Is this the boy for whom you gave up your arm, Major?"

"I—er, that was not my intention at the time, sir."

"It would seem you have something in common with my ancestor. You will not know it, but—"

"But Saladin had a deep love for children," interrupted Diccon. He saw the look of astonishment on the hawk face, and said with a grin, "I know quite a lot of him. He was a most remarkable gentleman."

Sheikh Ibrahim betrayed his Oxford education. "The devil you say!" he exclaimed, then sprang up as Marietta approached, her father, still talking earnestly, beside her.

She glanced uncertainly at Diccon. He nodded towards the sheikh, and ignoring Sir Lionel's frantic gestures, said, "Please examine it as minutely as you wish, my lord."

With hands that trembled the sheikh unwrapped the picture. When he held it up reverently his followers gave startled exclamations and each of them dropped to one knee. The sunlight set the gems on fire. Dazzled, the sheikh stared and stared.

Sir Gavin, also rendered speechless, made a fast recovery. "As you see, my lord, it is well worth the price!"

"It is beyond price," murmured Diccon.

Sir Gavin laughed. "You've not heard his bid, my dear boy."

"If I am become your 'dear boy,'" said Diccon ironically, "I've no doubt you already have named your share of the price."

Sir Gavin gave him a look of loathing.

Visibly shaken, the Arab returned the picture to Marietta. "For *The Sigh of Saladin*, and on behalf of my people, I will pay you the sum of five hundred thousand pounds, Major Paisley."

"Half a *million—pounds?*" gasped Sir Lionel, his eyes goggling.

Dazed, Diccon thought of Lanterns, proudly and graciously refurbished and set amid a groomed park and gardens. He thought of other things and, aware that his step-father waited with barely concealed jubilation, turned to Marietta. She was watching him, her expression grave. He asked, "Well, ma'am? Do you think I should accept his lordship's offer?"

A moment she hesitated. Then, she shook her head.

"Right!" exclaimed Sir Lionel heartily. "Good girl! Never accept the first offer, I told her! Beautiful thing like that; an object of antiquity. Worth a king's ransom. Ain't that right, Diccon?"

His face cold and closed, the sheikh said, "I do not care to haggle in this matter. I would point out, Major, that it could provide you with a new manor house. A new"—he glanced at Marietta—"and glorious life."

"Very true," said Diccon. "Still, I must refuse."

The guards muttered angrily.

The sheikh's jaw tightened. "Very well," he said, reluctantly. "But this is my absolute and final offer: One million pounds."

From Sir Lionel and Coville came simultaneous gasps.

Diccon gazed at Marietta for a long moment and it seemed to Sheikh Ibrahim that a silver flame lit those hitherto enigmatic blue eyes.

Diccon said quietly, "As I said before, *The Sigh of Saladin* is beyond price. It is not for sale, my lord."

The sheikh's lips curled back from his teeth in a soundless snarl. Three muscular hands reached for three murderous scimitars.

Sir Lionel said a dismayed, "Not for sale? But—my dear boy . . . !"

Sir Gavin yelped, "You're mad! There's a limit, even to Mr. Ibrahim's generosity!"

The sheikh demanded coldly, "Have you an explanation, sir?"

Diccon took *The Sigh of Saladin* from Marietta and held it

up to the light, marvelling at the beauty of it. "I have no doubt," he said, "that my ancestor considered this to be a prize of war. But to my mind sacred objects belong to the people and the nation of their origin." Unused to making speeches, he thrust the picture at the sheikh. "It's yours. But not because I believe it was stolen dishonourably."

There was an instant of stunned silence. Then, five howls fractured the quiet of the gardens. Two of rage from Sir Lionel and Sir Gavin; three of joy from the sheikh's bodyguards.

"One million pounds—*truly* a king's ransom—and you whistle it away?" roared Sir Lionel. "You're stark, raving mad!"

"If I had my way you'd be placed in Bedlam under strong restraint!" raged Sir Gavin.

Not daring to look at Marietta, Diccon knew that they were probably right. But it was too late for him to change now. He would undoubtedly be a stupid fool all his days.

⁕

Arthur knelt on the rug in Marietta's bedchamber and watched her arrange her shawl. "Why was Papa so cross with Sir G'waine yest'day after those men in the dresses were gone? I 'spect that's why he went home so quick."

"They weren't really dresses, dear. They're robes that men wear in the country they come from. And Papa thought that Diccon should have done something in a rather different way, that's all."

"Oh. You've tied your bonnet three times, Etta. He went away yest'day y'know. An' it's already today aft'noon."

"I know. But he's still not very strong, and I don't expect he'll go anywhere just yet. And besides—" Marietta started to fashion the bow again, then sighed and gazed at her reflection. "Oh dear. I suppose the truth is that I'm just a coward, Arthur. I never did anything like this before."

Ladies were awful strange, he thought. What was there to

be a coward about? All she had to do was talk. What was scary 'bout that? "If you're 'fraid," he said, "you'd better grid up the lions."

She turned and looked at him. "I'd better—what, dear?"

"Grid up the loins. That's what Lem told me to do when Sir Strut hissed at me an' I was scared. He says it's out of the Bible."

The light dawned. "Ah! So it is. Perhaps Lem didn't speak loudly enough for you to hear properly. It really says, " 'Gird up thy loins.' " She saw his mouth opening and added quickly, "Which means—gather up your courage."

"Oh. Why doesn't it say that, then?"

"Well, because we say things a little differently nowadays."

"Why?"

"Because times change. And time is changing very fast, so I'd better hurry, hadn't I." She tied the bow and took up the valise that lay on the bed. "How can this be heavy? It's empty." She set it down again and lifted Friar Tuck out. "Were you going to come and offer me moral support, moggy?" she asked, holding up the cat.

"We're both coming," said Arthur.

"No, dear. I really don't think—"

"We must, Etta! You might forget to grid your loins on the way!"

It was, she thought with an inner quake, very possible.

After a long and emotional reunion with Orpheus and Mr. Fox, Diccon left the paddock and wandered across the field behind the manor, irritated because he still tired so easily.

Vaughan came to meet him and called a greeting. Still Sir Lionel's house guest, he'd promised to come and look over the damage to the old wing this morning; something Diccon had not been able to bring himself to do.

"Beautiful day, Major, sir," he said, his eyes keenly appraising his friend.

"Very," agreed Diccon. "Well, what's your verdict? Am I alive?"

Vaughan laughed. "You look less like a corpse every day. I really believe you'll survive."

"I am still *persona non grata* at the Warrington establishment, I take it?"

"The old boy judges you ripe for Bedlam."

"Add to that my despicable conduct with regard to his heir."

"It was his heir who was despicable—not your conduct. I told him any self-respecting officer would have done the same. Myself included."

"Did you! That was good of you, Joss. But in the matter of the sheikh, did you also judge me ripe for Bedlam?"

"Oh, absolutely. But—I'm . . . Well, what I mean is—" Vaughan finished in a rush, "I'm jolly proud that you number me among your friends, dear old looby." Very red in the face, he mumbled something about "giving Mac an assist," turned to bolt, then stopped dead.

Seven horsemen were approaching at the gallop. Seven followers of the Sheikh Ibrahim, mounted on superb black Arabian horses, riding abreast, robes flying, and high-held scimitars glittering wickedly in the morning sunlight.

"Jupiter," muttered Diccon.

Vaughan sprang to his side. "And I left my pistol in the saddle holster," he said grimly. "Fiend seize the fellow! He's taking revenge on your blasted ancestor!"

The Arabs were upon them with a thunder of hooves and a chorus of ear-splitting battle cries. There was no chance to run; no hope of an attempt at defence. Side-by-side, pale but unflinching, Diccon and Vaughan faced that thundering charge, waiting to be cut to ribbons.

At the last instant the Arabs divided and circled the two men. Still shouting, they raced around them in a dwindling circle. Abruptly, they slowed, formed a single line facing the Englishmen, and were still.

The central rider walked his horse forward and, scant paces

from them, halted once more. The curving blade of the scimitar shot out. It was all Diccon could do not to recoil but then he saw that a small velvet bag was tied to the end of the blade. He reached out and removed it.

At once that deafening war cry rent the air. The riders who had sat as if carven from stone spurred their horses into another encircling gallop gradually widening until, whooping and howling they raced off and out of sight.

"Phew!" gasped Vaughan. "Life around you is never dull, old pippin! I suppose your almighty sheikh is demanding satisfaction, is that what those flamboyant manoeuvres were all about?"

Diccon took a piece of paper from the bag, scanned it, and held it out with a hand that trembled.

Vaughan was no less shaken and it was some moments before he was able to croak, "Oh . . . egad!"

❧

MacDougall smoothed the back of Diccon's coat and said approvingly, "Right bonnie ye look, and no mistaking!" He pulled out a chair. "Sit ye doon, sir, and have a wee bit brrrandy while I pole up the hacks."

Diccon took up the "wee bit brrrandy," stared at it, and put it down again.

He smiled foolishly at the open door, wondering what Marietta was doing on this bright and breezy afternoon, and what she would think of— A carriage was stopping outside. He took up his helm and crossed to the door. Mac had been speedy.

He was mistaken. There was no sign of his coach, or MacDougall. The dilapidated Warrington carriage, the roof piled with baggage, stood in the courtyard and Lem Bridger was handing Marietta down the step. She wore a bonnet and a travelling coat, and, as usual, at the sight of her his heart bounced up behind his teeth. He walked quickly towards her, and she turned and saw him. "My goodness!" she exclaimed. "Full dress regimentals? How splendid you look, Major. Are you summoned to Whitehall?"

"Yes. But never mind about that. Where are you going?"

"Away," she said with a sigh, walking to the house with him.

"Away? What d'you mean—away? Away where?"

She shrugged. "Something has to be done. Eric borrowed my—our—savings. We're properly in the basket now. So I've decided to take a post as governess."

He stopped walking and looked down at her, aghast. "That's the most nonsensical thing I ever heard! You won't make any money at it. And besides, you know Vaughan will provide for your family."

"I expect he will, when they are officially betrothed. But he wants a long engagement so that Fanny can have a London Season."

"Yes, but—"

"He has offered, of course, but Papa says we cannot take charity from a comparative stranger. He has his pride too, Diccon."

"Does he! I wonder that he didn't—" He bit back the angry words, and demanded, "Where are you going to look for this post, I should like to know? And what will you do until you find one?"

With brave but pathetic resignation she said, "Oh, I shall manage. Somehow. I have, in fact, already accepted a post—at least for a trial."

"You *have*? When did all this transpire? And where is this fabulous opportunity?"

"I wrote after it last month. I didn't tell anyone at the time. But I received a reply yesterday, and with Papa in such a taking, and my—my last hope . . . gone." She peeped at him from under her lashes. "I can at least spare my family the upkeep of a spinster daughter. So I'm off to Edinburgh, and—"

"*Edinburgh? S-spinster?* Oh, come now! You're doing it up too brown—What I mean is—"

"It's quite all right," she said wistfully. "I understand, Diccon. But you have been so good—I just had to—to say . . . ," she turned from him and dabbed at her eyes, saying on a sob, ". . . good-bye."

His eyes narrowed. He demanded, "Understand—what?"

"That I have no portion—"

"You mean dowry."

"Well, yes. And you need—or will want to find—a lady of wealth and position."

He looked down at her demurely bowed head, and drawled, "Like—Mrs. Maitland, perhaps?"

"She is very wealthy, I hear. And—you know she has always yearned for a title."

"Has she, indeed!"

"She may be a touch—scratchy. But I expect she will be willing to restore Lanterns."

"How very good of you to plan such a delightful future for me. And just think, I could stay here and see Arthur every day, and think of you in Glasgow, and be—"

"Edinburgh."

"—Edinburgh, and be perfectly content at long last!" He snorted. "Oh! If *ever* I needed two hands!"

She peeped up at him again and saw laughter mingling with the indignation in his eyes. "Why, dear Diccon?"

"To spank you." He dropped his shining helm, seized her arm with unexpected strength and pulled her to him. "Hard! A governess, indeed! Who put you up to this blatant attempt to force my hand?"

"Arthur," she admitted shamelessly. "He's afraid I'll let you get away and he wants you for a brother-in-law, even if you judge me unfit to be your wife, so—"

Much tried, Diccon uttered a ferocious growl and cut off her confession with remarkable proficiency considering that he had only one usable arm.

"And—besides," gasped Marietta when she was able to

speak. "He likes Mr. Fox, so you see I had to do as he asked, regardless of my own—"

After another blissful interlude they discovered to their mutual surprise that they were sitting on the step of the main entrance and that Marietta's head, bonnetless, rested comfortably on Diccon's right shoulder.

"Are you sure, my lovely one?" he asked, kissing her ear. "I'm not one of your London beaux always ready for an endless round of parties and routs and musicales."

"Nor am I," she said. "Even if we could afford it."

"And I'm not a brilliant conversationalist, but tend to stand about like a speechless dullard, besides being cursed with my antiquated notions—as you've seen."

"Well, that's true," she agreed, reaching up to touch his empty sleeve with a very gentle finger.

"Besides—and you must face it, Marietta, you're such a lovely little thing, and—well, I'm probably going to be a bit of a nuisance, which is easy to dismiss now, but will likely get tiresome after a while."

She nodded. "I expect it will. And I would be much wiser to refuse your splendid offer—"

"Which I haven't yet made."

"Which you have as good as made, sir! But the problem is that, though I searched the whole wide world, how could I hope to find another almost-nobleman to compare with the man I so love and honour and simply cannot exist without, or—"

She was interrupted at some length. With his lips brushing hers, he murmured, "So you came here to entrap me, you saucy schemer. I suppose all those portmanteaux and band boxes atop your coach are empty?"

"Yes. I would have come sooner in fact, but I couldn't very well entrap you when you owned an *objet d'art* worth a million pounds."

"But you would be willing to entrap me had I not a penny."

"Not *one* penny?" She chuckled. "I don't think you're quite that deep under the hatches, are you, my love?"

"Not . . . exactly." He took his arm from around her, and drew from his pocket the bank draft that had been most dramatically delivered by a troop of magnificent Arabian horsemen.

Marietta glanced at it, and her own breath was snatched away. "Oh! . . . Oh, *Diccon*! The sheikh?"

"He says it is the reward, and not even half what he was really prepared to pay." He pursed his lips. "Still, it's an enormous amount. Do you think I should refuse it?"

"*No!* I do *not*! Oh, my dear! How wonderful of him! We will be able to restore Lanterns, just as you've so longed to do! There will be room for all of us. And—"

"Oh, no there won't! On the estate—yes. At Lanterns, just you and I, beloved, and our staff. Er, for a while, at least." Marietta blushed, and he chuckled and kissed her temple. "Now I'll take you home in my coach, and Lem can follow."

In swift alarm she cried, "You're not going to start for Whitehall today?"

"No. In a month, perhaps."

"Deceitful man! Then why are you so magnificent in your regimentals?"

"Because I must call on your sire and make a formal offer for my lady, and the uniform makes me look—well, a little more impressive, I hope."

"You are always impressive, Major. Besides," she added with a giggle, "what you have in your pocket will impress my sire enormously."

They had reached the coach. Of Bridger there was no sign, but a trill sounded from the open door, and Friar Tuck yawned, and stretched his front legs over the edge of the seat.

"Arthur!" gasped Marietta, repentantly. "Oh dear! I quite forgot!"

"I knowed you would!" The little boy blinked at her. "I shouldn't of goed to sleep. Did you grid your loins?"

"Did she—*what*?" asked Diccon, intrigued.

"Never mind!" said Marietta.

He grinned and kissed her ear again.

Cheered by this demonstration, Arthur said, "Oh. Did she do it right, Sir G'waine?"

Diccon put his arm around his love and smiled down at her. "She did indeed," he said, knowing his lonely years were done. "She did it exactly right!"

"Good," said Arthur. "Then I think I'll go and see— I said—" He stopped. They weren't listening, but it didn't matter because there was no longer any doubt that he'd have Diccon for a brother 'law.

Accompanied by Friar Tuck, he skipped off happily in search of the Lord of the Larder.